Hollywell Stables
Omnibus Two

Samantha Alexander lives in Lincolnshire with a
variety of animals including her thoroughbred
horse, Bunny, and a pet goose called Bertie. Her
schedule is almost as busy and exciting as her
plots – she writes a number of columns for
newspapers and magazines, is a teenage agony
aunt for BBC Radio Leeds and in her spare time
she regularly competes in dressage and
showjumping.

The Mission, Trapped, Running Wild and *Secrets*
first published 1995
This omnibus edition published for Bookmart Ltd 1997
by Macmillan Children's Books
a division of Macmillan Publishers Limited
25 Eccleston Place, London SW1W 9NF
and Basingstoke

Associated companies throughout the world

ISBN 0 330 35529 5

Copyright © Samantha Alexander 1995

The right of Samantha Alexander to be identified as the
author of this book has been asserted by her in accordance
with the Copyright, Designs and Patents Act 1988.

1 3 5 7 9 8 6 4 2

A CIP catalogue record for this book is available from
the British Library.

Printed by Mackays of Chatham plc, Kent

HOLLYWELL STABLES

The Mission
5

Samantha Alexander

**MACMILLAN
CHILDREN'S BOOKS**

Chapter One

"I don't like him!" my little sister Katie said, screwing up her face into a tight frown.

My brother Ross and I were hovering behind the kitchen curtains, spying on our new YTS groom, Trevor.

"He's horrible!" Katie repeated, diving out of sight as Trevor glanced across the stable yard in our direction. "He's the most horrible person I've ever met!"

I must admit, I was inclined to agree. Not only was our new groom lazy, rude and sarcastic, but he didn't know the first thing about horses – and hadn't any intention of finding out.

He also looked like a nightmare. His hair was shaved at the sides, stuck up on top and dyed bright purple. Katie insisted that he'd frighten the horses.

"There's no doubt about it," Ross said. "We've just got to get rid of him!"

We had been running the sanctuary for horses and ponies for over a year now and we'd collected

1

so many waifs and strays that we couldn't look after them all ourselves. But we couldn't afford to employ an experienced, professional groom so Trevor had been our only answer.

Two hours later we found Trevor snoring in the hay barn with a smouldering cigarette hanging out of his mouth. Ross was very angry. "Come on, Mel, you're the practical one in the family. What are we going to do?"

"Maybe we ought to give him another chance?" said Mrs Mac, our official secretary and head fund raiser.

Trevor had turned up for work two days earlier while Sarah, our stepmother, was away at a writers' conference. Sarah was a romantic novelist and she'd already had quite a few books published. She'd looked after us single handedly since our dad died. Our real mother had run off and left us when we were quite young. The sanctuary had been our dream for years and Sarah was the person who'd made it happen.

"There's only one thing we can do," I snapped back at Ross whose face was getting blacker by the minute. It took him two seconds to read my thoughts.

"I can't," Ross protested. "I can't just sack him!"

"He's coming in!" Katie yelled, running away from the door and sending our cats, Oscar and Matilda, flying for cover. Even Jigsaw, our Golden Labrador, had his hackles raised in a state of uncertainty.

"I'm sure he's just misunderstood," Mrs Mac persisted, picking up one of Jigsaw's Bonios which had somehow found its way into the dishwasher. "Maybe he needs special guidance?"

"Special therapy, more like," Ross bristled, furious that we couldn't handle the situation by ourselves.

Trevor had spent most of the afternoon in the outside toilet (we'd had one fitted to accommodate visitors) reading the newspaper and a copy of *Amateur Mechanic*. We knew this because Danny had spied on him through the hole in the latch after we thought he might have had an accident.

He now stopped to look at himself in one of the stable windows and spike up his hair which bore a striking resemblance to a startled porcupine.

"Right, that's it!" Ross shouted, his patience finally running out. "If I don't return alive you can have all my CDs and my clothes can go to charity."

He marched across to Trevor with every intention of firing him. As it was, he didn't get the chance.

A Land Rover and trailer turned up the drive and I instantly recognized James's car following behind. James was our vet and family friend and he'd helped to save many of our horses' lives. Something must be terribly wrong for him to turn up unexpectedly.

"What is it? What's happened?" We all ran out to meet him, with our hearts in our mouths.

"I tried to ring," said James whilst frantically trying to undo the ramp on the trailer which was rusty and sticking. Beads of sweat stood out on his forehead and he looked worn to a frazzle. "Your phone," he panted, "is out of order."

That would explain why we hadn't heard from Sarah. We'd been too busy talking about Trevor to think of checking the line.

A farmer from the next village, who had been driving the Land Rover, pushed past James, yanked the chain up and out of the socket and pulled the ramp free. It creaked and groaned on its hinges and reluctantly came down to ground level. James was inside like a shot. There was a thick banking of dirty straw and a strong smell of pigs. Inside it was dark and dreary and I had to squint my eyes to get a better view.

What I saw shocked me.

"Oh no!" Ross whispered at my side.

Over the past year we had seen lots of cases of

4

cruelty but it never got any easier to bear. The little face that stared out at us was so sweet and amazingly friendly that I couldn't help but wonder at the nature of horses. How could they possibly stay so trusting when humans abused them to this extreme?

The tiny pony in the trailer was about 11 hands, dusty brown in colour and with a small white star on his forehead. His weak legs were shaking; his hindquarters were painfully thin. Where he should have had well rounded muscle the skin was taut and dry, dull and lifeless.

"I'll have to put him on a stomach tube," James said. "The poor little chap's got a parrot mouth."

No wonder he was so thin. Even if he'd been given plenty of food it wouldn't have been much use to him. Horses and ponies with very severe parrot mouths can't eat in the normal way. Their bottom jaw is undershot, which means they can't put their teeth together to pull at grass or hay. They can starve to death unless they are hand fed in a special way at frequent intervals.

"It's OK, little fella, we'll get you sorted out."

James, Ross and the farmer practically carried him into one of the stables. Even though he was so weak he did everything he could to help, shifting his weight and trying to walk as best he could.

He had the sweetest face I'd ever seen, huge dark eyes and a delicate head which tapered down into a tiny nose and nostrils. He looked as if he'd been bred for the show-ring – his parents could have been champions, but his parrot mouth would have put an end to his chances. He'd probably been sold on from home to home from the earliest possible age. Heaven knows what kind of life he'd had.

"It's all right, boy, you're safe now."

This was what Hollywell Stables was all about: saving lives, putting an end to misery.

"I swear I'm going to close them down!"

James leaned against the trailer after tending to Dusty, as we decided to call him.

"They're not getting away with this. Not as long as I'm a vet doing my job properly."

I'd never seen James so upset. He was close to tears.

Dusty had been rescued from the Leafton horse sales which were held once a year on the other side of town. Horses arrived from all over the country to be sold off for a pittance. They often came in batches, sometimes wild, straight off the moors, sometimes broken down and no longer of any use. We'd never been to this particular horse sale before but by all accounts it had a bad reputation. Although inspectors visited all the sales throughout the country some were better run than others. Leafton was definitely one of the worst. James had been there to check on the horses, to make sure they were well fed and watered and in proper condition. Dusty had been with a group of ponies brought in from a riding school. They'd been hidden round the back. James had to put three of them to sleep because they were so infested with redworm. Dusty had been one of the lucky ones. With proper care and lots of love he could have a good life.

"They're not getting away with this, Mel. I won't allow it."

Burning with anger, James leaned his head against the hard metal of the trailer. For quite some time now he'd been romantically attached to Sarah. We all thought the world of him and I knew for him to get this upset, the Leafton Sales must be pretty horrendous.

"We're coming with you." Ross's voice broke the silence.

James lifted his head.

"It's our job as much as yours," Ross carried on. "If Sarah was here she'd have done exactly the same. We can't let these animals suffer. We've got to do what we can."

James said nothing.

"You can't stop us," Ross said, getting defensive,

his dark hair flopping into his eyes. "We're coming whether you like it or not."

"Tomorrow morning," James said. "I'll pick you up at eight o'clock."

Chapter Two

"I'm coming with you!" Trevor plonked himself down on the side of the water trough.

"Oh no you're not!" Ross threw back at him. "You're not going to mess this up."

Trevor had arrived an hour early and had actually done some work for a change. Ross had then gone completely bonkers when he found him feeding grass cuttings to Big Boris. Everybody knew that grass cuttings could give horses colic. They swallowed them down without digesting them properly and the result could be fatal.

After that, Trevor was banned from going anywhere near Dusty and so stormed off in a huff.

"This isn't some pleasure trip you know," Ross said. "It's serious business."

We'd been to horse sales before and it wasn't a pretty sight. All those horses neighing to each other, lost and lonely, not knowing where they were going to end up. It was impossible to save them all.

"You're not coming with us and that's final," Ross said, sticking to his guns.

Mrs Mac was going to look after Dusty while we were away. She was getting really good at first aid and could even give an injection. James had shown her how – I was too squeamish to even try. We'd stayed up all night with Dusty, keeping him warm, giving him plenty of fluids. James was convinced he would get better.

"Where's my riding hat?" Katie screeched from inside the tack room. She was still dressed in her pyjamas.

"For heaven's sake, Katie, that's the last thing you need. Now hurry up!"

Danny plodded out of the house wearing Sarah's Sherlock Holmes hat and a false moustache. Trevor burst out laughing and Ross grinned.

It was important that we kept a low profile, that nobody realized we were from a sanctuary. Mrs Mac had drawn some money out of the bank in case we decided to bid for a horse under James's direction. If it were known who we were, the price would go sky high.

"Can we just try to look normal?" Ross said, running his hand through his hair in exasperation. "Is that so much to ask?"

James arrived at two minutes past eight. His car was so overloaded with veterinary equipment that the back bumper was practically touching the ground.

"Where on earth are we going to sit?" I asked.

Katie ended up perching on a box of worming powders and I crouched next to a pile of rope which James said he'd last used to deliver a calf. I was just wrinkling my nose up in distaste when Danny thrust a stethoscope on my chest and made me jump out of my skin.

"Can we have some order in the back there, please," James said, turning on the radio and listening to the local news.

We were just turning past the holly tree at the end of our drive when a figure leapt out from underneath it and James had to slam on his brakes. "What the dickens?"

Katie started coughing convulsively and said she'd just swallowed a boiled sweet whole; James wound down the window, looking far from amused.

It was Trevor.

"What on earth do you think you're playing at?"

Trevor grinned down at us, looking sheepish. James told him to climb inside.

One thing about Trevor, he was built like a house. If there wasn't much room beforehand, it was now like a tin of sardines there in the car.

11

"Can't you wear a woolly hat or something?" Ross said, looking distinctly irritated.

An hour later we arrived at the Leafton horse sales.

At first it looked like any other horsey event. There were horseboxes and old cattle wagons parked down either side of the road; lots of noise and bustle; people walking around with head-collars and programmes.

One man was trotting up a piebald mare who looked very much like Jakey, our Welsh cob, only he'd got more white patches and this horse appeared to be decidedly lame behind. Even so, a totally unhorsey person nodded his head and money was exchanged. A girl clapped her hands together and I wondered if she knew the first thing about looking after a horse.

Trevor headed off straight away for the hamburger stall and James went to check in with the officials. Three Shetland ponies scurried past us, running loose and heading for a patch of rough grass. Within seconds a huge woman bustled after them, waving a lead rope in the air.

There was a huge area cordoned off where saddlery was being sold. There were rows and rows of harnesses and bridles and more saddles than I'd ever seen. It was all second-hand and there was every gadget under the sun; martingales, breastplates, draw reins, cruppers. Katie held up a bit with reins running through it and I told her it was a gag.

"Come on," Ross said. "We want to be with the horses."

We wandered down rows of makeshift enclosures made out of iron gates, crammed full of ponies and a few old donkeys. There were a couple of shire horses standing dozing together with their bottom lips hanging open, resigned to whatever fate might bring them. Beyond them we saw a farrier hard at work and then more rows of horses. There were horses of every shape and size, every age and colour. But they all had one thing in common – they all had a lot number stuck on their rumps and were available to the highest bidder.

"If there are any dodgy batches they'll be round the back," Ross said, trying as hard as the rest of us not to get emotionally involved.

We were looking for cases of cruelty, wilful neglect. In the distance we could hear the auctioneer hard at work. Someone was frantically brushing the tail of a smart chestnut who was weaving from side to side, swinging his neck in a nervous twitch. On the other side of us a man in a tweed jacket was examining the teeth of a tired-looking hunter and someone else was looking at a children's pony. I already wanted to go home.

"Where's Trevor?" Katie asked, looking round at the hordes of people. Surely we'd spot him with that ghastly hair.

"Hopefully we'll never see him again," said Ross, keeping his fingers crossed.

As usual, he spoke too soon.

Trevor appeared from nowhere. He looked pale and strained and was out of breath as if he'd been running.

"You've got to come quickly," he gasped. "It's serious!"

"Whoa, slow down a minute. What's going on?" Ross looked suspicious.

"There's no time to explain," Trevor rasped.

Ross wasn't so easily convinced. "How do we know this isn't one of your sick jokes?"

"Because it's not. All right? Now come on!"

Trevor practically frogmarched us down past the hamburger bar and along a row of horse stalls which we hadn't seen before. There were scores and scores of ponies all crammed together. I wanted to give each and every one of them a hug but there wasn't time.

Trevor was running, urging us all on. "Hurry, come on. Hurry!"

We veered off to the right and found ourselves in what looked like a car park, only it was empty, except for a huge lorry which was parked in the far corner. The ramp was down and two men were holding a group of ponies.

"Get down," Trevor hissed, pushing us behind a pile of building materials. "Don't let them see us!"

We crouched on the cold concrete, hardly daring to breathe.

"What's going on?" Ross was itching to get a better view.

From what I could make out the men were loading the ponies into the lorry.

"They've got stacks in there," Trevor whispered. "They're herding them in as if it's a corral."

No wonder it was all being done in secret. It was a sad fact that the travelling arrangements from horse sales were often appalling. No food or water, and impossibly cramped conditions. It was obvious that was the case here.

"We've got to do something," Katie said in a small voice.

Trevor poked his head over some breeze blocks, just as the men drove in three more ponies.

"It's gone!" he blurted out, diving back out of sight. "It's disappeared!"

He then tried to explain what he'd originally seen. Apparently, he'd gone to the burger bar when we arrived and then decided to have a wander around. That's when he saw the two men dragging a little pony by its forelock towards the car park. It was neighing frantically and trying to bolt in all directions but the men just clobbered it over the head with a big stick.

"It was so thin and weak and they kept on bashing it."

I was bristling with anger. How dare anybody treat an innocent animal like that? They ought to be locked up and the key thrown away.

"And there was something else," Trevor went on. "It kept bumping into things which I thought was really odd and then it turned round and I saw its face."

"And . . ." Ross prompted after Trevor hesitated a moment too long.

"It only had one eye . . . It was blind!"

None of us said anything. We were all too shocked to speak.

"We've got to get inside that lorry," said Ross. His voice sounded husky and I knew he was just as upset as the rest of us.

Trevor looked vague. "I hear what you're saying but I just don't see how we can."

He had no idea how determined we could be.

It wasn't long before we saw an opportunity. The men were having trouble with the last pony. They had a thick rope round its neck and were trying to yank it up the ramp but it wasn't having any of it. Every time it got close it ducked out to the side and dragged the men with it. I'd never seen a pony so strong.

"That's because it's not a pony," Ross whispered, getting a better view between two oil drums. "Look at its tail and the size of its ears – it's a mule!"

Ross was right. A mule is a cross between a male donkey and a female horse or pony and has a horse-like body with donkey-like ears, tail, legs and feet. They are also as strong as an ox, quick-witted, calculating and incredibly stubborn.

"It's planning something," Ross said. "Just watch what it does next."

The mule moved towards the ramp as if he had finally decided to go in. His massive ears flopped forward and his head hung between his knees in submission. The rope fell slack. He put two hoofs on the ramp. The men dropped their guard. And that was when the mule struck.

At the very last minute, without any warning, he hurled himself backwards, somersaulted in the air and fell heavily on his side. Within seconds he was up on his feet, as quick as a stunt pony, and hurtled off towards the road with the rope trailing behind him.

"Way to go!" Trevor half shouted, forgetting for

a minute we were undercover. The men were too angry to notice.

"Come on, this is our only chance." Ross leapt up, dragging me with him.

The men ran after the mule and were soon out of sight. We didn't have very long; they could be back at any moment.

The car park seemed enormous. We ran across to the lorry, not really knowing what to expect. As soon as we got close we could hear scuffling and kicking. One pony screamed out in protest. There were far too many ponies in the lorry.

The ramp was steeper than on most horseboxes and there wasn't any matting to prevent them from slipping. No wonder the mule wasn't very keen on going in.

The plan was that as soon as we discovered ill treatment first hand, someone was to go and fetch James. Under no circumstances could we all leave the lorry together because the men could come back and disappear into thin air.

I was the first to peer round the corner into the lorry. There were some metal gates keeping the ponies in but nobody had bothered to fasten the catch properly. A little black pony with a white blaze had got his hind leg caught in the gap. No wonder the poor creature was squealing in panic.

"It's all right, boy, I'll get you free."

I had to clamber up the ramp on my hands and knees and even then I was slipping all over the place. Ross was right behind me. "It's OK, we'll get you out of there."

The smell from the straw bedding was appalling. I don't think it had been mucked out in months. Heaven knows how many horses had been transported for it to get in this state.

"Ssssh, boy, I'm here." I opened the metal gate and the black pony immediately pulled loose. "Ross, I think you'd better take a look at this."

There must have been over a dozen ponies crammed in that lorry. But my eyes immediately fell on a little 12-hand pony stuck in the back, lying on its side and desperately scrabbling to get back on its feet. It was incredibly pretty but with one eye missing.

"Oh Ross, it's the blind pony!"

We pushed our way into the lorry without a second thought. It was so dark and clammy I could barely breathe.

There were no partitions, nothing to offer any protection. At least in proper horseboxes each horse or pony was tied up and separated from the others with enough room to keep its balance. One wrong move here and they could all be down on their knees. It was a time bomb waiting to go off.

"Don't frighten her," Ross said, directly behind me.

"It's all right, baby, we're not going to hurt you."

She was lying on her right side with her off-hind leg caught underneath her body. No matter how hard she tried, she couldn't get enough leverage to heave herself up. It was heartbreaking to watch her.

"There's my girl, steady now."

I put my hand gently on her forehead but she flinched away, struggling even more. She was completely disorientated. Her chestnut coat was so matted and stained from neglect that she looked more a dull brown than a bright copper and her tail was so long that the other ponies were trampling it into the straw.

"Hurry up," Trevor shouted from outside where he was keeping guard.

"We need your help," I answered back, aware that it would take more muscle power to get her on her feet.

Trevor's idea of horses was that they kicked at one end and bit at the other. He looked very nervous as he pushed his way towards us.

"We've got to try and roll her over," Ross said. It was so unbearably hot, the sweat was running down the sides of his face.

"Just tell me what to do." Trevor stood stiffly.

I didn't know whether it would work or not but, as it was, we didn't get the chance to find out. Katie and Danny were in the lorry before we knew what was happening.

"They're coming!"

I froze to the spot. There was nothing we could do. The voices were right outside the lorry.

"Ger in there, yer stupid nag."

Suddenly one of the metal gates was dragged open and the mule came staggering up the ramp with some kind of coat over its head. These men couldn't have been so daft if they knew that horses are quieter in the dark – that's why racehorses are sometimes blindfolded to go in starting stalls.

"That's the lot of 'em," a deeper voice grunted, banging the metal gate shut.

"No, wait! Stop it!" Ross shouted. I suddenly realized what was happening. The men were lifting up the ramp! They were going to lock us in! "Wait! No!" There was so much noise – the creaking hinges, the squealing and kicking, the mule trying to bulldoze its way through all the other ponies – Ross's voice was just lost in the mayhem.

We couldn't move. We couldn't push past all the ponies in time.

The ramp crashed shut with a massive thud. It blocked out all but a crack of daylight.

"Help! Help!" I banged on the metal sides of the lorry until the palms of my hands stung.

Ross and Trevor joined in. We were desperate. We were locked in the lorry with a dozen ponies and nobody knew we were here. We could easily get trampled to death.

"Help, help . . . Someone!" Katie's voice rose with panic.

All I could feel around me was a sea of bodies.

"Hold on!" Ross grabbed my arm as the engine whirred into life and I was thrown back against a pony's shoulder.

Trevor grasped hold of a haynet and Katie screamed out that she was falling. It was impossible to stay upright.

"Help, someone! Help! Help!" We all banged on the side of the lorry together but it was useless. Even worse, it was upsetting the ponies. Any more noise and they were all likely to go crazy.

The lorry hurtled along, picking up speed, showing no sign of stopping. The vibrations from the engine rattled through the floor into my legs and I had to deliberately brace my calf muscles to stop myself falling. If that's the effect it had on me, heaven knows what it was doing to the ponies. No wonder horses had to stand with their legs apart when they were travelling. But here there was no room – there wasn't even room to breathe, let alone stand comfortably.

"Everyone stick together." Trevor could barely disguise the fear in his voice.

"What now?" Katie clung on to my hand.

The heat was stifling. The smell from the dirty straw was already making my eyes sting.

"There's nothing we can do," Ross half shouted above the engine, one hand holding on to a tie ring, the other wiping the sweat off his face. "We've just got to accept it – we're trapped!"

Chapter Three

The most important thing was to stay calm. The only way we were going to survive this nightmare was if we kept our heads. Our main concern was to keep out of the firing line of the ponies' hoofs. The last thing we needed was one of us ending up with a broken leg or arm.

We were desperately worried about the blind pony. She was still down on her side and making very little attempt to get up. Also her breath seemed to be coming in short gasps, almost like someone with asthma. The only ventilation was provided by a few small gaps in the roof and sides of the lorry.

Luckily we were protected somewhat by being in the back corner. At least we had two sides of the lorry to lean against. The rest of the ponies seemed to have settled down, almost as if they realized they had to be quiet for their own safety. All except the mule that is, who was still blundering his way through the tightly packed lorry as if his life depended on it. My eyes had adjusted now to the dark and I could make out shapes and at least get my bearings. It was easy to see the mule because his ears stuck out above everybody else's.

"Just what is it with him?" Trevor mumbled, obviously more nervous of the mule than of the other ponies. I kept forgetting Trevor was so inexperienced with horses. Up until a few days ago the nearest he'd come to a horse was a seaside donkey.

"Look!" Ross pointed to the blind pony who was suddenly trying to heave herself up by striking out with her near foreleg. The other ponies were shuffling away to give her as much room as possible.

"It's the mule," Ross whispered. "I think he's trying to get to her."

Every time the mule squealed, she seemed to try a bit harder.

"Trevor, get round the back of her and try and give her a lift." Ross moved across to her head and supported her shoulder.

"He's coming through," Danny whispered excitedly as one of the bigger ponies nipped the mule on his shoulder.

"Katie, stay behind me." Ross grabbed the back of her coat as she tried to reach the mule. "Mel, where are those horse nuts?"

I fumbled in my pocket and closed my fingers round a dried-up apple core. "Here take this."

"They know each other," Danny said. "They do – I know they do."

The mule flashed the whites of his eyes and glared at Trevor who probably reminded him of the men driving the lorry. Trevor was roughly the same build.

"Danny, move out of the way." Even though we'd had so much experience handling horses I wasn't sure how the mule would take to us. He obviously hated humans and I think he thought we too were the enemy.

The lorry suddenly lurched into a lower gear and sent us all flying forward.

It was just enough of a jolt for the little mare to work her leg free and stagger to her feet.

"She's up!" Ross yelled. "Trevor, watch out!"

The mule was right behind him and about to take a chunk out of his jeans.

"Let him get to the mare," Ross shouted. "He thinks we're hurting her."

As soon as the mule reached the blind pony he started sniffing her all over and curling up his top lip. She half whinnied in delight and leaned her bodyweight against him as if for reassurance.

"Is she really blind?" Katie whispered, not wanting to look at the empty socket which had once been an eye.

"It's likely to be cataracts," Ross insisted.

"Maybe with an operation she might be able to see again."

"What's happening?" Suddenly we were in total darkness. I couldn't see a thing.

"I think we're in a tunnel. Nobody move." Ross was right beside me.

I put my hand back against the side of the lorry and nearly leapt out of my skin. It was dripping wet.

"Condensation," Trevor whispered. "It's like being in a sauna."

I don't know how long we were in that lorry. Ross was the only one wearing a watch but he couldn't see to read it. It wouldn't have made any difference if we had known. We were trapped, and until that ramp came down there was no form of escape.

"I'm hungry," Katie moaned for the hundredth time. We'd shared out a packet of salt and vinegar crisps which Trevor found in his pocket but all they'd done was make us more thirsty. My shirt was clinging to my back it was so hot. I was worried about the blind pony who had broken out in a sweat on her neck and flanks.

Katie decided to call her Sally because it sounded pretty and Trevor named the mule Walter after his grandad.

We'd managed to pull a wooden gate which was

propped up in the corner across at an angle so it protected us, Walter and Sally from the other ponies. I was sure I heard one of them nearest the ramp fall but Ross refused to let me go and look. There was nothing we could do – not until the lorry stopped.

The engine droned on and on. My legs didn't just ache any more, they felt numb. Trevor started to tell us his life story.

I couldn't stop thinking about James. He'd be going out of his mind with worry. And what if Sarah was trying to ring home? And how was Mrs Mac getting on with Dusty and the other horses? They all seemed so far away.

"We will get out of here, won't we?" Danny sounded as anxious as I felt.

"Of course we will," I insisted, trying to keep the panic out of my voice.

But I didn't know then what really lay ahead of us.

"This is weird," Ross strained his hearing even more. The lorry had stopped and there were voices outside but the main noise, drowning out everything else, came from seagulls – hundreds of them by the sound of it.

"We're at the seaside," Katie whispered in an excited voice.

It was quite possible the ponies had been bought for rides up and down the beach. They used ponies as well as donkeys – but somehow I wasn't so sure.

"What's happening now?" Ross nearly lost his balance as we lurched forward up a sharp incline. I grabbed hold of the wooden gate to keep it upright and Danny slipped right down on his bottom.

There were other vehicles all around us and the noise of chains clanking together. There were voices shouting, "This way – stop – pull in here." More engines in front of us.

"Oh my God, Mel," said Ross. "I think we're on a ferry!"

"But we can't be!" I yelled. "We can't be, it's impossible!"

But it wasn't so impossible, as Ross clearly pointed out. Ponies were being bought cheap and shipped abroad every day of the year. It was well within the realms of possibility.

"But we haven't got any passports," Trevor croaked. "The furthest I've ever been was Blackpool and that was only for a weekend."

"Is this what you call being a castaway?" Danny chipped in.

"Stowaway," Katie corrected, and then com-

29

plained at length that she wanted the toilet and was passing out from starvation.

"It'll take at least an hour and a half," Ross calculated.

"What? To go to the toilet?" Katie looked flabbergasted.

"No, you dope, to cross the English Channel!"

We were on a ferry surrounded by other vehicles, heading for somewhere in Europe.

Trevor crouched in the corner with his head between his knees. Ross said it must be a rough sea but I couldn't imagine that in the middle of May.

I was still amazed that these horses had been loaded on to the ferry without anybody checking them. Surely there must be some kind of law to protect them? Ross said there probably was but that it wasn't enforced. All I knew was that it wasn't good enough.

"What's French for horses?" Katie ignored me.

"What's French for 'Help, we're in trouble'?" Trevor added.

We'd already agreed that no matter what we were going to stay with the horses. There was no way we were going to let anything happen to them. Sally nuzzled at my hair as if she knew what I was thinking and I vaguely wondered if she could smell my apple shampoo.

Katie commented that her horoscope for that morning had said something about a "trip over water".

A deep fog-horn blasted out somewhere above us and Ross said we must be nearly there.

"It's about time," Trevor groaned from the corner.

"*Vive la France!*" I added, seriously wishing I'd paid more attention in my French lessons.

"Ssssh," Ross hissed, and then we heard the chains clattering and car doors slam. Trevor said the chains were used to tie down the wheels, which I suppose made sense.

"Hold on," I yelled as the engine whirred into life, jolting my legs.

We felt ourselves moving down off the ferry and then come to a grinding halt for what seemed like ages.

"Customs," Ross said, and I slowly tried to extricate my big toe from under Walter's hoof before it dropped off from lack of blood supply.

Poor Walter. He didn't have a clue what was going on and his big woolly ears kept wafting back and forth at the slightest noise. Katie said if we stood close enough they would act as a sort of fan, but Trevor for one didn't want to risk it.

"God, he's an ugly mutt," he whispered, just

before Walter booted him in the back with his mottled nose.

I didn't think anything would be able to stop the sweat running down my back apart from a blast of fresh air and there didn't seem much chance of that at the moment. Surely they'd have to let down the ramp soon – these ponies were gasping for water and more hay. They couldn't keep them locked up like this for ever.

The little black pony reared up at the front of the lorry and Walter backed into a hairy cob and promptly started to bray. The noise was deafening and seemed to come wrenching out from deep within him. Once he started he wouldn't stop.

"Come on," Ross yelled. "This is our only chance."

Someone was bashing at the ramp and within seconds dazzling streams of sunlight gushed into the lorry and half blinded us.

"Come on," Ross yelled.

We squeezed past all the ponies like greased lightning.

"What the devil . . .?" A man with bleached blond hair and putty-coloured skin leapt back from the metal gates as if he'd seen a ghost.

"How the . . .?" His mouth moved up and down like a ventriloquist's dummy but nothing came out. He was so startled that he took a step back and slipped on the ramp and that was when we seized our chance to escape.

"Run!" Ross shouted, holding open the metal gate as Katie and Danny pushed past. "Run!"

I leapt off the ramp behind Katie, banging my knee on the metal springs but not even feeling it. We had to find an official, someone in charge.

"Run!" Trevor yelled, grabbing hold of my arm and dragging me forward.

My eyes squinted in the bright light and I could hardly focus. We appeared to be in a huge car park with lines of cars queuing up in all directions. There was a massive cafeteria or hypermarket, and to the right, rows and rows of pay phones and a sign which said Enquiries and the equivalent in French.

Suddenly the man with the bleached blond hair yelled out, "Get them!" and a man walking towards us looked up and dropped two plastic cups of scalding coffee and a bag of chips. He was the other driver!

A cold chill of terror raced up my spine. I could hear Sally neighing frantically from inside the lorry. We had to do something!

"Over there, quick!" Trevor pushed me in the back towards a car where a family were having a picnic.

Trevor banged on the window and the husband

nearly choked on a sausage roll. The wife looked horrified and locked all the doors.

"Come on, they're not going to help," I yelled and raced over to Ross who was trying to jump the queue to the Enquiry desk. Two Germans and an Italian family started screaming at him in foreign languages.

"Look," Danny pointed, grabbing hold of Ross's shirt.

"Oh no!" The lorry was backing out of the car park!

The men must have back-tracked as soon as they realized what we were trying to do. They were getting away and we hadn't even got their registration number!

"Taxi!" Trevor yelled. "Taxi!"

There was a row of taxis lined up alongside the pay phones but none of them took any notice of Trevor. Even Ross was getting desperate. Every taxi he came to was occupied or off duty.

"You want 'elp?" a Frenchman stepped out of the rank, looking hopeful. He had jet-black hair and a ferret-like moustache. He was also the only friendly face we'd seen.

"Get in." He pointed to a scruffy red Renault estate and we all clambered inside. To prove that we could pay, Ross showed him the wad of five-pound notes Mrs Mac had given us for the horse sale, and he quickly started the engine.

"Where to?" he asked in his heavy French accent.

"Just follow that lorry." Ross leaned across from the back seat, gasping for breath. "And step on it!"

We flew out of the docks and on to the main road. The Renault rattled like an old bus but kept on going. The Frenchman hissed and grumbled but I couldn't understand a word he was saying. Katie shrieked that we were on the wrong side of the road and for a minute I thought so too.

"We're in France, you idiot," Ross said, scouring the road ahead for the lorry.

"Can't you go any faster?" Trevor urged, hanging on to the dashboard.

"I 'ave my foot flat to the boards," the taxi driver assured us, but cars were zooming past us from both sides. Everybody seemed to drive like maniacs.

"There!" Katie shrieked, breathing down my neck as she spotted the lorry ahead.

"Just don't let them spot us," Ross said from the back seat.

"That eez very difficult with you all hanging out of ze window!"

Trevor pulled his head back into the car just as

two men drove past in a Mercedes saloon, pointing and waving at him like mad.

"They probably think you're part of the local culture," Ross grinned.

"No, I think it's ze smoke from ze back," the taxi driver corrected him.

Sure enough, black smoke was billowing out of the back of the Renault.

"What now?" Ross panicked.

"We take short cut, now 'old on!"

Without any warning, the taxi driver shot across two lanes of traffic and disappeared down a side street.

"Was that wise?" Ross croaked. Danny's face was pressed up against the window and my stomach felt as if it had just done the loop the loop.

"We'll lose them," Katie wailed in despair and the taxi driver banged down hard on the accelerator.

We were off the motorway and heading out into the country. Earlier on I'd spotted a green sign which said to *Dunkerque* and *Lille* but now I didn't have a clue where we were going.

"Hang on!" the Frenchman yelled and sprays of water battered the sides of the car as we dived through a ford at sixty miles an hour. Black smoke was still puffing out of the back like a thick fog and I had an uneasy feeling the Renault wouldn't last out for much longer.

"How much further?" Katie demanded as a gaggle of geese waddled into the road and we came to a screeching halt.

The thought of never seeing Walter and Sally again was too much to bear. We had to save them. Trevor leant over and bashed the car horn and we thundered off.

"I'm Katie and this is Ross." Katie decided to start introducing us all as trees sped by at the speed of light.

"Pierre – Pierre Duval," the Frenchman said with a hint of national pride, leaning over the front seat head-rest and trying to shake hands.

"Over there!" Trevor yelled.

"It's the lorry!" Katie shrieked.

Sure enough, just pulling out of a narrow cross-roads straight ahead was the lorry and judging by the speed they were going they obviously thought they'd given us the slip.

"We can still catch them." Ross yanked down the back window which got stuck halfway and Pierre pressed even harder on the accelerator.

We were heading out into open countryside now. There were no houses in sight, just winding lanes and flat, almost barren-looking fields. I always thought France was hilly and full of vineyards but this could have been anywhere in England.

We'd all decided to try to overtake the lorry and pull it to a halt. It was a common fact that ponies were sometimes transported non-stop right through Germany, Austria, even as far as Italy. We couldn't afford to follow them for that distance – we didn't have enough money. It was now or never.

"We're getting closer." Trevor's voice wavered as he frantically tried to scribble down the registration number on the back of a matchbox. More smoke puffed out of the back of the car.

"There's an extra hundred if we catch them." Ross wafted the wad of notes in front of Pierre's nose. Using the money was now the only way of saving Walter and Sally. We hurtled over a hump-backed bridge with such a burst of speed that all four wheels left the ground.

"We're gaining on them!" Katie bounced up and down on the back seat unable to control herself. Danny looked carsick and I suddenly realized I was sitting on a baguette.

"It's him, look." Trevor leaned out of the window at the same time as the man with the bleached blond hair stuck his head out of the passenger side of the lorry. We'd just entered two double bends and the lorry was forced to slow down.

"Gotcha now!" Trevor yelled out of the window, shaking his fist.

We were right behind the lorry. Pierre moved to the right to try to overtake. Then to the left. The lorry blasted forward as the road straightened out.

"Now!" Ross shouted, as a gap opened up on the left. Pierre slammed down his foot and we shot forward. We would have made it. We would have got past, apart from one slight hitch – the car broke down!

"My car!" moaned Pierre, throwing his arms up in the air. "This has never 'appened before!"

"I'm sorry, Mel," said Ross.

"We tried our best," Katie said in a weak voice.

"Yes, but it wasn't good enough was it?" Ross snapped.

Trevor gazed along the road at the vanishing lorry.

"We've lost them," he said finally, venting his anger by kicking out at a front tyre.

Chapter Four

"It's nobody's fault," I said, trying to keep Ross and Trevor from clawing each other's eyes out.

Ross carried on regardless. "You idiot, if you hadn't shouted for a taxi; if he hadn't come along with his death trap . . ."

Pierre sat in the passenger seat smoking a French cigarette and apparently ignoring everyone around him. He was more worried about the state of his car and whether he was going to get his money. Now that the excitement of the chase was over, reality hit us with an uncomfortable thud. We were stranded in the middle of nowhere in a foreign country with no passports and hardly any money. All we had for transport was a wreck of a car and a grumpy French taxi driver to act as our guide. It wasn't very good.

"Well, we can't stand around here all day," Trevor barked, determined not to be bullied by Ross. "What are we going to do?"

Pierre shrugged his shoulders, refusing to talk

and just rubbing his thumb and forefinger together which we took to mean money.

"How much?" Ross asked, doling out five-pound notes by the fistful.

"I'm off to have a look-see." Trevor flounced off down the road in his Doc Martens and heavy metal T-shirt. Heaven knows what the locals would think of him.

I suddenly realized that none of us had eaten anything since breakfast and it would soon be dark. As soon as I acknowledged my hunger I felt very weak; I thought I was going to pass out. Somehow we had to get back to civilization and find a decent eating place.

"I know how to light a fire," Danny piped up, proudly wanting to show off his Boy Scout skills, but the last thing we were at that moment was prepared. At least not for what happened next.

"Oh my God, I don't believe it," Ross groaned. "Where on earth did he find that?"

Trevor came grinding round the corner on an old rusty tractor.

"What does he think he's doing?" We all stood there with our months gaping open in amazement.

"But we can't just take somebody else's tractor." Ross was stunned by Trevor's suggestion.

"In case you hadn't noticed," Trevor answered, "we're stuck in the middle of nowhere and I don't know about you lot but I need a good feed."

Katie said she did too and she didn't fancy a night under the stars in a foreign country – you didn't know what might be lurking around.

"We're in France, Katie, not Africa, for heaven's sake." Even so, I could see her point. I didn't fancy it either.

Trevor said we'd return the tractor next morning and nobody would be any the wiser.

"What about me?" Pierre said suddenly when he realized we were leaving. "You cannot leave me 'ere." It was amazing how quickly he could stop sulking when it suited him.

Trevor found an old rope in the car boot and attached it to the front bumper. Pierre sat in the driving seat to steer and Trevor towed him along on the tractor. Ross, Katie, Danny and I sat behind Trevor on the tractor.

We all felt terrible about using the tractor but it was an emergency. Pierre said the nearest house was about fifty kilometres away and there were no roadside phones. Trevor insisted he'd found the tractor in a field so it wasn't as if he'd taken it from someone's drive. I was amazed that he'd managed to start the thing in the first place.

Katie had found the squashed baguette on the

back seat of the Renault and now dug in her teeth only to find it was rock hard. Danny wiggled one of her teeth and said it was loose, but I'd more on my mind than the state of Katie's teeth.

All I kept seeing was that lorry disappearing into the distance and not knowing where it was going. It could be anywhere by now and the chances of seeing Walter and Sally again were very remote. I couldn't stop picturing Sally's face and imagining those men handling her. She reminded me so much of Queenie, another pony we'd rescued, only Queenie was dark brown while Sally was a chestnut. But they both had that same sweet angelic expression and they'd both shared the same nightmare – ill-treatment. Only for Sally it wasn't over, not by a long chalk. We couldn't give up.

"I 'ave a brother called Jean-Paul," Pierre suddenly piped up. "He owns a big restaurant, we'll go there."

Maybe he wasn't so bad after all.

The restaurant turned out to be a dimly lit bistro with candlelit tables and pretty checked tablecloths. Jean-Paul came panting through from the kitchens, slapping Pierre on the back and playfully on both cheeks.

If Pierre was thin and weaselly, Jean-Paul was like an elephant in comparison. He must have been all of seventeen stone with a mountainous stomach and pudgy cheeks. His eyes twinkled like two black currants and he wore a huge chef's hat which towered upwards like the Eiffel Tower. He took it off in a sweeping gesture, revealing a shiny balding head and wisps of metal-grey hair. He talked at the speed of an express train, mostly in French, and wasn't happy until we were all sitting down with huge checked napkins thrust down our shirts and a glass of Coca-Cola in our hands. Danny finished his all in one go.

We all ordered *bifteck* and *pommes frites* (steak and chips) but I then changed mine to something called bouillabaisse, thinking at least one of us should sound sophisticated. Jean-Paul assured me it was *magnifique*. Pierre ordered *cuisses de grenouille* whatever that was, and Trevor horrified us all by adding *escargots* to his order which Katie at first thought was the name of a racehorse, only it wasn't, it was French for snails, and as soon as I told her, she looked sick and buried her nose in her Coca-Cola. Ross whispered behind his napkin that Trevor was just trying to be clever, but I honestly didn't think he realized what he'd ordered.

"We must phone home," Ross said, relishing the taste of a French bread roll.

But what we suddenly all remembered at the same time was that the phone was out of order.

James had said so. I racked my brains trying to remember Mrs Mac's number and then Ross said it was ex-directory.

"Maybe it's been fixed," Trevor said, blowing his nose on the checked napkin like a bugle which immediately caught the attention of three French girls sitting in the corner.

By the time the food arrived I was ready to start eating the table and Katie was still moaning about her loose front tooth. The *bifteck* and *pommes frites* were served with a flurry of pride from Jean-Paul.

"We've got to do something," Ross said. "We can't just sit here in a foreign country and pretend everything's all right."

Trevor looked down at his steak which was oozing blood.

"You'd think they'd cook it first," he said, having only just recovered from the sight of the snails he had ordered as a starter.

I tackled the bouillabaisse which had just arrived. It turned out to be a thick fish stew. I seriously wished I'd stuck to the *pommes frites*.

Katie was horrified when Pierre casually mentioned that he was eating frogs' legs and that they tasted very similar to chicken. They lay on his plate, stick-like and charcoaled, rather than green and frog-like and I wondered just how hungry I'd have to be before I ate those.

"So what are we going to do?" Ross sounded desperate as he hacked at his steak with a blunt-bladed knife and topped up on Coca-Cola.

Somewhere out in the dark Walter and Sally were battling for their lives.

"We need a car." Trevor stated the obvious.

Pierre grimaced and twiddled with his ferret-like moustache as if the very word "car" was causing him acute pain. Katie stabbed a chip and I discreetly covered up my bouillabaisse with my napkin. Jean-Paul brought more bread rolls.

"I'm going to try and ring Hollywell." Ross scraped back his chair, rubbing his face with a tired hand, the enormity of our situation beginning to sink in. "There's only one person who can sort all this out."

And at that moment I didn't think I'd ever missed her more.

Sarah wasn't just our stepmother but our best friend and without her we felt like a ship without a captain. She was as determined and passionate about the sanctuary as she was about her writing career and it was her refusal ever to be beaten that had kept us all going for this long.

Ross slammed down the phone in a state of exasperation. She wasn't there. Nobody was. The line was still dead – so the phone was still out of order. The international operator said three times that there was no connection. It took that long for the news to sink in. I was getting really frightened now. Everybody would be going crazy with worry. All James would know was that we had been at the horse sale one minute and the next we disappeared. Sarah would never forgive him. What if they'd rung the police? What if they were showing our pictures on the television?

"It'll be all right." Ross looked gaunt and worried. I knew it was the only thing he could think to say.

Katie came running in from the restaurant with Danny behind her and nearly went hurtling into the dessert trolley.

"It's Trevor," she shrieked. "He's gone!"

"I knew it," Ross glowered, pacing up and down, his eyes blazing blacker than Pierre's hair. "The good for nothing lazy lout, the miserable low life . . ."

"Ross, stop it, this isn't going to get us anywhere." We were in the back hallway of the restaurant beyond the kitchens and Danny and Katie were busy making friends with Jean-Paul's giant poodle Fifi.

47

They'd just told us the whole story and as far as I could make out, Trevor had gone off with the three French girls who had been sitting in the corner. One of his discarded snail shells had accidentally flown across the room and landed near their table. It was the perfect excuse for him to start talking, although Katie said none of them spoke a word of English.

"Doesn't stop him though, does it?" Ross fumed. "Talk about being insensitive! How could he think about chatting up girls at a time like this . . .?"

It didn't matter anyway. He was gone and that was that. But what hurt most was that I'd actually started to like him – he'd been slowly growing on me and now I felt cheated and let down.

"We were right all along," Ross said. "We should have known."

Jean-Paul, who had a heart of gold, immediately took pity on our situation. He told us to go upstairs to his bed-sit and he'd be with us in a moment. Pierre followed us up and immediately raided the fridge for a bottle of beer.

Ten minutes later we told Jean-Paul our whole story with Pierre interpreting whenever necessary.

"It's impossible." Jean-Paul could hardly believe it. But then, come to think of it, neither could we.

Katie sucked a continental chocolate and Jean-

Paul slapped Pierre on the head and demanded back our money.

"You 'ave to excuse my little brother – he is greedy and mean."

I felt momentarily embarrassed and didn't know where to look. Jean-Paul handed the crisp five-pound notes back to Ross and said he had an idea, a very good idea.

But, as it was, we didn't get a chance to hear it. There was a sudden pounding up the narrow staircase and the door burst open, flying back on its hinges. Trevor stood in the doorway looking elated, with pink lipstick smeared round his left cheek and his hair stuck up on end like a toilet brush.

"Well, don't just sit there," he said, waving a bunch of keys in the air. "I've got us a car!"

Chapter Five

It was a bright pink Citroën with more soft toys dangling from the rear-view mirror than I'd ever thought possible. There was a row of stuffed elephants in the back window and a sticker which said in French, "Save Oür World". It might just be possible they could save ours.

"You thought I'd done a runner, didn't you?" Trevor drove like a Formula One racing driver but we didn't seem to be going very fast at all.

Ross looked uncomfortable in the front seat and I mumbled that we had all given him the benefit of the doubt. Katie gave me a black look and I squirmed like a worm. The Citroën belonged to one of the French girls who was called Celestine and she'd gladly agreed to lend him her car when he explained our situation. I'd obviously underestimated Trevor's charm.

Jean-Paul ordered Pierre to go with us as he knew the French roads and could act as our guide.

We were heading back out into the country with the sole intention of tracking down the lorry. It was common sense that they'd have to stop to feed and water the ponies – they couldn't keep them travelling indefinitely. Pierre was sure he knew which road they would have taken and there was only one farmhouse along the way that he knew of. It sounded like a wild goose chase but we had once before set off into the unknown in search of a Falabella and got lucky. Maybe Lady Luck would shine on us again. I sincerely hoped so for Walter and Sally's sake.

"What was that?" Katie's fingers curled round mine.

"An owl, I don't know, some kind of French bird." Trevor pushed at the gear stick and we shot forward.

It was a pitch black night with no moon and no stars. Jean-Paul had given Ross a torch which looked about fifty years old and only worked if you kept your thumb pressed on the switch. A car whizzed past with two men in the front seat and their headlights on full blast. Trevor cursed and turned a corner.

And then it happened.

"What was that?" Trevor slammed on the brakes and veered into the grass verge.

A dense black object had just lurched in front of the car, narrowly missing the bumper. It had loomed up from nowhere and disappeared just as quickly. A split second earlier and we'd have hit it for sure.

"It's ze headless man!" Pierre half shrieked, crossing himself frantically and muttering what sounded like a dozen "Hail Marys". He'd just been telling us that this stretch of road was said to be haunted by a headless ghost who was still looking for his wife. Katie quickly started locking all the doors.

"Look, this is stupid," I said, trying to be brave but not really feeling it. I cranked down the window in a flash of courage and then screamed at the top of my voice. There was a face looking in at me!

It was black and hairy with pleading eyes and massive ears – it was Walter!

"I don't believe it!" We stumbled out of the car and raced across to the grass field where he'd galloped.

"Walter! It's OK, it's us!"

The poor thing must have been terrified. I didn't know who'd been more scared, me or Walter, but one thing was certain, my bloodcurdling scream must have frightened the living daylights out of him.

"Walter, Walter!" Ross flashed the torch under the trees and along a hedge but there was nothing. Some cows in the next field started mooing and pushing against a wooden gate. Katie fell down a rut and Ross panned the torch up and down for a third time. Still there was nothing.

"Mel, are you absolutely sure it was Walter?" Ross sounded doubtful. "You weren't imagining things?"

I might have vivid dreams and sleepwalk occasionally but I knew what I'd seen. It was Walter all right.

"But what's he doing out here? How did he get loose?"

I honestly didn't know.

"Look, over there!" Danny grabbed the torch from Ross. "Look, there, by that tree. It's him, it is – it's Walter!"

A lump caught in my throat as we walked slowly up to him. We all wanted to run and throw our arms round his neck but that would have scared him off.

He was standing in a hollow, trembling from head to foot, his head slung low and his great ears pinned back against his brown woolly neck. If mules could cry then I think he would have been sobbing his heart out. As it was, he just stood dejected and forlorn.

"Walter, sweetheart, it's me." I gently stretched out my hand and felt his whiskery nose. He jumped back as if in a trance and then lifted his great head and stared.

"Walter."

Recognition filtered through, slowly at first as if he couldn't quite believe it, as if it was all too good to be true.

"It's us, boy, it really is." Danny buried his head in his short, stubby, sticking-up mane. "We came back to save you."

He was OK. Physically at least. Ross felt him all over, down each of his sturdy legs and across his pony-like body. There wasn't a scratch. But what he'd gone through mentally was another story. Something awful must have happened for him to be this upset. And I couldn't help feeling it had something to do with Sally.

"Where is she, boy, what's happened to her?"

Walter butted me in the stomach and gazed longingly over the fields. His spirit was coming back in great waves. Trevor decided to wrap his trouser belt round his neck just in case he decided to take off. And not a minute too soon.

Suddenly, with a deep sigh, Walter bulldozed past us all and hurtled off up the field with Trevor in tow.

"Come on," Ross said. "We'll lose them . . . Hold on, Trevor!"

"What about the car?" I suddenly remembered the pink Citroën skewed across the grass verge.

"Wait for me!" Pierre galloped after us, terrified of being left alone just in case the "headless man" really did put in an appearance.

We crossed two fields and slithered down a bank before Walter finally checked his pace, sniffing the air and curling back his top lip.

"What is it, boy? Where now?"

This was madness, following a disturbed mule through the French countryside in the middle of the night, looking for two thugs and a lorryload of ponies. But if anybody could find them it was Walter. Mules were super intelligent, with an inbuilt sixth sense. I knew he could do it.

"Come on, boy." We set off downhill through kneehigh grass, Pierre panting after us, Trevor desperately holding on to the leather belt. All I could see in the torchlight was Walter's short tail swishing back and forth and his great ears stuck up like antennae. Presumably somehow he'd managed to escape and had set off to try to find help. It sounded far-fetched but I would have bet anything it was the truth.

"What's the matter?" Walter had suddenly stopped dead in his tracks.

"Look – down there." Ross flashed the torch.

There was a farmhouse. Outbuildings. A big white lorry.

"It's them!"

We had to be careful. It was no good blundering in like the Cavalry. There was no way we could take Walter any further. We'd be spotted for sure.

Trevor passed Pierre the leather belt. "Hold on to him. If we're not back in half an hour, fetch help."

I didn't know who looked the most horrified, Pierre or Walter.

We set off clinging close to a wispy hedge and praying that we couldn't be seen. The ground was terrible and it was all I could do to stay on my feet. Rabbits flitted out in all directions and in the distance a pony neighed, long and lonely – calling. It could be Sally.

"What was that?" A door slammed shut and a dog barked. I was sure I could hear a voice.

We kept on going.

It was a small farmhouse with a courtyard, a barn and some more buildings round the back. Luckily there weren't any outdoor lights and, as far as I could make out, nobody was in sight.

We crept slowly behind a hen hut and on to the first building. The lorry was over on the other side of the courtyard and impossible to reach in one go. Trevor switched off the torch and we shuffled forward, Katie and Danny right behind me. We were getting close to the house. We could hear singing. My ankle twisted in a rut and I nearly fell into a roll of chicken wire.

"Listen." Ross held up his hand.

A deep throaty whinny came out from one of the outbuildings.

"They've moved them inside," Ross whispered. "They're not in the lorry."

We crept forward, glued against a brick wall damp with moss, creepy to the touch.

"Over there." Trevor was sure he knew which building they were in.

We pressed on, my heart clattering against my rib cage. I couldn't stop thinking about the man with the putty-coloured skin and bleached blond hair – he looked lethal. I'd heard stories of sanctuaries following horses abroad and how if they got caught the men would stop at nothing to scare them off, from smashing up their houses to threats of physical violence. Nerves made the palms of my hands clammy. What were we doing?

Trevor pulled back a sliding door and poked in his head. My heart leapt. There were thousands of turkeys crammed inside.

"They're over here," Katie hissed impatiently, dragging us round the corner to an open-fronted barn.

There they were, all crammed in, hungry and dejected, the little black pony fighting off the attack of an aged looking cob.

"Sally, where is she? Sally!" Ross shook the torch which suddenly wouldn't cooperate.

"There." Danny pointed right at the back.

There she was. A dull brown coat and the long flowing mane and tail. She stood stock still with her head rocking back and forth, back and forth, like a disturbed child. There was no doubt about it, she was in a terrible state. Tears prickled like grit in my eyes. I tried to imagine what it must be like to be blind and surrounded by strange ponies, ill treated, and your one best friend and guide suddenly not there any more. Was it any wonder she was distressed?

"Oh Ross, we've got to help her."

"No," Trevor said. "Use your head, there's no way we can get her out of there without being caught, it's impossible."

"But we've got to," I almost shrieked. "I'm not leaving here without her."

"Mel, I hate to say it, but Trevor's right. We've got to fetch help."

"But we can't desert her a second time. It'll break her heart."

"She's not seen us." Trevor turned his back on the ponies. "And I think it's best we keep it that way. Let's not upset her any more than we have to."

The prickly sensation in my eyes increased ten fold.

"Come on, there's something I've got to do," said Trevor.

It was the first time I'd ever walked away from a pony in need. It hurt like mad.

"It's the only answer." Trevor insisted on going across to the lorry. "The way things are at the moment they could get away. We've got to stop them in their tracks."

I had no idea what Trevor proposed to do but I had noticed that he knew a lot about cars.

"Here, hold this." Trevor handed the torch to me. We'd crept carefully across the courtyard, one step at a time, and we were all now in front of the lorry. There was a fresh bout of singing from the house but nobody came out. Somebody struck up a tune on a guitar and somebody else switched on a light in an upstairs room.

"Hurry up, we've not got much time."

Trevor set to work. His plan was to disconnect the wires to what he called the stop solenoid on the fuel pump which would effectively stop the lorry going anywhere, but just to be extra sure he took out a penknife and started hacking away at the fuel pump.

The rich heavy smell of diesel swamped the air.

"Come on, Trevor."

We were running out of time. We also had no obvious way of escape. We were boxed in.

"Trevor."

"OK, another couple of minutes."

"Trevor!"

My voice rose to a high-pitched squeak. Just a few hundred feet away was the man with the putty-coloured skin and bleached blond hair. "Trevor!"

Ross pushed Katie and Danny behind him. I dropped the torch which smashed on the tarmac and Trevor stood rooted to the spot.

"Hi there," Trevor squawked. "Lovely lorry you've got here."

"Shut it, plankhead. You're dead meat."

This guy was mean.

Terror made my knees turn to jelly.

"Let's take him together," Ross hissed out of the side of his mouth at Trevor who had a cheesy grin fixed painfully on his face. He wasn't half as tough as he looked.

"OK, big bruv, let's do it."

Trevor charged forward hollering at the top of his voice, with Ross right behind him. It could have been a scene from *Butch Cassidy and the Sundance Kid*.

"Watch out!" I screamed as the bleached blond

thug pulled a short metal truncheon from behind his back. He slammed it over Trevor's head with such force I thought he'd smashed his skull. Trevor's legs buckled and he slithered to the ground in a heap. Unconscious.

Ross backed off.

"Come on, idiot, lost your bottle?" the man waved the truncheon in the air, taunting Ross with a look of disgust.

"Time you learnt a lesson or two like your mate here," he jeered, backing Ross and the rest of us into a corner. "You really shouldn't mess in other peoples' business."

"You're not going to get away with this," said Ross. "We're on to you, we know what you're up to!"

"Des, leave them be. They're just kids. I've called the police." Another man appeared from the house, older, more sedate, the other man in the lorry.

The blond thug dropped his guard. Just for a second. It was all we needed.

"Now!" Ross yelled and we all dived forward.

There was only one way out and that was past the lorry and straight down the drive. But what about Trevor? We couldn't leave him!

"Catch them!" The two men were after us, angry now, ready to do anything.

"Run!" Ross scooped up Danny who was lagging behind. Katie gripped on to my hand like a clamp. Great gasps of air filled my lungs but I still couldn't breathe. I was too scared. Ross was right behind me. It was pitch black ahead and all I could hear were heavy footsteps, getting closer. Help, somebody!

"Mel!" I went crashing down on my knees, sprawling to the ground with the hard wet gravel grating into my face. "Mel, get up!"

A car turned up the drive.

"It's the police!" I wasn't sure whether it was Ross's voice or Katie's but a great wave of relief washed over me.

Two police officers sprang out of the car. I could see their boots grinding towards me. I suddenly remembered my French lessons and the gendarmes; French policemen in blue trousers and black jackets with white belts were the good guys – only this time they weren't on our side.

"Mademoiselle, I afraid you are under arrest!"

Chapter Six

"Your passports, please," said a miserable looking gendarme with a shrew face and glasses.

We were in big trouble. Not only did we not have our passports but we were being accused of trespassing and attempted theft. Or at least that's what Ross said but I didn't entirely trust his grasp of the French language.

Trevor complained of a splitting headache and he'd been officially examined by the police doctor. The verdict was he was all right but he must have a head as tough as a nut and none of us disagreed. He washed back Paracetamol with scummy black coffee and said he could murder a cup of proper English tea.

The gendarme with the shrew face immediately picked up on the word "murder" and thought he had a confession on his hands until a lady police officer came through and gave the necessary interpretation.

"Phew, that was close," mumbled Trevor.

"Let me do the talking," Ross hissed.

"Are we going to jail?" Danny asked.

We were in a room with bare walls and just a desk and chairs and some old curtains and carpet. It was a long way from the Hollywell kitchen.

I'd never felt so low in my whole life and all I could think about was poor Sally and what had happened to Walter. The gendarme had found the five hundred pounds hanging out of Ross's jeans pocket and was convinced we'd stolen it. Nothing we said seemed to make any difference. I was beginning to think we'd be here for eternity. Katie and Danny looked petrified, especially when the gendarme kept glaring at them, no doubt hoping they'd break down and tell him the whole story.

"Let us go over theez once more," he said, trying to take off Hercule Poirot and failing miserably. "You all got stuck in ze lorry?"

Ross started at the very beginning and went through the whole story yet again. But it was obvious no one believed us.

The first thing Ross had done was give them the address and telephone number for Hollywell and anybody else he could think of who could get us out of this nightmare mess. All I wanted was Sarah to walk through the door and sort everything out. She'd put the gendarme in his place. Nobody ever got the better of Sarah.

"You have behaved in a reckless manner," he

droned on, twitching his head. "We will have to see."

We were left by ourselves then. Another lady brought in some rubbery eggs on toast and pots of coffee and the rest of the time we sat staring at the four walls. We were shut up for most of the night. We weren't locked in but it felt like a cell. We couldn't leave, which amounted to the same thing, and all we wanted to do was dive out and start our needle-in-a-haystack search for Walter and Sally.

"I hate this place." Katie was on the verge of tears. "I hate it, I hate it . . ."

"Ssssh." Ross cut her off in mid-flow. "Listen."

The voice was unmistakable. It had the authority of a sergeant-major and the cutting edge of a politician. The gendarme must have been trembling in his boots.

"Yes, madame, no, madame."

"Well, don't just stand there, man, where are they?"

Sarah burst through the opened door like a red tornado. We all felt very relieved. Ross couldn't stop grinning and Trevor couldn't stop staring.

With long red hair, glamorous good looks and a wild wacky manner, Sarah could almost be one of her imaginary romantic heroines. Trevor looked overawed and immediately impressed. Sarah looked at Trevor as if he'd just stepped out of the House of Horror.

"Where did you find him?" Ross and Trevor had just gone to the toilets and Sarah and I were standing in the foyer with Danny and Katie. "The lad's a nightmare. How can we be taken seriously as a sanctuary with a purple wonder like that around?"

Sarah had already given us a grilling for disappearing into thin air. "Have you any idea how worried we've all been?"

Apparently James had been going out of his mind and blamed himself for not looking after us properly. It took a while for him to realize we'd disappeared and when he did it was like all hell had been let loose. Mrs Mac was going frantic and since the phone lines had been repaired Sarah had been ringing the police every half-hour.

"Lucky for you that the French police called the moment you were arrested. I never want to go through that again," Sarah said. "Is that clear?"

We were out on the pavement now, breathing in fresh French air. Trevor lagged behind like a lame dog, suddenly shy and aimless, not wanting to intrude.

"Give him a chance," I whispered to Sarah. "He's all right really."

Sarah wanted to know every minute detail about Walter and Sally. We'd already interrogated her about life back at Hollywell. Dusty was doing very well and Mrs Mac had taken him to her heart. She was fussing like an old hen. Queenie was missing Danny, and Boris had been squabbling with Terence as to who was the head of the tribe. Fluffy had run off with one of Mrs Mac's slippers. "Honestly that foal gets more human every day." Fluffy was a Falabella whom we had rescued from two jugglers at a circus. He was a miniature horse, only the size of a dog and he spent more time in the house than out. Apart from that everything was fine.

"What now?" I said, realizing we were walking in no particular direction.

Sarah was striding along and shaking her head after hearing what we had to say. "How can horses be treated like that?"

Her red hair swirled out in the wind making her look wilder than ever. "I'm going to have that horse sale cleaned up if it's the last thing I do."

"Watch out!" Trevor leapt forward and saved Sarah in the nick of time just as she was about to step on to a pedestrian crossing. A cherry red van whistled by with no intention of stopping.

"Steady on, Mrs Foster, they drive like maniacs over here."

"I have been to France before, you know." Sarah

was more ruffled than she was letting on. Trevor turned bright pink.

"Now where's this Pierre bloke and who did you say, Jean-Paul?"

"But that's just it," Ross said in a heavy voice. "We can't remember."

"What do you mean, you can't remember?"

We were in a café drinking great bowls of steaming coffee (they didn't seem to use cups or mugs in France) and wallowing in our sorrows.

The fact was we had arrived at the restaurant in the dark and left in the dark. We hadn't thought to ask what it was called. We hadn't expected to get separated from Pierre. It was all a terrible mess. I stared down at a crisp croissant, wondering where we would go from here.

"We can't give up," Ross twiddled with a plastic spoon. "We've got to find them."

"I've got it!" Trevor leapt up, nearly sending the rickety table flying. "The street, it's the same name as an author because I remember asking Pierre about it, Rue . . ."

"Barbara Cartland."

"No, you idiot."

"Stephen King."

"No, no, one of the romantic ones."

"Danielle Steel?"

"That's it, Rue Danielle. We've cracked it!"

We dived out of the café as if they'd just announced a bomb and leapt into the first taxi we could wave down. Rue Danielle was just around the next corner.

"There, Valentino's, that's the restaurant."

I was nervous about stepping inside. To start with it looked twice as smart in the daylight and last night seemed but a foggy dream. Did it really happen at all?

"Come on, Mel." Ross gave me a firm push.

We found Jean-Paul pacing up and down his kitchen in a flurry of excitement. "At last you are here!"

He was very relieved to see us.

"Where's Pierre? What's happened to Walter?"

"So theez must be the beautifool Sarah, she looks like film star – no?"

"Wrong, she's an author – now what about Walter?" Ross was getting agitated.

Jean-Paul made a great show of kissing Sarah's hand. Pierre bounced into the kitchen and then tried to slink out like a rat.

"At last my brother has done the right thing. Come outside and we will show you."

I was really worried now. Jean-Paul was carrying on as if nothing was wrong. Surely Pierre must have told him what had happened. Sarah looked completely confused by the whole scenario. But then Jean-Paul was a pretty overwhelming character, in size as well as personality.

He opened a low wooden door and we stepped out into a small courtyard with hanging baskets and tufts of grass sticking up between the flagstones. There was what looked like a garage and a couple of storerooms with stable doors. One was overloaded with boxes of every description, from tinned oranges and tomatoes to toilet rolls and artichokes.

"Never tell that we sometimes use tinned food." Jean-Paul put his finger to his lips.

I noticed something else. A shadow at first. Then a big brown hairy head thrust over the other stable door and two womble-like eyes staring at us with obvious joy. It was Walter!

"You brought him back!" Katie was ecstatic.

Pierre grinned unexpectedly and Walter started braying at the top of his voice. It sounded like bedlam.

"Help," Katie shrieked. "My ears are about to drop off."

Sarah dived into the stable faster than any of us and gave Walter a thorough examination. Walter looked at her as if she was mad but seemed to realize that she was one of us. He had cobwebs round his ears and wisps of straw sticking out of his mouth but according to Jean-Paul he hadn't eaten anything since he had arrived.

I checked his water bucket which was half full and there were droppings in the stable. Sarah looked in his eyes which were a healthy salmon-pink colour and felt his pulse under his throat. Normal.

"He's as fit as a flea," Trevor said.

"His heart is sick," Pierre added in a solemn voice, momentarily holding a fist to his chest.

"You mean he's love-sick?" Sarah rubbed affectionately at Walter's massive ears and got stuck up with cobwebs.

"*Exactement.*"

Poor Walter. He looked like a lost soul. He must have been desperate to know what had happened to Sally and he probably blamed himself for leaving her. He let out a huge sigh as if he knew what we were talking about.

Pierre had led Walter back to the road as soon as he realized something was wrong. He'd heard the police sirens and thought the best plan of action was to run away. The funniest thing was that he'd leapt on to Walter's back and ridden him all the way home. It was hilarious. It was so bizarre, I couldn't picture it in my mind.

"What I wouldn't give to have seen that," Ross grinned.

"It was ze only way." Pierre looked deeply offended as we all burst into peals of laughter.

"But what about Walter?" Danny said in a small voice, still painfully aware of Walter's depression.

Walter stared out over the door with a sad expression.

"It's OK, boy, we'll find her, I promise." But I didn't sound very convincing.

Somewhere out there was a little brown pony with a terrible handicap and her fate was in our hands. There was only one thing I was really sure of – we had no time to lose . . .

Chapter Seven

"Blast and double blast," Sarah cursed as, back at the farmhouse, we stood in the middle of the farmyard looking over the iron gate into empty space.

They'd gone. Vanished. Just as we'd expected.

"Theez is not good." Jean-Paul stated the obvious.

Ross kicked out at a metal can and sent it hurtling against a breeze block wall.

The lorry was gone. The only sign it had ever been there was a purple-black patch of diesel that somebody had tried to cover over with a shovelful of sand. Trevor must have succeeded in delaying them while they repaired the damage.

"What now?" Ross looked at Sarah who was scanning the farmhouse with eagle eyes.

We'd all agreed to come out in force, thinking of safety in numbers. Sarah was intent on tackling the thugs face to face and offering to buy all the ponies. More often than not, we had to pay over the odds to get possession of a pony – it was the only way.

Pierre quivered with nerves and looked anxiously at his watch. Jean-Paul suggested it was time we leave while we were still in one piece.

Sarah had other ideas. We'd all arrived in Pierre's taxi which had been miraculously repaired by Trevor (even Sarah had been impressed) and Celestine's pink Citroën which Pierre had reclaimed earlier. Apparently Celestine had been round to the restaurant baying for Trevor's blood. Heaven knows what he'd promised the poor girl to get the loan of her car. Nobody had thought to return the old tractor which was still parked in Jean-Paul's courtyard.

"Trevor, over here quick." Sarah went up to the kitchen window and peered inside. Above the main window was a smaller one and it was flapping open.

"But you can't do that," Pierre squeaked in disbelief.

"Watch me." Sarah kicked off her shoes and climbed on to Trevor's shoulders.

"I'm right with you, Mrs F." Trevor staggered under her weight.

Sarah plonked a stockinged foot on his head and struggled to lever open the catch on the bottom window. "Gotcha."

It swung open.

"I'll go in," I said emphatically, determined not to be dissuaded. "You lot keep guard."

The men could be back at any time.

I clambered up on to the sill above a sink piled up with dirty pots. There was a wilting spider plant in one corner and a bottle of tomato sauce in the other with the lid left off and flies stuck all around it. On the table in the middle of the room was a heap of squashed lager cans and a half full tin of baked beans with a fork still propped in the middle. I wrinkled up my nose in distaste.

"Look at the paper," Trevor urged through the window, pointing to a newspaper lying on a chair. But it was no help at all. There was nothing written on it and it was open at the racing pages – no relevance to Sally and the other ponies. Underneath was a notepad and a message, scrawled in black biro: "Des, be back soon. Don't let them knock you down." In the bottom corner was a doodle of an aeroplane and the words, "Ten nags – £40 per hour."

It didn't make sense.

"Mel, get out of there, quick."

I scribbled down the message on a piece of kitchen roll in my pocket and scrambled out of the window as fast as I could. Luckily it was a false alarm.

"Come on, let's get out of here while we still can." Trevor was very jumpy.

We galloped towards the cars, nervous tension running through us like electricity. Suddenly the farmhouse seemed sinister and spooky and I had no intention of ever going back inside.

"Mel, get in." Ross held the car door open while Jean-Paul tossed a coin.

Pierre lost and so it was his turn to stay behind and look out for the lorry. He insisted on being by himself. Jean-Paul reassured Sarah that he could be trusted, and he gave him a couple of packets of cigarettes and three bars of chocolate.

The plan was that as soon as he saw anything he was to report back to Jean-Paul on the CB radio. In the meantime we'd decide what to do. I felt awful leaving but Jean-Paul and Sarah were adamant. We had to take it in shifts – it could be days before the men returned. I knew they were right but it didn't make it any easier. Katie said she was starving and Ross pondered the meaning of the message.

"Ten nags – forty pounds per hour. It sounds like a riding school."

I didn't know what to make of it. Neither did Sarah. All I knew was that £40 an hour seemed a heck of a lot.

"We're no closer to finding her, are we?" Danny

twiddled with one of Celestine's elephants which had black beady eyes. Unfortunately we had to admit that we weren't.

We pulled up outside Valentino's with mixed feelings until, that is, we saw a familiar white car parked outside with a GB sticker on the rear bumper. It was James!

"Monsieur Jean-Paul, come quickly, we have a big problem!"

It soon became clear what the problem was. Walter who had obviously got bored standing in his stable had escaped into the restaurant kitchen.

We ran through the push-through doors to find Walter with his head in a black forest gâteau and James desperately trying to get a grip on his short neck.

"Sarah, do something!"

It was funny. In fact it was hilarious. So it was no wonder that we howled with laughter and James just got redder and redder in the face. Jean-Paul bobbed up and down, puffing with exasperation.

In the end the only way we could get him out was to wheel the dessert trolley into the courtyard with Walter in hot pursuit.

Trevor grabbed hold of a woolly ear and I flung my arms round his neck.

"So this is Walter!" James appeared from the kitchen, looking the worse for wear.

Walter was furious that he was being dragged back into the stable and lashed out at James, very nearly clipping him on the knee.

"Walter!"

James dived to one side and said he now knew the true meaning of the expression "kicks like a mule".

Trevor was glued up with sticky fresh cream all down his front and Walter was slapping his tongue round his lips to devour every last particle of Jean-Paul's *specialité de la maison*, black forest gâteau.

"At least he's getting his spirit back," Trevor brightened.

"My beautiful kitchen!" Jean-Paul's wails could be heard from here to Paris.

"What are you doing here?" Sarah ran down the step leading into the courtyard and very nearly fell over.

James looked blank and then said he thought we needed help. He'd received a desperate phone call from Sarah at some unearthly hour of the morning to say that everything was fine, but all the kids were in police custody and she'd forgotten to bring her credit cards with her.

It was only now that I noticed her hair was tied back with one of James's old black socks and she hadn't got a scrap of make-up on her far too pale face. It looked as if she'd just dived out of the house straight on to the plane without a second thought.

"I can cope," she spluttered, looking anything but together.

Jean-Paul finally simmered down and realized there was no permanent damage to his precious kitchen and none of the customers lunching in the dining room had suspected a thing.

We all trudged upstairs to his flat where he prepared something called a *croque-monsieur* which was basically ham and cheese on toast and tasted absolutely delicious.

There was no word from Pierre.

"What do you think's happening?" Danny asked, pulling at a strand of cheese which stretched like bubble gum and refused to break off.

None of us knew. We could only hope and pray that Pierre was all right.

"Mrs Mac's coming across with the horsebox," said James.

The last time Mrs Mac had driven the horsebox she must have lost two stone in sweat alone and vowed she would never sit behind the wheel again. The lack of power steering pulled her arms out of their sockets for weeks and she still couldn't get the hang of second gear which was almost imposs-ible to find unless you pumped at the clutch.

Thank goodness we could at least take Walter back and hopefully the others without any kind of quarantine. Unlike dogs, horses very rarely caught rabies and if they did they didn't pass it on to humans or other horses.

We told James the whole story about Walter and Sally and the scribbled note I'd found in the farmhouse. It made no sense to him either.

"I think we've got to be prepared for the fact that Sally could be anywhere by now," he said in a tentative voice, knowing far more than us what happened to horses on the Continent.

Pierre was supposed to report in every half hour as to what was happening. We hadn't heard from him.

"Theez is not like him." Jean-Paul paced up and down getting anxious.

Jean-Paul was called downstairs to oversee the puddings which were in danger of sagging. James tried to keep everybody calm.

"That's it, I'm going back." Sarah leapt up, fran-tically rooting on the coffee table for Celestine's heart-shaped key ring. "He's probably fallen asleep . . ."

"We'll go in my car." James knew better than to

try to talk her out of it. "Mel, you'd better tell Jean-Paul."

"Hold on!" Trevor was at the window looking down into the courtyard.

"What is it? What's the matter?" I yanked the heavy velvet curtains back further. There was no doubt about it. A car had just pulled into the courtyard. A red taxi. And Pierre climbed out of it.

Oh no. He stood in the doorway as pale as paper and shaking from head to toe. A thick mat of dried blood clogged up his moustache and his nose had expanded to three times its normal size.

"They attacked me!" he squeaked, hardly seeming to believe it himself. "I theenk they broke my nose!"

Poor Pierre staggered towards an armchair saying he felt faint and Jean-Paul raided the fridge for some ice cubes.

"The low-lifes," Ross growled, as shocked as the rest of us.

I couldn't help thinking that if they were capable of this, they would stop at nothing. We could all be in danger.

Sarah said someone had once been put in hospital for three weeks when he tried to report horses being exported from Ireland in a double decker lorry. It didn't make Pierre feel any better.

Jean-Paul gave up on the ice cubes and brought the brandy. "Here – drink this."

Pierre tipped back the glass and drained it in one gulp.

"So what happened?" Danny stared at Pierre's nose in fascination.

Pierre started to tell us his story. He hadn't been waiting long when the lorry came back. He was going to ring in on the CB but then heard voices shouting and decided to get closer just in case he might overhear something important. He hid behind an old farm trailer and watched the ponies being herded out of the lorry. But there weren't as many, only five or six, and there was no sign of a pony fitting Sally's description.

" 'They fetched a good price,' the blond man shouted. I heard him clearly. Then he said the pretty blind one she gone to ze zimmerframe and fetched biggest money."

"What?" We were all shellshocked.

"What's a zimmerframe?" Katie asked.

To be honest, I wasn't so sure myself.

"It's a walking frame for humans," Sarah said. "But what's it got to do with Sally?"

James looked out of the window but didn't say anything.

"Pierre, you must have misheard him. There

aren't any zimmerframes for horses." Sarah was quite adamant.

"And there was something else," Pierre guzzled down another brandy and then closed his eyes for dramatic effect. Jean-Paul seized the opportunity and hid the brandy bottle back in the sideboard.

"Before they found me and beat me to ze pulp they said a name."

"Don't stop now!" yelled Katie.

"Ze name was, and remember, I risked my life for this . . ."

"Yes?"

Pierre closed his eyes again.

"Pierre, don't do this to us!" It was all Sarah could do to stop herself shaking him by the shoulders.

"Gently, gently," Jean-Paul whispered. "Pierre, my own sweet brother, you were saying . . ."

"Pierre!"

Suddenly his eyes snapped open.

"La place de la Josephine. That is where she is!"

Chapter Eight

It didn't exist. We searched phonebooks, ransacked tourist guides, rang the Information Bureau, not to mention the library. Nothing.

The only street vaguely familiar was rue Constantine. We drove there straight away, but it turned out to be a fruit tinning factory just outside Calais.

"This is crazy." Disappointment was etched all over Ross's face.

Pierre sat on the back seat trying to keep a low profile, which wasn't easy with a huge white pot stuck on his nose. Jean-Paul had taken him to Casualty where they'd confirmed a clean break and patched him up. Since then Pierre hadn't stopped whining and was convinced this meant the end of his love life.

"What love life?" quipped Jean-Paul.

Talking of love, Walter had gone into a decline, refusing to talk to anybody and even turning up his nose at Jean-Paul's black forest gâteau. He just stood at the back of the stable with his head between his knees and his eyes dull and staring. If we didn't find Sally soon I thought his heart would break.

"Time waits for no man," Pierre philosophized, sighing deeply.

Katie gave him a queer look and James said how right he was.

"If you find love, grasp it with both hands."

James looked thoughtful and Katie whispered that Pierre wasn't so bad after all – quite a softie really.

Another person we'd been wrong about was Trevor. Who'd have thought when he first arrived at Hollywell that he'd have become so passionately involved in our mission to save Sally? James said he was a rough diamond and even Sarah was warming to him. Katie said he was lonely and needed a family. I thought he needed a purpose.

"He's just called in." Jean-Paul shimmied across the courtyard in a turquoise polo neck carrying a huge carrot cake which he offered to Walter.

Trevor was posted at the farmhouse in Pierre's taxi to keep guard. We wanted to save the other ponies, not just Sally.

As of now, though, nothing had happened, the men were still in the farmhouse.

"I've got to go out." James surprised us all by this sudden announcement.

"Where to?" I asked without thinking.

Sarah was still in the kitchen helping Jean-Paul make strawberry cheesecake. She said it took her mind off Sally and it might trigger off some ideas. She'd already decided that talking reason to the men wasn't the answer.

"The town hall," James blurted out. "I'll be about an hour."

"You know something, don't you?" I put on my most questioning look.

James said he'd tell us all later and that it might be just a hunch.

I spent the next half an hour working at Walter's coat with a scrubbing brush. His winter coat was still flying out even though it was well into May. Outside the sun shone down in brilliant rays – it was going to be a fantastic summer, I just knew it.

Katie lectured me on the advantages of French chewing gum which came in a variety of flavours from peach to pineapple and blackcurrant. I asked her if she'd lost her tooth yet and she wiggled it about, opening her mouth like a hippopotamus. Danny helped me clean out Walter's feet with a penknife and wipe the gooey stuff out of his eyes with a handkerchief. He still looked depressed and defeated.

"Don't worry, boy, we'll find her,"

Before the words were out of my mouth Sarah

leapt down the steps into the courtyard. She was sprayed with lemon rind and cheesecake mixture but ecstatic all the same.

"We've just heard from Trevor. They're loading up the ponies. There's no time to lose."

We dived into Celestine's car in two seconds flat. It was a bit of a squash – Jean-Paul, Pierre, Ross, Sarah and myself. Katie and Danny were left in Celestine's care.

"Where's James?" Sarah asked as she started the engine and jerked forward.

"Never mind, I'll explain later."

We hurtled along the French lanes towards the farmhouse without any regard for speed limits. But then, as Sarah said, we could do with some police back-up. As usual, though, when you wanted the boys in blue they weren't anywhere to be found.

"He's not here," I groaned, when we turned a corner and found the secluded lay-by we had earmarked as a spy place empty. We'd agreed that Trevor was to keep watch in Pierre's taxi parked some distance away on the brow of a hill where Jean-Paul's binoculars could be trained on the farmhouse. That was the brief. But where was Trevor now?

"The fool must have gone in," Sarah said, sounding genuinely worried.

Fear dried up the back of my throat within

seconds. If Trevor had gone inside there could be real trouble. That thug with the blond hair had already broken Pierre's nose and knocked Trevor unconscious. Next time it could be fatal.

The late afternoon sun dazzled the windscreen in piercing rays and Sarah brushed irritably at her fringe and pulled down the sun flap. A packet of cigarettes and a bar of chocolate nearly fell on her head and I vaguely wondered what Celestine would think if she knew how many of us were crammed in her car. As it was, none of us said a word. We were too worried about Trevor.

We turned into a straight stretch of road. There was only one thing for it. We'd have to turn up the drive, into the farm that I had vowed I never wanted to see again. We had to, for Trevor and the rest of the ponies' sakes.

"It's the lorry!" said Ross, as a huge white vehicle turned into the narrow road in our direction and headed towards us.

What on earth were we going to do now? They'd recognize us for sure and there wasn't enough room for both vehicles to get past. Sarah slammed on her brakes and the car screeched to a halt as if in slow motion, but before any of us could think straight, Pierre's scruffy red taxi bolted out of a field opening and splayed itself across the road ahead.

Trevor leapt out of the driver's seat and stood almost Goliath-like in the middle of the road, his arms in the air, his feet rooted into the road like cement.

"He's going to kill himself," Sarah yelled, totally at a loss as to what to do. There was no time. There was no time for the lorry to brake; it was travelling too fast.

"Trevor!"

The idiot didn't move. He just stood in the middle of the road like a tree trunk.

"Get out of the way, you idiot!" Sarah's voice rang out like a siren. But it didn't do any good. Trevor didn't budge an inch. The lorry just kept on coming.

"I think he watches too many films," said Pierre, putting his hand over his eyes.

Jean-Paul was the first to run forward, jiggling up and down. All I could think of was the ponies in the lorry – were they still on their feet?

Suddenly a loud hiss of air brakes cut through the air.

"It's stopping!"

The wheels locked, skidded and screeched along the tarmac. Trevor backed up a pace, then held his ground. Still the brakes squealed, slowing, slowing, but not nearly fast enough.

Pierre let out a long low whine but I think he

was more interested in the plight of his precious taxi.

"Trevor!"

The lorry stopped with six feet to spare. Steam hissed out from under the cab. Sweat ran down the back of my neck. It was too close for comfort.

"Don't you ever do that again!" Sarah shrieked like a banshee. "We don't need any heroes . . ."

Trevor grinned from ear to ear but his hands were trembling and his neck was bright red.

The bleached blond thug leapt down from the cab, letting out a stream of curses a mile long. He came face to face with Sarah.

"I'm going to flatten you." He ignored Sarah completely and lunged at Trevor.

"You keep your hands off him." Sarah stepped in front of Trevor as quick as a whippet. "You lay one finger on him and you've got me to deal with."

"Who are you – his guardian angel?" He spat on the ground and leered at Sarah, fury bubbling dangerously under the surface. I felt sick.

Jean-Paul and Ross backed her up, one on each side.

"You're outnumbered."

He laughed out loud. "A bunch of kids, a beef-cake, and a jellyfish – don't kid yourself."

I was beginning to panic.

Sarah tried a different tack.

"Money – I'll double the price of every pony you've got on this lorry."

"Why all this interest in a few nags?" But his eyes were beginning to glitter. All Sarah had to do was reel him in.

I vaguely noticed Pierre disappear behind the lorry.

"So what do you say?" Sarah rolled out a wad of five-pound notes.

His greedy little eyes flickered over them.

There was nothing we could get him for legally. There was no witness to say he'd broken Pierre's nose. There was no proof the ponies in the lorry were being severely ill treated. And even if there was, how did we communicate that to the French police?

The only thing we could do was use Hollywell funds to buy the ponies, even if it was at a ridiculous price. We all knew for sure they weren't destined for good homes. What was left in the lorry were the rejects, the ones nobody wanted.

"Another hundred." The man held out his greasy palm with so much attitude I felt like hitting him. All I wanted was to get that ramp down and lead out the ponies as quickly as possible.

I heard something click behind the lorry.

Ross and Jean-Paul were temporarily distracted. Only for a second but it was long enough.

"Well, ta very much, I'll be seeing you in Heaven." The man made a dive for the lorry cab.

We should have known. We should have known he couldn't be trusted. He had no intention of handing over the ponies. He was trying to rip us off.

"Hey, stop!" Trevor was after him like a shot but Sarah was even quicker. She grabbed hold of his shirt tail and clung on for dear life.

"Get your hands off me." He swung his arm round and hit her on the side of the neck.

Trevor saw red. I saw a black police car with the siren wailing rattling up the road.

"Trevor, stop him!" Ross and Jean-Paul helped Sarah back on to her feet and I stood in a daze, not knowing what to do for the best.

Trevor left us all speechless. He grabbed hold of the man's shoulder, whipped him round and lashed out with his fist. Unfortunately he missed. There was just enough time for the blond thug to belt him in the stomach and scramble into the driving seat. That's when I noticed James and the policeman racing towards us.

"I'll stop him, Mrs F!" Trevor clung on to the driver's door for dear life and desperately tried to grab the keys to the lorry. But it was too late. The engine whirred into life.

"Mel, get out of the way." Sarah pushed me

back and the gendarme mouthed instructions but nobody could hear a thing.

The lorry edged towards the grass verge to get past the taxi.

"*Attention, attention!*" The gendarme jumped up and down on the spot and started frantically blowing a police whistle.

"What was that?" There was something else. A loud grating noise – and it was coming from behind the lorry. The ramp was down!

Pierre was standing in the middle of the road holding on to four hairy ponies!

"*Attention, attention!*" The gendarme was a dead loss.

"I've got him, Mrs F!" In the midst of all the confusion, Trevor dragged out the thug by the scruff of the neck.

"Ouch!" Pierre yelled as a bushy-tailed Shetland dug his teeth into his arm.

"We've saved them!" Ross said.

There was the Shetland, a big cob, a brown Welsh Mountain and the little black pony with the white blaze. They stared at us in amazement and then Pierre screeched that he needed help.

Jean-Paul, for once overcome with pride for his brother, ran up and kissed him on both cheeks. He then kissed the Shetland for good measure who scowled at him with beady eyes.

"Madame, why you not tell me you famous writer?" The gendarme's eyes gleamed with reverence and appreciation. "My wife, she read all your books."

This was a touch of good fortune. Sarah wasn't famous but her books had recently started selling in France.

"Your sister – she still doing the film in Hollywood, eh?"

Oh dear. He'd got her confused with Jackie Collins.

James winked at me and Sarah stifled a giggle.

"I see you very modest. I say no more. But you want police protection. Monsieur Renaldo can provide."

This was bizarre. We all agreed that we'd have to take the four ponies to a local riding school because there was no room at Jean-Paul's. It would take two trips on the ferry to get them all home. Jean-Paul said he knew a lady who taught children – she was a bit scatty but she treated her horses like royalty. Pierre backed this up by saying in the winter she wrapped them up in duvets. I didn't like to say we did exactly the same at Hollywell. Jean-Paul said he'd get it organized, and Renaldo fumbled in his brain for something to charge the blond thug with. The man said his name was Des

Chapman and he came from Manchester and what on earth were we playing at?

Renaldo marked him down for assault and reckless driving straight away. He refused to answer any questions about the other horses or the man he was working with. All he kept demanding was a solicitor.

What I wanted to know was what James had been up to and how he'd come to be with Monsieur Renaldo who was at present polishing his specs and staring at Sarah as if she were an international celebrity.

"Well, I've got a lot to tell you," James began. "And it's just as I suspected – "

"That's it!" Pierre grasped hold of a newspaper which he found on the passenger seat of the lorry. It could well have been the newspaper that I had been looking at earlier. It was folded back at a picture of a fairground with dodgems and high swings. Above the photograph I picked out a few words in the headline. "La Place de Napoleon."

"This is it!" Pierre repeated, his black eyes bulging and his long olive-brown forefinger tapping at the picture. "La Place de Napoleon, not Josephine – I remember wrong – It's her husband, Napoleon . . . That is where we will find Sally!"

"My God, he's right!" James grabbed hold of

the paper. "This would fit. That's where she is –
at the fairground."

Sarah grabbed the paper from James and Ross
grabbed it from Sarah. The fair was just outside
Calais.

"Well, don't just stand there," Sarah shouted to
everybody at once. "Let's get going!"

Chapter Nine

We stormed off down the road in the police car and the Citroën. Pierre and Jean-Paul stayed behind with the taxi so that they could contact their friend who would deal with the ponies.

James began to tell us what he had discovered. "I got suspicious when you mentioned forty pounds an hour and ten ponies. I knew it rang a bell, I'd read something somewhere. I just couldn't remember what, and besides, I didn't think they were operating in France." James zoomed through a red traffic light following the police car and Renaldo who was giving us a police escort.

"James, we're not with you – what are you talking about?" Ross grabbed hold of the front seat as we sailed over a humpbacked bridge. It was just like the first car dash when we ordered Pierre to follow the lorry, only that seemed like a lifetime ago. Now signs for Calais flashed by – we were going back to where it all began.

"I went to the town hall to ask questions and they confirmed my worst fears."

"Oh no." Ross went white. "Don't tell me you're thinking what I'm thinking." Realization flooded into his face.

"What? What are you talking about?" I hadn't got a clue. "James, will you please tell me what's going on?"

"Of course her being blind wouldn't make any difference. In fact it could be quite a bonus."

"Zimmerframe!" Ross shouted. "So that's what they meant. It all adds up."

"James?" I was practically going out of my mind by this point. I could see James looking at me through the rear view mirror – worried, strained – not sure how I'd react.

"A carousel," he said. "Sally's been sold to a carousel."

"Oh."

"Is that all you've got to say?" Ross looked surprised.

It was all I could say at that point. A lump had formed in my throat as big as a golf ball. Carousel. Carousel. Carousel. Of course. I should have guessed.

"Mel, are you all right? You've gone really pale." Ross was sitting in the back seat with me. Sarah and Trevor were travelling on ahead with Renaldo and a hand-cuffed Des Chapman.

Carousel. It was so obvious.

"But I thought they were only found in Spain," I said, not trusting my voice to sound normal.

Only a few weeks ago we'd all sat in the kitchen at Hollywell reading reports and deciding what we could do to help. Now we were going to see one face to face.

"So did I," James said in a grim voice. "But at the town hall they said they're spreading through Europe, just in the summer months, moving on every few days. That's why they're so difficult to track down."

"Oh." That same word again.

A carousel is a living nightmare for a pony. One of the first rides I'd ever had was on a musical carousel horse at a fairground. I didn't know how to ride and clung on, digging my shoes into its sides. But it was wooden and it didn't have any feelings. It didn't hear the loud music or the shouts and screams, the dodgems, the bustle, the over-whelming crowds.

The carousel we were talking about involved live ponies, ten of them usually, walking round and round in a circle all day long, often for ten to twelve hours without a rest. No water. No food. No kind word. Strapped into a metal frame with no escape. They couldn't move backwards or side-ways, they were dragged forward all day long – an equine zimmerframe.

"Of course it's hard to prove that the ponies are being ill treated," James went on. "They're usually up to weight, not emaciated. The actual floor is kept scrupulously clean, no droppings in sight. But it's the lifestyle which is the worst problem."

I could feel myself going numb as he explained. Dehydration. Flies. Exhaustion. Desperate boredom. Stupid tourists. Noise. Flashing lights.

"Most of these ponies turn into zombies. They switch off from everything and everyone."

A road sign flashed by – we were in Calais.

"There're two types of frame used, one where their head is pulled round on a very short fixed tether. The other..." James paused, unsure whether to continue.

"The other uses a metal harness."

"Oh." That word again.

"We'll stop them, Mel, and we'll get Sally. Trust me." Ross squeezed my hand.

"La Place de Napoleon." We were here.

"Just tell me one thing," I said to James. "Why?"

"Money. Ignorance. It's a lethal cocktail. The only way it will stop in Spain is if British tourists stop using them. Until everybody knows about the cruelty aspect it will carry on."

"Hurry, Monsieur James, there is no time to lose." Renaldo ran on ahead, pushing his glasses up his nose every time they slipped down, pinching his flared nostrils.

Des Chapman had been dropped off at the police station. He still refused to say anything. But it didn't matter, we could manage without him.

The disco music blasted out, sounding more like a rave party than a fairground. I was still wearing the same jeans and shirt I had put on to go to the horse sale and was smelling very much the worse for wear. Trevor was unusually quiet. Obviously Sarah had been telling him what James had been telling us. The grim facts.

"Over here." James plodded over some cable wires that led under a tent flap and we all followed suit. There were kids screaming all over the place, candy-floss stalls, coconut shies, a ghost train, a rocking boat.

Sarah was right beside me, scanning the rides, taking in every detail.

"Excuse me, where is the carousel?" she stopped a French boy who was more interested in ogling his girlfriend.

"*Je ne sais pas*," he said, and wandered off.

Renaldo was determined to be a hero, strutting here, there and everywhere, asking questions, terrifying everybody in his starchy uniform, not making any headway whatsoever. We'd just have to keep looking.

I'd never seen a fairground so enormous. It was going to take us ages to find Sally. Trevor was the first to spot something, a red and gold painted top with spiralled spokes coming down from the roof. We could just see it in the distance next to the bouncy castle.

"Come on," Trevor yelled, bulldozing his way through a party of people studying pocket-sized guides.

We barged through milling crowds with no time to lose. Renaldo streaked on ahead, and I heard one woman with a foreign accent say it was most likely a drugs raid.

Wrong. It was a wild goose chase. We turned the corner of the bouncy castle and saw the carousel. There were ponies, lots of them, but wooden with flaking paint and fixed expressions. Not alive and not Sally. They were also half empty.

"Blast." Disappointment dragged at our hearts. Trevor's shoulders visibly slumped. Maybe we'd got it all wrong. Maybe Sally wasn't here at all. It was beginning to look like a distinct possibility.

"There." Sarah's voice was flat and stony.

"What?" We whipped round quickly, expecting to see the bouncy castle. Instead, our attention was focused on something entirely different.

A cream, shabby-looking 11-hand pony clad in a scant harness was being led by the man whom we'd seen at the docks carrying the coffee and chips – the man who'd called Des off when he had us cornered at the farmhouse.

He didn't see us. His head was down and he was deep in thought. The cream pony trudged at his side, unresisting, just plodding on, one foot after the other.

"Sssh." Renaldo put his finger to his lips as if we were stupid enough to call out and give him warning.

We followed him, keeping well back, terrified of being spotted. He was going to lead us straight to the carousel.

We knew we were near before we even saw it. There were extra crowds, kiddies and mums, dads trying to show off. One man shouting "Tallyho", another complaining they weren't very big. There were ten ponies in all, lined up in a circle, heads low, eyes dejected. The cream pony was being put in the place of a little Welsh Mountain, cripplingly lame and unable to go anywhere. One of the tourists was shouting out, telling them to get on with it. I wanted to pour his can of beer over his head.

There she was. Round the other side, standing as still as a rock, but her ears were flicking back and forth, listening, frightened, alone.

"Is that her?" Sarah couldn't stop staring.

"Leave this to me." Renaldo puffed out his chest with importance. He took one step forward and hurtled over a discarded carton of chips.

Sarah snapped. She raced towards the carousel with her hair flying out wildly and James running after her. They were just about to start the ponies off again on their mindless trek to nowhere.

"Get away from her, you creep." Sarah grabbed hold of a middle-aged man with a camera round his neck and a straw hat on his head. She yanked him off Sally and nearly sent him flying into the dust.

The operator of the carousel was so shocked he just stood there open mouthed and unable to co-ordinate.

"I have eet on good authority . . ." Renaldo was having to shout above the disco music and he had to hold up his hand against the flashing lights. Sarah was frantically undoing all the ponies. I raced up and threw my arms round Sally's neck. Her ears pricked forward, straining as I repeated her name over and over again. But she didn't seem to hear.

"I'll get him." Trevor belted towards the dodgems after the man who had finally recognized us and was trying to leg it into the crowds. The cream pony was left standing among a family of three who offered him some popcorn.

"*Attention, attention!*" Renaldo blasted on his police whistle till he turned blue in the face. "*Attention, attention!*"

"I told you so," a voice piped up. "It's drugs every time."

Trevor hurtled through the crowds until all we could see was his purple head bobbing up and down.

"Go get him, Trevor," Ross yelled, flying off in pursuit.

Our main concern was Sally. We gently lifted the metal framework from her head and led her down from the wooden platform. More crowds were gathering, ten deep. There was nothing like a scandal to get people's interest.

"She can't hear!" I shouted at James, entwining my fingers in her long mane, horrified at the prospect that she might have turned deaf as well as blind.

James was examining her in an instant. I couldn't believe it when he pulled wet newspaper out of her ears by the handful.

"To keep her quiet," he said. "All this noise would have driven her crazy."

*

The next hour was chaotic. Pierre and Jean-Paul's friend from the riding school very kindly came and picked up Sally in her horsebox. James contacted the International League For The Protection of Horses who were based in Paris and who would see to it that the other ponies would be taken into care. Sarah stuck her neck out and said if they couldn't be found good homes we would find room at Hollywell. We never turned a needy case away. Not ever.

Renaldo had the time of his life ordering people around and charging Des Chapman's mate for causing undue suffering to animals. Trevor had caught him and dragged him back to the carousel with one arm behind his back.

Sally staggered up the horsebox ramp with us all guiding her and offering encouragement. She recognized our voices now that the newspaper was removed, but I knew the one voice she wanted to hear above all else was Walter's. We had to get back to the restaurant.

Parked slap bang in front of Valentino's was our wonderful old wooden horsebox, which Mrs Mac had somehow managed to manhandle on the longest drive of her life. She was standing on the pavement, waving frantically, wearing her Hollywell T-shirt, tracksuit bottoms and sweat band.

Pierre and Jean-Paul had returned in the taxi and were standing next to Mrs Mac, grinning from ear to ear and trying to wave us into a parking space.

"Coeee!" Mrs Mac yelled, coming up and giving Ross a huge kiss on the cheek, which left a fuchsia pink imprint. People were gawping from all directions and one woman with two poodles walked into a parking ticket machine.

"We'll have to unload her here," the lady from the riding school said. "We'll never get through into the courtyard."

Jean-Paul said Katie and Danny were with Walter and when could he see the beautifool Sally?

"Well, come on, let's get this ramp down," Trevor urged, bursting with impatience.

The whole front of Valentino's was covered up by the two horseboxes. It looked more like a race meeting than a busy street in a French town. Renaldo arrived, twitching like mad and bustling with importance, carrying a huge stack of his wife's books under his arm. "Later, Madame Jackie, maybe you sign ze books?" he enquired, the question of Sarah's true identity not yet having been mentioned in all the confusion.

Sally stood sideways on, gently munching some

hay and listening carefully to everyone's voices. It seemed really odd that she didn't turn her head to look at her new surroundings like any other horse would, but then any other horse wouldn't be totally blind.

"Ssssh," Renaldo whispered, having once read that you should be quiet around horses.

"OK girl, here we are. Now you're going to have to take it really steady." Ross held on tight to her headcollar as she carefully felt her way down the ramp one foot at a time.

Trevor fussed around, putting straw on the ramp and doing his utmost to make sure she wouldn't slip. Mrs Mac whispered in my ear that she always knew he'd come good – a misguided soul, that's all.

I grinned until my jaw ached and then went to fetch Walter who was spruced up like a new pin. Katie and Danny were arguing about who was going to lead him.

"Come on, she's here," I urged, bursting with excitement.

Walter shot out of the stable like a Grand National winner, looking around him, serious and suspicious. He knew something was going on. Sally came through the courtyard, still uncertain, then her nose quivered and flared and she half neighed, timid, unsure. Was it really him?

Walter wasted no time. He dragged the rope out of Katie's hand and charged up to Sally, almost bumping into her nose. Then he started braying at the top of his voice, trying to sniff Sally at the same time and bustle her back to the stable. Sally remained firmly put and Sarah said you could see who wore the trousers in this relationship.

Jean-Paul wiped his eyes on a red hanky and then passed it to Mrs Mac. Pierre puffed doubly hard on a cigar and Renaldo just stood and twitched.

"Love is being reunited," Katie said in a low voice.

"Love is being together for ever," James added, putting an affectionate arm round Sarah.

"Well, come on, we can't stand around here all day," I said, quelling emotion before it completely took me over. "We've got a ferry to catch!"

Chapter Ten

We decided to leave early the next morning. First there was a major celebration to organize. Jean-Paul was up to his elbows in cooking ingredients, whipping up a feast fit for a king. Even his staff were caught up in the excitement, smuggling out extra helpings of carrot cake to Walter and Sally who were eating as if there was no tomorrow. Walter insisted on standing nearest the door to protect Sally but nobody took any notice of his gruesome expressions. Who was he trying to kid, anyway?

Overall, Sally wasn't in that bad a condition. The worst news was she would never see again. There was nothing James, or any other vet for that matter, could do for her. One eye was completely lost and the other was the victim of cataracts. On close examination we could all see that the pupil was dilated and had gone cloudy. James said it went this way because no light was getting into the eye; although Sally could probably make out shadows she would never be able to focus properly. There was no cure.

"Never mind, old girl, you've got Walter." Ross rubbed her nose affectionately. Walter was as good as any guide dog. He never left her side.

James said it was important that she should have the same surroundings, the same stable and field. Gradually she would rely on memory and be able to lead a very normal life. She may be blind but she could still be happy. Looking at her contented expression as Katie and Danny brushed at her tangled mane with the scrubbing brush, I didn't doubt it.

The meal that night was fantastic, better than any food I'd had before. Jean-Paul strutted around bringing in dish after dish, waiting for praise and gratitude. Pierre reluctantly offered James a cigar and Mrs Mac went mad to have the recipe for the black forest gâteau. It would be the perfect addition to the cake stall at the Hollywell Gala Open Day.

"What Open Day?" we all yelled together.

James proposed a toast to Walter and Sally and Danny and Katie shouted out, "Mission accomplished." Anyone would think we were in a James Bond movie.

"But seriously," Sarah was about to make a speech when Katie bit into a toffee deluxe pudding and yelled out in excruciating pain. Her tooth had finally come out.

"Quick, make a wish," I shouted, eager for her to close her eyes and be quiet for a minute.

"But there's nothing to wish for." She grinned a toothless grin and then caught sight of James and Sarah looking romantically at each other and screwed up her eyes tight shut. For once she couldn't have made a better wish.

"This is beautifool." Jean-Paul dug into an ice cream bombe with relish and Mrs Mac said he'd got it exactly right. It was indeed just beautiful.

Celestine, who we'd invited along after returning her car, gazed into Trevor's eyes with adoring affection.

The next morning there was a tearful farewell. We loaded up Walter and Sally into our horsebox and Jean-Paul gave us a crate of French wine and a bag of cakes and sweets to be getting on with.

"Never farewell, *mes chers*, always *au revoir*." He kissed us all on both cheeks, weeping like a baby and Pierre went round giving us all a hearty smack on the back and grunting some unintelligible form of affection.

They both promised devoutly to come and visit Hollywell in the next few months, to see Walter and Sally and the rest of the crew. I had one last lingering look at Valentino's where all the staff were lined up in the doorway. I was going to miss France but, that said, I couldn't wait to get back to Hollywell. Hollywell was home.

"Well, come on, let's get this show on the road," I urged.

We arrived in England around lunchtime and started the long trek north. It was a beautiful hot day and we had all the windows down and the fresh air vents open. James said, "Oh, to be in England," and I said, "Oh, to be in a fresh set of clothes." Danny fell asleep and the rest of us pigged out on Jean-Paul's home-made sweets.

It was with contented souls that we turned up the Hollywell drive just as the sun was beginning to set, casting the house and stables in a warm orange glow. Oscar and Matilda, our two cats, were playing on the front lawn and Jigsaw, our Golden Labrador, was drinking out of one of the water buckets in between barking at Isabella, the pot-bellied pig, who was squealing with indignation. Nothing had changed.

Mrs Mac had gone on ahead in James's car to relieve one of the neighbours who'd been looking after the horses. Boris was dozing by the field gate, his bottom lip dangling open like a big soup plate. Queenie was standing next to him, old, wise and equally half asleep. It could have been an old people's retirement home.

"Wake up, you old cronies!" James shouted at them over the fence as we lowered the horsebox ramp. "We've got some new residents!"

The next week was chaotic. The rest of the ponies from France had to be brought across and settled in. We ended up with thirteen altogether and it was a full-time job just thinking up names for them. Walter escaped three times in the first four days, ploughing through the next door neighbour's vegetable patch and then heading off into the village where he terrified a group of women doing aerobics in the village hall. Ross said he must feel satisfied that Sally was safe or he wouldn't go walkabout. Sally had teamed up with Queenie and could already find her way round the paddock and into the field shelter. She was putting on weight.

Trevor fixed three new bolts on Walter's door and that seemed to keep him in for the moment. Often, though, I caught him with his woolly head deeply furrowed in a concentrated frown, no doubt plotting his next escapade.

James was flat out examining the new arrivals and working out feed charts and taking worm counts. He was acting very strangely but Sarah didn't notice because she was desperately trying to meet the deadline for her new novel. All we could hear was the typewriter bashing away and lots of cursing and scrunching of paper. James said we should leave her to her own devices but quickly changed his mind when he discovered salt in his tea instead of sugar.

Trevor was working like a slave and cooking up some scam with James, although we couldn't work out what it was. He just kept reading motoring magazines on classic cars when he thought we weren't looking and grinning to himself, altogether acting very peculiarly. Apart from that, he was a tower of strength and even took on the job of showing visitors round the sanctuary, explaining about each rescue case, although always spending the most time with Walter and Sally.

I was assigned the job of looking after Dusty whose condition had altered dramatically since we last saw him. He was the apple of Mrs Mac's eye and he was also the sweetest pony I'd ever known. Already his face was filling out and his ribs weren't quite as prominent. James had rasped back his upper teeth which were far too sharp and made eating practically impossible. Now he was managing loose meadow hay, sugarbeet and grated carrots. His parrot mouth wasn't that bad. He could survive.

"I've got it," Katie yelled, splashing white emulsion all over Danny who was busy fixing a daisy chain round Jigsaw's neck. We'd been home a week and Trevor had hit on the bright idea of painting the old stable block, as if we hadn't got enough to deal with already. "We'll organize a petition, it's the only way."

"And send it to the Prime Minister!" Danny shrieked, giving up on the daisy chain and peeling the wrapper off a chocolate cream egg.

We'd been discussing non-stop the serious issue of the carousels in Europe and particularly Spain. Something had to be done – we couldn't buy up all the poor ponies destined to a life of misery. The only way to go was to change the law or at least make sure it was enforced.

"She's right," Ross said, yanking the lid off yet another tin of paint. "But it's going to take some organizing – we'd better fetch Mrs Mac."

"It's going to take most of the summer," I pondered. "We'll need loads of signatures."

"But it will be worth it." Katie's eyes shone with enthusiasm. "Think of all those ponies we'll be helping."

"Speaking of horses," Ross meditated, "where's Walter disappeared to?"

Right on cue, there was a loud noise from the barn and Walter scuttled out with a red ribbon in his teeth and a look of sheer glee written all over his face.

"What on earth . . .?"

Trevor and James erupted through the side door, James holding a pair of scissors and Trevor up to his eyes in car grease.

"Just what is going on?"

Trevor had told us that he was working on a motorbike in the barn and we couldn't see it until it was finished. Now I wasn't so sure.

"Something's smelling very fishy," Ross whispered as James, who looked a nervous wreck, suddenly made a momentous decision.

"Right, it's now or never, Trevor," he said. "Fetch Mrs F . . . I mean Sarah . . . No, better still, I'll do it."

He marched into the house with purpose and intent and dragged Sarah out of her study, moaning like mad that she was on a creative flow and James had no right disturbing her. She still had a Biro clutched in her right hand. Sarah wrote everything in longhand and refused point-blank to get a word processor.

"Shut up, woman, and for once do as you're told," James dragged her towards the barn and demanded that we all follow. Something very very fishy *was* going on.

I shut Walter in his stable, still trying to get red threads of ribbon out of his front teeth, and then bolted after them. Trevor shot into the barn, flapping like mad and looking more nervous than James, if that was possible.

James put his hands over Sarah's eyes and Ross followed Trevor's instructions and opened the huge, green barn doors.

Sunlight dazzled in and for a moment I thought I needed my eyes testing.

"Wow!" Katie's eyes bulged in amazement.

"But . . ." Sarah's jaw moved up and down but nothing came out.

"How did you get it in here without us knowing?" Ross was the first to say something intelligible.

James held up the car keys and Sarah took a tentative step forward.

We were looking at a beautiful bright red old-fashioned sports car with a soft top which James promptly said was an MGB and used to belong to Lord somebody or other and he'd seen it when he went to examine his horses.

"It was just rusting away in a chicken shed. Trevor assures me we can get it going."

Sarah ran a hand over the newly polished body-

118

work which was in amazing condition. Trevor hid the duster and polish behind his back.

"I figured you needed a new car," James hurried on, "I thought this would fit a writer's image . . ." His words tailed off as Sarah moved to open the driver's door. Trevor was winking at me non-stop and Katie asked him if he'd got something in his eye. As Sarah opened the tiny door a piece of paper dropped down from behind the interior mirror.

"Open it," James said, looking worried.

"Well, don't keep us in suspense," Ross finally shouted, when, what seemed like hours later, Sarah was still gawping at the piece of paper.

"Yes," she said in an emphatic voice. "Yes, yes, yes and double yes!"

James's face lit up like a Christmas tree and he ran forward and twirled Sarah right off her feet. Katie grabbed the paper and shrieked at the top of her voice.

"Trevor, the ring, the ring!" There were tears in James's eyes as he put Sarah down for half a second to take hold of the small black box. There were tears in my eyes as I suddenly realized what was going on.

"Well, I'd be a fool not to marry the local vet, wouldn't I," Sarah grinned and I couldn't have agreed more.

Mrs Mac came rushing out of the house to

admire Sarah's sapphire ring and Katie was quickly jotting down names for the wedding list. "Of course we'll have to invite Blake and Rocky, and then there's Pierre and Jean-Paul, Dom and Cassandra . . ."

"Steady on," Sarah said. "We've only just got engaged."

"When are we going to fit in a wedding?" Ross asked, perplexed.

"In between the horses' feeding times," I laughed.

"I can wear my new hat," Mrs Mac half sobbed.

"I can be a bridesmaid," Katie whooped.

"We'll be like a proper family." Danny looked wistful.

Queenie and Sally gazed at us from the field gate as if we were stark raving bonkers and then went back to their afternoon nap.

"What did Jean-Paul say?" Ross said, "Theez eeze, what eez the word?"

"Beautifool," Trevor said, flinging an arm which felt more like a tree trunk round my shoulder.

And at that moment, as Mrs Mac trooped back into the house to get Jean-Paul's crate of French wine, I had to agree with Trevor – life truly was just beautifool.

HOLLYWELL STABLES

Trapped
6

Samantha Alexander

MACMILLAN
CHILDREN'S BOOKS

Chapter One

"You've got to help me!" A spiky-haired girl wearing Doc Martens and a cut-off T-shirt sat in our kitchen looking washed out and desperate. She said her name was Hazel. "You're our only chance," she sobbed. "I don't know where else to turn."

Sarah, our stepmother, passed her a tissue and Ross, Katie and I didn't know what to say for the best.

"He's just a baby," Hazel said, "he's only four years old."

Hazel had turned up on the doorstep at eleven o'clock that night, deeply distraught and hardly making any sense. We had taken her in, listened to her story and tried to get her to calm down. In the beginning all she kept saying was that we had to save him. Then she had started to open up and the full details came out; it was even more bizarre than anything we could have imagined.

1

My brother Ross asked what we'd all been wondering: "Surely a horse that young couldn't be crippled with arthritis?"

"He had an accident – about a year ago – twisted his fetlock. It never healed properly. He was put back into work too soon, it's all that woman's fault!" Hazel broke down in a fresh bout of tears and Sarah suggested she stay the night as she'd missed the last bus home.

"Arnie's the only thing I care about," she said. "Without him there's no point carrying on."

Arnie, it turned out, was a seventeen hand German bred Hanoverian and the best horse in the world. He was steel grey, as strong as an ox and liked a pint of Guinness a day. We still had no idea who he belonged to or where he was being kept.

"You've got to tell us more, Hazel, we can't help you unless you help us!" Sarah knelt down in front of her, wiping her eyes with a tissue. "Who is Arnie? Who does he belong to?"

It was our job to save horses. This is what we were here for: to listen to people's stories, help, come to the rescue. We'd done it time and again, but it never got any easier. The idea of this beautiful young horse facing a death sentence made my blood boil.

Hazel pulled a creased photograph from her pocket and handed it to Sarah. "Here, this should tell you all you need to know."

It was a tatty picture about the size of a school photograph but it obviously told a thousand stories. The colour drained from Sarah's face.

Ross took one look and passed the picture to me. It was a portrait of a woman dressed up in top hat and tails holding on to the head of a huge grey horse. The woman was Jennifer Beaumont, affectionately known as Bo in horsey circles. She was a famous dressage rider. She was blonde, thirty-something, and extremely well liked. She was smiling, oozing star quality and looked totally above reproach. The horse was nuzzling against her hair. It was the perfect photograph.

"That's Arnie," Hazel said in a strangled voice. "That's my baby."

"I don't believe it," I said, stroking Oscar who was purring half asleep on my knee. "I always thought she was so nice."

Hazel had gone off with Sarah to get some aspirin. The poor girl was heart-broken and I couldn't blame her. Apparently she'd looked after Arnie since he was first born. He was always a

3

big-boned thing, clumsy and gawky and they'd given him the show name Goliath. Hazel called him Arnie, after Arnold Schwarzenegger, the film star, because he didn't know his own strength. He was as gentle as a lamb but always getting into trouble. He was easygoing, somewhat lazy and totally unco-ordinated. But amazingly when he was in the dressage arena and forced to work he could perform beautifully. He was so powerful even Jennifer Beaumont found him difficult to sit on. He was a rising star and destined for the top, that is, until the accident.

"It's so tragic," I said, looking at the photograph again and the horse whose career had been so cruelly cut short.

"But he doesn't deserve to be put down." Ross collapsed into an armchair, raking a hand through his jet black hair. It was well after midnight but we hardly seemed to notice.

"It's all about money." Sarah came back into the kitchen with Hazel. "Apparently the lovely Ms Beaumont is in debt, she's having to sell horses left, right and centre. Arnie is insured for a lot of money. Now he's classified unfit to work she can have him put down and claim the full insurance payment for loss of use."

"But that's dreadful," said Ross, struggling to

4

come to terms with what Sarah had said. "Arnie has literally become salvage."

"But why can't she let someone have him for hacking and just pottering around?" I suggested. "He could have a really good life."

Sarah put some teabags in the pot and turned round to face us with tears glistening in her eyes. "Because he's insured for ten thousand pounds," she said, "and he's worth more to Ms Beaumont if he's not around."

"But what kind of woman is she?" I said, my voice quivering.

"Heartless," Ross answered, folding over the photograph and placing it back on the table. "Completely heartless."

I couldn't have agreed more.

"So are you going to help me or not?" Hazel's eyes stared unblinking at Sarah, defiant, trying to hide the fear of us saying no.

It was seven o'clock in the morning. We had talked well into the small hours as to what we could do to help, how we could save Arnie's life. Hazel had just come inside – she'd been up with the lark and had already mucked out six stables. She was a total professional and left us all standing.

5

"So?" she said, her elfin face smudged with dust and sweat.

"You didn't have to do the stables," Sarah said.

"I know. I wanted to. So have you made a decision?"

"It won't be easy," Sarah began.

"I know that already," Hazel snapped . . . "Look, maybe I'd better just go . . ."

Hazel turned for the door, nearly stumbling over Jigsaw, our golden Labrador, who was sprawled out on the stone floor. She reached for the latch and stopped in mid air.

"You'd better write down the address," Sarah said. "We haven't got much time."

Chapter Two

"Somerset Stables, it's just outside Staunton – here, turn left here!" Hazel leant over the front seat giving instructions to Sarah.

We flew over a tiny crossroads and then came to a grinding halt as Hazel tried to get her bearings.

"Mel, pass me that map, I think you're sitting on it."

"It's at the right page," I said, sticking the map under Sarah's nose.

"She's bound to listen to a sanctuary," Hazel's voice tailed off.

I didn't like to tell her I wasn't so sure.

Somerset Stables was every bit as impressive as I imagined: superb immaculate stables, two all-weather arenas surrounded by white fencing, picture-book fields with beautiful mares and foals.

"This must have cost a fortune," Ross said,

who was sitting next to me and gaping through the window like the rest of us. Only Hazel was oblivious to it all, wound up and uncommunicative.

"She's there," Hazel pointed to a woman on a big bay horse. "It's her."

There was no mistaking Jennifer Beaumont. She was the centre of attention.

"Darling that was wonderful." A blond horsey-looking chap sat on a shooting stick, shouting encouragement across the arena.

One of the grooms ran across carrying a mobile phone and the bay horse momentarily shied away.

"He's over here." Hazel moved across to the first stable in the row and a big grey head appeared with soft brown eyes and a floppy bottom lip. "This is Arnie!"

Before we had chance to draw breath, "Bo" Beaumont had ridden across, talking into the mobile phone. "Hold on, sweetie, we seem to have got some kind of school party here." She put her hand over the mouthpiece and looked daggers at Hazel. "How many times have I told you that we simply don't tolerate visitors."

Her voice was acid-sharp, spiteful. She was not at all how she appeared in magazine pictures and on television.

"We're from Hollywell Stables." Sarah's voice was level and reasonable.

"Oh," Bo said. "I see."

Bo had dismounted and was shaking her long blonde hair. "I don't see that it's any of your business."

"Anything to do with horse welfare is our business." Sarah was holding her own.

"The horse is a waste of time," Bo said, getting angry. "He's no good to anybody."

Arnie nodded his head over the stable door, flapping his lips to amuse himself, totally unaware of the significance of the conversation.

"Give me ten thousand pounds and you can have him with pleasure." Bo picked up her reins as if to dismiss us.

"You know we don't have that kind of money," Sarah insisted.

Bo just shrugged and turned her back.

"I'm appealing to your better nature." Sarah was fighting a losing battle.

"Forget it, I've said my piece."

"Come on, darling, go through it once more and then we'll call it a day." The guy on the shooting stick tried to get Bo's attention again – he didn't even acknowledge us.

9

"You'll regret this," Sarah shouted after her, but she didn't seem to hear.

Hazel threw her arms round Arnie's neck while he gently butted her in the face.

"We won't let you down," I told him, finding a soggy mint in the bottom of my pocket.

"Too right we won't," Sarah said, narrowing her green eyes as she watched Ms Beaumont flounce back into the arena. "We'll re-group and come up with Plan B. And if Miss Fancy Pants wants a war, then that's exactly what she's going to get!"

Trevor, our full-time groom came bounding across the yard as soon as we opened the car doors. "Where have you been? I've been trying to contact you all over the place."

"Trevor, what is it? What's happened?" Sarah asked, worriedly.

With purple hair, Union Jack shorts and builder's boots, Trevor was the most unlikely groom anyone could imagine, but he'd proved himself to be loyal and was now a bonafide member of the Hollywell team.

"You mean you didn't see that bloke in the Jag shoot down the road?" he asked.

"Trevor, you're not making any sense," I complained.

"Oh my God, but he is," Sarah groaned, filled with horror and dropping her car keys on the cobbles. "That was . . ."

"Maxwell Curtis," I said, suddenly putting two and two together.

"Maxi Crowface more like," Trevor scoffed.

Sarah groaned even louder.

Maxwell Curtis was the local MP and extremely wealthy and influential. We'd been trying to arrange a meeting with him for weeks with the idea of him putting a bill forward in Parliament to stop the live export of horses for meat, but it was like talking to a brick wall. He'd finally agreed to a meeting but with all the excitement over Arnie we'd completely forgotten. Now we'd proved unreliable and he'd had a run-in with Trevor. I was convinced he'd never take us seriously again.

"Well it's no good crying over spilt milk," Sarah bounced back. "I'd better go and give him a ring."

"Oh and some geezer left this." Trevor held out a business card. It was for an insurance firm and someone named Derek Hatfield. "He said he'd call again."

11

We didn't give it another thought.

"Coeee!" Mrs Mac, our official secretary shouted from the office.

"She's going round the bend," Trevor grunted, about to make a quick getaway. "I think she's had too much sun."

Poor Mrs Mac did look mildly hysterical, but then not without good reason.

"I don't think any of you realize the gravity of the situation." She was waving a wad of papers up and down as a make-shift fan while she reached for a lemon bon-bon. "We've been let down in a big way."

"I see what you mean." Ross checked the figures.

"But I thought we were doing so well," I said. This was the last thing we needed – a major crisis.

Ever since we had come back from France with a lorry-load of rescued ponies we had been organizing a petition to stop the export of live horses abroad to be sold for meat. We had appeared on radio and local television. We had appealed to every riding school in the country. The weekly paper had collected ten thousand signatures; Trevor had single-handedly collected a thousand traipsing round pubs and bowling alleys; I had spent every Saturday in the High Street with a clipboard and pen – everybody at school had put down their name.

But according to Mrs Mac it wasn't enough. We had set a target of one million signatures and we were three hundred thousand short. What's more, the presentation was at Number Ten Downing Street in just under a week's time.

"What are we going to do?" Mrs Mac started to panic.

"I wonder if we'll have a police escort?" Katie carried on regardless. "We might even be invited in for afternoon tea."

"Get real, Katie," Trevor barked. "You'll be lucky to see a secretary, never mind the PM."

Katie insisted her "stars" for that day predicted something out of the ordinary, but I was more concerned about the horses escaping into the streets of London. We were taking Queenie, our lucky mascot who was partially deaf and brilliantly behaved on special occasions, and Colorado, who was now a famous show-jumper and used to lots of noise and flashing cameras. Katie said she was going to wear her Hollywell Stables T-shirt, and I planned to buy some new jodphurs and jodphur boots. Heaven knows what Trevor was going to turn up in – his purple hair was bad enough, but we couldn't possibly exclude him.

13

"This is serious." Ross sat back on a box of Hollywell mugs.

"We'll just have to get out there and make up the shortfall," said Trevor, optimistic as ever.

"The whole reputation of Hollywell Stables is at stake," Ross said. It was the truth.

"I know." Mrs Mac sounded at the end of her tether. "You don't have to remind me."

A few hours later, Roddy Fitzgerald raced up the Hollywell drive in his clapped-out Mini, tape recorder, paper and pen at the ready. Roddy was a reporter on the *Weekly Herald* and a really good friend. We'd never forget his heroic attempts in dealing with a hunt saboteur called Zac, and although he wasn't very good with the horses, he really liked them. In fact Roddy had been the first person to join our fan club.

"So where's the big white chief?" he grinned, as he unfolded himself from the car and rubbed his knees. "She's promised me an ace story."

This was Plan B. To go to the media with a vengeance. Sarah had been on the phone all morning, and we had already raised quite an interest in Arnie's plight.

"Sounds a real character," Roddy commented.

"Who, Arnie or Hazel?"

"Both."

Jigsaw finally got the message that Roddy didn't really want him jumping all over his nice clean suit, then Katie dragged him off to see some of our new arrivals, in particular Walter, our wayward mule, who promptly snorted all over his starched sleeve.

Mrs Mac said she didn't recognize him with his trousers on (last time she'd seen him, Roddy had been stripped to his boxer shorts – but that's another story).

"I'm ready for action now." Roddy pointed to the tape recorder, and I had to admit he did look more professional.

Sarah came out of the house, deep in thought, clutching on to six dripping ice-cream cornets and nibbling at one of the flakes.

"There's been a development," she announced. "And it could be in our favour."

We all held our breath in a state of expectancy.

"It's Hazel – she's been given the sack!"

Chapter Three

"It's unfair dismissal." Hazel had arrived at Hollywell in a desperate state and nothing we could say would calm her down.

"I'm not leaving Arnie with that witch, I'm *not*. I don't care if they have to drag me bodily out of his stable."

As soon as we had left the yard, Bo had gone berserk at Hazel and given her two days to pack up her things and go.

Sarah was straight on to the Industrial Tribunal, and Roddy was literally writing the story as we spoke. Hazel gave him the picture of Arnie and one of herself at the National Championships, and Roddy promised a page lead in tomorrow night's paper. Sarah was keeping her fingers crossed that one of the major Sunday papers was going to ring back, and the local television station was at that moment informing their crew of the situation.

"This is what we need," Sarah insisted. "The

16

last thing Bo Beaumont wants is bad press. It'll kill her perfect image stone dead."

"But it's not enough." Hazel wouldn't be convinced. "It's all going to take too long – we've got to do something now!"

Ross passed her a cup of sweet tea, which she refused, and I tried to reassure Jigsaw, who was wondering what on earth was going on.

"Hazel, you've got to trust us, we know what we're doing." Sarah tried to calm Hazel down.

"But do you?" She took us all by surprise. "You've not been open that long, have you? Can you honestly say you've dealt with this situation before?"

Sarah was as cool as a cucumber. "Go and look at the scores of happy faces out in the fields, I think you'll find your answer."

Hazel burst into floods of tears and ran out of the room.

"Trevor, go after her," Sarah said, after a few minutes of deathly silence. "She's upset, she didn't mean it."

The rest of the day was a lot less frantic. I managed to scrub down two winter rugs and hang them on the washing line to dry, and to take the pressure off Mrs Mac, Katie and I spent some time packing up orders for fan club members. We'd recently started a new line in Hollywell Stables pencil cases and bags and they were selling really well. I couldn't believe the amount of money people would spend, but I certainly wasn't complaining. It was the general public who were the life-blood of the sanctuary. Ross showed some visitors around the stables: a family with four children. The mother was nearly in tears when she saw Sally, our little blind pony, and heard her rescue story.

Trevor had disappeared with Hazel. I was beginning to wonder whether he'd be back for evening feeds. We were all worried and upset for Hazel and Arnie but I had every faith in Sarah – she wouldn't let Arnie be put down. I also knew that if anyone could console Hazel, it was Trevor: he had a heart of gold.

"That was the police on the phone." Ross had answered it in the tack room. "Apparently a donkey has been stolen in the area. It's pure white. They just want us to keep a look out."

Both the police and the RSPCA tended to keep us informed of missing ponies, or of anything that might be of interest to the sanctuary. I always felt a pang of heartache whenever anyone mentioned stolen animals. I could still remember vividly when Bluey had been stolen from our field and the heartbreak we'd all gone through. I wouldn't wish it on anyone.

"Not much chance of us finding it, though," Ross said. "It could be anywhere by now."

Trevor rolled up just as Mrs Mac was putting the final touches to a huge home-made pizza, and I knew something was wrong when he didn't immediately drool at the mouth. He even refused a portion of Mrs Mac's apple crumble which had always been his out-and-out favourite.

"Trevor, if you were a horse I'd be seriously worried."

"But only if I were a horse, eh?"

I didn't have time to give him an answer. Katie shot through the door like a startled whippet, her face as white as a sheet and her mouth gaping open.

"I've seen it!" she finally managed to shriek out, dropping a tub of chocolate ice-cream all over the floor, which Jigsaw thought was wonderful.

"The axe man! I've seen him!"

"Katie, what *are* you talking about?" Mrs Mac demanded. Katie had always had an over-active imagination, but this was ridiculous.

Trevor coughed uncomfortably in the corner

and suddenly became intent on burying his head in the fridge.

"Trevor, have you been filling her head with tall stories?" Mrs Mac was determined to get to the bottom of this.

"It was a ghost! At one end of the upstairs windows. Just staring out. Watching. Waiting to get me."

Katie's dark eyes expanded to the size of two flying saucers, and it was a full ten minutes before we could coax her to say anything else.

"There's no such thing as ghosts." Mrs Mac flung the dishcloth at Trevor which clipped him on the ear.

"Trevor was just winding you up." I tried to reassure her. "He does it sometimes. He thinks it's called a sense of humour." I pulled a face at him for being so irresponsible.

Apparently Trevor had told her that the Old Rectory, an eight-bedroomed, almost derelict house on the edge of the village, was haunted. The axe man had murdered his family and then killed himself, and his ghost roamed the empty rooms unable to come to terms with his guilty conscience.

"You didn't see anything," I insisted. "It was just your imagination."

"Funny though," Mrs Mac meditated, when Katie had left the room. "I could have sworn that old house was boarded up years ago."

"Mel, leave me alone, I'm not telling you," Trevor and I volunteered to do evening feeds and we were bringing in three ponies each from the fields and being dragged all over the place. We didn't bring all the horses in, just the ones who were really old, or needed special treatment. We were all convinced that any day now we'd have terrific thunderstorms. This heat-wave couldn't last for ever: the grass was disappearing away to nothing, and it was so oppressive.

"You'll find out tomorrow," Trevor insisted, not giving anything away. He'd asked Sarah for the morning off and I knew he was up to something but he wouldn't tell me what.

"It's to do with Hazel, isn't it?" I asked, grabbing hold of a hairy Welsh pony who was trying to devour a tub of begonias.

"No," Trevor answered back, a little hastily. "Now mind your own business."

*

21

It was Katie who first spotted the huge red horse-box trundling up the lane taking up the entire road and brushing against the over-hanging trees.

"It's Blake!" She came tearing across from one of the fields, Jigsaw going crazy under her feet. "He's back!"

My heart leapt in the air and did three triple somersaults. Blake was back.

I dived out of Queenie's stable, nearly colliding with one of the free-range hens and suddenly became painfully aware of my unwashed clammy hair, my bright red face and a spot in the middle of my chin. I looked a mess. No, even worse, I looked awful, and there was no time to get changed – the horsebox was already turning up the drive.

"Don't worry, sis, you don't look any worse than usual," Katie quipped.

I lobbed a dandy brush at Katie and then gave a low groan of despair. Blake was in the driving seat still dressed in his white shirt and show-jumping jacket and wearing dark sunglasses. He looked as if he'd just stepped out of a Hollywood film set. If anything he was more gorgeous than ever.

"Life's just not fair," I whined, trying to cover

over a patch on my left knee. "Why can't I look like Michelle Pfeiffer?"

"You're fine just as you are," Trevor grunted, filling up a water bucket and causing me to go redder than ever – I didn't realize I'd been speaking aloud.

"Move the wheelbarrow!" Ross ran forward as it nearly disappeared under the huge modern cab. "More to the right." He waved his hands like a traffic warden. "Watch the wall!"

The horsebox finally came to a halt with a swish of airbrakes and Blake leapt down, grinning all over his face. He looked different somehow, more confident, more sophisticated – but still the same Blake. He and Ross were very similar, extremely dark, although Blake was a few inches taller and altogether leaner.

"Well don't just stand there," he said. "What about a proper welcome?"

"You look so different," I managed to say when Sarah had finished hugging him to death.

I was still worried that my hair was all over the place and I'd got my chin tucked into my chest in the hope that my spot wasn't glowing like a beacon.

"Come here, you daft thing," Blake leaned across, almost in slow motion, and ruffled the top of my hair and then gave me a massive hug. My face turned scarlet and I could have throttled Katie when she started singing, "Here Comes The Bride." Trevor looked really uncomfortable, and Ross asked wasn't it time we got Colorado out of the box before he kicked a hole in the side?

Colorado was a beautiful 14.2 hand skewbald, half wild Mustang, half thoroughbred, who we'd rescued from a girl called Louella. He was now a grade A show-jumper and one of the best horses in the country.

Blake had just returned from the Royal International Horse Show. He and Colorado had been away since Easter competing on "the circuit" and hadn't been due back for another three days. I knew because I'd been counting them off on a calendar.

Colorado came pounding down the ramp like a champion. He looked even more powerful than ever and twice as spirited.

"He's getting very cocky," Blake joked. "It's all the attention."

I led him into the stable next to his old friend, Queenie, who was neighing at the top of her voice, and Colorado whipped round and very nearly followed me out again. We left them together to catch up on old times while Sarah said we had enough of that to do ourselves, and what did Blake know about Jennifer Beaumont?

"There's no dirt on her, if that's what you mean." Blake sat down at the kitchen table. "At least not that I know of. She's always been so squeaky clean. Unfortunately it's not against the law to have a horse put down because it can no longer do its job."

"We've got four days," Sarah said, revealing that she'd just spoken to Roddy and that Bo had decided to extend the deadline on Arnie's life by an extra two days. "She's just trying to take the heat off herself, make it look as if she's doing all that can be done. Her vet is trying a new form of treatment but according to James if arthritis has set into the joint, there's nothing that can be done."

James was our local vet and Sarah's fiancé. He was brilliant because he could answer any question on anything.

"One thing's for sure," Blake said. "Bo will hate you for any bad publicity, especially at the moment, when she's trying to get a new sponsor."

"I know," Sarah said with a thin smile, "which is exactly why we're going to step up the campaign."

Mrs Mac plied Blake with more food than he'd seen in two months. On the road Blake said most up-and-coming showjumpers ended up living off hamburgers and what they could cook in their horseboxes.

Katie was fascinated with stories about Hickstead and wanted to know if the Derby bank really was as steep as it looked. Blake said he'd never ridden down it but it was even worse than it appeared on television.

Mrs Mac nearly fainted with relief when Blake passed her a box of nearly one hundred thousand signatures. It was a fantastic achievement and totally unexpected. Apparently the petition had been passed around audiences at all the major shows and behind the scenes.

Katie was bowled over when she read some of the names. "Half the Olympic team have signed!" she squealed.

"And there are some eventers, too," Blake added. "There's even Mark Todd."

"So when are we setting off for Downing Street?" Blake grinned.

"As soon as we find another two hundred thousand signatures," Sarah said. "Anyone believe in miracles?"

*

"Trevor fancies you," Ross hissed in my ear as soon as we were alone together by the sink.

"Don't be so stupid," I hissed back, nearly dropping one of Sarah's best plates.

"He's not said a word all night and he keeps glaring at Blake."

"Well I haven't noticed," I lied, feeling the colour welling up in my face.

"No, because you've been too busy drooling over Blake."

"I have not!"

"Sssssh," Ross nearly pushed the tea towel into my mouth. "The question is, what are you going to do about it?"

We returned to the table just as Sarah was giving Blake a rundown on all the latest residents.

"And at least Sally's cataracts don't seem to be getting any worse, and the ponies from France are all doing very well."

"And Mrs White's daughter's getting married next week." Mrs Mac brought out yet another one of her chocolate cakes. "And the Post Office is up for sale."

"So who's moved into the Old Rectory?" Blake asked quite innocently.

We all stared at him with our mouths open.

"A big man," Blake said. "I saw him at one of the upstairs windows as I drove past in the box."

Katie's face drained of colour. "You've seen him, too," she said in a small voice.

"The question is," I joined in, *"who is he?"*

Chapter Four

"Trevor has been arrested," Sarah said as she put the phone down.

It was the following morning and I'd just sat down with a pile of biscuits and a cup of hot coffee. It was half past ten, and Blake had promised me a ride on Colorado. I was just about to change into my jodphurs.

"You're joking," I said. "You've got to be!"

Trevor had left at the crack of dawn and I'd been itching to find out what he was up to, but getting arrested – Trevor?

"Come on," Sarah started frantically shutting windows and locking doors and accidentally stood in the cat litter tray. "We've got to get to Somerset Stables as quickly as possible!"

Blake drove while Sarah filled us in on the story. It had been Bo Beaumont on the phone and she was spitting with fury.

"That woman's got an evil temper," Sarah said,

practically bursting a blood vessel herself as she ransacked her purse for some change.

"Not a bit like you then," Ross grinned as we turned down a lane, which Blake insisted was a short cut.

It was another boiling hot day and I could already feel my T-shirt sticking to my back. A DJ on the car radio said, "Hi groovers, isn't this weather just great?" I said I wished it was snowing, and Katie for once agreed with me.

"You still haven't told us what's going on." Blake crunched the gears and started hanging out of the window as some horses came into sight.

"I think there's your answer," Sarah said in a solemn voice as we rounded the next bend.

Somerset Stables had an impressive entrance with huge iron gates and wonderful lion statues on either side. But it wasn't them that we were staring at. It was the hordes of protesters grouped outside the gates chanting and marching up and down with placards and banners. And in the thick of them was Trevor.

"What on earth does he think he's doing?"

Hazel was leading the show, sitting on the bonnet of a blacksmith's van, refusing to let him through the gates. Two other girls waving a wooden board started shrieking even louder,

"Save Arnie! Murderers! Animals have rights, too!"

The blacksmith looked bewildered. Suddenly I noticed Bo, with two police officers, strutting through the fray with a face that looked as if it was going to crack with rage.

"It's all their fault." She pointed accusingly at Sarah.

One of the police officers with ginger hair, who I vaguely recognized, put his hand on Trevor's shoulder. "You're going to have to move on mate, this is private property."

He wasn't under arrest. Obviously Bo had been exaggerating.

"But this is a peaceful picket," Hazel objected, refusing to get away from the van.

"Come on, duckie, it's time to clear out."

"But you don't understand." Hazel started fighting him off. "This is our only chance."

"Hazel, listen to me, this isn't the way to save Arnie." Sarah had rushed forward and was trying to grab hold of her free arm. "What use are you going to be in a police cell?"

"Well, at least I'll get some decent publicity," she yelled back, tears streaking down her face.

The blacksmith continued to stare and the

police officer rubbed his knuckles where they'd sliced against the wing mirror.

"Breaking the law, is that how you're going to win the public's sympathy? Use your head, Hazel, for God's sake!"

Most of the other picketers had left as soon as they saw the police officers. Trevor was the only one left holding a banner. I noticed that the paint had run on the word "Arnie."

"But it's not fair," said Hazel. "It's just not fair."

"Here, you can take these with you!" Bo Beaumont flung a rucksack, a horse blanket and a pile of clothes on to the gravel. "And if I ever see you on my property again, I'll set the dogs on you, do you hear?"

"But you can't just throw her out," Trevor protested. "She's got nowhere to go!"

One of the grooms who had fetched Hazel's stuff rushed forward and pressed a necklace into her hand. "Don't lose it," she whispered. "It was for your birthday."

We took Hazel back to Hollywell. Sarah said she could use Danny's room as he wouldn't be back for two weeks because he was staying with his mother. Gradually Hazel calmed down, and Roddy confirmed that the story was going in the paper that night. Hazel insisted on making herself useful outside and spent the next couple of hours grooming Jakey, Walter, Dancer and Queenie. I'd never seen anybody bring the body brush down in such regular even strokes. She was amazing. Katie was fascinated when she got a full demonstration on how to plait up, while I sidled off to Colorado's stable, drained and exhausted and in need of five minutes to myself.

I sank down in the deep straw with my eyes closed and Colorado nuzzling at my hair. It was another ten minutes before I realized Blake had come in and was sitting beside me.

"You must be getting old when you can sleep during the day," he joked.

"I've missed you," I blurted out, instantly regretting it.

"Me, too," he said, taking hold of my hand. "And he'll be all right you know, we will save him."

There wasn't much we could do about Arnie but there was something we could do about the petition.

"We can't just leave it all to Mrs Mac," Blake

reasoned. "Besides, it'll help take our minds off Arnie."

We decided to go out collecting signatures, all round the local villages. It wouldn't make a tremendous amount of difference but it was a step in the right direction, and it would please Mrs Mac.

Trevor refused to come with us. What's more, he was downright rude to Blake. It all started when I wanted to put Colorado in the field. Blake asked Trevor to fetch the headcollar. It was an innocent remark and I knew Blake didn't mean anything by it. But Trevor went off the deep end.

"Fetch your own gear," he yelled. "I'm not your servant. Next thing you'll be wanting me to valet your horsebox, or would it be to polish your boots?"

Trevor stormed off in a temper and Blake just gaped in total shock.

"I knew something like this would happen," Ross said, putting an arm round my shoulder. "You've got to sort it out, sis, you can't string them both along."

"But I'm not," I protested. "Trevor's my friend and Blake's my . . ."

"That lad's got an attitude problem," Blake

came back from the tack room carrying the head-collar.

"No," Ross said, opening Colorado's door. "He might be a bit rough around the edges, but Trevor's the most loyal person I've ever met. He'd stick with you through thick and thin, and that counts for a lot."

Ross, Blake and I eventually set off with a clipboard and pen. Katie stayed behind with Hazel who was busy showing her how to make a bat box, of all things. Katie had been watching a wildlife programme on television and was determined to attract more bats to Hollywell. Ross said all she had to do was stand in the orchard after dark and they'd all come flocking.

We had hardly got to the end of the drive before a car turned up and a bald man in a suit wound down the window. He asked if Sarah Foster was on the premises. We told him to knock at the front door. He said his name was Derek Hatfield. Yet again, I didn't give him a second thought.

It was so hot. I was wearing a cropped white T-shirt, denim shorts, which showed off my white legs, and scruffy old trainers. I was still boiling hot.

"Where now?" Ross said after we'd knocked on a dozen doors and had nearly been attacked by three Jack Russells. We still had the old part of the village and three cul-de-sacs to complete. Blake suggested a choc-ice each from the local shop, and I said it was the best idea he'd had all day.

"Talking about ideas," Blake went on, "what about a visit to the Old Rectory?"

I dropped my choc-ice on the pavement, "You *are* joking?" With all the panic over Arnie I'd completely forgotten about the new mystery resident.

"That place gives me the creeps," Ross said, visibly shuddering. "Whoever's moved in must be mad – it's like a morgue."

"I agree with Ross," I said. "Wild horses wouldn't drag me up that drive."

"Well that's settled then," Blake said. "Come on before you lose your nerve."

The drive was circular, very elegant, with a huge poplar tree in the middle of the front lawn, and acres of neglected garden and rose trees running wild. In its day it must have been fantastic but now it was just falling to pieces.

Ross pushed open the iron gate which creaked on its hinges. Everything was so quiet. All I could hear was my heart pounding and my feet crunching on the gravel. I felt like I was taking the yellow brick road in the *Wizard of Oz*, only I was the lion and I'd have given anything to run back home to safety with my tail between my legs.

"I don't think this is such a good idea," my voice rattled, somewhere in my throat.

"Don't be silly." Blake grabbed hold of my hand and we marched forward. "There's no such thing as ghosts."

The front of the house was stone grey with steps up to the main door and most of the lower windows boarded up. Lichen and moss were growing all over the place; it had that damp, clingy feeling that made you think of graveyards.

"Look, over there." Blake pointed to the back of the house. "Somebody's definitely living here."

There were sprinklers turned on, gently rotating over the shrivelled brown grass.

"Doesn't he know there's a hosepipe ban?" Ross took hold of the huge door knocker and rapped it up and down three times. I gripped the clipboard until my knuckles turned white and broke the top off the pen with my other hand.

Nobody answered the door. Ross knocked again. Nothing.

"I think it's a fair assumption to say he's not in," Blake said, swivelling round on his heel and looking over the vast lawns and flower beds.

Ross moved towards the back of the house.

"I don't think we should be doing this," I said, my knees starting to quake. A cloud passed lazily over the sun, and it became more creepy than ever.

Blake and Ross didn't even hear me. They'd found a ladder leaning up to one of the back windows which was wide open. The ground around the base of the ladder was strewn with ivy clippings. A tatty piece of netting was wafting back and forth in the breeze. It was impossible to see inside the ground floor windows.

"Look, let's get out of here before he comes back." My voice was rising to a screech now. "This is stupid!"

Blake put one foot on the bottom rung.

"Maybe she's right." Ross was the first to change his mind. "Whatever's going on in there, it's none of our business. We don't want to be done for breaking and entering."

"Yeah, you're right, but you've got to admit, it's pretty weird," said Blake.

We turned round with every intention of leaving. I was practically falling over myself to get down the drive. Then we heard an eerie sound.

"What was that?" Blake stood stock still with his hand on my arm. I looked up at the open window but there was nothing to see but the flapping netting. Surely it couldn't have been what I thought . . .

"Listen . . ." Blake put a finger to his lips.

Time almost stood still as we strained to hear the slightest noise.

There it was again. No doubt about it. And it was coming from inside the house.

"Oh my God." Ross's face turned white.

Horror slowly filtered through my body.

The donkey kept on braying for a full five minutes.

We were climbing the ladder after three.

"Hurry up," Ross shouted as he clambered through the window. Blake followed him in and then leant over to give me a hand.

We were in a bedroom with an old brass bed which was covered in cobwebs. There was no carpet, just floorboards and the door was ajar. We slipped through not knowing what to expect.

The hallway was huge, dark, murky, with a kind of musty smell which pointed to years of neglect. I put my hand on the banister and felt the dust clog under my fingers.

"Come on Mel, quick!"

Blake and Ross were already tearing down the stairs. I could hear the donkey now as if it was right next to me, I could hear the panic in its voice.

Blake flung open a door. Ross was right behind him. Suddenly there was a loud clatter from a room on the right. Blake swung round and took a step forward.

"No!" I shrieked, wanting to reach out and stop him. I had a crazy notion that the donkey was a ghost and it was leading us to some terrible fate.

"Blake!"

He pushed open the door.

I was bounding down the stairs now, two at a time. All I knew was that Blake and Ross had disappeared and the donkey had stopped braying. It was deathly quiet.

The room looked like an old library, only there were no books on the shelves and all the furniture had been pushed to one side and covered with a big dust sheet. There was a huge bay window looking out over the back gardens and a door on the opposite side of the room leading to heaven knows where.

Blake and Ross were kneeling down in front of the fireplace. That's when I saw the donkey. It was snow white with the cutest face I'd ever seen and it turned and stared at me as if I were its guardian angel. It wasn't a ghost at all – it was a real live donkey, and by the looks of it, not very old.

"He's gorgeous," I said, burying my hand in his white coat mingled with flecks of grey. He pricked his ears up and tried to push his nose into my pocket. I offered him a mint and he wolfed it down and started pawing at the floor with a foreleg. "Oh, you poor baby, who's done this to you, eh? Who do you belong to?"

Blake gently examined his teeth and said he was probably not much more than a year old. He'd got a full set of deciduous teeth.

Behind an old sofa were two saucepans full of water and there was a wedge of hay lying near the fireplace. Somebody must be looking after him, he obviously hadn't been abandoned. But what was he doing locked in the library of an old deserted house?

"Put two and two together," Ross said. "Remember what the police said, 'A white donkey has been stolen.' I think we've just found him."

I didn't know much about donkeys apart from the fact that a male is called a jack donkey and a female a jenny, but why would somebody steal a donkey and hide it away? How much were they worth?

"We'd better call the police." Ross stood up and moved towards the door. "We've got to get the little guy out of here before he hurts himself."

I didn't see the shadow in the doorway. Neither did Ross. Not until it was too late.

"What the hell do you think you're doing?" The voice was well spoken, but high pitched, out of control.

I wheeled round, panic grinding inside me. We were trapped with nowhere to run.

A six foot bloke in a pin-striped suit loomed in the doorway, glaring at us with white hot anger.

But it was what he was holding which filled me with cold dread . . . a shotgun, and it was pointing straight at us!

Chapter Five

"I've got to do this." The man yanked a piece of baling string tight round Blake's wrists. "You do understand, don't you?"

Understand? Understand that a man with a shotgun was tying us up in a deserted house? What were we supposed to do, sit back and thank him?

Ross kicked my ankle and hissed under his breath. "Cool it, will you, we don't want to get our heads blown off."

Panic was rising inside me. This couldn't be happening! The baling string dug into the soft flesh above my wrists.

"Do as you're told and you won't get hurt." The man propped us up against the settee and stood back to look us over. He was about forty years old with blondish hair. His suit was soiled and ripped around one of the pockets and his shirt was open at the collar with the tie pulled loose. "One wrong move and you're done for, do you hear?" His hands were trembling; he was as panic-stricken as a cornered animal, but he wasn't joking.

I cringed back against the settee hardly daring to move. I was frightened now, petrified, but I couldn't help blurting out, "But you can't leave us here, you can't do this!"

The door slammed shut with a sickening thud. We heard his footsteps on the stairs and then silence. He was gone. Only the donkey carried on munching at some hay as if nothing had happened.

"We've got to get out of here." Ross tugged at the string to get his hands free but it was no good, it was too tight. Our legs were bound, too.

"I think he's locked the door." I started dragging myself forward on my bottom.

"Listen, wait," Blake said. "It's no good wasting energy uselessly. We've got to stay calm. Work out a plan."

"But he could come back any minute and kill us." Tears were stinging at the back of my eyes. "Blake, I'm frightened."

"Well he's definitely a nutter," Ross said. "Did you see how his eyes were all glassy?"

"What are we going to do?" I was nearly

crying. "Everybody's going to wonder where we are."

"Exactly – we just sit tight and wait."

"I don't know whether you've noticed," said Ross, "but we haven't got much choice."

We didn't know whether the man was coming back; we didn't have a clue what all this was about. If Katie were here she'd be convinced he was a drug smuggler or an axe murderer. All we knew for sure was that we couldn't escape. We literally couldn't move.

It was really odd. Somehow the reality of the situation hadn't hit me. It all seemed like a terrible nightmare and any moment now I'd wake up and be back at Hollywell. Only I didn't wake up. The door opened instead.

The man walked in carrying a tray and I could smell baked beans before he'd even got near us. There were three tins of coke on the tray and a bar of chocolate.

He didn't untie us. He took a spoon and hand fed us, one mouthful each, one at a time. I felt like a baby bird in a nest, totally helpless. He wiped some tomato sauce from the corner of my mouth with a napkin. Then he held up a can of coke so I felt the cool liquid drain down my throat.

"I can't let you go," was all he said. His hands were still trembling and veins in his neck stood out like cords. In fact his whole body was set rigid, a time bomb just waiting to go off.

"Why are you doing this?" Ross asked.

But the man didn't answer. He just gave us a look of disgust, picked up the plates and marched out of the room. Once again we were left by ourselves.

"Any ideas?" Blake said eventually, after we'd discussed all the reasons why we were here, talked endlessly about Hollywell and dreamt about Mrs Mac's apple crumble.

It was dark outside. I'd got pins and needles in my arms and Blake said his hands had gone numb.

"I don't know how much more I can stand," I croaked.

"If only we hadn't climbed up that ladder," Ross said.

"But then we wouldn't have found the donkey." I tried to be positive.

"I hate to say this, guys, but I honestly don't know what we're going to do." Blake at least was being honest.

"I wish I'd paid more attention to murder mystery movies," Ross joked.

46

We had no ideas – we were trapped in a room with a donkey, no food, no water and no hope. All we could do was sit and wait . . . That's when I must have dozed off to sleep . . .

The banging at the front door jolted me awake like an electric shock.

"Somebody's found us!" Ross tried to heave himself up.

The door knocker rapped hard up and down. The man came flying into the room carrying a roll of masking tape.

"Shut it," he growled, tearing off a strip and slapping it across Blake's mouth and then Ross's. I pulled my head away and tried to yell out, "Hel . . . p" but he grabbed hold of my hair, and before I knew it the tape was across my mouth, too.

"Be good," he threatened, straightening his tie. I noticed that he'd had a shave and brushed his hair. I also saw that he had pulled a curtain across the main window so nobody could see in.

The banging at the door continued.

"Hello, can I help you?" I heard his voice at the door. He sounded so normal. "I'm sorry I didn't hear you, I was watching television."

"I wonder if you can help us. We're looking for three teenagers, two boys and a girl with long blond hair. They should have been back hours ago." It was Mrs Mac – her voice was starting to break. "We're desperately worried."

I was silently screaming now, pushing at the tape with pursed lips but it was not making the slightest difference. I now knew what it must be like not to be able to talk.

"I'm sorry, I haven't seen anything. I've been at work all day, only just got in, actually."

Blake tried to reach a coffee table leg with his ankles.

"Have you recently moved in?" This time it was Trevor.

Blake inched his way forward.

"Only been here a few days, I'm renting it off Mr Johnson. Bit of a dump really."

"You've got your work cut out." Trevor was being friendly.

Blake wrapped his ankles round the ornate wooden leg.

"So if you see them you'll let us know?" It was Mrs Mac. "We're from Hollywell Stables, just down the road."

Blake tugged at the leg but nothing moved.

"No sweat, they've probably just lost track of time."

"I dearly hope so," Mrs Mac said. "But it's so unlike them."

Blake pushed with both feet and the coffee table and a huge antique lamp went crashing to the floor.

But it was seconds too late. The front door thudded shut, blocking off any noise or disturbance. Mrs Mac and Trevor might as well have been three thousand miles away. The man came in, took the tape off our mouths and left.

"It's twenty-four hours before the police can do anything." Ross sounded so defeated.

I'd never felt so sore in all my life. The only respite we'd had was when the man took each one of us to the toilet, but always holding on to the gun. There was no escape in the bathroom. The window was boarded up, it was all so hopeless. It was now the middle of the night and we were trying to get some sleep.

The donkey dozed near the fireplace, every now and then snorting and shuffling to keep his balance. He didn't seem at all bothered about us in the corner. I think he realized we didn't have any food for him. He'd been left some carrots and vegetable peelings and he'd munched his way through those.

I shuffled my position to get more comfortable and leant on Blake's shoulder. Outside an owl hooted and I thought I heard a cat on the roof. I shuddered even though I wasn't cold and Blake turned his head and kissed my hair.

"Sweet dreams," he said, half asleep. "And keep thinking it can only get better."

The sunshine streamed in through the window the next morning and the man burst in, full of beans, shouting, "Rise and shine!" as if it were perfectly normal to keep people tied up all night as prisoners.

"I've got a special treat for you this morning," he grinned like a totally different person, reaching for the donkey's saucepans to fill them with fresh water. "You're going to really like it."

He came back with a steaming bowl of lumpy porridge as if it were a special gourmet offering. "Just what you need to keep your strength up," he said. "Susan used to love my porridge."

Who was Susan? And why was he suddenly being so nice?

He held out a spoonful in front of me and I didn't dare refuse. It tasted revolting and I was sure the milk was off but I just moved my jaws up and down and swallowed. The last thing we wanted to do was upset him.

"How long are you going to keep us here?" Blake was trying a new tack. "You're going to get in serious trouble you know, you'll end up in prison."

There was no answer.

"What's the donkey's name?" Blake asked.

"Snowy, his name's Snowy. And I'm Joe. Now cut the questions."

He told us he was going out for a little while and that we were not to try to escape because there was no way out. He left us with a radio which was a link with civilization at last. The DJ whom we had heard yesterday came back on air. "Another fantastic hot day out there, groovers. Perfect for just laying back and doing nothing." It seemed a lifetime since we'd been to see Arnie.

He played a couple of romantic ballads and then some heavy metal from a local band who'd just landed a record contract, and then it was straight to the news at eleven o'clock.

"Three teenagers by the name of Mel and Ross Foster and Blake Kildaire have been reported missing after setting out to collect signatures for a petition to stop cruelty to horses. Blake Kildaire is a bit of a local name, an up-and-coming show-jumper, and Mel and Ross are from the well-known horse sanctuary, Hollywell Stables. If anybody's seen or heard anything, please report it on this number . . ."

He then gave out our home telephone number, and I felt like shouting, "We're here, help, do something!" But a bright, breezy pop record came on next. Nobody could hear us. Not even the birds outside.

"We've got to come up with something," Ross said, trying to shake his hair out of his eyes. I'd got a terrible itch in the middle of my back and a fly was irritating me to death as it kept trying to land on my arm.

"If only we could get Snowy to come across here and undo us," I said, wallowing in wishful thinking. But things like that only happened in books and this was real life. We had to think of something practical.

Slowly as the hours ticked by, and there was still no sign of Joe, we formulated a plan. It wasn't a very elaborate plan but it was the best we could come up with in the circumstances.

What we didn't expect was the unexpected.

Snowy had been dozing in his favourite spot by the fireplace, resting on three legs. The smell from his droppings and staling was now getting pretty bad, but in our situation it seemed the last of our worries. Joe came back into the room with a bundle of hay and started shaking it out on to the floor. I don't know whether it was the way the sunlight slanted, or Joe's hand movements, but Snowy suddenly leapt back, jerking his head up and stepping into the hearth.

His near hind-leg locked tight. I don't know how it happened but it terrified me. The whole length of his leg was paralysed and just hanging stiff as a rod. Fear rolled around in his eyes, his nostrils flaring in panic. He tried fighting against it but nearly lost his balance. Joe had his hands up over his eyes.

"Keep him still," Blake shouted out, instinctively fighting to free his hands. "For God's sake man, hold him still!"

Joe was getting hysterical. "Not again, oh not again, I can't stand it."

Snowy was breathing heavily but his own good sense stopped him from struggling. Ross looked as horrified as me. I'd never seen anything like it!

"Let me go," Blake demanded. "Undo me and I can fix it."

Joe didn't seem to hear him. He just started silently crying to himself and refused to look at Snowy's leg.

"Joe!"

Minutes seemed to drift past. But it was only seconds.

"He's dislocated his patella – he's in pain, Joe. Let me put it back," Blake insisted.

That seemed to do the trick. He fumbled across to Blake and started undoing the knots. "No funny business though, do you hear me?" His fingers clasped firmly around the gun which was lying on the chair. "I mean it!"

"It's happened before hasn't it?" Blake examined Snowy's leg. "There boy, steady, it's going to be OK. The ligaments haven't developed properly. Look, we might need a rope."

Joe held the gun. "It normally just goes back by itself."

"Not this time." Blake was down on his knees. "It's too bad."

"No rope." Joe released the catch on the gun. The tension was unbearable.

"I'll do my best. Now you'd better hold his head."

Snowy was quivering all over. His huge ears had flopped back and he was watching Blake out of the corner of his eye.

"I'm going to count to three and then I'm going

to try and push it in. Hold him tight . . . one, two, three . . ."

The sudden snap made me wince.

"It's in," Blake breathed.

Joe went ecstatic. For vital seconds he completely forgot that we were his captives. He just kept patting and rubbing at Snowy's neck, laughing and crying at the same time.

That's when Blake seized his chance.

He grabbed Joe from behind and lurched for the gun.

"Traitor," Joe screamed out and dug back with his elbow.

"Blake," I yelled.

Joe spun round with superhuman strength. Blake regained his balance and moved forward. I could hardly watch any more. The gun was suspended in the air with them both wrestling for a stronger grip. Blake's foot tangled in a ruck in the carpet and I could see his knee buckling. Joe was pulled down with Blake's weight. It was all a horrible situation, a terrible accident. And it happened so quickly.

"No," Joe yelled . . . and the blast filled the room.

Chapter Six

"Blake!" I stared down at his wan, lifeless face. "Blake!"

The blood slowly seeped through his white shirt.

"You've killed him." I was verging on the hysterical. "You've killed him!"

"Calm down you silly nit-wit, I'm still here." It was Blake. He was talking!

"Get an ambulance," Ross shouted.

"Blake, if you bail out on me now I'll never forgive you." Tears were pouring down my face. "Blake, do you hear me? Don't you dare leave me. Who's going to teach me to show-jump if you're not around and who's going to ride Colorado? Blake, are you listening to me? I . . ."

"I know." He was still alive.

As soon as Joe had untied us, Ross started ripping Blake's shirt open. "It's just a graze, it's caught the top of his arm," he said. "I'm going to make a tourniquet."

Thankfully, Ross had been on a first aid course. It didn't look like just a graze to me. There was blood all over the place.

"Did you hear that, Blake, you're going to be all right."

"Well, I could have told you that," he mumbled.

"In that case there's no need for an ambulance," Joe was standing directly behind us with the gun.

"You've got to be joking." Ross could hardly believe it. "He needs proper medical care, surely you can see that?"

"It was his fault," Joe said. "He shouldn't have been so stupid. Now he's got to pay the price."

I was starting to get really frightened.

Ross rolled up a strip of the shirt and tied it at the top of Blake's arm.

"At least get us some water and antiseptic," I pleaded, silently deciding that when the police did catch him they should throw away the key for ever.

I dabbed at Blake's forehead which had broken out in a sweat and prayed that an ambulance would magically appear, but I knew there was no chance of that happening – Joe had no intention of dialling 999.

"There's some cartridge lodged in his arm." Ross washed the blood off his own hands in one of Snowy's saucepans. "If he doesn't get help he could get an infection, maybe even blood-poisoning."

Joe's face didn't even flicker.

"You monster," I yelled, standing up, my hair all over the place, my whole body grubby with dirt and sweat. I'd had enough now. I was fed up with being bullied by this madman. I wanted to go home. "I hate you," I yelled. "I hate you, I hate you! I hope you rot in hell."

Ross put his arms round me and I started crying, sobbing, all the fear and panic of the last twenty-four hours coming out.

"If you don't sit down and be quiet I'll tie you up again." Joe's voice was jittery, on edge – he was starting to lose control.

"Do as he says, Mel, it's our only chance." I couldn't believe how well Ross was handling all this. Usually it was me who stayed calm and together.

Joe pulled something out of his pocket and handed it to me. It was last night's paper and on the front page was a picture of Arnie, his big goofy face staring out at me. "Does this horse deserve to die?" – Roddy had really gone to town with the headline.

"Tell me about Hollywell Stables." Joe sat back in a chair, nursing the gun.

I didn't have a choice. So I started to talk. He wanted to know every little detail. Every horse we'd rescued. All about Sarah and Mrs Mac and Trevor. I was exhausted.

That's when he started to cry. I was embarrassed at first, I'd never seen a grown man cry before.

"The bleeding's stopped," Ross said, examining Blake's arm. "Keep him talking," he hissed at me.

But it was Joe who took up the conversation.

Susan was his wife and Snowy belonged to her and their two children, Charlotte and Emily. A few days ago she'd walked out on him, taking everything. In a fit of anger he'd stolen Snowy from the garden late at night and brought him here. He knew she'd report it to the police. If she was going to take the kids, then he was going to have Snowy, it was only fair.

It was obvious something must have flipped in his mind – the gun, keeping us tied up here – for the first time I realized he must be a very unstable man.

"At Hollywell we give good homes to animals like Snowy," I said. "You can't keep him shut up in here for ever, it's not good for him."

"If I did take him to your place, would you promise not to let her get him?" There were tears glistening in his eyes, and he looked ready to drop.

"We promise," I said. "Cross our hearts and hope to die. He'd be safe with us."

Joe fiddled with his finger-nails, scraping the dirt from under his thumb. I felt a trickle of sweat run down my back. It was so hot.

"Maybe," he said, rubbing his hand over his temples. "Just maybe."

"You've got to get help." Ross was insistent. "The bleeding's started again, and he's losing far too much blood." Ross held a pressure pad over Blake's arm, but it soon turned bright red. "I mean it Joe, he needs help."

Blake's face had gone grey, his breathing was shallow and irregular.

"OK, OK, I'll go." Joe finally saw sense. He was running his hand through his hair, his eyes bulging. "I'll go to the chemist's, get some pain-killers."

"That won't do any good," Ross retorted.

"Well it will just have to do."

Nothing we could say would change his mind.

"Just be grateful I'm doing something, OK?"

He was panicking now, unable to cope with the situation, squirming at the sight of blood. And that's when he made a mistake. "I'm going to lock the door. If you make any attempt to escape . . ." He thrust the gun in my direction but he did not tie us up again.

"Just go Joe, hurry." Ross pulled a cushion off the settee and placed it under Blake's head.

The door slammed shut and the key turned in the lock. It was a few minutes before we heard a car engine start up.

"Right Mel, quick – try that door over there." Ross was totally in charge; I was a nervous wreck.

"It's locked," I screamed. "It's locked."

"Don't panic, is the key still in?"

I closed one eye and peered through the hole. "No, it's not, I can see right through. It looks like some kind of store-room."

"OK, now try the window, if that's locked, try and find some wire, anything, a coat hanger. What about that flower arrangement over there?"

The window wouldn't open. "We can't smash it," Ross said. "The glass would fall back on Snowy, besides, it's double glazed, it's too thick."

"There's no wire!" I threw some dried flowers on the floor.

"Come on, think, think, something to pick that lock . . ."

"My hair grip!" I suddenly remembered that I'd pinned back my fringe before we left Hollywell because it was so hot. The grip was still there, half hanging on a clump of blond hair. "I've got it!"

"Just keep calm." Ross was talking me through picking the lock. "Don't panic, just keep twiddling."

"But it's not doing any good." My hand was shaking like a leaf.

"You come and mind Blake and I'll have a go," Ross offered.

Something clicked. "It's worked!" I grabbed hold of the door handle and it swung open.

Ross was right behind me. "Come on, we haven't got much time."

Inside was a load of piled-up furniture. It wasn't a very big room and the first serious disappointment was the lack of window.

"The skylight." Ross pointed to the ceiling. "It's the only way."

We pulled out a table and piled up some boxes on top. All the time I was straining to hear the noise of a car engine. The nearest chemist was six miles away. It wouldn't take that long. What if he changed his mind, what if he came back early?

"Mel, you've got to do it, you're the only one small enough."

I looked up at the skylight with a feeling of dread.

"What about Blake?"

"He's OK, he's holding the pressure pad himself."

"Wouldn't you be better going? You can run faster than me."

"No way. I'm not leaving you here for when he gets back. There's no telling what he might do."

"But Ross . . ."

"Don't think about it, just fetch help!"

I clung on to his hand, my big brother, my safety net, the one person who was always there for me.

"Be careful," I said, "big brothers aren't that easy to replace."

"Come on, I'll give you a leg up."

I scrabbled up the boxes, ignoring my aching muscles and concentrating on keeping my balance and unscrewing the metal lock inside the skylight. It was quite straightforward; luckily it wasn't rusted up. I pushed hard and the whole thing creaked open.

The waft of fresh air was wonderful but I didn't have time to enjoy it. I heaved myself up, straining my arms, grasping, scratching, desperate to get a foothold. One shoulder was through, then the other. I was looking out at a flat roof.

"Good luck," Ross shouted, but I was too out of breath to answer. I was on my own now – it was all down to me.

I had to keep a clear head. The flat roof was a reasonable size, it looked as if it was an extension of the main house. It was still pretty high up though.

My head was swimming when I looked down at the ground. There was no way I could jump. The only chance was the drainpipe, but I was terrified of heights. I'd never even climbed a tree, let alone shinned down a drainpipe.

The thought of Ross and Blake still locked in the house was enough to send me down the metal pipe. "Dear God, let this work out," I prayed. If it came away from the wall I'd be done for.

My hands were sweating so much I didn't think I'd be able to keep a grip. I banged my knee as I swivelled round trying to get a hold with my ankles. The pain made my eyes water. "Come on Mel, you can do it," I urged myself on.

I slid down, a foot at a time. That's when I noticed the red burn marks round my wrists. It hadn't been a bad dream. Somewhere a dog barked in the distance. I could hear the church clock chiming. It was normality and it gave me the strength to carry on. The relief when my feet touched the grass was incredible. But there was no time to lose. The quickest way home was over the fields. If I went down the drive and out on to the road I might run into Joe and that didn't bear thinking about.

I set off across the lawn, scuffing across molehills, racing as if I was in the eight hundred metres, not daring to look back.

I scrambled across a metal gate and then flew through a field of meadow hay, the long stalks whipping at my bare legs. But I didn't feel it, the pain inside my head was far greater. I had to get to Hollywell.

Everything looked deserted as I came on to our land. Boris and Dancer were standing under the chestnut tree scratching each other's withers. There were no cars in the yard, nobody in sight.

"Trevor! Sarah!" My lungs were rasping as if

I'd got asthma. My head was pounding with pumping blood. "Somebody! Somewhere!"

Jigsaw was sitting in the yard trying to catch flies on his tummy. I had to force back the tears – I'd thought I'd never see him again.

"Mel!" There was no mistaking the voice. It was Trevor.

"Trevor! Trevor!" He came out of Colorado's stable carrying the grooming box which he promptly dropped on the concrete. Hoof oil leaked out all over the body brushes. But I didn't care because he was running towards me, catching me in his arms, hugging me like a sumo wrestler, kissing me non-stop, on the hair, on my cheeks, as if any minute I'd vanish in a puff of smoke.

"Just look at you." He held both my hands and stared into my face in shock. Heaven knows what I must have looked like, I can only guess.

"There's no time," I croaked. "Ross, Blake, the gun . . ." My voice disappeared altogether, I was just gasping for air.

"What is it, Mel? Where are they?"

"The, the R-Rectory!" My knees were buckling and Trevor had to hold me up.

Mrs Mac appeared at the back door with the

bald man in a suit. Just seeing the suit freaked me out. I thought it was Joe.

"Ring the police and call an ambulance," Trevor was telling Mrs Mac. "Get them to the Old Rectory as fast as poss. Tell them there's an armed man there."

"Derek, get your car!"

"I'm going with you!" I wasn't going to stay behind now, not after I'd come this far.

We leapt into Derek's car and he turned the ignition key. The dry, grating cough of the engine was the final straw.

"I don't believe it," said Derek. "This can't be happening."

"Quick, out, we'll go in Sarah's." Trevor was out of the car and pulling back the barn doors before I could speak.

The bright red MG roared out of the barn in a cloud of smoke.

"Come on, jump in," yelled Trevor.

"But we can't take this, it's not finished," I protested.

The sports car was Sarah's engagement present from James, and Trevor was doing it up. At the moment it had no exhaust and no bumpers.

"It's a life or death situation," Trevor shouted. "Now, come on."

I couldn't argue with that. We had to get back to the Rectory before Joe. I calculated it would take him twenty minutes to get to the chemist's and back, half an hour if he hit heavy traffic. It had taken no more than ten minutes to run from the Rectory to Hollywell, we were still in with a chance.

Trevor put his foot down and we zoomed off down the drive.

"I only hope you've fixed the brakes," I shouted, the wind whipping my hair right across my face.

Derek said he didn't have that problem, hair he meant, and I wondered how we could be having such light conversation at a time like this. But Sarah always said in tough times you could either laugh or cry. I only wished I could feel something. At the moment I was numb with shock. I felt as if all this was happening to someone else.

We hurtled down the main village High Street at fifty miles an hour. People were stopping and staring – one lady dropped all her groceries. I had to admit, we must have looked a peculiar sight.

Trevor took a corner practically on two wheels. The noise coming from underneath the car was more fitting of a juggernaut. The trees in full bloom blocked our view. I couldn't see a thing. All I noticed was a grey squirrel scampering across the road directly in front of us. Trevor swerved and we missed it by inches.

The green Land Rover was upon us before we knew it.

We were just approaching the Rectory. The Land Rover was coming from the other direction. It slowed down and switched on its right indicator. It was a full ten seconds before my brain swivelled into gear.

"That's him," I shrieked. *"That's Joe!"*

Chapter Seven

He didn't recognize me.

He was so busy concentrating on the road ahead that he didn't see me bouncing around in the back of the MG.

Not until it was too late.

Trevor had always had the ability to think fast, now he made a split second decision.

We were on the left side of the road nearest the Rectory. Joe was on the opposite side about to turn in. Without any warning Trevor slammed down the accelerator and we shot forward.

"Trevor!" I screamed.

I don't think he meant to crash the car. But then I don't think he expected Joe to deliberately ram into us.

"How the hell . . .?" Joe leapt out of the Land Rover with his eyes on me and me alone. It gave Trevor and Derek just enough time to get the upper hand.

And they didn't waste a second. Trevor charged

at Joe like a bull, slamming him back against the Land Rover bonnet. Derek whipped round to the driver's door, seizing the shotgun.

The police sirens were wailing at us from all directions.

"It's all over, matey, just give in peacefully." Trevor relinquished his arm-hold.

"You're a maniac," Joe gasped, badly winded, bending over double.

"You're under arrest." Two police officers moved in. "You do not have to say anything . . ." They were reading him his rights.

"But you can't arrest me! Who's going to look after Snowy?"

Joe was frog-marched off to a police car, his head cast down, his shoulders slumped. Just once he turned round and stared at me: dull, lonely eyes, and I almost felt sorry for him.

Sarah's car was a mess. The whole front wing was smashed in, crumpled like corrugated cardboard. It only took a few minutes to push it out of the way so that an ambulance could get past. All I was interested in was Blake and Ross. I was running blindly up the drive. A policewoman grabbed at my arm but I shook her off. I had to get to Blake.

"Mel!" It was Trevor's voice behind me.

The blue lights of the ambulance flashed round and round.

"Blake!" I shouted. He was there, coming down the steps from the front door. Safe, alive, still in one piece. Ross was at his side. "Blake!" He grinned a watery grin back at me, and one of the paramedics opened the ambulance door. "He is going to be all right, isn't he?" Tears were welling up inside me now, burning to escape.

"Mel!" Sarah appeared from nowhere, her arms enfolding me just when I needed her most. Her mascara had run and her cheeks were wet. "Thank God you're all right," she said. And I sobbed into her shoulders: it was as if a dam had just burst.

"She's in shock, it's only to be expected." At the hospital the doctor was looking down at me with a friendly face and a warm smile.

We had been told that Blake would have to stay in hospital for a few days. "But what if he's got an infection?" I said, terrified at the mention of blood-poisoning.

Sarah squeezed my hand and said it would be all right. Ross came back from the drinks machine with three cups of insipid cold tea. "The only thing we can do is go home and rest," he said, sensibly.

I knew it made sense, but I couldn't bear the idea of leaving Blake.

"He's asleep, it's what he would want," Sarah insisted.

She looked so tired, the agony of the last twenty-four hours showed on every line of her face: the not knowing, the uncertainty must have been terrible. When I managed to escape back to Hollywell she had been out in the car searching with James. They had been out all night. It was Mrs Mac who told her about the Rectory; car phones were the best thing that were ever invented.

Ross took my arm, saying, "Come on sis, let's hit the road."

Hollywell was cast in the warm glow of the sunset as we turned up the drive. Everything appeared as normal, only the empty stable next to Sally was now occupied. Two white ears protruded over the top of the door.

James had brought Snowy back to Hollywell and settled him into our medical unit, checking him over and taking a blood sample. "He needs an operation on his near hind," he told us later in the kitchen. "Apart from that he's in fine fettle." The kettle was already boiling on the Aga that James had recently fixed.

I collapsed in a chair and Oscar immediately sprung on to my knee, purring in a deep baritone.

"The man needs locking up," Sarah said, fighting off exhaustion. "To think what might have happened . . ."

"I don't think he's a particularly bad person," I said. "He's just mixed up. He loves Snowy, that must count for something."

Snowy was finding the whole experience of being in a stable both novel and bizarre. He kept wandering around, sniffing at the manger, the walls, even the haynet, as if it was all rather too much for him. James said he'd given him a bran mash and that he'd soon settle in.

"I hope we can keep him," said Katie. "He's so sweet and cuddly and he's the first donkey we've had."

She insisted on taking me out to the orchard where she and Hazel had erected a bat box on one of the apple trees.

"That reminds me," I said. "Where's Hazel?"

"We don't know," Katie answered in a low voice. "She went off to see that Beaumont woman and we've not seen her since."

"Oh," I said, feeling the rough bark of one of

the apple trees and thinking how it would be there probably long after all of us. I was so tired I didn't have the energy to worry about Hazel.

Back in the kitchen, Mrs Mac was cutting a portion of her apple crumble and drowning it in fresh cream. I'd suddenly developed a craving for her home-made special. It represented safety and security and it was just what I needed. I didn't think I'd ever be able to face baked beans or porridge ever again.

"Sometimes it helps to talk about it, you know," Sarah knelt down, looking me straight in the eye, full of concern.

But I didn't want to talk about it. I didn't want to dwell on the worst ordeal of our lives. It had left me ragged, empty and frightened, and I just wanted to put it all behind me.

"I – I thought I was going to lose them both," I said.

"I know," Sarah took hold of my hand, pressing it to her face. "I know."

I woke up at six o'clock the next morning with bells clanging in my head. Only it wasn't bells at all – as soon as I'd got my senses together I realized it was a series of massive "e-yore"s which threatened to wake up the whole neighbourhood, if not the entire county.

"Snowy!" I pushed up the window and felt like lobbing a book at him. He momentarily stopped and stared at me, an "e-yore" strangled in his throat, and then he started again with renewed gusto, his jaws open, his ears pricked forward.

"What's going on?" Katie stumbled into my bedroom in her pyjamas looking like a sleep-walker in a horror film. "It's only ten past six!" she squawked.

Sarah said we might as well all get up and decided that a good home-cooked breakfast was just what we needed. Katie went off to collect the eggs and I sorted out Snowy who had not only finished off his hay, but most of the clean straw in the stable as well.

"We might have to put him on woodshavings," I said to Ross who was still yawning.

Straw tended to blow horses up and make them cough. We'd never had a bed eater before.

Snowy grinned wickedly and his whole head disappeared into a bucket of coarse mix.

"I think this little fella's a bit of a character," I

said, fighting desperately to hold on to the bucket handle.

"You and me both," Ross grinned. "He's definitely starting to find his feet."

After I'd cleaned him up – he'd got pieces of straw stuck all over him, even in his ears of all places – I moved over to Colorado who looked uptight and on edge. He kept watching the back door as if Blake would appear at any minute and I noticed his bed had been trampled down where he'd marched round and round in a circle.

"Poor lad," I breathed into his nostrils. "He'll be back, he hasn't left you."

How do you tell a horse that his master has been shot and is in hospital but he's going to be all right? Colorado just stared past me uncomprehendingly, and I tried to send him telepathic messages but it didn't work.

Trevor came out with his purple hair stuck up like Snowy's mane and his jumper on back to front. "Nobody said anything about six o'clock starts," he grinned, adding that he'd collect the haynets if I did the water buckets.

It was a glorious sunny morning and the wood-pigeons were cooing nineteen to the dozen and a cuckoo was trying to compete somewhere over in the woods. I was already feeling ten times better. I seemed to be viewing everything through fresh eyes, it really was good to be alive.

"Mel come on, fetch Trevor."

Ross loaded my plate with everything from mushrooms to scrambled eggs and crispy bacon. Jigsaw got told off for slobbering at the table, and Sarah said she was way behind on her novel and that the typewriter was on the blink.

Everything had clicked back into normality and it was as if Ross and I had never been tied up and gagged in a deserted house by a madman. The peace didn't last for long. By nine o'clock the police were back on the doorstep, wanting to ask more questions even though we'd told them every little detail the night before. Roddy wanted to cover the story with me giving my own personal account but I told him quite emphatically that Ross was the hero, not me. Without him I'd have gone to pieces. The local television stations were on the phone wanting to put us on film but Sarah was as protective as a bodyguard and told them we were in no fit state to talk. Trevor even had to chase a photographer down the drive who was trying to climb up one of our trees to get a better view.

"Wouldn't it be lovely to have a quiet, uneventful week." I said to Ross, swiping at a midge which had just landed on my neck.

"No chance of that at Hollywell," he said. "You'd have to book tickets for Timbuctoo to get away from it all."

We were intent on visiting Blake. Sarah had rung the hospital and his condition was stable. We were supposed to be there two hours ago, but Walter, our mule, had escaped and pulled back the bolt on Snowy's stable. The two of them had sloped off when we weren't looking, and we found them munching runner beans in Mrs White's garden and drinking out of the fish pond. It's lucky that Mrs White was a friend, and even more lucky that the goldfish didn't have heart attacks.

We arrived at the hospital hot and bothered and I nearly freaked out when I saw Blake's bed empty with the sheets pulled back.

"It's OK, he's in the day room," a nurse shouted across, carrying a bedpan which made me squirm.

The day room was bright and breezy with a huge television and chairs lining the walls. Blake was talking to two old ladies, one who was discussing her back pain and the other complaining about gout. They looked as if they were in seventh heaven.

"Ooh, what a lovely young man," one of them said, obviously besotted with Blake.

"This is Ethel and this is Margaret." Blake introduced us, looking amused and not nearly as washed out as the night before.

Katie and Ross overloaded him with everything from grapes and chocolates to magazines and a Dick Francis thriller.

"I think I've had enough thrills to last me a lifetime," he said, plucking off a grape and sticking it in Katie's mouth.

Sarah said she thought we ought to take everything back to the ward so we left Ethel and Margaret with a packet of coffee creams and went down the corridor. We must have looked more like a coach party than hospital visitors.

The only person missing was Trevor. He had insisted on waiting in the canteen. His last run-in with Blake over the headcollar hadn't been very pleasant and he didn't know how to face him. I told him he was being stupid, but he wouldn't listen.

"How's Colorado?" was one of Blake's first questions. "And what about Snowy?"

"What about Downing Street?" Sarah said,

putting her hand up to Blake's forehead to check his temperature, and pulling down his eyes as if he were a horse.

"I'll be fit enough," Blake touched at his bandaged arm. "And if I'm not you'll just have to go without me."

"But . . ."

"The petition's the most important thing," he said. "The show must go on."

"He's right," Ross said. "We've got to get that petition to Downing Street, there are thousands of horses out there relying on us."

"Hear, hear," Katie shrieked, and then nearly choked on a Walnut Whip.

"Can you keep the noise down?" A matron strutted past looking severe. "There are patients sleeping in here."

Someone at the top of the ward was snoring so loudly I thought it would take a bomb to wake them up.

"What shall we do with Colorado?" Sarah whispered.

Trevor was behind us before we even realized.

"Listen mate," he said, scratching his head and looking embarrassed.

"It's all right," Blake butted in, "let's call it

quits, and for God's sake help me eat some of these chocolates."

We drove back from the hospital feeling a lot better and confident that Blake was going to be all right, although it would be a while before he was riding again.

"Somebody had better tell Mr Sullivan," Ross said.

Mr Sullivan was Blake's sponsor and he'd supported him through thick and thin for the last year. I only hoped his patience hadn't run out. In show-jumping the expense was colossal and the rewards few and far between.

We were all taken by surprise when we saw the car and pony trailer in the drive.

"What's going on?" Ross was suddenly serious.

I didn't have a clue but something told me it wasn't good.

"My name's Mrs Wilson." A stringy-looking woman approached us with two kids. "Mrs Joe Wilson."

"Oh." We hadn't expected this.

"I can't say how sorry I am about . . ." she broke off, fumbling for words. "Anyway, the thing is . . ."

"You're here for Snowy." Sarah took the words right out of her mouth.

"Yes, I am."

"But you can't, he's ours," Katie was devastated.

"No, love, it was good of you to look after him but we're going to take him home now. He belongs to Charlotte and Emily."

The two kids shuffled their feet and looked as if they couldn't care less one way or another.

"Yes, of course," Sarah said, and I couldn't believe what I was hearing.

"We've got no choice," she hissed when Mrs Wilson had gone across to Snowy's stable. "He's not an ill-treated animal, he's not neglected. She's every right to take him back."

This was the last thing we needed. I put my arm round Katie's shoulders, who was trembling.

Snowy pottered out of the stable behind Mrs Wilson wondering what on earth was going on.

Sarah explained about his leg.

"No way, he's not having an operation, I'm not wasting good money on that, it always goes back into place."

"But, Mrs Wilson—" Sarah began.

"I've made up my mind," the woman butted in.

"If he doesn't have it sorted out he'll develop arthritis, is that what you want?" Sarah retorted.

"We'll cross that bridge when we come to it, now come on, I haven't got all day." Mrs Wilson was not to be convinced.

We coaxed Snowy up the ramp. Walter banged frantically on his stable door wanting to follow his new friend, but for once he couldn't have his own way. Snowy looked across at him with sad bewildered eyes. I tied his leadrope to the ring and rubbed my hand through his stubby mane. "Look after yourself little fella."

Katie clung on to my hand as the ramp thudded shut.

"But I don't want a donkey, I want a video game," Emily blurted out.

But it didn't do any good. Mrs Wilson was not going to change her mind.

"I hate her!" Katie screeched as the trailer rattled down the drive. "I hate her, I hate her." Hot tears bubbled over her cheeks, and she ran full tilt towards the house.

"Leave her," Sarah said to Trevor. "Let her be."

*

The phone rang as we were having a cup of tea.

"It's Jennifer Beaumont," Ross came through. "She wants to speak to you, Sarah."

Chapter Eight

"But that's bribery," Ross was gobsmacked.

We were all discussing Sarah's phone conversation with "Bo" Beaumont, outraged at what had been said.

"We should have taped her conversation, put bugs in the plant pots, that kind of thing," Katie said.

"I don't believe the cheek of the woman." Sarah flopped down in the deck-chair which had somehow found its way into the kitchen.

Katie grabbed some chocolate eggs from the fridge and started gnawing on one like a squirrel. I did the same. Heaven knows we needed something.

Boot-faced Beaumont, as Trevor called her, had just offered Sarah five hundred pounds to drop the campaign to save Arnie's life.

"What kind of people does she think we are?" Sarah steamed.

"Can't we report her?" Katie broke off some chocolate for Jigsaw.

"As usual we don't have a shred of evidence." Ross was absolutely right.

"If the dressage selectors knew about this . . ."

"But don't you see," Sarah said, standing up, "we've got her on the run. She's seriously rattled. All we've got to do now is put on more pressure."

Apparently Bo had been inundated with irate phone calls after the article in the paper. She'd had to take the phone off the hook, and when Sarah told her we hadn't even started on the national papers, she went through the roof.

"The bad news is she hasn't seen Hazel. In fact she thought she was here."

"Well if she's not at Somerset Stables, where is she?" I was beginning to get seriously worried.

"That girl's in such an emotional mess she's capable of anything." Sarah was right, I had to agree.

"Oh my God!" Ross looked through the window down the drive where a pick-up truck was hauling the red MG sports car behind it like a limp dog. "Now keep calm Sarah, it's not as bad as it looks . . ."

But it was – even worse in fact. The whole right wing was a crumpled heap. The wing mirror hung broken and dejected, and the paintwork was just a criss-cross of scratches.

"Oh dear," Trevor murmured.

"Do you honestly think I'm bothered about the car?" Sarah squeaked. "It's you lot that are most important for me – a car can be replaced . . ."

"I can rebuild her Mrs F, I know I can," Trevor offered.

"Yes, Trevor, whatever you say," Sarah sighed.

"All it needs is some expertise and some spare parts," Trevor persisted.

. I couldn't help wondering for the zillionth time how we could have been so wrong about Trevor. He was, as Katie put it, a forty carat dude and totally indispensable.

The car wasn't the only black spot. Sarah finally decided to open a backlog of mail which started with a monstrous overdue bill from the blacksmith and finished with a letter from Maxwell Curtis, or rather his secretary, beginning: "I am sorry to inform you . . ." He didn't want anything to do with our campaign.

"Who does he think he is?" I barked, feeling quite put out.

"Well, we don't need him." Sarah tore up the letter and sent it flying into the foot bin alongside last night's potato peelings.

"I think it's time Maxi Crowface and I had a little chat," Trevor said, a thunderstorm brewing across his face. But he didn't get a chance to elaborate.

An unexpected phone call threw us into such pandemonium that Sarah had to sit down with the dishcloth over her forehead and I just wanted to silently scream. Dominic, the producer of the Saturday morning children's programme, *The Breakfast Bunch* had just thrown a spanner in the works; he'd rearranged our plans completely. *The Breakfast Bunch* were going to film us handing in our petition which was going to be shown in September along with an update on the sanctuary. This was a real coup for Hollywell Stables – most of the viewers had become avid supporters and it would give us a chance to promote the Fan Club and to show off our new range of pencil cases and bags.

The problem was, Dom's boss was insisting he jet off to Florida to interview a pop band at the end of the week. So they'd come up with an alternative plan – we were to go to Downing Street tomorrow!

"Do tell me he's joking!" Sarah groaned.

But according to Dom it would be in our favour. He'd managed to talk one of the big feature writers from a daily paper into covering the story, and Dom insisted he might have an extra surprise up his sleeve.

"Well that's that then," Sarah said. "We must do as Master Dom commands!"

"I think we'd better start packing," said Ross.

Mrs Mac's office was a mountain of boxes. Each one contained thousands of signatures and had to be packed into the horsebox. It's a shame we hadn't reached the million target but maybe we'd been just too ambitious, there was nothing we could do about it now.

Trevor and Ross agreed to load the horsebox while Katie and I made a start on Colorado and Queenie. We had to get them gleaming like conkers, which wasn't easy when the weather was tropical, and sweat was running off my face like a stream.

"We're going to have a thunderstorm," I predicted.

"You've been saying that for weeks," Katie bantered, banging the curry comb against the wall, leaving a dusty imprint.

Queenie nodded her head up and down. I didn't know whether she was agreeing with me or Katie. Small, fluffy clouds drifted across a clear blue sky. Maybe I had got it wrong after all.

"Ouch!" I yelled, as Queenie plonked a hoof on my left foot.

"Serves you right for wearing sandals instead of jodphur boots," Katie said in her know-it-all voice.

"I wonder what this surprise is that Dom's got lined up." I had to admit, I was intrigued.

"I've told you," Katie said, "we're going to meet the Prime Minister."

"Oh yeah, pull the other one, it's got bells on," I sneered.

"Mel, you're such a cynic," Katie retorted.

"Hey, watch it," I yelled as she squirted fly spray on to Queenie's head, only she missed and it went all over my hair.

"No flies on you, big sis," she joked, and I swiped her across the legs with the stable rubber.

"It's unbelievable." Mrs Mac was thrown into a state of near delirium. "How can Dom do this to me?"

We'd sent her into the house as soon as she'd arrived, to make up some orange squash, only she'd left the door open, and now we were chasing Sarah's hens out of the kitchen. One of the oldest, a mangy cockerel, had plonked itself on Mrs Mac's new cotton cardigan.

"If I didn't know better I'd swear he was laying an egg." Mrs Mac looked as if she was going to cry.

"When the going gets tough, the tough get going," said Sarah, vaguely, wandering in from her study, sucking an ice-cream.

"There's no problem," Ross gasped, complaining that his arms felt six inches longer after carrying the boxes. "Just stay cool, hang loose."

Derek, the insurance man, arrived in the yard looking hot and stuffy, with his shirt sticking to his back.

"At least his head must be cool," Katie said, referring to his baldness. And this time I really did clip her behind the ear.

"What does he want?" I said to Trevor when Derek had been in conference with Sarah for nearly an hour. I'd tried listening at the door but Sarah had sprung me and booted me out.

"Beats me," Trevor grunted. "Maybe he's trying to sell insurance. One thing's for sure, he doesn't give up easily – this is his third visit."

Mrs Mac looked frantic as she scooted Oscar

off the ironing board and started ironing my special brick-red Hollywell T-shirt until it could have stood up by itself.

"For tomorrow," she said. "And don't dirty it."

I gave her a weak smile and then the study door slammed shut and we all tried to look busy. I buried my head in Katie's pony magazine and Ross started whistling.

"Don't even think of asking," Sarah said. "I'm sworn to secrecy, I've given my word."

"It never crossed our minds," Ross blatantly lied, as Derek's car turned out of the drive.

"It must be something important though," Katie whispered. "Did you see how she kissed his bald head?"

Colorado's white bits ended up so white I felt like entering him for a washing powder advert. Even though I say it myself, both Queenie and Colorado looked radiant, fit for the Queen, never mind the Prime Minister.

I was just finishing off polishing the bridles, picking out the dirt from the buckle holes with a matchstick just like Blake had shown me . . . Blake: that was a huge disappointment. The doctor had said Blake was in no fit state to go to

London. He had to stay in hospital another twenty-four hours. At this rate I'd never get to see him.

By late evening we thought we were ready. The horsebox was packed, phone calls made. Sarah had made a list of things to do: diesel at the first garage; tell James to pay the milkman; leave an extra bale of hay in the field. We were all sorted. We spent the rest of the night picking faults in an eventing video and devouring pizza and popcorn.

"It's all going too well." Sarah pushed back the foot stool. "Something's bound to go wrong, it always does."

We thought she was just being paranoid. But we should have known better.

It was one o'clock in the morning when the phone rang and I was still awake, dreaming about Prime Ministers and romantic summer evenings. I was the first to reach the phone.

It was Hazel. She was in a phone box and she sounded desperate. She told me where she was, and then the pips started going. All I caught was her saying, "I've done something really stupid . . ."

Chapter Nine

The rain poured down in slanting sheets. A crack of lightning lit up the blackened sky, and I shivered inside as if someone had just walked over my grave.

"Hazel?" I called out. The torchlight flickered over some rough scrub.

"Are you sure this is where she said she was?" Sarah came up beside me, rain sliding off the brim of her sou'wester.

"Look – over there," Ross scrambled down a bank, taking the torch with him and plunging us into instant darkness.

"Ross!" I stumbled forward, tripping over the surcingle which surrounded the weatherproof rug I was carrying, and cringing as warm rain drops funnelled their way down my neck and back. It was a first class storm, just as I'd predicted.

Sarah took my elbow and we half slithered, half tumbled down the steep slope, a clump of nettles biting into my hand as I groped for extra balance.

"There!" Ross held the torch still and I could vaguely make out the old railway tunnel and the figure waving frantically at its entrance.

"We're over here!" The voice echoed for ages, eerie and high pitched. It was Hazel. "Before you say anything, I know it was a crazy thing to do."

Arnie stood under the huge arch looking like a drowned rat with his forelock stuck to his ears and his tail clamped down between his hindlegs. I think he would have given anything to be back in his warm stable with a full haynet and a dry bed and I didn't blame him.

"You certainly pick your nights," Ross said, casting the torch over Arnie's near fetlock which was starting to swell.

"Hazel, what on earth did you think you were doing?"

We were a mile from Somerset Stables, and Hazel explained how she couldn't bear leaving Arnie with Bo for a second longer. She'd been camping rough on the edge of a wood overlooking the Beaumont land, determined to keep watch, a pair of binoculars trained on his stable. The other grooms had gone into town to a nightclub; Bo and her man friend were at a dinner party. There was only the housekeeper on the premises – it was too good an opportunity to miss.

"I'd led him out of the stable before I'd even thought what I was going to do with him." She was visibly shivering from head to foot and Ross took off his jacket and wrapped it round her shoulders. "And then it started thundering . . . Arnie hates thunder, it scares him to death."

I was beginning to get the picture. "You poor old boy." I rubbed at his ears which were cold and wet and Ross slung the rug over his hindquarters.

"You see what I mean?" Hazel said.

Arnie's head was practically between his knees and he was trembling even more than Hazel. If it hadn't been so serious it would have been comical. He was almost trying to hide behind us all as a roll of thunder rattled ominously over the tunnel. If he could have leapt into Hazel's arms I think he would have done.

"It's OK boy, it's not going to hurt you."

"We've got to get him out of here." Sarah stated the obvious. "This rain, and his arthritis – he soon won't be able to walk."

Hazel's bottom lip quivered and I could almost feel the agony she was going through. "I would have done the same thing in your shoes," I said, trying to make her feel better.

I could still remember vividly when Blake and I had kidnapped Colorado and hidden him in the cow shed at the bottom of the field. It was stupid and irrational but when you're desperate you do anything.

"We can't go breaking the law," Sarah said, looking out at the driving rain. "There's only one course of action—"

"But I thought you'd take him back to Hollywell?" Hazel's voice had almost become a screech.

I was pretty speechless myself.

"It's got to be as if nobody knew this happened," Sarah insisted. "We've got to take him back to Somerset Stables."

We plodded along a bridlepath, Sarah, Ross, Hazel and myself, and Arnie crawling along looking as if the sky was going to fall on his head at any minute.

"If only it would stop thundering," Hazel shuddered.

"At least we're all wearing rubber wellies," Ross said as lightning lit up the sky.

"And just think what this rain will do for the grass." I tried to make conversation but it fell flat.

"It's not doing much for Arnie's nerves," Hazel groaned as Arnie caught sight of a fluttering crisp bag and carried on as if it was a fire-breathing dragon.

Somerset Stables was just at the bottom of the dip; all we had to do was cross a road and we could go in the back way through the dressage arenas and into the stable yard. We passed the telephone box where Hazel had contacted us and where she said Arnie had nearly strangled himself trying to get in the door.

"Oh no." Hazel stopped dead in her tracks.

The whole of Somerset Stables was lit up and a car was parked at an angle across the drive.

"They're back." Hazel's voice was a whimper. "Angela said they were staying out all night. What are we going to do? They're back!"

Panic set in like a suffocating fog. We had to get Arnie into his stable.

"It might not be as bad as it looks," Sarah said, taking charge. "Hazel, you said they don't check the stables last thing at night?"

"That's right, they usually just go straight to bed. It's the grooms' job to check the horses."

"But they're not here, only Bo doesn't know that."

"Exactly."

"OK, this is what we'll do." Sarah took off her yellow sou'wester, shaking off the streams of water and stuffing it in her pocket. She said it was too bright and she might get noticed. "Hazel and I will take Arnie, Ross will keep watch, and you, Mel, will go up to the front door and distract them."

"You've got to be joking!" I nearly twisted my ankle in a rut as I swivelled round in shock. My voice-box seemed to have dried up to sawdust.

"Mel, it's the only way. You can do it, I know you can."

"But why me, why not Ross?"

"Because you can talk better, and besides, you've got a better imagination."

"What for?"

"For whatever you're going to tell them." Sarah said, unhelpfully.

Oh, great, this was all I needed. I was beginning to think Arnie would have been better off at Hollywell after all, even if it did mean breaking the law.

The front door was ivory white with a doorbell that chimed like a cathedral and dogs that barked like the Hound of the Baskervilles. I wanted to run for it, but that wouldn't be enough of a distraction – I had to keep them talking. Besides, my legs were rooted to the spot.

Jennifer Beaumont opened the door, looking every inch a charismatic star in a black velvet dress and diamanté jewellery. She was holding a brandy glass, and unless it was my imagination, swaying slightly in her high heels.

"Yes, hello?" She looked at me enquiringly.

Anybody would be shocked to see a bedraggled teenage girl on the doorstep at two in the morning. Especially someone from Hollywell Stables who was more likely to put a poison pen letter through the letterbox than ask to come in.

"I don't understand, what's going on?" Her clipped, staccato voice sounded nervous. I think she was actually apprehensive of me.

A fleet of sooty black labradors hurled themselves round the corner and descended into the hallway, all slavering tongues and wagging tails.

"Darling, what's going on?" It was the man who'd been on the shooting stick.

I stepped inside and said it was of the utmost importance that I speak to her. I had a message.

"So why didn't she come and do her own dirty work?" Bo screwed up her face in distaste. I had to admit she was rather glamorous. "Somebody ought to have a word with that woman. Who does she think she is, telling people how to run their lives? She needs to get a grip."

"Darling, let's hear what the girl's got to say," the man said, trying to calm her down.

"Well, that's it really," I stuttered. "Just that we've decided to call off the campaign to save Arnie. Sarah wanted me to tell you straight away."

"At nearly three in the morning? Couldn't it have waited until a respectable hour?" I decided that she looked better in photos than she did in real life.

"We were coming back from an emergency call and we saw the light on." It sounded pathetically weak, but she fell for it.

"I knew she would see sense in the end. Tell her from me to stick to what she can handle: little ponies and seaside donkeys," Bo sneered.

I bit my tongue so hard it stung my eyes. I still had to buy time. "Can I have your autograph?"

Jennifer Beaumont almost smirked in surprise. "Well I don't suppose it's your fault you've got such a troublesome mother."

"She's not my mother, she's my stepmother."

Jennifer swirled out of the hallway and came

back two minutes later with a signed photograph of her riding her best horse, Solitaire.

"I hope you appreciate that," she said, opening the door.

I heard the owl hoot I'd been waiting for and raced out of the house as if the devil himself were behind me.

"We did it!" Ross hissed, lifting me off my feet in relief. "Arnie's ploughing through his haynet and you wouldn't suspect a thing."

"Apart from his muddy feet," Hazel said. "But I think I managed to wipe off the worst."

"There's only one thing to do now," Sarah said, looking completely whacked. "Let's go home."

"I promise you, Hazel, give me twenty-four hours and Arnie will be at Hollywell for good." Sarah was trying to console Hazel.

"How can you say that?" Hazel had broken down in tears as soon as we sat in the kitchen. Jigsaw was slobbering over her knees and Trevor and Katie wanted to know everything that had happened.

"I can't say exactly," Sarah stalled. "Let's just say it was vital that Arnie be in his stable tomorrow morning."

"*This* morning." Katie looked out of the window where dawn was just breaking.

Ross and I exchanged meaningful looks. There was no doubt Sarah knew more than she was letting on, but it was so unlike her to keep secrets; we were all normally so honest and open.

"I think Mrs F's got something up her sleeve." Trevor, as usual, said what he thought.

"Trevor, the milk!" Sarah leapt up to switch off the boiling milk before it ran all over the old Aga which was now her pride and joy. It was also a good way to change the subject.

Hazel looked grey and worn to a frazzle and Trevor plied her with hot cocoa and home-made cookies. She admitted that she'd been living off muesli bars and stewed tea from a flask. Camping out, even in summer, wasn't all it was cracked up to be.

"That wouldn't keep a flea going," Trevor snorted, taking a handful of cookies and demolishing them.

"You should have told us where you were," Sarah said. "We've all been worried."

"I figured you had enough of your own problems, locked up in that house – I heard it all on the radio."

Ross and I clammed up. It was something we

still didn't want to talk about. It was all shut away in the recesses of our minds, not for dwelling on.

Trevor went to fetch a towel for Hazel's wet hair and Sarah gave her a bundle of dry clothes. Oscar went flying through the air off a kitchen unit on to Ross's shoulder looking desperate for an early morning feed. I opened a tin of cat food and asked if it was really worth going to bed when we had to be up in an hour and a half?

The last time we'd been in London was to appear on *The Breakfast Bunch* and I couldn't wait to see Dom and Cassandra again in the flesh. They were completely wacky and bizarre but great fun, and they really cared about Hollywell Stables.

"I vote we stay up," Katie said, leaning back against the units and accidentally plonking her hand in Oscar's food.

"Oh no, Katie, not Snakes and Ladders." The last thing I was in the mood for was being thrashed at Snakes and Ladders by my little sister. "Let's just sit here and doze," I suggested, yawning and letting my eyelids shut. Jigsaw barked as if this was the best idea.

"Oh no," Katie said, looking in the sugar tin. "I've lost my four-leaf clover!"

We spent the next hour looking for Katie's plastic clover which went on all the big occasions, and which she had convinced us brought oodles of luck.

"Well think when you last had it," I snapped, having finished emptying the magazine rack and scouring the carpet.

"It's here." Ross held up a chewed plastic lump which he'd found in Oscar's cardboard house, but something else distracted our attention and had us all frozen to the spot.

"It can't be," I said.

"I don't believe it." Ross shook his head.

"It is!" Katie shrieked, leaping up and flinging open the back door.

Two huge white ears plunged forward and we were deafened by the loudest "e-yore" this side of a donkey farm.

"Snowy, what are you doing here?"

The poor little guy was in a terrible state. His coat was covered in burrs and was all crinkled from the storm. His nose was badly scratched and he had a deep gash down his shoulder where it looked as if he'd run into something.

"He must have escaped," I said. "He must have been wandering around all night."

Even worse, his near hind leg was fixed straight at an agonizing angle. It had happened again.

James was with us at the speed of light. "OK, little chappie, let's get you into a stable."

"I'm going to operate on his leg," James said. "There are complications – it's got to be done. And he needs stitches in that shoulder."

Snowy huddled up to my body as if he needed the contact. He looked sad and forlorn and I just wanted to hug him and tell him it was going to be all right. James rigged up some extra lighting and Trevor said he'd be the assistant and pass over the instruments.

James pulled on a pair of fine plastic gloves and said Snowy would be all right with a tranquillizer and a local anaesthetic. It was only a small operation.

Sarah was flying round the house trying to get ready and Ross and Hazel were feeding all the horses. Buckets were clanking like an army canteen and then Ross remembered someone had better warm up the horsebox, and then there were Queenie and Colorado to bandage and rug up for the journey.

Sarah came hopping out of the house in a

daffodil yellow two piece suit, with one shoe on and the other half-off and a piece of toast in her mouth.

"Mel, we've got to leave in twenty minutes."

Snowy nuzzled at my hand and I felt his nose which was all rough and grazed.

"Well then, you'll have to go without me," I said. "I'm staying here with Snowy."

Chapter Ten

"OK, Mel, hold his head," James moved forward with the scalpel. Trevor backed off looking pea-green.

"Basically all I'm going to do is cut the patella ligament inside the leg." James carried on talking as he worked. "I've never seen this condition in a donkey before."

Luckily I couldn't see anything and Snowy just stood, drowsy and well behaved, not aware of anything.

"Under normal circumstances I'd advise building up the muscle in the hindleg, that usually does the trick, but in this case . . ."

"Gee, James, I don't know how you keep your hand steady." Trevor's were trembling like a road digger.

"Here, you can start threading me that needle." James pointed to some thread in his black case.

The wound on Snowy's shoulder was open and gaping and James said he'd have to clean it up first. He took a pair of surgical scissors and moistening some cotton wool in antiseptic, he placed it inside the wound.

"That's to stop the cut hair falling in," he said. I just winced and looked the other way.

The proper word for stitching is "suturing". I couldn't believe how quick and neat James was. Trevor said he put his Granny to shame and she'd been embroidery champion at her WI club for the last ten years.

"There, all done." James snipped off the thread. "He'll be as right as rain in a few days, won't you, fella?" James patted his neck and said somebody ought to contact Mrs Wilson but we didn't have her phone number and when we rang Enquiries they said she was ex-directory.

"That's that then," Trevor said.

We settled Snowy down in the stable, the tranquillizer already wearing off. James put his things in the car and Mrs Mac arrived with a pile of cookery books and one of Sarah's romantic novels. She hadn't wanted to go to London in case Dom had caught her on film, and besides, she said, it was too hot for travelling. Her job was to horse-sit, but now we were here there was no need.

"It's a shame you had to miss the big occasion," she said.

The house was deathly quiet with just Jigsaw wandering around wondering where everybody had gone. My over-pressed, brick-red Hollywell T-shirt was still on the back of a chair.

"Snowy needed us more," I said and meant it, although I wished sometimes everything wouldn't happen at once.

"Here's somebody who needs you, too," Mrs Mac looked out of the window as a taxi pulled into the yard.

A dark-haired tall young man got out with one arm in a sling.

"Blake!" I went hysterical. "It's Blake!"

I shot out of the back door like a whippet and practically careered into his arms just as he was paying the taxi driver.

"Steady on," he grinned, looking more like the old Blake.

"But how did you get out?" I made it sound like a prison.

"Simple," he said. "I just checked out."

"But what did the doctor say?"

"I told him I'd got a better nurse here, besides I was fed up with fish, jelly and ice-cream."

I thumped him on his good shoulder and then told him about Snowy and Arnie and Hazel and how we'd been up all night.

Mrs Mac came outside and shook his hand, saying he needed feeding up. Trevor said he was probably going to be fussed to death and he hoped he could stand the pace. I couldn't stop grinning and didn't feel half so bad about missing the trip to London.

"Eh up, what's this?" Trevor was the first to notice the red Royal Mail parcel van coming up the drive.

"Beats me," I said, mentally checking that it wasn't anybody's birthday.

"Mrs Foster?" The parcel man looked at Mrs Mac. I signed the clipboard in Sarah's place and nearly flipped when I saw who the boxes were from – *In The Saddle*, one of the top pony magazines! They'd collected a mountain of signatures, and we hadn't known anything about it.

"You realize this pushes us over the million mark." Trevor read the letter which was attached to one of the boxes.

"It's incredible," I said, looking over his shoulder.

"It's a terrible shame." Mrs Mac dabbed at her

112

eyes with the tea towel. "All that work, and it arrives an hour too late."

"The cruel twist of fate." Trevor developed that glazed distant look which I knew so well. He was plotting something, no doubt about it. "I've just got to have a yarn with someone on the dog and bone," he said, meaning the telephone.

"What's he up to?" Blake whispered ten minutes later as I made him a cup of tea. James had rushed off to see a bull in distress so there was just the four of us.

"Right get your glad rags on." Trevor barged into the kitchen looking flushed. "We're going to London."

"Trevor, don't be stupid, if we set off this minute we'd still be hours late. There's no way we can get to London in time."

"Stop complaining," Trevor barked. "Anyway, we're not going by car."

"I don't see why you have to be so mysterious." Mrs Mac drove her car out of the village, Trevor in the front, Blake and I in the back. "Why can't you tell us what's going on?"

The biggest shock had been Trevor's suit. I couldn't believe it when he raced down the stairs doing up a fancy tie and white shirt and looking like the cat's whiskers. As we'd only ever seen him in extra large heavy metal T-shirts and King Kong sized boots, it was like a make-over on day-time telly, only ten times more dramatic.

"Here!" Trevor screeched and Mrs Mac slammed on the brakes.

We were parked slap bang outside the country estate of our Member of Parliament, Maxwell Curtis.

"Well, don't waste time, come on, up the drive!"

I'd never seen a house so big, or a drive so vast – it must have been acres across.

The helicopter was on the lawn, the propellers already turning.

"Glad you could make it." Maxwell Curtis strode out of the house looking confident and immaculately groomed. "I'll have to ask you to hurry, we haven't got a minute to lose."

A fleet of staff helped us carry the boxes of signatures towards the helicopter. Mrs Mac waved frantically and Trevor's hair blew up in the vacuum of air so he resembled a startled cockatoo.

"I don't believe this is happening," I mumbled, and took Blake's advice to just go with the flow.

The helicopter soared up over the patchwork of fields and my stomach flipped over, half with nerves and half with excitement. Blake held my hand and we stared out at the view of England with something amounting to patriotic pride.

"So as I was saying," Trevor shouted over to Mr Curtis who was actually doing the flying. Locked in like an insect in a bottle Mr Curtis had no choice but to listen to Trevor's never-ending spiel about the importance of improving awareness of equine welfare. Trevor successfully bent his ear from the moment of lift-off to seconds before landing.

"Look, the Houses of Parliament," Blake breathed as we hovered over London feeling like royalty. This was a journey I would never forget.

As soon as we landed, someone slid back the doors, and there was a car waiting some distance away with a chauffeur in full uniform.

"Number Ten Downing Street," Mr Curtis shouted and then climbed into an identical car parked behind.

Blake, Trevor and I piled into the back seat with the boxes in the boot for the five minute drive to Downing Street.

"All we need now is some cucumber sandwiches," Trevor joked as the car set off with barely a murmur.

"I want a full explanation and I want it now," I eyed Trevor with eagle-like intensity. "Just how did you pull this off?"

As usual he was as slippery as an eel but after five minutes in a traffic jam he told us that he had saved Maxwell Curtis's dog from being run over and that Maxwell had owed him a favour.

Mr Curtis had gone on to the House of Commons and had actually invited us back to take tea in the Members' Dining Room if we had time.

It was pandemonium. Black taxis were pushing out of queues, honking horns, trying to do U-turns; there was every type of car, and tons with foreign number plates.

"This is ridiculous. It's only just round the corner," Trevor said, pulling at his shirt collar which had turned his neck turkey red.

"Deep breathing," Blake said to me as I really started to flap.

"Blake, believe me, this is no time for meditation," I said.

The sun was getting hotter, and out on the streets people were stripping off to the bare minimum. I saw every kind of T-shirt, from holes in the back, to holes in the front and bare midriffs. I even saw one woman wandering along in what looked like her best bra.

"It's called culture," Blake grinned.

Trevor asked if we realized that we were in the middle of an international city, and where was Pall Mall and Buckingham Palace? I don't think he'd been to London before. I had to insist that we wouldn't have time to go to Madame Tussauds.

"OK, here goes," the chauffeur piped up. "Let's take the bull by the horns."

We dived down a side street, narrowly missing a powder blue Rolls-Royce, and scorched along at the rate of knots.

Blake grinned at a woman carrying a poodle into an exclusive looking veterinary clinic – she was unloading more baskets and bowls from the car than you'd find in a pet shop.

"Sure is different from the country." Trevor scratched his head, looking completely fazed.

We sailed down street after street trying to drive around the traffic until in the end I surrendered to the fact that we were going to miss the presentation.

Trevor was just about to apologize for what seemed like a good idea when I suddenly caught sight of our horsebox and Colorado in his best show rug.

"We're here," I shrieked, grabbing hold of

Blake's injured arm and causing him to wince. "We're just in time!"

There was little Queenie, her brown coat shining, and Katie holding on to her looking about to burst with pride. Sarah was flying around in her yellow suit, as fizzy as a lemon sherbet, and Hazel was frantically oiling Colorado's feet, only he wouldn't stand still and he kept barging into someone in a striped shirt.

"That's Andrew Davison," I hissed, "the top National Hunt jockey, and look over there, by the ramp, it's Daniel Lamond." I couldn't believe that so many famous people had turned up.

Sarah practically flipped her lid when she saw us running towards her. I think she thought we were a vision. "But that's brilliant!" she said. "There's a reporter from *In The Saddle* here somewhere."

Already there were loads of people milling around, cameras everywhere, tape recorders. Blake went across to Colorado who was getting more skittish by the second.

"The Minister of Agriculture should be here any minute," Sarah said, pulling out her speech and rehearsing it just one more time.

I helped Ross pull out a white board from the horsebox which we'd had specially made. It said:

"Here Are One Million Protests Against The Live Export Of Horses For Slaughter."

I'd never felt so elated as at that moment. It was the sense of achievement, the actual doing, the making a difference. It was something I couldn't describe.

"Here, hold Queenie a minute," Katie stuffed the lead rope into my hand and ran off to chat up Andrew Davison.

"The little minx," I said, under my breath, as I'd been planning to do exactly the same thing.

Queenie found some mints in my jeans pocket and I put my arm over her neck and thought how far we'd come since that night we'd found her, near to death in a scrap-yard. It seemed a lifetime ago, and now she was the best lucky mascot any sanctuary could wish for.

Sarah strutted up the ramp in her high heels, ordering Ross and Trevor to reorganize some of the cardboard boxes so that they were in better view of the cameras. On each box we'd slapped a Hollywell sticker, just for some extra publicity – you could never stop trying.

The feature writer from one of the daily papers was chasing Sarah around with a tape recorder asking meaningful questions. He'd got a pony tail and wore burgundy glasses and didn't look like a top writer at all.

I was just about to ask what had happened to Dom and Cassandra when a familiar *Breakfast Bunch* car whizzed up, screeching the tyres, and the long gazelle legs of Cassandra leapt out of the back causing a ripple of excitement. Then the rest of Cassandra followed, along with Dom who was half her size and as usual wearing the gaudiest bow tie and silk skirt anybody could find this side of the tropics. But we loved them both to death and Sarah was the first to race forward and hug Cassandra.

"Is everything fixed?" Dom fussed, organizing his own camera crew and wiping a smudge off Katie's face which she didn't appreciate in the least.

I had a word with the sound man to keep the sound boom away from Queenie and Colorado. The last time we'd had one near the horses Boris had devoured it in one go. I didn't want the film going out on telly resembling a silent movie.

"OK, get ready to roll." Dom ran a hand through his hair in typical producer style. Reporters shuffled for position as the countdown began.

Sarah wiped her hands on her skirt and prepared to knock at the door of Number Ten. Katie stuck up her thumb in a good luck sign, and I hissed at her to be careful, you never knew where the cameras were lurking.

I was so proud of Sarah, she looked so beautiful and sophisticated as she approached the huge famous door. The Minister of Agriculture seemed like a really nice guy. He posed for pictures with Sarah on the horsebox ramp in front of the boxes. Sarah said her speech word perfect, and there was just the right amount of feeling and passion without going overboard. She'd been practising in the kitchen for the last few weeks with James acting as adviser. He'd given loads of speeches on medical matters.

"Bravo," Cassandra cheered when it was all over and the cameras had stopped rolling. Everybody gave a round of applause and then there were more pictures to be taken with Queenie and Colorado. I nearly died when the whole Hollywell team had to pose. I'm sure I had my eyes closed on most of the photographs.

Colorado wouldn't stop neighing. Katie said he could probably hear the Queen's horses but I denied this as a load of rubbish. It was more likely over-excitement.

It was all an incredible success and I prayed

from the bottom of my heart that it would do some good. It was only when we'd got trapped in the lorry going across to France that we'd really discovered the conditions in which many horses were transported abroad for slaughter. It was so terrible that something had to be done and fast. Public awareness was the best approach – Sarah always said that the general public could move mountains if they really wanted to. They just had to care enough and be brought together. I wanted to say a personal big thank-you to the one million people who had signed our petition. It was fantastic.

"Penny for your thoughts," Blake said coming up to me, holding a very restless Colorado.

"You know, Blake, life really is wonderful – it's just the best!"

"You weren't saying that an hour ago when we were stuck in that traffic jam," he joked, and I couldn't help agreeing.

Reporters started to drift off and we loaded Queenie and Colorado, who were starving and tore at their haynets as if they hadn't been fed for a week.

I showed Cassandra some photographs of the Hollywell residents: Fluffy, our little Falabella, who had made an amazing recovery; Isabella, the pot-bellied pig who was now a major attraction but still getting into mischief and still as greedy as ever; Jakey, the lovely piebald cob now retired and enjoying a quiet life.

Tears were welling up in Cassandra's eyes as we reminisced on times past. It was so good to see her again. She'd always be welcome at Hollywell Stables even if she did like seaweed-tasting tea and kept trying to convert us to rabbit food and sunflower seeds.

"OK, we're on." Dom raced up, looking more excited than I'd ever seen him.

"Could somebody please tell me what's going on?" Sarah said.

Sometimes in life things change so dramatically that just when you think it can't get any better it does. I'd read in a magazine that sometimes you had to go through really bad times to enjoy the good; life was like a pendulum – and looking back over the last week I think they'd got a point.

As Sarah approached the brass knocker of Number Ten for the second time that day we were all trembling in our shoes. The whole Hollywell team was present, Blake, Trevor, even Hazel. The policeman at the door stood aside and a secretary showed us in. We stepped into a hall and my immediate thought was how small it was. I'd imagined Number Ten to be a bit like a Tardis.

"Ssssh," Sarah whispered as we were left alone in a room. Unbelievably the *Breakfast Bunch* cameras had been allowed in and Cassandra was bickering with Dom about exactly what kind of angle to aim for.

I looked around the room, which was beautiful with masses of impressive pictures on the walls. Katie and Ross flicked through some outdated magazines on a coffee table. My knees were buckling underneath me, it was almost like waiting at the dentist's but a hundred times worse.

The door opened just as I was staring at a picture of Disraeli. We were shown up a narrow staircase with endless photographs of past Prime Ministers. The camera was right behind me and I felt vaguely like Anneka Rice and became acutely aware of my bottom.

"Step inside." The lady showed us into a study. It was dimly lit and had a lovely cosy atmosphere. The palms of my hands were sweating and my heart was hammering like ten thousand pistons. I didn't notice the man at the window, not until he turned round and looked straight at me. It was the Prime Minister!

Chapter Eleven

"We had tea with the Prime Minister!" Katie shrieked into the mobile phone. Mrs Mac was completely stuck for words at the other end.

Dom had said that it was the best film ever and Sarah was saying that Hollywell Stables had finally "arrived," although where, I couldn't quite work out.

"Did you see the way he was looking at the photographs?" My heart was still banging like mad.

"He's definitely an animal lover," Katie insisted, talking nineteen to the dozen.

We were on our way home in the horsebox, all squashed in, Trevor's jacket slung in the back of the cab and his spotted tie hung up next to some of Blake's rosettes.

Blake, Ross and Hazel were following behind with Cassandra who was going to stay at Hollywell for a couple of days. She said she had some time owing, and Dom could manage Florida by himself. Besides, she knew which place she'd rather be.

"We are the champions," Katie started to sing.

We heard Snowy braying before we reached the stables. Mrs Mac said he was as perky as a tom cat in spring and he'd taken a particular shine to her new "extra rich" recipe for flapjack. Sarah stopped off at the Bottle And Pig to buy a bottle of champagne and Cassandra went on ahead driving as if she were blasting her way along the M25. I saw Mrs White's curtains twitch and the colonel who was across the road cutting his privet hedge nearly chopped off a clump of hollyhocks.

"We're home!" Katie yelled as the diesel engine died out and we climbed down as stiff as boards.

Walter yawned over his stable door and Oscar carried on watching for mice.

"Well thanks for the welcome, gang," I said, suddenly feeling an overwhelming love for the countryside and all it represented. I couldn't live in a big city for all the tea in China – it just wouldn't be Hollywell.

The sweet fragrance of new mown grass wafted up and James appeared from the front garden with his hair stuck on end and a slick of oil across one cheek. Sarah gave him a hug and told him he smelled of elderberries and asked what he had been doing.

James ignored her and said practically the whole county was chasing her, namely Mrs Wilson and Derek who said, and he quoted, "Everything was on course – just give him the word."

What on earth did that mean?

"Oh and about the elderberries," James followed her into the house looking vague, "I thought I might try making a drop of home brew . . ."

The kitchen was full of plastic tubes and strange looking bottles and a manual on how to make wine. Sarah said he wouldn't have such a free rein when they were married and buzzed off to the hallway to use the phone.

She was on the line to Mrs Wilson for a long time. She said that Snowy had panicked when the storm began and had ploughed through a wire fence.

Cassandra made a cup of herbal tea and looked twitchy, and Katie cut out a picture of a white donkey and stuck it on the wall.

Mrs Wilson was probably at this moment going bananas that we'd operated on Snowy. It was amazing how he'd managed to find his way back here, but then they always say that equines have a mysterious sixth sense.

"Well?" Cassandra said as soon as Sarah came into the kitchen.

Sarah's face was grave. Joe was out on bail and undergoing therapy. He was quite obviously mentally unstable and this would figure largely when his case came to court. Mrs Wilson said they were selling the family house, which had a monstrous mortgage and was partly why their marriage had broken up in the first place. Joe had been cracking up under the pressure for quite some time. She was going to stand by him and give their marriage another go, not just for the sake of the kids but because she still loved him.

"And where does this leave Snowy?" I had to ask, I was bristling with tension.

"Well I hope you can stand being woken up every morning," Sarah said. "Because Mrs Wilson wants him to stay right here!"

"You're joking!" we chorused.

"No, straight up," Sarah assured us.

"You're serious?"

"Every bit."

"Yippee!" Katie shrieked and ran out to tell Snowy.

Cassandra wanted to know if they could use

Snowy for *The Breakfast Bunch*'s Christmas play and Sarah said they'd have to watch Walter didn't lead him astray in the meantime. Heaven knows what the mule would get up to next.

James thought it was seriously time for a party and what about a barbecue? Sarah said she'd invite Roddy and then of course there was Derek . . .

"Mrs Foster?" Hazel came in from outside. "You haven't forgotten about Arnie, have you?" Her face was a picture of desolation.

"I never break a promise, Hazel. I said he'd be here within twenty-four hours and he will be."

"Sarah?" James caught her elbow and frog-marched her into the study. All we could hear was a torrent of urgent whispers and then James's voice partially raised. "Just what is going on?"

"I thought we could put his water bucket in an old tyre to stop him kicking it over, and maybe some sacking on the inside of the door to stop him banging." Trevor was being innovative as ever. Snowy glared at him with beady eyes.

"I think he knows what you're talking about," I said.

"Of course he does." Katie came out of his stable. "He's a donkey, isn't he?"

Trevor finished with the idea of a swede or

sugar beet suspended on a piece of rope as a play toy, anything to stop him getting bored, and then there was a cloud of smoke from the front garden and Mrs Mac shrieking like a banshee.

"It'll be the charcoal on the barbecue that's damp," Trevor said, as a column of black smog curled its way up over the house. "Oscar's been using it as cat litter tray for the last few months."

Cassandra insisted on making up some high fibre veggie-burgers and discussed at length the nutritional value of sesame seeds on bread buns. Roddy arrived clutching a bunch of wilting carnations and promptly sat in one of the plastic chairs outside which was still harbouring a puddle from the storm.

"Oh dear," he said, plucking at his trousers.

Sarah was like a cat on hot bricks, getting more nervous by the minute. She'd changed out of the daffodil yellow suit into something cooler and was now wrestling with a tossed salad.

"I hope you know what you're doing about Arnie," I said. "Hazel will be heartbroken if it goes wrong."

"Wrong? Don't be so silly," she screeched and tossed the salad a little too intensely so that the iceburg lettuce went sailing through the air and plopped in Jigsaw's basket.

It was a beautiful evening, slants of sleepy russet sun dying out like the embers on a fire. It was warm without being overpowering and fresh and balmy after the torrential rain.

"Fancy a walk?" Blake asked, picking up a stick for Jigsaw and throwing it towards the orchard. There wasn't much we could do to help out: James was scuttling around in Sarah's frilly pinny and Cassandra was getting quite carried away with the bellows.

"A good draw, that's what it needs," she said, coughing as the smoke veered back towards her.

It was cooler among the apple trees and I took off my trainers so I could sink my bare feet into the long grass.

"It's been a dramatic week," Blake said, watching Jigsaw run on ahead, frisking around like a puppy.

"The worst," I said, pulling at a strand of my hair which had fallen loose.

"But this is nice, though."

We carried on walking, looking at the clover and the buttercups which were closing up their heads ready for the approaching night. All but the last rays of daylight had disappeared.

"I wonder what the Prime Minister would

think of this," Blake said, throwing Jigsaw's stick so it skipped and spun over the long grass.

"I think he'd think it was pretty fantastic," I said. "Maybe he'll call in one day like he said."

"Maybe."

Blake slowed down his pace so we were walking side by side.

"Listen," I suddenly said, catching his shirt sleeve. "Ssssh." There it was, a high-pitched squeak, a swoop and flutter, a black shadow. "It's a bat."

We listened intensely in the dusk, and I swore I saw more than two.

"Don't tell Katie," Blake whispered, "but there have been bats here as long as I've lived here."

"Oh," I said, and that's when he bent down and kissed my lips and bells erupted in my head and it was just like in Sarah's romantic novels, only better because this was for real.

"So where have you two been?" James grinned, shovelling blackened sausages from side to side; Cassandra was waiting for her veggie-burgers, vulture-like.

My face coloured up bright red and Blake

started to say something I couldn't hear, and that's when Sarah let out a half strangled shriek.

I turned round as if in slow motion to see a big steel grey horse bouncing up the drive with poor Derek hanging on to the lead rope for dear life.

"Do something!" he gasped as he was nearly scraped against the wall. "Help!"

"It's Arnie!" Hazel finally clunked into gear. "It's Arnie!" She put down a tub of coleslaw and leapt over a rose bed just as Arnie was about to wrap Derek round the nearest telegraph pole.

"He's all yours, love, you can have him with pleasure." Arnie butted Derek in the stomach and then proceeded to slobber all over Hazel's hair. Precariously balanced around his neck was a big red bow which had been half eaten but it was the thought that counted.

"I don't believe it," Hazel mumbled, tears welling up in her eyes. "I honestly don't believe it."

"Anyway the bottom line is that the insurance firm preferred you to take him than obtain their carcass money," Derek explained. "I talked it all over with Mrs F . . . He really is a lovely horse."

"But why all the cloak and dagger stuff?" Ross asked. "Why didn't you tell us?"

"Mainly because I didn't want Hazel building

her hopes up," Sarah explained, handing out the burgers. "It was all up in the air until a few hours ago. Jennifer Beaumont thought Derek was having him as a pet – she'll hit the roof when she finds out the truth."

"So she's still getting her ten thousand pounds?" I asked.

"Absolutely," Sarah said. "But we get to keep Arnie."

It all sounded very complicated to me. Roddy said he'd heard of this before when an insurance company paid out on a greyhound but the Managing Director fell in love with it and took it home to his wife.

"I don't think Jennifer Beaumount could fall in love with anything," I said, thinking it wasn't fair that she'd got her money after all.

"What goes around comes around," Blake said. "She'll get her comeuppance."

James ran his hand down Arnie's injured leg and said it shouldn't be too difficult to treat. "He'll always have to be on medication though," he added.

Hazel fed him some lettuce and Derek asked if he always stood as if he'd got two left feet.

"Just about," Hazel grinned. "He's pretty gormless really."

Cassandra said she thought he was lovely and carried on devouring the blackened sausages.

"I thought you were a vegetarian?" Katie caught her on the hop.

"Only at weekends," she blushed, and reached for another chicken leg.

"Wait till we tell Maxwell Curtis about this." Katie hadn't stopped talking about him since we called in at the House of Commons. He'd finally come round to the idea of supporting our campaign, especially now the PM had given it his blessing.

"That reminds me," Sarah said, opening a can of lager and passing it to Derek, "he's coming round here tomorrow night, wants to go over some papers with Trevor."

"What?" Trevor was momentarily caught with his mouth full and could only grin and wave his arm up and down. "But I can't," he finally spluttered, looking seriously rattled.

"Go on, you tell them." Hazel had suddenly become extremely coy.

"It's Hazel's birthday," Trevor fidgeted and then blurted out in a rush, "and we're going on a date."

James wolf-whistled and Ross patted him on the back. I dreamily thought how Trevor and

Arnie had a lot in common – they both had hidden depths.

Sarah said it was time we put Arnie to bed but Arnie had other things on his mind, namely Derek's lager.

"He thinks it's Guinness!" Hazel laughed hysterically. "He's so used to his daily pint."

Derek let out a howl as Arnie suddenly bulldozed after him, straight down the garden.

"Hadn't we better go and help him?" I tried to smother a giggle.

"We'd better send you-know-who to Alcoholics Anonymous," Sarah laughed.

As it was, Arnie finally settled for a cup of tea with lots of sugar.

The sun went down on one of the most momentous days at Hollywell Stables and Sarah finally managed to uncork the champagne bottle.

"Welcome to Hollywell!" We all toasted Arnie.

"We'd better read him the house rules," Ross grinned as Arnie butted him in the stomach. But somehow I didn't think Arnie was going to take the slightest bit of notice.

HOLLYWELL STABLES

Running Wild

7

Samantha Alexander

MACMILLAN
CHILDREN'S BOOKS

Chapter One

"I'm telling you, there's a wild horse out there!" Binny Alderidge plonked herself down at our kitchen table, ready to take on the whole world. "You don't believe me, do you? You think I've lost my marbles."

For months now we'd been reading newspaper reports of a "Black Beast" roaming Bordman Moor. People had been on television talking about a panther, a leopard, a llama, even a giraffe.

"It's better than the Loch Ness Monster," said my little sister Katie. Her best friend Danny sat beside her, his eyes wide and his bottom lip quivering.

Binny Alderidge had come to us with the story of a stallion running wild on Bordman Moor. She'd seen him from her bathroom window in the middle of the night, strong, powerful, but nervous, looking for something.

"You've got to understand—" said Sarah, our stepmother.

"Are you calling me a liar?" Binny leapt up,

glaring defiantly. She was an old lady but she was tough and wiry. She was the grittiest and most strong minded person I'd ever met.

She crumpled a faded picture of a Palomino pony in her hand, her eyes bloodshot and angry. "He's got my Angel! I know it – in here." She clasped her hand to her chest. "Something's wrong, terribly wrong!"

"Mrs Alderidge," said Ross, raking a hand through his jet-black hair, "let's just say . . ."

The air hung with tension. I didn't know what he was going to say next.

"Let's just say, we believe that you believe it. And that's a start."

"She's a bit prickly, isn't she?" Trevor, our full-time groom marched into the tack room later that day, drenched with rain, carrying Oscar, our youngest cat, who was poking his nose out from under his oilskin.

We were huddled in the tack room trying to analyse the situation.

"I like her," said Katie.

"Mel?"

"I honestly don't know," I answered. I thought she was odd from the moment I saw her. She had dyed bright ginger hair which stuck up in tufts, trendy tartan trousers covered in grass stains and dog hairs, and spectacles round her neck on a chain. Her birdlike eyes were piercing.

"I can just about swallow the wild horse bit, but for it to have taken her Angel?" Ross looked as bemused as the rest of us.

Angel was a Welsh Palomino mare who had disappeared without trace a year ago. I vaguely remembered seeing pictures up in the village shop and a reward being offered. Mrs Alderidge had taken out full-page adverts in the local paper, but to no avail. Wherever Angel was, nobody came forward with any information.

"Surely a horse loose on the moor would be seen by somebody?" I said, rolling up a stable bandage. If it had been any of our horses they'd have been round people's gardens in a jiffy – they loved human company.

"Not if it's wild, it wouldn't," Trevor said.

"But this isn't the Dark Ages, there are no wild horses, not on Bordman Moor anyway."

"Maybe it's a unicorn?" said Katie.

"Oh, get real, Katie." Ross threw a sponge at her which bounced off the saddle rack. "Next thing you'll be saying that Angel was taken by aliens."

"Maybe it came from the New Forest?"

"What?"

"The stallion."

3

"Look, this isn't going to get us anywhere." Ross was exasperated. "Wherever Angel is, she's not on Bordman Moor and she's certainly not with this mystery stallion. If you ask me, it's all in Binny Alderidge's imagination."

Even so, I shivered to think of an old pony out on the moors in all this rain. Ever since we had come back from Downing Street, it had poured down in steady, persistent sheets. Purple clouds banked up against each other, water spattered out of the gutters, the drains gurgled. It didn't seem like the middle of July.

"Eh up, what's this?" Trevor peered through the drizzle-misted window across the yard to where Sarah was plodding towards us with her head held down, not even bothering to protect herself from the rain.

"I need to have a word with Danny." She stood in the doorway, sopping wet, her red hair pushed back and her eyes glistening with tears.

Danny followed her out, looking confused and anxious, and the rest of us were left to wonder what had happened.

She came back a few minutes later and told us that Danny's mother was moving to Brighton and that Danny was going with her.

We were all taken aback. Danny's huge dark eyes seemed magnified and he looked terrified, as if he'd done something wrong. Danny had been at Hollywell Stables right from the very beginning. He'd led us to Queenie who'd been suffocating and starving to death in a scrap-yard, with wire caught round her neck, and no water or food. He was part of the team.

"I'm not going, I'm not, I'm not!" Danny buried his head in Queenie's neck.

"You can come back for holidays." It sounded so pathetic, I could have kicked myself.

"How is he?" Trevor whispered over the stable door. He came in and placed his hand on Danny's shoulder.

Why did life have to be so cruel? This was Danny's home, this was where he belonged, not with a woman who suddenly decided she wanted to play mother.

Blake came in after a long hack on Colorado looking deadly serious. "I've just heard," he said. Blake was my closest friend and confidant.

"It's just not fair," I said. "Blake, it's not fair!"

I was gritting my teeth so hard it made my jaw hurt. He folded me up in his arms and my eyes started stinging. There was nothing we could do.

"Life's not fair." Trevor clanked down some

water buckets and switched on the outside tap full blast.

"She's coming tomorrow morning," Ross said.

When Danny first came to live at Hollywell he'd had a carrier bag of belongings. It was pathetic and pitiful and Sarah had been moved to tears. Since then we'd watched him blossom with confidence and happiness. He'd gone to school every day with Katie and he was even losing his stutter and learning to read properly.

"Mel, you've got to accept it. When all's said and done, she's still his mother." Blake lifted Colorado's show-jumping saddle on to the top of the door and tickled me under the chin. How was it he always knew how to make me feel better?

Danny was far calmer after having a long talk to Trevor and by the time we'd finished lunch and watched an Australian soap he was even smiling.

Chapter Two

Mrs Mac, our chief fund raiser and secretary, telephoned later to say she'd call round that afternoon and what about a welly-wanging competition, whatever that was, or a Donkey Derby?

"She's panicking," said Sarah, writing down an idea for her latest novel on the back of the electricity bill. "I can just tell, she even called me Sandra."

In ten days we were holding the very first Hollywell Stables Gala Open Day and although none of us would admit it, we were all terrified. We'd tried to gauge how many people would be coming by putting a form in the last newsletter, but it all seemed to be getting out of control. There was so much to organize: craft stalls, burger bars, cream teas, entertainment, car parks to rope off and where to put the portable loos. Sarah was decidedly fraught and the paddocks were just one great muddy swamp. To top it all, our famous patron, Rocky, had gone on a safari in Africa and couldn't be traced.

"Are you sure you told him it was July and not September?" Sarah said, looking pointedly at me as I tried to slope off to find Blake.

It was always difficult getting through to Rocky because he had such an entourage of bodyguards and personal managers. When I'd last spoken to him he'd just come off stage after performing in Los Angeles for the President of the United States. His voice was hoarse, and he said he could barely hear me after all the noise of the concert. His ears were ringing. What if I had got it wrong? It didn't bear thinking about.

Ross suggested scrubbing up the last of the winter rugs and surcingles and I dived out of the kitchen. Jigsaw was sprawled on the only dry bit of concrete in the yard, and Walter our wayward mule had let himself out of the stable and was devouring one of Sarah's hanging baskets.

"This is the life." Katie perched on the edge of the water trough. The rain had stopped, which was a miracle, and a huge rainbow stretched from our fields right over to the other side of the village.

"Aren't they supposed to be lucky?" Danny asked.

"Only if you want a pot of gold," said Katie.

"I just want one wish," Danny sighed.

A lime-green Mini Metro shot up the drive like a rally car and Binny Alderidge got out.

"You wanted proof," she said. "Well, I've got it." She slammed a brown file down on top of the wheelbarrow.

"Aye, aye," Trevor whispered as Binny Alderidge braced herself in front of Ross as if he were the sworn enemy.

A pack of small dogs yapped non-stop inside the Mini Metro and Jigsaw looked completely unnerved and tried to blend into the stable block.

"Let's go inside," suggested Ross, and we all followed him.

"So you see, it is possible," said Binny, showing us a newspaper cutting. It was dated a few months back and the headline read: WILD PONIES FOUND ON MARSH. It told the story of four ponies which had been discovered living wild on a marshland. They were in terrible condition and one had to be put down. The only rational answer was that they'd been dumped.

"I can't believe we haven't heard about this." Sarah didn't know what to say.

"It only made local news." Binny twiddled her spectacles. "I only saw it because I was visiting my sister."

"Listen to this," I said, reading aloud. " 'People are thought to be increasingly turning horses loose as soon as the novelty wears off. Just like people dumping puppies, they want to get rid of the responsibility and have no thought for the consequences.' "

"This is serious," said Ross as he reread the article.

"That stallion has been dumped – I would bet on it!" said Binny.

Cogs slowly began to click into gear in my head. Stallions were the hardest horses to look after. They were a common victim of neglect; it all started to add up.

"This is one of the worst things I've ever heard of," said Sarah, flopping back into the armchair with Jigsaw. "It's terrible – how can someone do that?"

"Just like they can dump cats and dogs," said Trevor. "There are some really cruel people out there."

"And there's more," added Binny, her face softer now that we were listening, now that someone was taking notice.

"Here's the first sighting of the Black Beast." She passed us another newspaper cutting. "And here's when Angel went missing, just two weeks later. That's got to be more than coincidence."

"How exactly did she escape?" Sarah asked.

"The fence was smashed to smithereens. The police said it was obvious she'd been stolen – there was a professional gang going round at that time so they put two and two together."

"But you never believed them?"

"Not really. I've always had a feeling that she was alive and very close by. In the same way that I now have a feeling she's in trouble."

"I see."

"Were there any hoofprints?" Katie was using her detective brain.

"It was raining all night. If there were they'd been washed away hours before. It was just rotten luck."

Poor Binny. I was beginning to see why she'd been so desperate when she'd first visited us. For a year nobody had believed her about the Black Beast; they thought she was a dotty old lady. She'd turned to us as a last resort and we still hadn't taken any notice.

"I've got to get her back," she said. "She belonged to my husband. She's all I've got left, since he died two years ago."

Sarah put the kettle on and Katie fetched the biscuit tin. Blake came in from sorting out Colorado and Binny joked about how many handsome young men there were at Hollywell Stables. Trevor preened and Ross just went scarlet. Katie said she ought to see James, Sarah's fiancé, he could have his very own television programme. James was our local vet and spent much of his time at Hollywell Stables.

"My Frank was a head-turner in his time, a real Rhett Butler."

"OK, down to business." Sarah dropped sugar lumps in everyone's tea. Katie now insisted we use lumps instead of granules so we could give them to the horses.

"Bordman Moor covers hundreds of miles. It's desolate and it's easy to get lost. Anybody could hide out up there. It's like a wilderness."

"So what you're saying is we haven't got a hope," said Ross.

"Let's just listen, shall we?" Binny winked at him and reached for a coffee cream.

"It's no good us trying to find them," Sarah paced up and down the kitchen. "Somehow we've got to get the stallion to come to us."

"But that's what I've been trying to tell you. He came looking for me last night. He stood at the edge of the paddock for a full half an hour. Something's wrong – it can only be Angel."

"How big is he?" Katie asked.

"Oh, I'd say fifteen hands, no more. An Anglo Arab."

My heart flipped with excitement. We hadn't rescued an Arab before.

12

"But he's wild," Binny added, "as wild as the wind, and that means dangerous."

"OK, so we'll stay at your place tonight, we'll have to stake out. James isn't working tonight, and we might need a tranquillizer gun." Sarah's mind was racing.

"Anybody good with a lasso?" Trevor asked.

"He came at midnight last night," Binny said. "But we'll have to be ready earlier, just in case."

"What if we don't catch him?" Katie asked.

"We don't want to catch him," Binny said. "We want him to take us to Angel."

"And if he doesn't?"

"He will, I know he will."

I honestly wished I had Binny's faith, but it all sounded so over the top. Blake caught my eye and I knew he was thinking the same thing.

"To tonight, then," Binny raised her mug of tea, "and I promise you won't be disappointed!"

Chapter Three

"Well, that was a waste of time," Ross said as soon as we were out of earshot.

Binny kept saying that she couldn't understand it.

"So you'll give us a ring?" Sarah opened the car door. "As soon as you see something?"

Binny lived in a pretty cottage right on the edge of Bordman Moor. The views were fantastic. We'd stayed up all night, taking it in turns to watch, but nothing had happened. Wherever the stallion was he didn't come to the cottage that night.

"Do you think she's all right?" Blake whispered as we climbed into the car.

"I think she's lonely," I said, "and this business with Angel is tearing her apart."

The disappointment was etched all over Binny's face. She seemed to have aged ten years.

"I feel such a fool," she'd said when dawn broke and there still wasn't a sign.

The cottage was full of photographs and portraits of Angel, some showing her being driven by

Binny's husband, some just loose in the paddock. There was one of Binny feeding her a carrot with Frank in the background.

"I'm worried about her," Blake said. "She's clinging to the past."

"Naah, she's a tough old bird." Trevor threw a sweet wrapper through the window and Sarah gave him a lecture on littering the countryside.

"Sorry, Mrs F."

I slapped his wrist and Blake looked at his watch. It was just after 9 a.m. We'd be home by 10. There were no prizes for guessing what we were all thinking. Danny's mother would be on the doorstep at 11 o'clock. After that we might not see him for months, if ever again. Brighton was a very long way away.

"Poor little shrimp," said Trevor.

"Blood's thicker than water," said Sarah.

Not in my book it wasn't.

We'd left Danny and Katie with Mrs Mac. The last thing we wanted was for Mrs Barrat to hear that Danny had been up all night on a wild goose chase.

Danny was with Queenie when we arrived at Hollywell. Mrs Mac had made a leaving cake and Katie had strung up some balloons and streamers.

"How is he?" Sarah asked, dumping down a pile of sleeping bags.

Mrs Mac just shook her head and turned away, choked with tears. Danny meant the world to Mrs Mac, and she'd taken him under her wing as if he were her son.

"Blake's with him now," Sarah said. "Maybe he can find the right words."

We all tried to pretend everything was all right, that nothing awful was happening. The only good thing was that the rain stopped. These last few weeks it had been like living in a monsoon.

"Put your false smiles on, everybody." Sarah glanced through the window. "Danny's mother has just arrived."

The reason we didn't trust Mrs Barrat was because she didn't show any affection for Danny. When he'd first arrived on our doorstep he was living by himself while she was staying with her boyfriend. He was nine years old and his arms and legs were like sticks. I don't think he'd ever known what it was like to sit down to a home-cooked family meal.

"Here she comes, brace yourselves," Sarah hissed.

The sharp rap at the front door was immediately answered by Trevor, who hadn't yet had the pleasure of meeting Mrs Barrat. He stood at the door blinking with shock, and I must admit I could see why.

Last time we'd seen her she'd looked like something the cat had dragged in; now she was dressed in a shell-pink summer dress and jacket and her hair was all coiffed up in an elegant style. The false eyelashes and dangly ear-rings were gone in place of a more sophisticated look.

"Fine feathers don't make fine people." Mrs Mac was not taken in.

"Earl Grey tea if you don't mind, Sarah," she said.

"What's wrong with her voice?" Trevor whispered. "She sounds terribly posh."

"More like she's read a manual on how to talk properly," I giggled, rooting through the cupboards for the tea.

"I say, this is rather nice." Mrs Barrat's husband dithered in the background. He was about twice her age and totally under her thumb. What was someone like him doing with someone like her?

"Of course, we've got the company car now." Her voice was beginning to grate on my nerves.

Mrs Mac grudgingly cut her a piece of Danny's leaving cake and Trevor searched for a clean plate. Within seconds she'd wolfed down two pieces.

Sarah's jaw was set so rigid she could barely speak and I thought she was going to explode when Mrs Barrat said she was planning on becoming a novelist, as if it was the easiest thing in the world to do.

"You could fit everything she's got to say on the back of a matchbox," Mrs Mac hissed from the walk-in pantry. "Have you noticed she's not even asked about Danny yet?"

I tried to keep a straight face and then Sarah suggested they find Danny – I don't think she could stand being cooped up with her any longer.

The stable yard was empty and so was Colorado's stable. We found Blake in the back field slowly cantering round on the beautiful skewbald with Danny perched in front of him on the pommel of the saddle. They looked so happy and content and in perfect balance. My eyes welled up. This was just too much to take.

As soon as Danny saw his mother he burst into tears and clung on to Blake.

"Come on, Buster, it's time to get down."

"You can come and visit any time, Danny." Sarah was very pale.

"I'll write every week and send you photographs," said Katie miserably.

I gave Danny a hug and realized I couldn't stop trembling. A single magpie scuttered away up the field. One for sorrow . . .

Mrs Mac passed him a bag of food and goodies she'd prepared. "We love you, Danny, and just remember this will always be your home." She stepped aside so that Danny could have one last word with Queenie.

The old pony nuzzled his hair and whickered for a biscuit. When Danny climbed into the car his face was streaked with tears.

"Oh, I nearly forgot." Katie ran forward and pressed her plastic four-leaf clover into his hands. "I want you to have this."

The car rolled out of the drive and out of sight.

"He'll be back," said Sarah, "just wait and see."

The rest of the day dragged by like the last week of term. Katie kept saying that she felt as if half of her was missing, that she was minus an arm or leg. Trevor joked that anybody would think they were an old married couple, but nobody really laughed. Ross made it worse by finding Danny's book, *Black Beauty*, balanced on top of the oven, where he'd obviously forgotten to pick it up.

"We've really got to start applying ourselves." Mrs Mac was breaking out in a rash over the Gala Open Day. "Now here's some notes I've made on the parade, who's going to lead which pony and so on. Ross, I really wish you'd pay attention!"

Sarah was going to read out a brief history of all the rescued horses and ponies over a loud-

19

speaker and we were going to lead them round for everybody to see and admire.

"Timing is going to be essential, and we could really do with more helpers. Any news on the Rocky front?"

All we'd managed to find out was that Rocky had last been seen playing polo on the back of an elephant and had then been rushed to hospital with severe sunburn. Since then, he seemed to have vanished into thin air.

"It's vital we sell as much merchandise as possible." Mrs Mac ticked something else off her list, ignoring the Rocky problem.

The official Hollywell shop, which was once a stable, was now up and running and packed to overflowing. We'd had the inside plastered, a new window put in and a proper door. There was even a cash till.

"I'm expecting big sales of the new baseball caps and Christmas cards. It may only be July but people plan ahead."

Mrs Mac passed round a list of all the craft stalls which were going to be set up in the empty stables – horsehair jewellery, pottery, basket-weaving, sign-writing . . .

"Just so there's no confusion," Ross said, puckering up his brow, "just what is a welly-wanging competition?"

"There's nothing we can do," Sarah insisted later that evening as she broke off from rattling out her next chapter on the electric typewriter. "We can't sit up every night on the edge of a moor waiting for a phantom horse that might never appear. We're needed here at Hollywell Stables."

She had wandered in, looking for her reading glasses which she hated anyone seeing her wearing. She always lost things when she was feeling on edge and since Ross had mentioned the black stallion she'd been positively jumpy. Blake was filling in the entrance form for the local county show and he found the glasses under some papers.

"But this *is* Hollywell business." Ross carried on the argument. "Binny really believes in this stallion."

"So do I, but we can't make it our major priority. What if a real rescue comes in? Bordman Moor is a good hour's drive away. We can't be in two places at once."

"So that's your final word, then?"

"Yes. Of course if Binny sees something else in the meantime, we'll be there like a shot. But we've got to keep a sense of perspective."

I knew Sarah was trying to be sensible. We couldn't stretch ourselves in too many directions, and we still had a sanctuary to run.

"Did you know," Katie read out, "that a horse's

stomach is only the size of a rugby ball, and that's why they can't eat a lot of food at once?"

She was reading from James's veterinary article which had just been printed in the pony magazine *In The Saddle*. James had just dropped it off and we were all incredibly proud. It was the first time his name had appeared in print and he'd kept the whole thing a big secret.

"Or," she went on, "that the kidneys are behind the saddle and the lungs are between the rider's knees?"

"It's a wonder they let us ride them at all." Trevor looked shocked.

"That's because they're noble and majestic creatures," said Sarah.

Rain hammered on the windows like an evil spirit. What had happened to the summer? What had happened to the heatwave?

I stared blankly at a quiz show on television and then switched over to the sheepdog trials. Oscar thought these were a hoot and kept leaping at the screen.

The telephone sat black and ominous in the hallway, as quiet as a Sunday morning.

Sarah plumped up the cushions for the umpteenth time and then decided to drag out the vacuum cleaner which only got used during severe attacks of writer's block.

"We won't hear the phone," Ross bellowed, switching it off at the mains.

"OK, you win, where's her phone number?"

But Katie didn't get a chance to reach for her horsy diary – the phone began to ring, causing us all to leap out of our skins. Sarah picked up the receiver and Binny Alderidge's clipped staccato voice shrilled down the line.

"He's here, he's at the paddock gate – it's the stallion!"

Chapter Four

Binny waved us down at the end of her drive, an oilskin slung over striped pyjamas, rollers clinging precariously to wisps of sodden hair.

"Quick, turn your engine off." She stuck her head through the window. "We don't want to scare him away!"

Sarah immediately switched off the headlights and grabbed her sou'wester. The rain was falling in relentless sheets. At least it managed to muffle any noise we might make.

Slowly, sliding along on the greasy lawn, we edged towards the paddock. The moon was totally hidden by cloud and the only light came from a feeble lamp outside the back porch.

Binny's fingers clutched my arm as a shadow moved in the distance. I only hoped it was a horse and not a burglar. I could feel Blake's warm breath on my neck. We all sounded as if we'd just run a hundred-metre sprint.

"There, I can just make out his ears," said Sarah. "Can you see his head?"

"We need a torch," Blake hissed. "He may run off but we can't do anything in this light."

The deep husky whicker from over by the gate told us all we needed to know.

"Quick, get the torch," Sarah urged.

Ross ran back to the car and Sarah took a couple of steps forward.

"I told you." Excitement caught in Binny's voice. "That's Bordman's Black Beast."

I could practically smell horse sweat and fear in the dank warm air. The hairs on the back of my neck were rising. He was out there, watching us, waiting. Seeing us far better than we could see him.

"He's been there for nearly two hours," Binny whispered. "He wants me to follow him, I know he does."

We heard a squeal and then a hoof stamping. Ross came back with the torch and flickered it towards the gate. "There he is," he murmured. "Look."

The head was well bred, dished, with flared nostrils running into a powerful neck and shoulders. He was as black as charcoal, with a tail so long it was trailing in the mud even though he had it arched over his back like a typical Arab.

"He doesn't look hurt," I said, trying not to move a muscle.

The stallion suddenly trotted off a few paces, stopped, wheeled round and neighed out loud.

"What is it, Blackie, what is it that you want, eh?" Binny shot forward, clinging to the paddock fence, her feet squelching ankle-deep in the mud.

"No!" Trevor, who up to now had been speechless, dived after her. "This is no task for an old lady."

"You're only as old as you feel, now let me go." Binny struggled to free her arms, her voice rising to a screech.

"Don't scare him off." Sarah lunged forward. "For Heaven's sake, this is no time for heroics. Now, Binny, go back into the house. If Angel's out there we'll find her."

"But you don't know the moors." A gust of wind and rain swept the words away like confetti.

"We'll manage. Go inside and ring James. Get the number from the directory – he's on emergency call. Now hurry!"

"Come on," Ross urged. "He won't wait much longer."

We set off across the moors, Ross and Trevor going ahead with Sarah, Blake hanging back, looking after Katie and me.

The stallion kept its distance; it stayed about twenty metres ahead, but trotting back and forth, anxious and fearful, trying to tell us to go faster.

"It's OK, boy, we're going as fast as we can." Sarah tried to settle him. "Just bear with us."

I was shivering like a puppy and sopping wet but it didn't matter. The yellow light of the torch picked up the vast acres of scrubby land pocked with boulders and heather. The wind was icy cold and all around us was barren wasteland; it was so bleak it made my teeth chatter.

"It's not as pretty as it is from the road, is it?" Blake grinned.

"It's wild," I shuddered.

"Anything could happen out here and nobody would know." Katie held on to Blake's hand until her knuckles turned white.

"Whoever dumped that Arab out here needs locking up for ever," Blake's voice was venomous. "Imagine a hot-blooded horse wintering out in this?"

It didn't bear thinking about.

"Where now, Blackie? Come on, you've got to do better than this." Sarah stopped up ahead, her sou'wester tilted to one side and her red hair hanging in drenched rats' tails just like the stallion's.

For half a minute the horse didn't seem to be able to make up his mind. Then he tore down a steep ravine and disappeared from sight.

"Come on, we're going to have to go down."

I slid along on my bottom, grasping clumps of

heather as I went. It was sharp and stung my hands but it was better than falling into the unknown.

"Is everyone all right?" Sarah shouted from the bottom, and then let out a shriek of terror.

Ross quickly shone the torch and we vaguely saw the fuzzy figure of a sheep brush up against her leg. We'd stumbled into a whole herd of them.

"They must be sheltering out of the wind," Sarah muttered. "Come on, the stallion's waiting."

We were still going downhill and the ground was getting more and more sodden. My wet socks clamped around my feet like blocks of ice and I didn't think I could go on much further; we must have travelled over two miles.

Suddenly the stallion stopped and started pawing the ground. There was a faint tinkling of water in the shadows and Ross's torch lit up a small stream. And something else . . .

"Oh my God!" Ross's hand started trembling helplessly.

"Don't panic," said Sarah. "Just don't panic."

We clambered forward into the black peat.

"It's OK, little girl, we're on your side." Sarah's voice was honey-smooth and gently coaxing. "We'll soon have you out of there."

A cream-gold head turned to look at her with eyes paralysed by fear. It was Angel.

"How the hell did she get in there?" Trevor couldn't believe it.

Angel was stuck up to her shoulders in thick black cloying peat next to the stream. No matter how frantically she struggled it pulled her down like quicksand and she couldn't move an inch. The rain had soaked her back and neck and her ears were pressed flat against her head. She looked utterly terrified.

"She could have been here for days." Trevor was really shaken.

"She's frozen up." Blake whipped off his jacket and threw it over her back, up to his waist in bog.

"I don't know what to do," said Sarah. "For the first time I haven't got a clue how I'm supposed to handle this."

"I don't want to speak out of turn, Mrs F, but I think we might need the fire brigade."

"Yeah, Trevor's right." Blake fought his way back to us, his shirt already rain-soaked. "I've seen something like this happen once before, and they had to lift the horse out in a sling."

"We need James." Sarah was desperately trying to get a grip. "Someone's going to have to find their way back to Binny's."

I ran full pelt across the moors towards the flickering light in the distance. Ross was just behind me, gasping for breath, stumbling, cursing, trying to go faster – Angel's life was in our hands.

Seeing the Land Rover bumping over the rough ground towards us was like seeing the star over Bethlehem.

"Ross, look, it's James!" My face became streaked with rain as I stood heaving for breath.

"What's happened, where is everyone?" James's soft brown eyes were filled with panic.

"It's all right," Ross wheezed, holding his hands on his knees. "Nobody's hurt." And he then told James the whole story.

"Ross, go back to Binny's. Get the fire brigade, we'll need at least two crews. Tell Binny to get some warm blankets. Hurry! Mel, you're coming with me!"

I clambered into the back of the Land Rover behind the driver, a mountain of a man with a thick beard.

James quickly introduced him: "This is Binny's neighbour, Jimmy. Now which way?"

James sank into the deep bog up to his armpits. Blake followed, holding up the black medical bag.

"Be careful," Sarah shouted, her eyes never leaving James's back. I felt exactly the same about Blake.

Jimmy angled the Land Rover so that the head-lights shone on Angel. She was transfixed with fear, like a startled rabbit. In the distance, the stallion whickered and snorted, pacing up and down then stopping and tossing his head. There was no way he was going to leave Angel.

"It's all right, little love, just stay calm." James gently ran his hand down Angel's sweating neck.

We stood watching, huddling together for warmth, Sarah, Trevor, Katie, me and Jimmy – without Jimmy I don't think we'd have ever got the Land Rover down into the ravine. He knew a back route and handled the terrain like a pro.

"Why don't you sit in the Land Rover?" he said to Katie and Sarah. "We're going to be here a long time yet."

James was feeling all over Angel's body, running his hands over her back, loins and flanks. The bog had her legs and most of her underside totally submerged in an evil grip, but at least she hadn't sunk down any further. James inched round to her tail and Blake passed him the thermometer. The lights from the Land Rover were a godsend as James gave Angel an internal examination.

"What is it, what's wrong?" Sarah's voice rose sharply.

"Listen." Katie held her breath. "They're here!"

The blue lights suddenly came into view, following the path Jimmy had taken. Five firefighters leapt out of the first engine and ploughed across to us. Two other engines pulled in behind it.

"Angel!" Binny appeared from nowhere, clutching a pile of blankets. She was horrified when she saw her, and I could actually see the old lady start to shake.

"It's not as bad as it looks." Sarah put an arm round her but didn't sound very convincing.

"Angel, sweetheart!" Binny's voice rose and cracked.

Blake waved at her and Angel looked up and squealed delightedly.

"Come on, I think you ought to get into the Land Rover, you'll catch your death out here." Jimmy manhandled her into the front seat next to Katie. "Now don't argue with me, Binny, I know what's best."

James pushed his way back through the bog, leaving Blake by Angel's head, keeping her calm. Two firefighters grabbed hold of his bag and an arm each and dragged him free. He was plastered in mud right up to his shoulders and was even spitting it out of his mouth.

"How is she? Tell me the truth, I want it laid on the line." Binny strained her head out of the Land Rover window, suddenly looking very old.

"She's extremely weak, Binny. I think she's been

there for a couple of days." James's voice was soft, gentle, a medical voice, and a cold finger of dread ran up my spine.

"I'm going to put her on a drip and give her some cortisone and Finadyne, to help reduce the shock and any pain—" James broke off and glanced towards the stallion who was still hovering by the edge of the trees.

"But?" Binny urged.

"There's an added complication."

"Well, tell me, then. Don't drag it out."

"She's in foal. It's on its way!"

Chapter Five

"She's in the very first stages of labour, so it's going to be a while yet."

Jimmy was gripping hold of Binny's hand.

"But it doesn't look good, I'm afraid. It's a breech. The foal's coming out backwards."

Binny's face contorted with shock, her eyes disbelieving. "She's twenty years old and it's her first foal."

"I know," James answered. "But she still has a chance."

And it was that chance, that single ray of hope which kept us all going.

Ross eventually swapped places with Blake at Angel's head where he'd been trying to keep her calm. Blake trudged over to the Land Rover, mud-blackened and exhausted. "I don't know how Angel's standing it," he whispered to me out of earshot of Binny. "It's a nightmare out there."

I'd got my fingers crossed for good luck and Sarah sent Jimmy and Binny back to the house to make flasks of tea, in the hope that it would take her mind off Angel. The firefighters were using Jimmy's chainsaw to cut down some trees so they could manœuvre the engines nearer to the bog.

"Time's running out," Blake whispered. "We've got to get her out of there."

I wiped a smear of mud from the corner of his mouth, then he went back to help Ross.

It was vital to get the drip into Angel as soon as possible, and James gathered his equipment together. "I only hope this works," he said.

"It will." Sarah was being a hundred and ten per cent positive.

Trevor came back from the tree-cutting with specks of wet sawdust all over his face.

Angel had sunk deeper into the bog. It was now up to her neck.

"Let her be all right." Katie clung on to my hand.

The options weren't very hopeful. They could either pull her straight out, which would endanger her life, or they could try and get hold of a crane and hoist her out. Either way it wasn't going to be easy.

Jimmy and Binny came back from the house with flasks of tea, which were over-sugared, but it didn't really seem to matter.

"It's no good pretending," she snapped. "I might

be old but I'm not stupid. I know it doesn't look good."

At least the drip was working. Angel had started to perk up and even tried to neigh to the stallion, who was still hanging around, unsure as to what was going on.

"See, where there's life there's hope." Jimmy put an arm round Binny's shoulder.

"I don't need your philosophy on life, Jimmy. If you want to be useful, just say a prayer."

"We'll get her out, you know, love," said one of the firefighters. "We haven't lost one yet."

But they didn't know anything about horses, and Angel must be getting exhausted.

It continued to pour with rain and we could barely see what was going on. Nobody seemed quite sure what to do, and there was still no way of getting the fire engines nearer to the bog. One of the firefighters tried to locate a crane on his mobile phone but everyone eventually agreed that the ground was just too wet. They'd never get it anywhere near the bog.

"So what do we do?" Binny was panicking. "We can't just sit here like lemons and watch her suffer."

"It's no good losing your temper, Binny. These gentlemen are doing their best." Jimmy tried to put a coat round her shoulders, but she shook it off.

36

"She's my little baby." Binny put a hand up to her face, the tears streaming down her cheeks. "I can't stand it any longer, I should be with her." She pushed past two of the firefighters and stumbled forward.

"Binny, don't be so stupid. Leave it to the professionals." Jimmy whipped her round like a rag doll and dragged her back towards the Land Rover. "All we can do is wait," he said. "That vet knows what he's doing and so do these guys. Now trust me, she's going to be all right." Jimmy wrapped his huge arms round her frail body and wouldn't let go until she'd stopped crying. "Now, come on, you silly old goose, let's just try and think positive – for Angel's sake."

"Jimmy O'Connor, don't you dare call me a silly old goose."

"Now that's more like it," Jimmy chuckled. "Mel, what about a cup of tea for this OAP?"

Another hour dragged by. Blake brought the empty drip bag and coil back up to the Land Rover but it didn't look good. When I asked him how she was, he just shook his head.

"See, I told you," Binny murmured.

Sarah was being a real brick, laughing and joking with the firefighters and trying to keep up morale. They'd managed to get an engine within a few metres of the bog, with the idea of putting a rope round Angel's neck and dragging her out. But James eventually decided it was too dangerous.

"The vet's coming out," said Jimmy, and I could just make out James being pulled out of the bog by two firefighters. "Now we'll find out what's going on."

Sarah gave James a cup of tea and he drank it all in one go. His hands were blue with the cold.

"She's improved enormously in the last half hour. The drip's done its work and she's certainly stronger. But we've got to move fast. Time's running out, and we've got to get her out of there."

The firefighters pressed round to listen to James's plan.

"There's going to be a lot of kicking and thrashing," he continued. "The main thing is that no one gets hurt, so we've all got to work together. She's a lot calmer now. I think it's possible."

All the firefighters were going to move into the bog and try to lift Angel out. It was bizarre but James said it was the only way. He was worried that the foal was lodged in such a position that it might suffocate. He had to do something.

"If we can just give her a kick-start," James said, "if we could just get the front legs out, she might be able to do the rest herself."

"I'm going in with you." Jimmy stripped off his jacket and marched forward.

38

"Jimmy, don't be a fool, what about your rheumatism?"

He wouldn't listen. "I'm going in whether you like it or not. I wasn't called mammoth muscles for nothing, you know."

"No, but that was twenty years ago," said Binny, arching her eyebrows at him.

"OK guys, are we ready?"

Six firefighters got behind Angel and four on either side. She might only be thirteen hands but she would still be incredibly heavy. Added to which there would be suction from the bog. Even with all that manpower it was an incredible task.

Binny was wringing her hands together in desperation. "What do you think, Mel, has she got a chance?"

They all heaved together. It was a massive effort. I could just make out Angel's head and her ears flicking back and forth. She looked as if she was fighting for her life.

"Come on, Angel, you can do it!" Binny clutched my arm.

"Come on, Angel," screamed Katie, at the top of her voice.

For seconds all we could hear was scrabbling, paddling noises, grunting and heaving. Trevor and Jimmy were right in the thick of it.

"I can't see anything," said Binny, frantic with frustration.

Someone yelled out. Then we heard a thud.

"Someone's hurt," I yelled.

It was pandemonium. Angel was plunging all over the place. Men were falling back into the bog.

"What's happening?" Binny shrieked.

"She's out!" Sarah went berserk. "Look, you can see her shoulders."

Angel made a last valiant effort and dragged herself on to firm ground.

A huge whoop went up from the firefighters and Trevor punched the air with his fist.

"She's out!" Binny screeched and hugged Sarah violently. We were all leaping around, tears mingling with the rain, emotion brimming over. "I don't believe it," Binny cried. "I thought I was going to lose her."

James and Blake were at Angel's head, examining her as we ran towards them.

"I should have brought a Jammy Dodger," said Binny. "She loves Jammy Dodgers."

"There'll be plenty of time for that later," said Sarah. "Let's see how she is first."

Angel was standing with her head down, trembling all over, her cream coat blackened and her tail a wet wisp. She looked so bony and pathetic it made my eyes sting. James was feeling over her stomach and looking in her eyes.

As we went towards her Binny was overcome. "Oh my poor little baby, what's happened to you?" She reached out her hand and touched the soft pink nose. "Remember me, girl, it's been a long time, hasn't it?"

Angel turned her head, stared at Binny and then dropped her nose and sniffed at her sweater. A flood of recognition lit up her eyes and she started whickering excitedly, lifting up one of her forelegs, and then the other.

"She's always done that," Binny said. "Frank taught her years ago and she's never forgotten it."

"Horses never forget anything," Sarah grinned. "Especially people – they always remember a good deed, and a bad one for that matter."

Binny kissed the pink nose and brushed away fresh tears. "I always knew you were alive," she whispered. "I never gave up on you, Angel, not for one second."

James gave me a worried glance and reached for the stethoscope. All the firefighters crowded round, quiet and anxious, wondering what was going to happen next.

"I've got to deliver the foal here," James announced. "There's no time."

It wasn't long before Angel lay down on her

side. Binny took off her coat and pressed it under her head but she was in too much pain to notice.

It was then that we heard the stallion screaming out from under some distant trees. He reared up and pawed the air as if to say he was worried about Angel too. Up until that point we had completely forgotten about him – we'd been too busy trying to save Angel's life.

"He is the father, after all," Ross said. "He's got a right to be concerned."

"While he's still hanging around," James said, "it might be an idea to contact the local zoo for a marksman. We can't leave him here."

"James is right," Sarah said. "Somehow we've got to get them both back to Hollywell and a newborn foal as well."

"Which is just starting to make its way into the world," James said, examining Angel.

At least the rain had stopped, and the firefighters drove the three engines towards us so they acted as a windbreak and gave James more light.

"Now then, my little girl," James stroked Angel's damp coat, "let's see if we can do this together, shall we?"

Usually a foal is positioned with its forelegs forward, and these come out first with the head following and then the rest of the body. Angel's foal was completely twisted the wrong way. Somehow

James had to push the foal back in, grab the hoof of a hindleg and flex and pull it into the right position. He explained this as he was working but I still couldn't picture in my mind what he was trying to do.

"It's OK, darling, I'm here." Binny crouched down next to Angel's head. "Mummy's here, it's going to be all right."

I'd never watched a birth before apart from on television and it was hard to imagine a new life was about to appear.

"I hope it's a girl," Katie said, watching eagerly.

"Katie, I don't know whether you should be watching this." Sarah was concerned.

"It's educational," Katie said. "Besides, Trevor's the squeamish one."

"I am not."

"Well, I don't care if it's a boy or a girl," said Binny. "I just want Angel to be all right."

"We all do, Binny." Sarah put a hand on her arm. "We all do."

Angel half lifted her head and then gave a huge sigh. She was sweating more now, and Binny was wiping her eyes and nose with the corner of her sweater. "Hang in there, darling, it'll soon be over."

James was working like mad to try and correct the breech, but it was still no good. "Come on,

Angel, don't fight against me." Everybody was willing her on.

Minutes ticked past and there was still no progress. James once told us that unlike humans, foals are often born very fast, in as little as ten to fifteen minutes. It was only because Angel had problems that it was taking this long.

"It's no good." James looked up and across to Binny. Rain, mud and sweat ran down his face. "It's the worst breech I've ever seen. I hate to tell you this, Binny, but I think we're going to lose the foal."

A huge wave of hopelessness swept over me. Angel couldn't have come through all this for her foal to die, fate couldn't be that cruel. Katie gripped my hand and I knew she was thinking the same thing.

"Keep trying, James." Sarah's eyes were desperate.

"Just save Angel." Binny stroked the drenched cream-coloured coat. "Do what you have to do but don't let her die."

A short distance away the stallion paced up and down, neighing every so often. He looked defeated, as if it was all his fault.

James went back to work.

We all waited.

Binny was stroking Angel over and over. I

wondered how she'd cope if she lost both the foal and Angel. Oh please, God, save them. It just wasn't fair. It would be too much of a tragedy for anyone to bear.

Suddenly a huge grin burst across James's face. He was scrabbling for extra leverage, his whole body stretched out on the ground. "I've got it!" he yelled. "I've got the leg, the foal's still alive!"

"Yippee!" Katie shouted and everybody started cheering and clapping and then just as quickly fell quiet again. There was still work to do.

"Look!" Katie's mouth opened in astonishment. A tiny nose and head had just appeared. It was so beautiful. It was the foal. It was being born!

The next few minutes were magical. I wasn't a bit squeamish. I just couldn't take my eyes off that tiny bundle of life.

"You've done it, girl," Binny shrieked. "You've done it!" Angel lifted her head and then sank down again.

But something was wrong. The foal wasn't moving.

James went to work like a shot. "It's not breathing."

With cool calm efficiency, he yanked the body up by its hind legs, shaking it, slapping it, then rubbing its tiny body. "Come on." Vital seconds ticked by. "Come on!" James started blowing into its nostrils, giving it the kiss of life.

"Breathe, please breathe," I prayed.

Suddenly it gave a couple of spasmodic gasps and a shudder, then it struggled on to its side. Each breath was shallow and weak at first but then it grew stronger.

James sank back on his knees, looking close to collapse. "It's a filly!" he grinned. "A chestnut filly."

A huge whoop went up from all the firefighters and everybody started shaking hands and slapping each other's backs.

"Where's Trevor?" Katie said, and then we saw him stretched out unconscious like a felled tree. "I think he's fainted!"

The next few moments were truly beautiful. Gingerly the newborn foal tried to find its legs, all spindly and giraffe-like, and James eased it round to its mother's milk.

"The mother's first milk is vital," Katie informed the firefighters. "It's called the colostrum and stops the foal getting germs." She never could resist the chance to show off.

"She's so tiny." Binny couldn't take her eyes off the foal.

James rubbed her dry with a towel and Angel

started taking an interest, watching, whickering, eyes filling up with motherly love.

"Sssssh." James held a finger to his lips as the foal wobbled towards Angel's head. Nearly, nearly, and then plopped to the ground. Angel looked almost shy and then reached out her nose and sniffed the tiny damp ears.

Reassured, the foal thrust her face into Angel's as if to say, "Hi, Mum, it's me, I've arrived."

"Isn't it wonderful?" I was almost choked up as I whispered to Blake.

Binny tenderly reached out and touched the delicate tapered nose and dinky little ears.

"She's a little beauty." Blake bent down next to Binny and put an arm round her shoulders.

He told her that it was in the first hour of life that you could tell a future champion. After that it was difficult to predict because they were constantly changing shape. "This little mite is up with the best of them," Blake said. "There will be nothing to outclass her, you can take my word on that."

I felt my body tingle all over. It was a special moment for all of us.

"Two for the price of one," Binny laughed. "But how am I going to cope?"

We decided to give mother and daughter a few moments to themselves and collapsed inside the

Land Rover completely exhausted. James wiped his hands clean and Binny kept saying how could she ever thank him. Sarah told her to be careful or it would all go to his head.

"What I wouldn't give for a hot bath now," Sarah groaned, trying to wring her hair dry with a paper tissue then giving up. All the towels Binny had brought from the house were soaked and the only thing I could find in the Land Rover was a ragged bit of oily sack which Ross said wasn't much use to man nor beast.

"I propose a toast," Sarah said through chattering teeth, holding up a mug of stone-cold tea. She pushed open the Land Rover door and yelled out, "To the best firefighting team in the country – well done, lads."

"Hear, hear." Katie backed her up and there was a general chorus of grunts and groans and an anguished yelp from Jimmy who'd hurt his leg in the bog and not said a word until now when he'd turned green with pain.

"Probably a chipped bone," James announced. And Jimmy shrugged it off, saying it was all in the line of duty.

"This will probably go down as one of the most incredible rescue operations of all time." Ross put the plastic lid back on one of the flasks.

"We're bound to be on television." Katie's eyes glinted.

"Oh, not again." Ross put a hand to his forehead in mock despair. "But seriously," he went on, "the discovery of the real Black Beast after all this time is bound to cause a sensation."

James gave both Angel and the foal a shot of antibiotics, and the firefighters took one last look then climbed into their vehicles. But not before Sarah had given them our address and made them all promise devoutly to come to our Gala Open Day.

"What about transport?" Sarah said when the last engine disappeared from sight. The thought of moving an exhausted mare, a newborn foal and a wild horse back to Hollywell was daunting. It would take far too long to fetch our horsebox. Jimmy came to the rescue with the suggestion that he hitch his trailer to the Land Rover for Angel and the foal and then he had a cattle wagon we could use for the stallion. It sounded like a good plan.

"Always handy to know a farmer," Binny winked.

Sarah said she'd drive the lorry if Binny could manage the Land Rover. Jimmy would have to go with them because he couldn't remember where he'd put the lorry keys.

"Hang on a minute." James punched out the number for Bordman Zoo on his mobile phone to find out exactly what was going on. Every minute that ticked by I imagined the stallion would disappear.

Relief spread over James's face. "You'll have to stop off at Binny's cottage. Look out for a white van. It's the marksman," he said. "He's on his way!"

Chapter Six

It wasn't going to be easy.

The stallion stood hunched under the trees, oily-black from the constant rain, his hindquarters bunched up and his legs splayed out in the mud. Ross and Blake had tried to get near him earlier but he'd backed off immediately, his ears pressed flat and his tail swishing. He hardly ever took his eyes off Angel and the foal.

"The poor thing," I said. "He's got nobody, he's so alone."

Almost as if he heard me, the stallion pawed at the ground and neighed to Angel, but she was busy nuzzling the foal who was still trying to stand up.

"He's not very friendly." I think Katie had been imagining a Black Beauty lookalike who, after leading us to Angel, would happily let us catch him and live happily ever after at Hollywell Stables.

James was convinced that he'd hardly had any contact with humans, that he'd probably been left in a field since he was a foal. It was the only explanation. I must admit, I didn't think there were many horses who would pass up the chance of some food and shelter in preference to a cold desolate moor. Even the wild Dartmoor and New Forest ponies were tamer than this.

"I'll tell you something for nothing," said the marksman, who had arrived ten minutes earlier and was busy loading the special rifle. "You've got your work cut out there. I've never seen a horse with such a look about him – he wouldn't trust his own shadow."

"If it wasn't for him my Angel wouldn't be in this state." Binny was getting more and more anxious. Angel still hadn't got to her feet and the foal was clamouring for more milk.

Trevor was helping the marksman set up a special battery-operated floodlight. It was all being done in a matter of minutes but it seemed to take for ever.

We were trying to be as quiet as possible but I knew the stallion was getting suspicious. He kept looking from us to Angel and pacing up and down, tossing his head and snorting with distrust.

"He's a strong fella. I'd say it's going to take ten to fifteen minutes for him to go down." The marksman explained how the dart had to hit the top of a hind leg where there was the largest muscle mass. He was going to use an anaesthetic called Immobilon which would knock him out completely. "We won't switch the light on until the very last minute."

The tension was unbearable.

"As soon as he drops, we'll get a rope round his neck." James folded the rope like a lasso.

I'd never seen a horse being darted before. I didn't know what would happen.

James said if we didn't catch him now, we might never have another chance. It was nearly imposs-ible to catch a wild horse on an open moor and the only reason he was hanging around at the moment was because of Angel. It was now or never.

"So does everybody know what they've got to do?" As soon as the stallion was hit we were to spread out in a circle and try to keep him from charging off until the anaesthetic started to work. "It won't take long," the marksman said.

"Everybody ready?" James fiddled with the switch on the floodlight and suddenly a whole clump of trees was illuminated, dazzling the stal-lion who wheeled round, squealing in fright, won-dering what on earth was happening.

"It's OK, boy," I whispered under my breath. "We've got to be cruel to be kind."

The marksman closed his fingers on the trigger and the first dart went sailing out. "Blast, it's no good, the lamp's frightening him. We'll have to wait for daylight." The marksman clambered to his feet in defeat.

"No." James was adamant. "We can't wait that long. I want Angel in a dry stable as soon as possible. We haven't got another two hours. Please, at least give it another try."

The marksman shrugged his shoulders and loaded another dart.

"We've got to catch him," James urged. "There's no two ways about it. He's got to go back to Hollywell."

Sarah squeezed my hand and our hearts thumped anxiously. Some distance away, Jimmy sat in the rusty cattle wagon waiting. That would be another nightmare – how to get the stallion up the ramp?

"Ssssh," Blake hissed, looking to where the stallion was tentatively moving out from under the trees. One step at a time, getting closer to Angel.

"Here's our chance," James whispered. "Let's not blow it."

The marksman knelt down and took aim. It was a clean, perfectly targeted shot and the stallion cried out with anger and fear.

"Blimey, he's going crazy," Trevor shouted.

I'd never seen a horse react like it: he was carrying on like a bronco.

"We've got him! Come on, move in on him quick!" said James, as he and Blake ran forward.

Somehow Binny managed to trip over the cable to the floodlight and it blacked out, leaving us all in complete darkness. I heard the stallion fall and scrabble to his feet again.

My feet squelched and pulled in the mud and I could hardly see where I was going.

"Where's Mel?" It was Blake's voice, anxiety filtering through. "She's not here!"

Trevor bawled in the distance. "He's all over the place! It's not working!"

The stallion appeared from nowhere, a black solid shape coming out of the darkness with his head down and his teeth bared. He was staggering about, foaming at the mouth, gasping for breath, but it didn't stop him. He just kept heading straight at me, charging like a bull.

"Mel!"

It suddenly dawned on me that I'd wandered between the stallion and Angel. I remembered from wildlife programmes that that was something you should never do.

"Mel, run!" I heard Blake's voice but my legs just froze like two concrete posts. It was all happening in slow motion. I couldn't do a thing about it. The dart should be working, why wasn't the dart working?

"Melanie!"

Stone-cold fear clogged my throat. I couldn't scream, I couldn't breathe, I couldn't move. He was going to kill me.

Blake's body hit mine just seconds before the stallion would have run me over. We both went hurtling to the ground in a rugby tackle and my head fell back against a jagged stone with a sickening thud.

"Melanie!" I could feel Blake's breath on my neck and his eyes boring down on me. "Melanie, don't do this to me!"

Blood started slowly seeping down my neck and I tried to smile but then a black wave engulfed me and all I could do was lie there and listen to a voice from far away.

"She's unconscious!"

I woke up in my own room at Hollywell, staring at a picture of Milton, the famous show-jumper, and wondering what on earth had happened. My head felt on fire and I couldn't stop shivering, and then the realization hit me like a ton of bricks. The stallion; the hospital; waiting around for what seemed hours for X-ray results; Sarah worried and strained; Blake carrying me into Casualty with a strip of his shirt pressed against my head. It was all coming back – every gory detail.

I plumped up the pillows and winced as a stab of pain shot up my neck. Someone had opened the window and there was a massive display of carnations on my bedside table. Propped up against the vase was a sherbet-lemon-coloured card which read in bold type: "Get Better Soon. From all your fans at Hollywell." There was a cat's paw mark in one corner which looked suspiciously like Oscar's.

"So you're awake, then. It's about time." Blake poked his head round the door, giving me a huge smile. "We all thought you were auditioning for Sleeping Beauty."

He sauntered into the room, grinning boyishly, and I suddenly became aware of my sticking-up hair and washed-out pyjamas, and sank further under the duvet feeling very self-conscious. He then told me how Binny had made up some kind of herbal concoction and I'd been sleeping it off ever since.

"It completely zonked you out," he said. "We could hear you snoring for hours."

I nearly hit the roof when he told me I'd slept solidly through the next day and night and it was now the following morning.

"But how could you let me stay in bed this long?

And where's Angel, and what's happened to the stallion?" I tried to move my legs but they felt like planks of wood.

"Whoa, whoa, one thing at a time." Blake stood over me, suddenly really worried and I knew I looked terrible. I forced a smile but my face felt like cardboard.

"Angel and the foal are in the intensive care unit and Blackie's round the back kicking Queenie's stable to smithereens. There's nothing to worry about."

"So why does my throat feel like sandpaper and why can't I stop shivering?" I didn't tell Blake that I felt sick too.

"The doc says you've got a temperature after all that rain. Trevor's just as bad – he's walking round like a bear with a sore head."

"So nothing's changed, then." My head felt as if a hundred little hammers were drilling away inside it.

"I'll go and fetch Sarah," Blake said, concern still etched on his face. "Remember, you've had a nasty knock. You've got to take it easy."

"Yes, sir." I saluted him, and then felt dizzy and wished I hadn't moved so suddenly. My mouth felt as if I'd got fungus growing on my teeth, and my head was about to blow off my shoulders.

"Oh, and by the way," Blake said as he levered

himself out of the chair, "you look just like normal."

I threw the pillow at him and he dived out of the door just as it clipped off my prize cactus.

A few minutes later Sarah led a small procession in to check on me.

"Mel, you've got to take this seriously," Sarah said. "You can't just get knocked out and then act as if nothing's happened."

I was trying to get out of bed but somehow my legs wouldn't co-operate.

Trevor followed Katie in, his nose throbbing like a bright red hooter and a huge length of toilet roll screwed up in one hand. "I can't breathe," he groaned. "I feel terrible."

Sarah told him to be a man and put a thermometer into my mouth.

"I'm getting up whether you like it or not," I squeaked.

There was a cool breeze outside and it brought me round no end as we approached Angel's stable.

"Ssssh, don't make too much noise." Trevor tiptoed closer to the stable door looking like a proud father.

The foal was sucking hungrily at Angel's milk

and swishing her short fluffy tail. She looked as if she'd grown a foot since last time I'd seen her.

"She's going to be a right little madam," Sarah said, reaching for the water bucket to refill it. Angel looked exhausted but never once lost her temper with the foal, who wouldn't leave her alone for a second.

"James said she might turn grey in a few months," Katie whispered excitedly. "He said it's more than likely with a Palomino mother. I didn't know they could change colour."

The foal stared at Katie with huge brown eyes and then scuttled round the back of Angel and peered out from underneath her tummy. She looked so comical that we all burst out laughing.

"I don't think she knew that either," Ross said. "You'll be giving her a complex."

I insisted on seeing the stallion.

"I'm not sure you should." Blake and Ross exchanged worried glances but it was too late, I was already shuffling round to Queenie's stable.

What I saw filled me with cold dread. I'd never seen a horse look so angry, so mean and distrusting. His eyes were like empty shells and as soon as I put my head over the door he ran at me with his yellow teeth snapping.

"I did try to warn you." Blake rearranged the metal grille which covered the top half of the door to stop him jumping out.

"He's sedated at the moment." Ross came up behind me. "He was literally climbing up the walls when we first put him in here. James was nearly crushed to death."

The stallion started kicking out at the breeze-block walls, as if to reinforce what Ross had just said. His coat was dull and brittle and most likely infested with lice. There were spiky burrs stuck in his mane and tail, and his nose was scratched and bleeding.

"So what aren't you telling me?" I knew Ross and Blake probably better than anyone else in the world and it was as plain as day that they were hiding something.

Ross shuffled his feet and Blake stared out over the paddocks.

"Has he got some disease or something?" Sweat was running in rivulets down my back and my hands suddenly felt clammy.

"James told us . . ." Ross broke off, looking awkward.

"James said what?"

"Mel, you've got to be rational about this. It's no good getting all sentimental."

"Ross, will you stop talking in riddles and tell me what's going on?"

"He might have to be put down." Blake almost spat out the words. "He's dangerous and quite frankly I agree with James, he's got no place at Hollywell Stables."

"I don't believe you've just said that." Blood rushed to my head and I staggered to keep my balance. "How could you even think such a thing?"

"For God's sake, Mel." Blake spun round. "He nearly killed you!"

"But he didn't, did he? I'm still here. He deserves a chance. That's what we're here for, to help horses that nobody else wants, not to give in as soon as we come up against a hurdle."

"He's not a hurdle, Mel, he's crazy." Ross was right on Blake's side.

"I don't care what you both think, it's not going to happen, not if I can help it." I turned on my heel, fury pumping at my temples, and suddenly felt my knees give way like jelly beneath me.

"Will you stop being so flaming stubborn." Blake scooped me up in his arms just as I was about to crumple in a heap, and started carrying me towards the house. "You shouldn't even be out of bed. Now shut up for at least two minutes and do as you're told."

Ross ran on ahead and opened the back door

and Sarah came rushing through from the hallway looking worried sick.

"I'm OK, it's just Blake making a fuss," I gasped, and was then overcome by another wave of nausea.

"Trevor, phone the doctor. I knew something like this would happen. Blake, take her upstairs. I'll get a hot-water bottle."

The doctor arrived and immediately prescribed antibiotics and bed rest. Trevor was seriously miffed that he'd just got a common cold.

Jigsaw lay on the end of the bed licking my feet and whining endlessly as if it was all too sad for words. Katie brought me some pony magazines and half a chocolate egg. I sat there fuming, not interested in anything but the stallion and what was going to happen to him. Sarah refused to talk about it.

Blake brought me some watery scrambled eggs and stood staring at me as if he had something deep and meaningful to say. We had another row about the stallion and then he said he'd come back when I'd calmed down, which would probably be the end of the next century.

Trevor slunk into my room, hovering by the bed

looking more bunged up than ever. I was getting so many visitors it felt like Piccadilly Circus.

"So he's told you, then?" Trevor shuffled nervously. "No, not about the stallion," he added. "About the job offer." My face must have frozen over. "Why does something tell me I've put my foot in it?" Trevor was turning purple.

"Not one foot, Trevor, both of them."

Blake stood with his back to me, looking out of the window, struggling to find the right words.

"I was going to tell you, Mel, but I didn't know how to and there never seemed to be the right moment."

He'd been offered a job in Ireland, in one of the top show-jumping yards, where he'd get to ride some of the best horses in the world.

"It's a fantastic opportunity, it could make all the difference to my career. I'd be a fool to pass it up."

Scalding hot tears burnt at the back of my eyes and my head throbbed.

"I'd be leaving in a week's time," he added.

I felt as if somebody had just punched me in the stomach.

"It sounds as if you've already made up your mind."

He gave me one of his probing looks but I kept my eyes down and refused to look at him.

"How long have you known?"

"Three weeks."

"And you've only just decided to tell me?" I was incredulous. It was the fact that I had to hear it from Trevor that really hurt.

"It wasn't like that," he said. "I didn't want to hurt you."

"Well, you have all right, so I hope you're satisfied."

"I don't know what to say."

"Don't say anything," I spluttered. "Just go, please, just leave me alone."

I didn't think he was going to take any notice. Long seconds dragged past and he made no effort to move. I could feel his eyes burning into my face looking for any sign that I might not mean it. But I did. I couldn't stand being in the same room as him. I felt utterly betrayed.

"Well, if that's what you want . . ."

"Yes."

"OK, then." He marched out, the door clicking shut behind him. I heard his footsteps on the stairs. He was gone.

I turned and buried my head under the pillow just like I used to when I was small and had no control over anything that was happening.

I didn't hear Katie sneak into the room, not until she'd come across and perched on the end of the bed, fiddling with my stuffed toys and looking as desolate as I felt.

"Sarah's just been speaking to Mrs Barrat," she said. "Apparently Danny's having a wonderful time and didn't want to come to the phone. He won't be visiting in the holidays."

I squeezed her hand and forced back a sob which was stifling my throat.

"You know," Katie said, "Trevor's right. Sometimes life can be really unfair."

Chapter Seven

The next couple of days were fraught with emotion. I was barely talking to Blake, and Katie was wandering around like a lost sheep.

Sarah had agreed to give the stallion another week to see if there was any improvement, providing only James or Blake went near him. At the moment he wasn't eating anything and would soon be as weak as a kitten. Even so, James said he'd never seen a horse so vicious. Blake had to literally chuck some hay into the stable while Ross held the stallion back with the yard brush. The only way we could get to the water bucket was by feeding in the hosepipe. It only went to prove that at some stage in his life the stallion must have been grossly mistreated.

On top of all this, the old-fashioned tractor we used for moving the manure collapsed completely and even Trevor couldn't do anything with it. Everybody had to spend hours extra pushing wheelbarrow after wheelbarrow, and all the loose straw blowing around made the place look more like a farm.

Walter and Arnie escaped twice to the local pub, the Whistle and Pig, where the landlord gave them Guinness by the bucketful. They were becoming a familiar sight wandering around the pavements, a wily mule and a seventeen-hand Hanoverian dressage horse. Sarah said we'd have to put them in strait-jackets before the week was out.

The whole structure of our lives seemed to be breaking down into chaotic bedlam. And all the time I was ticking off the days until Blake's departure. How could he turn his back on us like this?

The Gala Open Day was now only a week away. The paddock cum car-park was a mud bath and three of the craft stalls had pulled out at the last minute. The burger bar had also pulled out, going instead to a big three-day event in the next county. We were stuck with no refreshments apart from cream teas, and hundreds of people to enter-tain. It couldn't get much worse.

And then Angel started having problems. James said she wasn't providing enough milk for the foal. He was going to try a course of treatment but in the meantime there was only one option. We'd have to handfeed the foal.

He brought us a supply of dried mare's milk substitute and two bottles with teats. It was going to be a major job.

"She needs a feed every two hours, day and night." James was grim-faced. "It's going to be a heck of a task."

It was touch and go as to whether the hormonal injections James had given her would bring down her milk. James said if it didn't he would contact the "foaling bank", which was a system designed to locate a foster mum somewhere in the country, a mare who had recently lost her own foal and might adopt Angel's. We all hoped it wouldn't come to that but as each day went past it seemed more likely.

I was now beginning to understand why Angel looked so tired. After the first two nights of hand-feeding we were all walking round with huge dark bags under our eyes. The foal was loving every minute of it and I'd managed to talk Sarah into letting me do my bit. I was feeling a lot better although still really shaky and I'd lost half a stone in weight.

It was three o'clock on the third night when I crept downstairs to join Trevor in Angel's stable. We'd put her in the intensive care unit because it was twice the size of a normal stable and had special heated lights. It was also nearest to the house and Trevor had rigged up a sound system so we could hear the slightest noise. Mrs Mac had been terrified when Trevor first switched it on and she heard Angel munching at some hay – it sounded as if it was coming from directly behind the sofa.

The kitchen floor felt like the North Pole under my bare feet and I quickly pulled on my wellies and glided across the yard as quietly as I could. Boris, our old hunter, was snoring so loudly it was amazing he didn't bring down the rafters.

"Trevor, is that you?" I poked my head over the door, shivering from head to foot but glad to be doing my shift with Trevor and not Blake.

Angel was lying at the back of the stable resting, her heavy eyelids flicking open every now and then to watch us. She really was the most lovely pony with a sweet nature. When she arrived we'd spent hours brushing off the thick black peatish mud and had to literally pick it off her stomach but she hadn't minded one bit and had looked so incredibly grateful.

The foal swished her tail and started trying to eat Trevor's hair. I pulled an apple quarter out of my pocket and offered it to Angel.

"You know, Mel, you can talk to me, we're supposed to be friends." Trevor always had a way of getting right to the heart of what I was thinking. I couldn't hide anything from him.

"I just can't believe he'd go off to Ireland like

that," I blurted out. "After all we've done for him, after all we've been through."

Trevor quietly watched me, letting it all come out, letting me pour out all my thoughts and feelings. Just being a good listener, a best friend.

"I don't know what to say to him any more, Trevor, it's like there's a brick wall between us." I bent down and stroked the foal who was staring at me with huge brown eyes, sensing that something was wrong.

"He's a show-jumper, Mel. He wants to get to the top. He's got something to prove, to himself and to the world. If Ireland can give him the chance to do that, then he's got to take it. If he doesn't he might regret it for the rest of his life."

I knew Trevor was right but it didn't make it any easier.

"Good friends shouldn't desert each other, not by choice, not because something better has come along."

"I know, Mel, but sometimes when you really care about someone you have to learn to let go. That way they stand more chance of coming back to you."

We talked for ages about Hollywell, the horses, Angel and Binny. How much money we needed to raise, how much the Open Day would make. It was so quiet and peaceful it was like another world. I couldn't imagine being anywhere else.

Angel and the foal heard the noise first. They pricked up their ears and stood stock still, straining to see in the dim light. Angel whickered to the foal who anxiously ran behind her out of harm's way.

Trevor was looking straight at me, his fingers folding round the torch. "What was that?" he mouthed.

Goose pimples sprouted on my arms and I didn't know why.

"I was sure I heard footsteps." Trevor was slowly easing back the bolt on the stable door.

We quickly turned off the infra-red heat lamps and waited for a few minutes in the darkness, listening for the slightest noise. What if it was a burglar or a horse thief?

Nothing.

"Honestly, Mel, I heard footsteps, I would bet my life on it."

We switched on the torch and decided to go walkabout, clinging to each other for moral support.

"Maybe we ought to wake the others?" I hissed, shaking like a leaf.

Snowy blinked at us from his stable and Isabella snorted in her special pen. There was no sign of any disturbance. Even so, I had a feeling someone was out there, something wasn't quite right.

Suddenly a dustbin lid clattered from behind the house and a strange black cat shot off with its coat stuck on end.

Relief made me breathless.

"It must be that knock on the head." Trevor jokingly put the blame on me. "You've started hearing things."

The next morning dawned bright with thin rays of yellow sun attempting to dry out the sodden ground. For the first time in days I actually managed to laugh at one of Katie's jokes and sing along to the radio. Katie insisted that Angel found Radio One therapeutic.

Sarah came back from an early morning walk with a buttercup behind her ear and a pen still clutched in her hand. She'd got the worst attack of writer's block and nothing she did would give her the slightest inspiration, not even the banana and salad cream sandwiches which had worked a treat on her last book. James said it was because she'd got too much on her mind what with Danny, the Open Day, and all this business with Angel.

The previous night she'd worked herself up into a terrible stew over Mrs Barrat who was supposed to have rung her about Danny starting his new school. She hadn't done, and when Sarah had contacted her there was no answer.

"There's something wrong, Mel, I just know it."

I must admit, I was inclined to agree.

"Ross, Blake, you finish the morning feeds. Mel, you're coming with me!" Sarah flounced off towards the house, her red hair tumbling loose down her shoulders and her green eyes flashing, which always meant trouble.

Jigsaw was sprawled in the kitchen doorway, dreamily chewing on a bone, which nearly caused Sarah to go flying and made me stub my toe on a box of Hollywell mugs and teapots.

"Well, they've got to be here somewhere." Sarah had lost both her reading glasses and her address book, which was why she'd dragged me into the house after her. "Come on, Mel, you're the practical one, where would I put them?"

I rescued her address book from among the vegetable peelings and torn-up show schedules in the bin liner but there was no sign of her glasses.

"Now come on, let's get hold of Mrs Barrat and find out what's really going on."

I dialled the number for her and she nearly dragged the phone out of its socket pacing back and forth.

"I want to speak to Mrs Barrat now ... What

74

do you mean she's not there?" Sarah's temper was hitting boiling point. "Why the hell didn't you tell me this sooner?"

Jigsaw suddenly looked worried and started burying his bone in the laundry basket.

"So where is he now?" Sarah sounded murderous.

I crept out and half closed the door behind me, then picked up a screwed-up letter I'd found among the rubbish. The address at the top read: Salthurst Stud, County Clare, Ireland. "Dear Blake . . ."

I couldn't drag my eyes away.

"He's missing!" Sarah blasted through the door minutes later. "He's run away. Danny's gone!" Her whole body was trembling with shock.

"What do you mean? Where? How?" I couldn't believe it.

Apparently Sarah had been talking to Mr Barrat who couldn't take the strain any more. Danny had run away on the first night. Mrs Barrat had refused to tell anyone, especially Sarah. She figured Danny had tried to make his way back to Hollywell but he didn't have any money and she thought he'd soon give up and come back with his tail between his legs. But that had been nearly a week ago.

"Can you believe it?" Sarah screeched. "A nine-year-old boy sleeping rough and she hasn't even contacted the police. What kind of woman is she?"

My head was still reeling with shock. It brought back memories of when we'd first met Danny, how he'd been looking after himself because his mother was staying with her boyfriend. We should never have let her take him.

"Mel, there's a little boy out there completely defenceless. Anything could have happened." Sarah crashed into a chair and buried her head in her hands. "It's all my fault, I should never have agreed . . ."

"Danny's tough," I said. "He's used to fending for himself, if anyone can survive he can." I tried not to let her hear the icy fear in my voice.

"Sarah!" Blake bounded into the kitchen, breathless and as white as a sheet. I'd never seen him so shaken. His hands were trembling.

"What is it? What's happened?"

He leaned against the doorframe gasping for breath. "Quick, it's serious!"

All thoughts of Danny shot out of my head. I'd never seen Blake like this before – he looked as if he'd seen a ghost. Sarah was at the door before I'd even pulled on my boots.

"Blake, wait!"

We dashed out into the stable yard not knowing what to expect. The outside tap was running over and the yard brush was just slung down on the concrete; everywhere looked deserted. It was obvious something terrible must have happened, it could only be one of the horses . . .

"Blake!"

He ran on ahead towards Queenie's old stable where Ross was standing at the door frantically waving for us to be quiet.

That was it, then, the stallion must have died in the night or escaped. It was so quiet you could hear a pin drop, no kicking or wild neighing or marching round and round. I hated myself for suddenly feeling glad it was the stallion and not Queenie, or Snowy or Boris or Jakey – one of the old favourites.

"Ssssh, don't say a word." Ross put a hand on Sarah's shoulder. "One wrong move and it could set off a timebomb."

Blake dragged back the bolt on the stable door and it grated open a few inches at a time. Sunlight flooded in. I could hardly bring myself to look.

I imagined seeing the stallion laid out in the straw or maybe having a fit or a bout of colic but it wasn't anything like that. For the first time in my life I was completely stuck for words.

"I couldn't believe it either," Blake whispered behind me.

Sarah breathed in sharply and her hand flew up to her mouth.

"Trevor wasn't imagining footsteps after all," I murmured.

The bundle of horse rugs fell back to reveal our mystery intruder.

"Danny!" Sarah gasped.

There was no mistaking that tousled brown hair. It was Danny. He'd come back home.

"Well, you could have used the front door like ordinary people instead of frightening the life out of me and Mel." Trevor poked his head round the stable door, loaded up with crisps and chocolate from the village shop. "Gee, Mrs F., he looks awful!"

Danny grinned at us from inside three horse rugs, straw stuck to his hair and streaks of grime down both cheeks. He looked washed out and exhausted, but at least he was alive and in one piece. He also seemed to have made a new friend.

The stallion was standing over Danny, relaxed and happy, nodding his head up and down, every so often nuzzling Danny's neck. He was being so gentle, so inquisitive, his eyes full of tenderness and concern. He was a completely different horse.

"It's a miracle," said Sarah. "Is that the same horse? You know, the one that tried to crush James to death?"

"And charged at Mel." Blake gave me a warm look.

It *was* pretty amazing.

"Where did he come from?" Danny threw his arms round the charcoal-black neck and nearly gave us all palpitations.

"Danny, be careful, you don't know anything about him. He's not all he appears."

"Danny!" Katie pushed past Ross, immediately dropping a box of eggs and a loaf of bread on the brick floor. She screeched so loud I honestly thought the window was going to cave in. "You're back!"

"Here." Sarah shovelled heaps of glucose into a mug of tea and passed it to Danny. "Get that down you, it's good for shock."

"But I'm not in shock." Danny was hugging little Oscar to death.

"A proper breakfast, that's what you need. Now where are those eggs?"

"Where is he?" James rushed in and went sprawling over Jigsaw's bone. "I got here as soon as I could."

"He spent the night with the stallion." Sarah flicked margarine everywhere as she waved the knife around like a baton.

"Now then, my little shrimp, how are you?" James put his hand on Danny's head.

Danny rolled his eyes at Sarah, who was fussing like a mother goose and busily putting the teapot inside the microwave. James chuckled and pulled her back by the hair, plonking the teapot on the table and taking her in his arms. It was only then that I noticed her T-shirt was on inside out and back to front and her pump laces were both undone.

"Oh James, what are we going to do?"

Danny's eyes grew to the size of tractor wheels as we told him about Angel, the foal and Blackie.

"But he's so gentle," he said.

Mrs Mac arrived carrying a bundle of Hollywell sweatshirts and dropped the whole lot as soon as she saw Danny. "Good heavens, he's as thin as a blade," she said, slapping a pudgy hand on his forehead.

"It seems to me," James said, after listening to the whole story, "that that mad cracker of a horse has finally found a friend." It was really weird how the stallion had taken to Danny.

"Maybe," Katie said, stuffing her mouth with bread and strawberry jam, "it was because Danny went in there thinking it was Queenie and he didn't have any nerves."

"Possibly," Blake joined in. "Horses can smell fear a mile off."

I avoided his eyes and dug the dirt out of my finger-nails. "Should somebody contact Danny's mother?" I blurted out.

I might as well have dropped a bombshell if Danny's face was anything to go by.

"I'm not going back," he quivered. "I'm not, I'm not, not ever!" He bolted upstairs and slammed his bedroom door.

"I'd better take these up." Katie fetched a bag full to bursting from the pantry. It contained all the odds and ends that reminded her of Danny. "I didn't think he was ever coming back."

Chapter Eight

The rest of the day zoomed by. Danny helped bottle-feed the foal, who insisted on sniffing his hair and all his clothes. Danny said she was gorgeous and what were we going to call her. We couldn't keep saying "the foal".

"I think it's rather up to Binny," I said. "After all, they will be going back to her place when they're both strong enough."

Katie's face blackened and I knew she'd been harbouring hopes of them staying at Hollywell. She'd been spouting on about how to train foals and Sarah had caught her reading a youngstock handbook under the duvet at one o'clock in the morning.

"There's no way an old lady can look after her," she snapped. "It's not fair."

The Open Day was looming and there was still a mountain of things to do. I took my antibiotic tablet, put on an extra sweatshirt and threw myself into organizing the photograph displays – it helped take my mind off Blake and how ill I was starting to feel. I was just sorting through some before-and-after pictures of Jakey, an old piebald cob we had rescued, when James came into the office looking exhausted. He'd just been examining Blackie and giving him a tetanus and multi-vitamin injection.

"I don't know what's happened to that horse," he said, "but it's a transformation."

We'd had a Hollywell meeting earlier and all agreed that as soon as Blackie was strong enough he'd have to be gelded. We couldn't cope with a stallion, not with all the mares that were at the sanctuary. Sarah had phoned the blacksmith to have his feet trimmed and James was going to treat him for lice. In the meantime Danny was practically living in his stable.

"Mel, I really think we need to talk." Blake came in, still in his jodhpurs and riding boots, his hair glistening with sweat. "We can't go on like this."

I thumped some Blu-Tac on the display stand and marched off to Angel's stable. I knew if we started talking I'd lose my temper and I didn't want to say anything I'd regret.

Katie was leading the foal round in the head-collar slip Binny had bought, and was about to give her a feed. She tried to convince me that her mane had grown at least two centimetres, but I wasn't really listening. I was too busy thinking about the crumpled letter in my pocket and all the things Blake hadn't told me.

Ross came out of the house looking ponderous, with Jigsaw diving around his ankles. "Mrs Barrat's on the phone," he whispered. "Something's up, I just know it. Sarah's doodling like mad on the telephone pad."

At least while Mrs Barrat was on the phone we weren't being plagued by reporters. News had got out about the capture of the Black Beast and it was causing a sensation right through the country. Some people were still insisting it was a big cat or a llama and we'd even had sightseers gathering at the bottom of the drive in the hope of seeing something.

Sarah appeared looking exhausted, and cursed when she saw that James's car had gone. "Blast, just when I really needed to speak to him."

"You've missed him by seconds," I said. "He's gone back to the surgery."

We all tried to find out what Mrs Barrat had said but for some reason Sarah was being unusually mysterious. "I've got to speak to James first," she said. "It's something very important." She dived into her car and shot out of the drive.

Danny was sitting on an upturned bucket in Blackie's stable, telling him his life story and sharing a cup of tea. I listened outside the door for a few minutes and then sloped off with a lump in my throat. For a nine-year-old boy he'd been through too much. But then so had the stallion. Sarah was intent on giving Danny a lecture on running away, as soon as he was back to his normal self. It was a really stupid and dangerous thing to do, and running away from your problems never solves anything, it usually just makes everything a hundred times worse.

"Hey, look at this." Trevor nudged my arm and we turned to where Danny was leading the stallion into the main yard. Both of them were moving really slowly and hesitantly, finding their feet. Danny only came up to the stallion's shoulder. He'd looped a piece of baling string through the headcollar and was clinging on with both hands, looking at Blackie. I don't think Blackie planned on going anywhere – he was glued to Danny's side.

Jigsaw barked and waved his paw and Snowy dropped the mouthful of hay he was eating. Even Isabella stopped rooting, and stood and stared with her beady eyes.

But it was Angel that Blackie was really interested in. As soon as he heard her whinny he dashed over to the stable, plunging his head over the top and burying his nose in her cream mane. He sniffed her all over, from the tips of her ears to the tip of her nose, and then it was the foal's turn.

She was scrabbling up the door determined not to be left out. They were the perfect family unit and it was so obvious that Angel and Blackie were in love.

"Isn't it great?" Danny grinned, patting the thick black neck.

"It's straight out of a Barbara Cartland novel." Mrs Mac had appeared from the office with tears running down her cheeks. "I wish Sarah was here to see this."

"I honestly thought he'd have to be put down." Ross stopped Jigsaw from getting too close.

"He's a real looker." Blake took in the fine Arab lines and beautiful chest and hindquarters.

We could see his beauty now he was out in daylight. All the other mares seemed to be thinking the same thing because I'd never seen so many heads pop up over the stable doors. They were queuing up at the field gate. Snowy was glaring at Blackie as if a Hollywood film star had just walked into the yard.

"He's only got eyes for Angel." Katie looked really dreamy.

I ran and fetched a Jammy Dodger from the tack room and broke it in half for Angel and Blackie.

"Isn't he just the best horse you've ever seen?" Danny was patting Blackie's shoulder and pulling burrs out of his long tangled mane. "He's going to stay here for ever and ever. He's never going to be ill-treated again."

Sarah came back an hour later saying that she hadn't managed to track down James. He was out at a racing stables and he wasn't answering his phone.

"So what's the big mystery?" Ross couldn't wait any longer. "We've never kept secrets before, you can't tell us that nothing's happened."

Sarah put some frozen pizzas in the oven for lunch and turned round to face us.

"OK, I get your point. I'll tell you what I know, which isn't much."

"And Danny as well." Ross put his hand on top of Danny's head. "He's part of the family, too."

We all sat down with cheese and pineapple pizza and Sarah started to open up.

"It's not just your mother, Danny, there's something else."

Apparently a Mr Parker had been in touch with Sarah early that morning. Blackie's story had leaked to all the national papers and a couple of them had been prompting people to come forward with any information about the Black Beast. Mr Parker hadn't minced his words. He'd got our number from the RSPCA and he had a very serious claim. He insisted that a year ago his black horse was stolen from its field near a main road. He was

87

saying that Blackie was his and he wanted him back.

"Of course he's got to prove it first." Sarah was trying not to sound worried, but it was hopeless. Her knife and fork clattered against her plate. "I'll have to be honest though." She pushed the pizza away. "It doesn't look good."

If Mr Parker could prove that Blackie was his horse and he had the right facilities to keep him then there was nothing we could do. We'd have to let him go.

"He knows his age and size," Sarah said. "And I checked with the chief constable – there was a horse reported missing at his address a year ago."

"Oh great, that says it all, doesn't it?" Ross screwed up the kitchen roll in frustration.

"There was one other thing though," Sarah said. "His horse has a scar on his neck underneath his mane – something to do with a road accident."

"So does Blackie." Danny's voice was on the verge of desperation. "I saw it this morning."

"Do you really think Mr Parker will take Blackie away?" Katie had followed me into one of the fields where I was frantically pulling up some ragwort. It seemed almost symbolic that if I could rid the fields of every trace of poisonous plants it

88

might somehow clear all the bad stuff from our lives. And Heaven knows, there was enough of it.

Mrs Barrat was due to arrive tomorrow morning. Apparently she had something very important to discuss with Danny, but Sarah refused to tell us any more. She said she had to talk to James first.

Danny was trying very hard to put on a brave face. He insisted on dousing Blackie with the lice powder all by himself even though he ended up more de-loused than Blackie. Trevor said at least nobody could accuse him of having nits and Sarah sent him straight upstairs to have a bath. I never realized that you could actually see the lice moving around in the coat and it was no wonder that poor Blackie was scratching himself silly.

Poor Danny. Two blows in as many minutes and he was walking around as if someone had hit him with a sledgehammer.

"It'll break his heart if Blackie goes." Katie had never sounded more serious.

"I know," I said. "But what can we do?"

They say trouble always comes in threes but none of us was prepared for what happened next. In hindsight we should have known – it was so obvious.

*

That evening we decided to make the most of the dry weather and have a barbecue. Ross kindly told me I looked like something the cat had dragged in, and Blake went off to see Mr Sullivan about his sponsorship deal and no doubt to inform him that his new address would be in Ireland.

We organized the night rota for feeding the foal. Katie and Danny were to do the two o'clock shift and Trevor and I the four o'clock. Sarah said it was good to give Danny some extra responsibility and it would take his mind off Blackie. If they had any trouble they were to wake me at once. As my bedroom was nearest the stables I was sure to hear them anyway.

I threw some chicken legs on the barbecue and took another antibiotic tablet. Binny had arrived and was fussing Angel to death and rearranging her straw bed and her hay net. Sarah was wandering around with a bottle of barbecue sauce and the synopsis for her next book.

"Mel, what on earth's the matter? You look awful!" Sarah said.

I didn't remember much after that. I was completely knocked out, and I hit the pillow like a ton of bricks.

*

"Mel, Mel, wake up!" It was gone four o'clock when Trevor shook my shoulders until my teeth rattled.

"What is it? Leave me alone. I want to sleep."

"Melanie!" There was something in Trevor's voice which suddenly made me sit bolt upright and force my eyes open.

"It's Danny. And Katie. They've gone. They've taken Blackie!"

Chapter Nine

"But they can't have run away. They're not that stupid."

Blackie's stable door was swinging open. Empty.

"Maybe they've just taken him for a walk. It's more than possible."

"Look at this." Ross picked up a pink envelope from inside the manger and ripped it open.

Inside was a note in Katie's handwriting: "We didn't have a choice. Don't try to find us. We'll be in touch."

"It's all my fault." Sarah broke down in tears. "I should have told him. If only I'd said something this would never have happened."

We regrouped in the kitchen feeling completely shell-shocked. This was the last thing any of us had expected.

Sarah started to explain how Mrs Barrat wanted her and James to take Danny on full-time, to foster him.

"I didn't want to say anything until I'd spoken to James. I didn't want to build up Danny's hopes."

"And now it's too late." Ross clenched his fists.

"Listen, guys, they can't have got that far." Blake stood up, pushing back his dark hair, trying to think logically. "Surely somebody's seen two kids and a black stallion, they're hardly inconspicuous, and they've only been gone a couple of hours."

We dived into the car, not even aware that it was only 5 o'clock in the morning. All our thoughts were on finding Danny and Katie. Trevor stayed behind at Hollywell in case they came back.

"And Blackie. When all's said and done," Sarah said, "he's still a wild horse, he could turn at any time."

The village High Street was completely deserted, not a person in sight.

"It's my guess they'll have headed for the bridle-paths." Blake was scanning all around him. "Danny wouldn't have wanted to take Blackie on the roads. Not once the traffic starts to build up."

"They could be anywhere," I said, feeling helpless.

"We've got to think positive." Ross squeezed my hand. "It's going to be all right."

"Knowing Danny, he won't change his mind," I said. "He's got nothing to lose."

The early morning mist was starting to lift and

a clear blue sky shone through. It was going to be hot.

We checked out two of the local bridlepaths and farm tracks where we went riding, but there was nothing, not even a fresh hoofprint.

"Mel, are you sure they didn't say anything to you, any clue, anything that might give us an inkling?" Sarah slipped the car into fourth gear and we headed for the next village.

"I can't think," I almost shrieked. "I've gone blank."

"Here, stop! There's a milk float!" Ross dived out of the car and held up a milkman coming out of someone's front gate.

"Have you seen a young boy and girl and a black horse?"

It was hopeless. Nobody had seen anything. We stopped three people leaving early for work and one woman walking her dog. They all looked vague and shook their heads. A paperboy thought he'd seen someone riding a black horse but it turned out to be a riding instructor from the local livery stables. She hadn't seen anything either.

"It's a wild goose chase." Blake got back in the car and yanked the seatbelt across his front. "I can't believe nobody's seen them."

We scoured the next four villages, all the back lanes and tracks for miles around. Not a glimpse.

"I think we ought to go back home." Blake was the first to say what we were all thinking.

"Maybe they've come back." Ross sounded hopeful.

Our spirits were low as we made our way home, and it was already half past seven by the time we reached Hollywell.

"The phone's not rung once." Trevor was in the kitchen with Jigsaw, trying to stay calm.

"There's only one thing for it." Sarah collapsed in the armchair looking exhausted. "We'll have to contact the police."

"We'll do everything we can." The police officer stood in our kitchen taking down all the details including Katie's note. "I'll put out an alert. We'll pick them up in no time. The best thing is not to worry."

Sarah looked more drained than I'd ever seen her. "They're only kids, officer, they don't know what they're doing."

I thought back to what Danny had told me about his trip up from Brighton. How he'd thumbed lifts from lorry drivers and devoured half-eaten burgers from waste bins outside transport cafés. It was no way for a child to live.

"Katie's never done anything like this before." Sarah told the officer.

"Danny will look after her," I said. "She's his best friend. She wanted to stick by him."

"Don't worry, love, we'll find them."

Despite the crisis, life had to go on. Trevor and I went out to feed the horses and the foal. Sarah rang round all of Katie's friends to see if they knew anything. Blake and Ross went out for another search.

"I feel so useless," I said, picking bits of straw out of Angel's mane while Trevor finished feeding the foal. "I should have known something like this would happen."

"Eh, come on, now don't be so daft," Trevor said. "You can't go blaming yourself. It's nobody's fault. We've just got to cope. That's what life's about – coping."

He gave me a massive hug, which felt like being squeezed by a grizzly bear and I instantly felt better. "You now, sometimes, Trevor, I don't know how I managed without you."

By eleven o'clock there was still no news and we hadn't heard from Blake or Ross. Sarah was listless with anxiety and Jigsaw kept moping around with his tail between his legs. Trevor and I finished off Angel's packet of Jammy Dodgers which had gone soggy and made some coffee which was too strong.

"It's Binny." Sarah looked through the window. "I wonder what she's doing here?"

"It's no good, Sarah, I'm just not happy with the situation." Binny marched into the kitchen very much like the first time we'd met her. She was bristling with anger and took us all off guard.

"Angel's my baby. It should be me who's looking after her. But since she's been here, you lot have just taken over. It's as if I don't exist." Binny stood, trembling, wringing her hands together. Everything had been bottled up and now suddenly, came pouring out.

We all just stood and gaped. I knew Binny was really fussy about how we were looking after Angel, but we were the ones who were sitting up night after night feeding the foal until we couldn't think straight with exhaustion. It was Hollywell that up to now had paid for all Angel's treatment and the foal milk.

Sarah was livid. She slung down the tea towel and looked Binny straight in the eye. "How dare you march into my house and talk to us like that? Angel might be the only thing on your mind but we've got two children missing. At the moment we don't know where they are, what's happened, they've been out all night . . ." Sarah's voice caught in her throat with emotion. She turned away and stared out of the window, her whole body shaking.

"I'm so sorry, I didn't realize, I had no idea." Binny gave a little sob and stumbled for the door. Trevor went out after her, keen to check that she was all right.

I went across to put my arms round Sarah. She hadn't meant what she'd said, she was just so upset.

"Oh, Mel, I should never have told Danny about Mr Parker. What kind of mother am I?"

"The best," I said, hugging her as hard as I could. "Without you there wouldn't be a Holly-well, we wouldn't be a family, Danny would still be with that awful woman. It's going to be all right, I know it is."

Trevor came back in, followed by two officers in uniform. "It's the police," he said. "They want to ask more questions."

Mrs Barrat arrived in the afternoon with her husband, but surprisingly they took the whole ordeal in their stride. I quickly worked out that Mrs Barrat was keen to keep on Sarah's good side. They both wanted Sarah to have Danny while they moved to Scotland. Mr Barrat had been offered a promotion with a new executive car. There would be loads of functions, travelling abroad. Danny wouldn't fit in.

It sounded to me as if the novelty of having Danny had quickly worn off. Mr Barrat just seemed eager to get rid of the whole problem. He didn't seem to be quite the wimp I first thought.

"Now Sarah, you sit down, dear, and I'll make you a cup of tea." Mrs Barrat was trying so hard to be nice it was almost funny. She didn't know what to make of the pots piled in the sink or Oscar's half-eaten food or the foal's bottles sitting next to the dirty mugs ready for washing. "It's so nice to be in the country." She gritted her teeth.

She wasn't a bit worried about Danny and Katie. "They'll turn up when they're hungry."

Ross and Blake came back looking defeated and Sarah was a lot better since James had managed to call round in the afternoon. He'd been a hundred miles away vetting some pigs and he didn't have a clue what was going on.

The only phone call we had all day was from Mrs Mac to say that Rocky had been located and he'd just arrived in London. He'd be at Hollywell to officially open the Gala Day.

At the moment, that seemed a million miles away. But James and Sarah said we couldn't cancel; too many arrangements had been made. The show must go on.

It seemed incredible that two children and a horse could completely disappear like this. The whole of the local police force was out looking for them and still hadn't found a thing.

In the end I decided to go for a walk outside. The Barrats were driving me mad and Sarah had decided to start spring cleaning even though it was July.

It was a cool moist evening and I went right round all the stables and then switched the light on in the tack room and sat down.

"Is the Wicked Witch of the West getting too much for you?" Blake poked his head round the door and grinned at me.

I looked down and felt like bursting into tears.

"Here, I think you dropped something." Blake put the crumpled letter from Ireland in my lap and stood back and watched me.

My eyes were welling up. "You could have told me," I said. "I deserved to know the full story."

"Well, you hardly gave me much of a chance, did you?" Blake came and sat down beside me. I could smell his aftershave.

"That's the trouble with you, Blake, you're always so distant and mysterious. How can we be close when sometimes I don't think I even know you?"

He didn't say anything. He just stared ahead.

100

I opened out the letter and reread the scrawly handwriting. It was from a woman called Tina who had helped Blake enormously when he first started out as a show-jumper. He owed her a lot. She was writing to tell him that she had broken her back in a riding accident. The bank was threatening to close her down, and she had twenty horses and nobody to show-jump them. She really needed Blake to help her out.

"You will write, won't you?" I was having to bite on my lower lip to keep back the tears.

"Oh, Mel." Blake grabbed hold of me and I buried my head in his neck, feeling the warmth of his skin. I felt better than I had done in days. I didn't want him ever to let me go.

"Anyway, there's something I haven't told you." He gently kissed my forehead and held me closer. "I'm not—"

The door blasted open. Trevor loomed in the doorway, urgency written all over his face.

"They've found them!" he yelled. "They're both safe, but they've lost the stallion!"

Chapter Ten

"It's all right, Danny, you're not in trouble, nobody's going to shout at you."

Danny and Katie clambered out of the police car looking scared and bewildered. I never thought I'd be so pleased to see my little sister. "I thought you were a goner." I ruffled the top of her hair.

"You've got to find Blackie." Danny could think of nothing else. "He's all by himself, anything could happen."

Gradually, over Mrs Mac's apple crumble and extra thick chocolate cake, the whole story came out.

A policewoman took down notes in her black book and gently urged Danny for more details. There was a policeman with her who'd been driving the car and he stood and listened. Mr and Mrs Barrat had gone into the sitting-room out of the way because Danny had freaked out as soon as he saw them. If the policeman hadn't been standing near the door I think he would have bolted.

"So we hid out in the wood behind our old house." Danny carried on his story. "And then Blackie got restless, he wouldn't stand still."

"So we decided to head for the road and keep to the grass verge," Katie took over. "We were going to go to Birmingham and join the circus. It was my idea, I thought we'd be safe there."

"Katie, how could you be so irresponsible?" Sarah was pacing up and down, about to erupt, but the policewoman urged her to be quiet.

"So what happened next, Danny?"

They'd been picked up by a patrol car outside a telephone box. They'd been trying to ring Hollywell but the phone was out of order. Thank God the police car came along when it did.

"We were going along the road," Danny said, "when this car slowed down and these lads started shouting and jeering. They said they wanted a ride on Blackie and then they . . ."

"They got out of the car and tried to take Blackie," mumbled Katie. "Two of them got hold of his neck and one of them pushed Danny to the ground. He's got a big bruise on his back to prove it."

"Blackie went berserk," Danny murmured. "He charged at them until they were terrified and then ran off. We thought he'd come back but he didn't.

103

He just disappeared. That's when we decided to ring home."

"And this was how long ago?" The police-woman jotted down more notes.

"You've got to save him, Mrs F., he's scared, he could do anything."

"It's all right, sonny," the policeman said, "we'll do our best. He's bound to turn up somewhere, they always do." Right on cue his bleeper went off and he spoke into the special mobile radio. I could actually see his face turn a pale shade of grey.

"I think we've located him," he said in a grave voice. "There's a horse loose on the motorway galloping down the central divide. He's black and apparently completely wild."

"That's him!" Danny leapt up. "That's Blackie!"

"There's something I've not told the young lad," the policeman whispered to Sarah outside and I could just hear their conversation. "The horse has gone stark raving bonkers. He's jumped two cars and already caused a pile-up. They've called in a vet. He might have to be . . ."

"No, not that, not if we can get to him first." Sarah was shaking with emotion.

Blake was already unlocking the car.

"Come on, gang." Sarah dragged open the door. "We've got a horse to catch!"

The police siren wailed out ahead of us and

I clung to the seat as Sarah pumped at the accelerator.

"Dip the lights." Blake reached over and fiddled with the switch but it was stuck on full beam. Cars were tooting like mad at us but we hardly noticed.

"I know a short cut." Sarah swung round a corner practically on two wheels and we roared down a narrow lane.

"Sarah, I don't know whether this was a good idea."

"Of course it is." She crashed the gears. "I know what I'm doing."

We'd lost all sight of the police car and I had no idea how far we were from the motorway.

"Turn right here." Ross banged on the indicator and we went hurtling along what looked like a disused airfield.

"I should have brought my flying hat," Ross joked but none of us were in the mood for laughter. Somewhere Blackie was running wild and we had to save him.

"He won't trust anyone," Danny said, "he'll just keep running."

We flew over a concrete mound and Ross said he thought we'd lost the exhaust. We didn't have to look, we could hear, it sounded as if the whole rear end of the car had collapsed.

"Just keep going," Blake said.

We came out at a criss-cross of junctions and Sarah didn't hesitate for a second.

"I hope she knows what she's doing," Katie whispered, clinging on to my arm. I could feel my watch strap pressing into my flesh under her fingers. Time was short, and each passing minute could mean the end.

Ross wound down the window to listen to the exhaust, or lack of it, and a sharp blast of air blew Sarah's hair right across her face.

"Good one, Ross, what are you trying to do, kill us all?"

We charged on at full pelt.

"There it is!" Sarah eventually yelled. "The motorway!"

We screeched to a halt on top of a flyover to get our bearings. We knew we were in the right place because a crowd of people had got out of their cars and were craning to see what was going on.

"Make way, make way." Ross pushed past them all. "We're from the police, Special Branch."

What we saw brought us all up short. There was Blackie, a dark speck, heading towards us, darting from one lane of traffic to another, sliding, careering all over, squeezing past on the hard shoulder, completely demented.

"He's flipped his lid," Danny said in a small voice. "We'll never catch him now."

All the traffic in both directions had slithered to a halt and men were getting out and waving their arms.

"Never say never," Sarah muttered.

"We've got to do something." Ross stood and stared.

It was no good us going down on to the motorway. There was so much traffic we'd never get near him.

"Oh no." Blake drew in his breath. "They've brought in the army."

A helicopter suddenly appeared, hovering towards us, a man leaning out with what looked like a rifle. Some people on the flyover started cheering and one woman said Blackie had demolished three cars and caused a tailback for ten miles.

"For goodness' sake, have a heart," Sarah snapped. "Can't you see the poor horse is terrified?"

The helicopter was trying to shunt Blackie off the fast lane on to the slip road where we could just see a barricade and police officers.

Blackie saw them too. His mane and tail flew up in the breeze from the propellers and he darted and swivelled round, his hind legs at one instant dipping right underneath him.

"He's going up the bank," Danny screamed. "He'll never make it, it's too steep!"

He was scrabbling up the bank in sheer terror,

his whole body lunging forward in a series of cat leaps.

"If he falls he'll break his neck."

"It's just like on television, isn't it, dear?" One woman turned to an older one. It was probably more excitement than she'd had in the last twenty years.

"Way to go, Blackie!" Danny was pumping the air with his fist.

"He's done it, look, he's reached the top!"

"Run, Blackie, run!" Danny's eyes were filled with tears.

"Come on," Sarah yelled. "We've got to get to him first!"

We belted across a roundabout, not even bothering to check for oncoming traffic. Everything was pandemonium, with police cars going in all directions.

"He's gone that way!" A man walking his dog was pointing like mad.

"Poor Blackie, he must feel like a hunted animal," I said, almost sick with pity.

"Come on, Blackie, where are you?" Sarah drove down a dual carriageway leading into the town centre. Two police cars overtook us, burning rubber.

"There's Trevor, in the back of that last car," said Ross.

We set off in pursuit.

"Sarah, I hate to say this but you've just gone through a red light."

"Not now, Blake, I'm concentrating."

Trees and telegraph poles were whipping past in a blur.

"Turn right, they've all gone right," Ross yanked the indicator so hard it dropped off.

We were heading into a built-up estate. Anything could happen now: Blackie could knock somebody down. What if he ran into a child?

People were racing out to their gates, lights were going on right down the streets. Two police cars had loudspeakers and were telling everybody to stay inside, there was a wild horse running loose and potentially lethal: "Under no circumstances step into the road."

All the activity was coming from a road signposted as a dead end.

"Oh no," Ross groaned, "they've got him cornered."

We turned down the road not knowing what to expect. The first thing we saw was Trevor arguing with a police officer. And then we spotted Blackie, drenched through with sweat, trembling uncontrollably, cornered in someone's front garden, snapping his teeth and snaking his neck at anybody who dared go near.

The police officer nearest Trevor loaded a rifle.

"No!" Sarah yelled, bursting out of the car, the engine still running.

"I can catch him," Danny pleaded with the police officers. "I know I can, just give me five minutes. He's my friend."

Danny edged towards the stallion, all the time talking and holding out his hand.

"If anything happens to that young lad . . ." One of the officers looked terrified.

"It won't, he knows what he's doing." Sarah didn't take her eyes off Danny's back.

"You shouldn't have run away," Danny gabbled on to the stallion, "you've brought this all on yourself. I know those lads scared you and then all those cars, but you can't keep running away. I've learnt that. It doesn't solve anything. It doesn't make things better."

The stallion snorted and pawed the ground. He was listening, he'd recognized Danny and that was a start.

"You can have a good life at Hollywell," Danny said. "I didn't mean it when I told you about Mr Parker, that's all sorted now," Danny lied. "He's not going to take you away."

A huge great lump caught in my throat. Of course the stallion didn't know what Danny was saying. He was responding to the tone of his voice, like all horses do.

"I'll just stroke your neck like that and we can be friends again." Danny reached up to the huge black crest. "It's all right, nobody's going to hurt you, I'm just going to slip on this headcollar, like we did in the stable."

The stallion lolled his head, utterly defeated, trusting Danny to look after him.

"What a hero," a police officer whispered to Sarah. "He must have nerves of steel."

"No," Sarah said, swallowing back the tears, "he knows what it's like to be totally alone with nobody on your side. It's not very nice."

The stallion edged forward across to Trevor and the rest of us, sore-footed from all that galloping and still trembling, but not quite as much.

"You poor old soul." I reached up my hand to his flared nostrils and Sarah fetched a rug from the boot of the car and laid it over his back to stop him getting cold.

"I think," Sarah said, putting an arm round my shoulders, "this is when we fetch the horsebox, don't you?"

"Hip, hip – hooray!" Sarah and James raised their glasses.

"Hip, hip," Katie shouted.

"Hooray!" we all yelled.

We were all sitting in the kitchen toasting Danny and demolishing the remains of a congratulations cake. Jigsaw was under the table crunching on some icing and Danny was trying to pick a model of a horse off the top of the cake but it was stuck in the jam.

"I can't believe it," Katie said for the hundredth time. "It's the best happy ending we've ever had."

"It's purrfect," Ross drawled, stroking Oscar who was flicking a pickled onion across the tablecloth.

It really was the perfect ending to a traumatic week. It was seven o'clock the night after we'd rescued Blackie and since that moment it had been like a whirlwind. Blackie and Danny had been on television and in the local paper. Luckily nobody had been injured on the motorway and there was just the headache of sorting out the insurance. Mr and Mrs Barrat had set off for Scotland, and Danny was still trying to take in the news that he could stay at Hollywell. James and Sarah were even talking about adopting him.

"It's just the best." Katie gobbled a sausage on a stick. We hadn't heard any more from Mr Parker so we presumed he'd changed his mind or it had all been a hoax in the first place.

"Here's to Blackie and Danny," said James.

"And the Open Day!" Danny added and we all groaned out loud.

In precisely sixteen hours we'd be welcoming the first flood of Hollywell fans through the gates. My stomach was curling up at the thought of it. And we still had half a dozen horses to wash tomorrow morning. We'd been flat out all day making the final arrangements.

We'd just got the caravan and loudspeaker set up when Rocky telephoned to say he'd be there to cut the red ribbon, wild horses wouldn't keep him away.

"He's obviously not heard about Blackie," Ross joked.

Everything was ready and just waiting for the morning. The only fly in the ointment was the lack of burger bar, but I guess we couldn't have everything. If it all went to plan we could make enough for next winter's hay bill and more besides.

"I wonder how many people will turn up?" said Katie.

"Thousands," Danny munched and we all laughed out loud.

"Who's this?" Blake fiddled with the curtain and suddenly became unusually quiet. "It looks like we've got company."

The blue pick-up truck pulled into the yard and

we all piled outside. We didn't suspect anything out of the ordinary; I thought it was someone wanting to leave a horse with us. Since Hollywell Stables had become famous we'd received calls every week about ponies needing good homes and in the main we managed to foster them out to loving families.

"I want to see the guv'nor." A man with slate-grey hair and big dealer boots with steel caps stood in the yard looking round as if he owned the place. There was a girl with him but she stayed in the truck, almost slithering down the seat so we didn't spot her. Then again, that was quite normal – people often got embarrassed when they came to ask for a home for their horse, especially if they didn't have any money, which was usually the reason they were turning to us.

But I didn't like this man – there was something unsettling about him. They say first impressions are usually the right ones and from the moment he turned and faced me I felt myself cringe with unease.

"Yes, I'm the guv'nor, as you call it." Sarah bristled with distaste.

"Good." The man quickly rubbed a hand on his trouser leg and held it out to Sarah. "The name's Parker," he said, "Dave Parker. I've come for my horse."

We all looked devastated. We should have known, suspected at least, but as it was, it hit us like a bolt out of the blue. Trevor scratched his head looking gormless and Ross nearly choked on a sausage roll.

"Oh," Sarah said, "I see."

"So come on, where is he, then? Look sharp."

He was horrible. He was probably the worst person we could ever have chosen to take Blackie. He wouldn't know a sensitive thought if it jumped up and bit him on the nose.

"What are we going to do?" I whispered to Blake as Mr Parker blundered off to look in the nearest stable. Sarah was frantic. Ross had his jaw set and Blake had a nervous twitch in his cheek.

"Do something," I hissed, not having a clue what to suggest.

Thanks heavens Danny and Katie were in the house. James came out sizing up the situation and immediately taking charge. "There's no way that horse is to be moved for a few days. He's had too big a shock."

"That's right," Sarah said, "he's not going anywhere."

"Aye, but you can let me have a look at him. Check that he's the right horse. That's not so much to ask."

Sarah pursed her lips, which always meant she

was unsure, and then finally agreed to lead him round to Blackie's stable. With any luck he might have got it wrong.

"Yeah, and pigs might fly," Ross whispered behind me.

"He's always been a wild one, you know, I always said he was soft in the head." Mr Parker marched along at Sarah's side rubbing his hands together and gawping at everything with his tight piggy eyes.

"He smells more fishy than a fish and chip shop." Blake bent closer. "He's a conman, Mel, I would bet my life on it."

"Yeah, so how does he know so much about Blackie?" Blake didn't have an answer.

Mr Parker shoved his head over the door and his eye lit up like headlights. "That's him all right, the big black 'un, we call him Jet."

I felt sick to the bottom of my stomach.

I was just about to turn away when Blackie lunged at the door, snapping his teeth inches from Mr Parker's face. He was going berserk.

"Shut him in," Sarah yelled, "he's going crazy!"

All we could hear was lashing hooves and splintering wood. I honestly thought he was going to break down the door.

"Get away from him!" James yelled at Mr Parker who was still standing in a daze. Sarah grabbed him by the arm and dragged him away before Blackie went completely hysterical.

The girl had got out of the truck and stood staring at us. She had streaks of tears down both cheeks and she was trembling like a leaf. "Satisfied now? Satisfied at what you've done to an innocent animal? He was as sweet as pie when we first got him . . ." she cried.

"Rachel, I'm warning you."

"You've done this, you and your filthy temper. I hate you!" She was crying, her face bright red, no older than her late teens.

"Rachel, I've told you to keep your mouth shut."

"You don't scare me any more. I've had it with you, you disgust me."

She was gasping for breath and James moved forward to try and calm her down. Blake, Ross and I stood with our mouths open gaping.

"Don't you see, it was Dad!" she flared up again. "He took him to the moor and he dumped him. He was *my* horse but he didn't care. Now he thinks Jet's worth a fortune, he's only interested in lining his own pockets."

She broke down sobbing and James led her back to the truck with one arm round her shoulders. The truth was finally out. It was Mr Parker who had abandoned Blackie.

"Get off my property." Sarah turned on him

with pure loathing. "You miserable worm of a man. If I ever see you again I won't be responsible for my actions."

The truck rattled down the drive and disappeared from sight. Blackie was ours, nobody would ever threaten to take him away again.

We all stood gathering our wits, taking in what we'd just heard. It was the last piece of the jigsaw to fall into place.

"Mel, Sarah!" Katie and Danny came running up from the main yard, totally oblivious to what had happened, still thinking it was just a man offering us a horse.

"It's Angel," Katie shrieked, still on cloud nine from the party. "Her milk's come down, she's feeding the foal!"

Chapter Eleven

The alarm clock went off at precisely two minutes past five and from that moment onwards it was complete bedlam.

"I told you we should have washed their tails last night." Ross was storming round the house, eating toast and complaining that nothing ever went to plan.

Katie charged in to announce there was no more horse shampoo and could she use washing-up liquid instead? Sarah threw her some of her own apple blossom conditioner and howled when she saw the dirty footprints all over the floor.

James had taken the whole day off work and was clearing the breakfast dishes. Sarah said she hoped he'd buy her a dishwasher when they were married, and started squirting around with air freshener until none of us could breathe and my eyes were stinging.

"For Heaven's sake, Sarah, they're visiting the stables, not the house."

One of the first tasks of the day was to clean up

the horses who were going to appear in the parade. As usual Snowy was plastered in stable stains and his pure white coat had turned a dirty green. Walter had escaped into the greenhouse and was dreamily chewing on a cucumber plant and Big Boris had just slung his bucket over the stable door in a temper because somebody had forgotten his extra oats.

"We'll never be ready in time," Katie whined, gushing a river of hot water over Snowy's back and scrubbing like mad. Danny was flicking soap out of his own ears, never mind Snowy's.

I went across to Angel who was happily chewing at her hay and feeding the foal. We'd moved Blackie next door to her and I was convinced if he strained his neck much more to look at her he'd end up having to wear a surgical collar.

"A small price to pay for true love." Blake put down the wheelbarrow and stood and gazed at them.

I dived into the tack room feeling emotional because Blake was leaving straight after the Open Day. He'd been shut in his room for hours last night, no doubt packing his things. Life was never completely perfect.

"Mel, where's the sweat scraper? And all the towels are wet!" Katie suddenly realized she'd used Sarah's brand-new peach bath towel and turned beetroot, especially when Sarah shouted she was just popping into the shower.

We scrubbed and toiled for what seemed hours and ended up with aching muscles and pricked fingers from plaiting up manes. Katie still couldn't get her plaits any smaller than gold balls and I had to admit it wasn't as easy as it looked.

By eight o'clock a pale pink sun was poking through a reddish tinted sky casting the whole horizon in a warm glow.

"It's going to be a scorcher." James came out with pint mugs of tea and piles of Jammy Dodgers. Since Angel had arrived we'd been living off them.

"We're on course," I said. "The craft stalls should be arriving any minute."

Blake decided to put out a few more straw bales round the yard for people to sit on and Katie rooted out another couple of "No Smoking" signs – you could never be too careful. Ross was getting all tied up in bunting and streamers and Sarah had come to the rescue with the garden shears. "Has anybody seen that peach towel?"

Twenty past eight and Mrs Mac swept in with her team of WI helpers, and stalls selling everything from cakes, plants, home-made wine and bric-à-brac, and a tombola. It was starting to feel like a real Gala Day.

"That was Binny on the phone." James came

out of the house carrying all the clean headcollars. "She's asked us if she could come over – she sounded really edgy."

Sarah immediately dropped a plastic flag she was tying to the outside tap and stepped back into a half-empty haynet. "I think," she said jumpily, "this is when I start eating humble pie."

"By the bucketload." James gave her a meaningful look.

Binny marched across the yard looking as if she'd just been dragged through a hedge or at best had a bad night. Sarah had contacted her straight away about Angel now having enough milk to feed the foal, but Binny had been offhand and according to Sarah downright crotchety. The two of them went into the house and we could all imagine the scene. They were both as stubborn as each other and James feared that neither would back down.

Angel had her eyes glued to the back door waiting for Binny to appear and Blackie made it quite clear he was jealous.

"Here they come!" Danny leapt up off a straw bale and tried to look busy.

"I've made a decision." Binny gave Angel a hug and tried to stroke the foal, but she was leaping around the stable like a spring lamb.

Sarah winked at Danny and I looked away when

I saw Binny's eyes welling up. She loved Angel to bits and what she said next couldn't have been easy.

"I've decided to leave Angel here for the next six months, at least until the foal is weaned." Katie's eyes tripled in size. "I've been stupid, possessive, expected too much. I don't know, it's never easy accepting that you're too old to do certain things."

"But there's still life in you yet." Trevor looked terribly earnest and Binny put a hand on his shoulder.

"I'm not on the scrap heap yet, Trevor, but I'm no match for that young thing." The foal stared at her, then swished her little tail and started chewing Katie's welly.

"I'm giving her to Hollywell Stables – you'll know what to do with her."

We all stood gaping like fish.

"You m-mean...?" Danny couldn't get his words out.

"She's ours?" Katie's voice was so high it could have broken glass.

"I think that's another way of putting it," Binny grinned.

"Our very own foal!" Katie looked as if she was going to pass out.

"For ever?" Danny was shaking his head, hardly able to take it in.

"And I've made a decision about my own life." Binny went on. "Loneliness is the worst disease of old age so I've finally agreed to marry Jimmy – the man must have the patience of a saint."

"Yippee!" Katie yelled and then half jumped out of her skin when the foal bit her bottom.

"Way to go, Mrs A." Trevor shook Binny's hand vigorously and I thought he'd never let go.

"We're going on a cruise and then of course I'll be back to see Angel. You can't get rid of me that easily."

"You've done the right thing," Sarah said.

"I think Frank would have approved," Katie added, showing oodles of maturity.

"So, as far as I can see, there's only one thing left," Binny said, "and that's, what are you going to call the foal?"

"Blossom, Brandy, Lola, Kizzy . . . or maybe Red or Saffron or what about Sabre or Honey?"

"Katie, not now, we're in the middle of a major crisis!"

We really were up the creek without a paddle as Trevor put it. People were pouring through the gates in a constant stream. There were so many families, so many cars, so many children wanting to see every single horse and pony. The Hollywell shop was doing good business and Mrs Mac had to keep sending Blake to the store room for more supplies. Everybody seemed to be walking round in Hollywell baseball caps and T-shirts.

"It's heaving," Ross shouted across a sea of bobbing heads. "We can't keep up with the teas and coffees, it's like watering the five thousand."

There was a tailback of cars right down the lane as far as the eye could see and one of the neighbours had rung up to tell us all the main roads were jam-packed and traffic was moving about ten miles an hour. People were turning out in their hundreds.

Stalls were set out in each stable and we'd even got the blacksmith giving a display of how horseshoes are made. The cake stall sold out within an hour and loads of people were walking round with bottles of home-made wine and beer. James and Mrs Mac's husband were serving people left, right and centre.

Binny had miraculously set us up with a burger bar at the very last minute, Mr Pirelli's Mobile Munchies, and the smell of tomato ketchup and sizzling sausages was wafting out around the stables. I was just making my way over to grab a burger when Sarah appeared, flushed and desperate, waving her hand in the air.

"We really are in trouble now," she said. "Rocky's just phoned on his mobile – his limousine is stuck in the traffic, it doesn't look as if he's going to make it."

Rocky was supposed to be here in the next hour to cut the red ribbon and officially open a new row of stables we'd had built. We also had everything set up for him to sing "Chase the Dream", the number one record which Rocky had dedicated to Hollywell Stables. He had to get here – without Rocky the whole thing would die a death.

"We'll have to start the parade soon," Sarah squeaked. "All we need now is the loudspeaker to go on the blink."

"Have you ever heard of something being too successful?" Blake pushed past a family with three children and a pushchair and nearly got daubed with strawberry ice-cream. "We ought to get them into the field," he said, "make more room."

"Isn't it wonderful!" Katie came up wearing a pair of huge dangly ear-rings still complete with the price tag, and Danny wandered past reeking of men's aftershave.

"What are we going to do?" Sarah almost screamed. And short of dressing Ross up in a wig and disguise I honestly didn't have a clue.

"Just go with the flow," said James.

I spent the next hour pointing out some of the ponies in the field and telling crowds of people their life stories. A year ago I would never have had the confidence to do that and now nobody could shut me up. In fact Ross said if I kept going on like that I could talk for Britain.

Everybody seemed to be having a fantastic time and still more people were piling in. I vaguely saw Mrs Mac, bright red in the face and guzzling lemonade, and Jigsaw loping off from the Punch and Judy stall with a very lop-sided Punch. The car-parks were causing a few problems and already two cars had got stuck. Even though the sun was shining it still wasn't enough to dry out the ground. Heaven knows what we were going to use to tow them out. Some of the portable loos were causing problems because the canvas sides hadn't been pegged down nearly well enough and one poor woman went scarlet when a gust of wind caught her unawares.

"Mel, where's Sarah? We're all ready for the parade." Trevor tried to fight off a horde of kids with a water pistol.

"Now we'll have none of that round the horses," I said. I could do with a badge marked "Official".

Blake fetched me an ice-cream and said I'd

earned a rest, and we nipped into the house for a ten-minute breather.

"It's incredible out there," he said, drinking some water from the cold water tap.

I bumped into a chair and then realized I was still wearing my sunglasses, which was why everything was so dark.

"Mel, will you stand still for a minute and listen to me. I tried to tell you the other night. I'm not going to Ireland. I've found Tina somebody else. I'm staying right here with you and the horses."

My jaw moved up and down a couple of times but nothing came out and I was still squinting, trying to adjust to the light.

"If you keep holding your head down you'll get a double chin," Blake laughed.

"I could murder you, Blake Kildaire. Have you any idea what you've put me through?"

Suddenly the loudspeaker burst into life and we could hear Sarah's voice and then some music.

"Come on." Blake grabbed my hand. "We'll miss the parade."

Everybody was moving out of the yard into the roped-off ring where Katie and Danny were hanging on to Queenie and Bluey and the rest of the helpers were trying to do their best with the other horses.

"Walter's eaten the flower display and someone's

hat." Ross came up carrying a straw hat with no rim. "And somebody's been feeding Isabella cheeseburgers and now she won't move."

"It doesn't matter." I gave him a cheesy grin. "Everything's just perfect."

"And the first pony to lead the parade is Queenie, our lucky mascot." Sarah did the commentary from the Pony Club caravan. Then came Bluey, Colorado, Terence and Dancer. Sarah gave each one a case history and progress report and they were trotted round the ring to a round of applause. James had somehow found a camcorder and was trying to video it over someone's shoulder.

"Dancer is a pure thoroughbred, an ex-race-horse who we found neglected in a field in the middle of winter with pneumonia." Sarah's voice was brimming with emotion and everybody was straining to hear every word. It was wonderful.

A lot of the crowd were members of the fan club with badges and knew each horse and pony by name. One young girl had knitted a patchwork quilt for Queenie but she'd got carried away and it was a size more suitable for Big Boris.

"Never mind, dear, you can do another one for next year."

"I don't think I can take this in." Blake looked up at the powder-blue sky, one hand shading his eyes. "Do tell me I'm seeing things."

Everybody had suddenly fallen quiet and was looking up at the sky.

"This is just so typical." Sarah came out of the caravan and nearly fell down with shock.

A huge bright-red balloon was hovering over Hollywell with two people in the basket, one of whom we recognized immediately. He was waving like mad and trying to shout something but we couldn't hear.

"It's Rocky!" a big burly man yelled out from behind Blake.

"Good Lord, he's right," someone else piped up.

"What an entrance!" A chorus of voices struck up. "Rocky!" Everybody thought it was part of the show.

Rocky stepped out of the hot-air balloon, as athletic as a teenager and oozing star quality. He swept across the grass, his long dark hair rippling down his back and his white streak glinting in the sunshine.

"Rocky!" Everybody was shouting and screaming like mad and then they all remembered the horses and quietened down.

Rocky bowed as if he'd just done a stage show and then Sarah ran up and grabbed his arm and hissed, "Why didn't you tell us what you were up to?"

Apparently Rocky had got fed up sitting in the

back of the limousine and then he'd noticed a crowd of people with hot-air balloons in a huge field off the road. It was some special club and it didn't take two minutes for Rocky to explain his situation and one of them came to the rescue.

"They were fantastic," Rocky said. "I've even decided to buy one of my own."

Sarah groaned, and I suddenly had visions of Rocky popping in for afternoon tea in a big balloon and groaned too.

Rocky was whisked off to sign autographs and then he popped into the caravan to make a speech. "As patron of Hollywell Stables . . ."

"Isn't he just delicious?" A woman fanned herself with a hanky and then recognized the straw hat I was holding and gave a little sob.

Trevor, who was completely starstruck, became even more overcome when somebody drove a brand-new tractor up the Hollywell drive, decorated all over with pink toilet roll.

"Mrs Mac and I had a little chat last time I was here," Rocky explained guiltily. "I couldn't resist."

"But Rocky, a brand-new tractor." Trevor's eyes were still spinning.

Rocky wanted to know where the welly-wanging competition was, and the skittles – Mrs Mac had told him all about it – but Sarah insisted it was time for "Chase the Dream".

"Look, it's the fire brigade," Ross said, and we all recognized the burly men walking around with their families, now out of uniform.

Rocky picked up the microphone and the backing band struck up the first notes. It had taken ages to get a makeshift stage set up but it was worth it to hear Rocky sing what had become our theme song.

"I'm so happy," Danny breathed beside me and we all swayed to the music and joined in with the chorus.

When it was over Rocky cut the red ribbon and then joined Sarah in the caravan for the second half of the parade.

Boris, Jakey, little Fluffy, Walter, Sally, Snowy, Arnie, even Isabella was there – all the ponies we'd brought over from France and all the scores of others we'd rescued since we'd opened the Hollywell gates to any waif or stray.

"Look." Blake held my hand as Blackie gingerly walked alongside Danny to finish off the parade. Angel was ahead of him with the foal and Blackie never took his eyes off either of them.

"Danny calls him Superdad," Blake grinned. "Can you believe the difference?"

I rammed my sunglasses on quickly because there were tears streaking down my cheeks.

"This is the best day out I've ever had." I overheard an old lady talking to Ross and happily munching away on a bag of home-made fudge.

"Mel, Mel!" Katie came tearing along like a sprint runner after leaving Angel with Binny. She was gasping for breath when she finally reached me.

"Mel, I've thought of a name for the foal, and Binny agrees and Sarah—"

"Whoa, whoa, one thing at a time. What's the name?"

Katie gasped a couple more times and then grinned from ear to ear.

"Holly," she said, "after Hollywell Stables. What do you think?"

What could I think? It was perfect. The best.

"And we could call her Hollywell Daydream for her show name." And then she raced off again because she said Holly would be missing her.

Rocky went back on to the makeshift stage to give another burst of "Chase the Dream", and we all stood and cheered until we were hoarse.

Hollywell Stables was a success story ... and I'd never felt more proud in my whole life.

HOLLYWELL STABLES

Secrets
8

Samantha Alexander

MACMILLAN
CHILDREN'S BOOKS

Chapter One

"It's a death trap, Mel. There's no way I'm jumping it!"

We were standing in the main arena of the local county show looking at a new show-jump which anyone could see was downright dangerous.

It was a wooden bridge called a ha-ha with a stile at the end and Blake said it was there to draw in the crowds, to create a spectacle. There had already been an article in the local paper comparing it to a bank which had been used at Olympia, where a horse had been killed.

"I'm pulling out, I don't care about the prize money." Blake screwed up his entry number with contempt. "Somebody's got to make a stand!"

"Mel, Blake!" Sarah, my stepmother, came charging across the arena waving a catalogue at us, her red hair flying back, making her look more like a film star than a romantic novelist.

"Of all the pigheaded old fossils," she fumed. "They won't change their minds, they won't budge an inch!"

We'd left her wrangling with the stewards while we went to have a second look at the ha-ha. I couldn't believe any course designer would expect a horse to canter over such a flimsy bridge and then somehow jump the four-foot stile at the end. It was ridiculous.

"They say it cost a fortune to build and it's perfectly safe." Sarah was beside herself with frustration. "They won't take a blind bit of notice."

The loudspeaker crackled into life. "Would all competitors now leave the arena as the grade A championship is about to commence."

"Not if I can help it." Sarah whipped round and marched out of the arena.

I knew exactly how she felt, I was boiling up with fury too. "Blake, you've got to do something!"

Back in the collecting ring, grooms and competitors were milling round, apprehensive and trying to make a decision. Blake marched up to Daniel Lamond, one of the top young riders, who was leaning against the rails signing autographs, his groom already warming up his horse.

"Forget it, Kildaire, there's no way I'm pulling out. There's too much money at stake."

Sarah came out of the stewards' office shaking her head.

My brother, Ross, pushed through the crowds leading Colorado, a beautiful skewbald who was only 14.2 hands but rated as one of the best jumpers in the country. He and Blake had already taken the show by storm, winning a speed class with a scorching round which left the others standing. If he'd gone into the championship he'd have probably won best horse in show.

"I'm not jumping," said Blake, as he led Colorado back to the temporary stables.

"Mel! Mel!" A purple mohican hairstyle burst through a crowd of onlookers and Trevor, our full-time groom, appeared at my side, hot and gasping. "It's chaos on the stall." He tried to get his breath. "They're all going dotty over the fan club – I can't cope. Where've you been?"

I suddenly remembered that I was supposed to relieve him half an hour ago, but I'd got totally taken up with the show-jumping.

We'd had the Hollywell Stables, Sanctuary for Horses and Ponies, stand on the showground for the full two days. We'd completely sold out of Hollywell T-shirts, baseball caps and mugs and it looked as if we desperately needed more membership forms. Poor Trevor – he'd been left by himself all morning.

"But what about the show-jumping?" I said, but he was already dragging me by the arm through the throngs of people back to our stand, which luckily wasn't too far from the main arena.

"Excuse me dear, how much is this?" A woman

in a multicoloured hat thrust a Hollywell tea towel under my nose. There was a queue of people clutching merchandise and I could immediately see what Trevor meant. My little sister Katie and her friend Danny were supposed to be helping but Trevor said they'd sloped off to the goat tent hours ago and he hadn't seen them since.

"The first rider in the ring, ladies and gentlemen, is number 28, Daniel Lamond, with the very experienced Earl Grey."

My hand froze in mid-air as I handed a woman her change. I could hear the hoofbeats on the hard ground, and the crowd fell silent as he went through the treble combination. It would be the bridge next.

"Mel, come back!"

I pushed my way through the ten-deep crowd and felt the sweat starting to run down my back from the heat. I nearly fell over a man sitting on a shooting stick and then ducked behind a television camera.

The huge grey was lumbering down to the bridge with his ears pricked forward. Daniel held him between hand and leg keeping up the impulsion and leapt on to the bridge off a perfect stride.

One-two-three. Check, check. Earl Grey bunched his hindquarters underneath him and popped out over the stile, making it look easy. A

4

huge whoop went up from the crowd and the commentator complimented Daniel's superb riding. A clear round.

"Blake, what's going on?"

Blake, Ross and Sarah were standing at the entrance to the collecting ring with their eyes glued on the next horse in the ring, a heavy dun cob who didn't appear to have any brakes.

"He'll never hold him over the bridge," said Blake, raking his hand through his dark hair, as edgy as a cat on hot bricks.

Daniel Lamond swaggered across the collecting ring looking smug. A reporter from the local radio station stuck a microphone in front of him and he said, "It's no problem at all. It just separates the men from the boys." He swung a quick glance in Blake's direction.

"The jumped-up little nerd," said Sarah; and I couldn't believe I had once thought Daniel Lamond was the biggest hunk in Britain.

"And that's another clear round," said the commentator, sounding almost disappointed that there hadn't been any spills or thrills. The crowd clapped mechanically and started drifting towards the shire-horse parade in the next ring.

The big dun horse ploughed back into the collecting ring, streaming with sweat. Maybe the bridge wasn't so bad after all. Maybe we'd over-reacted?

"I don't believe it," said Blake, staring at a pretty chestnut mare warming up over a cross pole.

"What is it? What's the matter?" Ross whipped off his extra-dark sunglasses and followed Blake's gaze.

"It's impossible," said Blake. "It can't be."

A man wearing a cowboy hat scuffed across the deep sand and put the jump up by at least a foot. "Now hold her together," he barked out at the inexperienced looking girl on top. "Come on Goldie, you can do it!"

Goldie was the chestnut mare. Blake told us that her show name was Gold Crest Lady, and that she was an old hand on the show-jumping circuit. She'd been around for ever and had never refused in her life. Next to Colorado she was the bravest horse he'd ever known.

"But that's just it," he growled. "I saw her only last week at the Royal. She was so lame she could barely walk. How could she have recovered this quickly?"

"How dare you tell me what to do? It's none of your business!" The man with the cowboy hat glared at Blake as if he was completely mad and grabbed hold of Goldie's reins. "Haven't you lot caused enough trouble already?"

Goldie jerked her head back in alarm, her soft

6

brown eyes filling up with panic. It was impossible to see if her legs were swollen because she was wearing protective boots.

"But I saw this horse only last week." Blake tried again. "She can't possibly be sound enough—"

"Are you going in or not?" An official stepped forward, anxious to get the next horse into the ring.

"Dad, I don't think I want to . . ." The girl on Goldie's back looked a nervous wreck and was frantically entwining her fingers in Goldie's mane.

"Go on, off you go, I've not spent all this money for nothing." The man yanked Goldie forward and they entered the main ring.

The crowd fell silent and the bell clamoured into life. Any minute now and the girl would have to start her round. Goldie moved obediently forward and cantered towards the first fence.

"What's happening?" Trevor appeared at my side, clutching the cash box. "I couldn't stand it any longer," he gasped. "I can't see anything back there!"

Sarah held up her hand, shielding her eyes from the sun.

Goldie turned towards the double gates, her ears cocked forward, her stride lengthening. The girl on her back was completely hopeless; she couldn't ride for toffee.

"Goldie's carrying her round," Blake breathed. "She's totally outclassed."

"So how's she going to tackle the bridge?"

We all held our breath as Goldie launched herself over the wall off a wrong stride.

"Good girl," Blake murmured under his breath. "She's doing it all by herself."

The girl bounced up and down, becoming more unbalanced with every jump. This is what I hated to see; parents so keen to do well that they spent a fortune on expensive horses just so their children could enter the big classes. It was an attempt to buy success and it was pointless. This girl would have more fun on a riding school horse doing the minimus.

"She's on the wrong leg." Ross's voice was as taut as a tightrope as Goldie fought to keep her balance round a tight corner. There was no sign of any lameness. Her bold stride was eating up the ground.

Through the treble combination. Perfect timing. Goldie was trying her heart out. Now the bridge. Steady. Steady her. She was going too fast. Goldie's head came up – a moment's hesitation.

The girl immediately started flapping her arms and legs. It was the worst thing she could have done. Goldie lunged forward. She was going much too fast, totally unbalanced, her legs were all over the place.

The whole audience gasped in horror as Goldie plunged on to the narrow bridge and her entire hindquarters slipped underneath her. It was horrible to see. She was sliding all over, scrabbling to stay upright. It was like a skating rink.

"Oh no!" Sarah's hand flew up to her mouth.

"She's going to fall!" Trevor yelled out.

Goldie hit the ground with a sickening thud. Thankfully the girl was thrown forward, clear of the flailing hoofs, both her feet coming out of the stirrups.

"I told you something like this would happen," Sarah screamed at one of the officials.

"She can't get up!" Blake shouted. Ross was already ducking under the ropes, Trevor right behind him. "She's hurt." Blake was glaring at the man in the cowboy hat. "Goldie's hurt!"

Chapter Two

"She's broken her leg." A new vet in the area called Tom Drummond stood in the arena and gave his verdict.

"But it doesn't have to mean the end!" Sarah gave Mr Drummond an eyeball-to-eyeball glare. To our horror he'd already advised Goldie's owners to have her put down on the spot.

"She deserves a chance." Blake held on to Goldie's reins, rubbing her ears, trying to get her to relax. Her injured foreleg was held up at an awkward angle, the sweat was running off her in streams. "It's all right darling, everything's going to be OK."

The girl had been taken off to the first aid tent immediately although there was nothing wrong with her apart from shock, but she was so hysterical she wouldn't have been much use to Goldie anyway. Her dad was more interested in examining the expensive show-jumping saddle which had been slung on the ground than looking at Goldie's leg.

Three stewards in identical bowler hats talked

into walkie-talkies and within minutes the horse ambulance came trundling across the arena, a white trailer with a blue cross on the side and, according to Sarah, specially padded inside just like our Hollywell horsebox.

"Get the screens across," one of the stewards yelled, looking scathingly at the gathering crowds. "Next they'll be taking photographs."

"It's all right Goldie, we'll soon get you out of here." The poor mare was shaking convulsively and her breathing sounded terrible.

It was a nightmare. Her near foreleg was just dangling in the air, the fetlock and hoof waving limply like something out of a horror movie. If I looked at it too much I knew I'd be sick, so I concentrated on stroking her nose and trying to ease the fear and the pain.

More men appeared, struggling with green canvas sheeting and propping up poles. Suddenly the whole showground was blotted out and all we could see was the inside of the horse ambulance and the ropes and pulleys ready to winch her in.

The message went out on the loudspeaker for a second time. "Would all acting veterinary surgeons please make their way to the main arena. Thank you."

It was a standard procedure to seek a second opinion and there were three vets on duty that day. James happened to be one of them. He also

11

happened to be Sarah's fiancé and our local vet. And there was no way he'd let Goldie die.

"Where is he?" Sarah hissed, wracked with nerves and well aware that all the stewards were in agreement with Drummond that Goldie should be put down.

Ross had last seen him attending to a prize-winning bull who'd cut his leg open on a car bumper, and that was right over the other side of the showground.

"Come on James, come on."

The tension in the closed-off area was becoming unbearable. The girl's dad had turned white and didn't seem to know how to handle the situation. Tom Drummond looked thunderous and it was obvious the stewards just wanted the whole problem to go away. Goldie hopped on three legs and then stood gasping, her pretty, delicate face contorted in agony. Surely the injection she'd had should start numbing the pain soon? The smell of churned-up grass, fear, sweat and blood made me feel nauseous. How much longer?

"Poor old lady," said Blake, mopping at the sweat which was running into her eyes. "She doesn't deserve this."

"Broken legs can be mended," Trevor blurted out. "What about that dressage horse, Rembrandt, or whatever his name was?"

Mr Drummond looked at him as if he was

12

something the cat had dragged in. "When I want your opinion I'll ask for it."

"You might be a vet," Trevor flew back at him, "but we're from Hollywell Stables – we believe where there's life there's hope."

"Sentimental money-wasting trouble-makers if you ask me." Mr Drummond turned round muttering under his breath just as Sarah was about to fly to our defence.

"It's James!" I'd never been more pleased to see the familiar tousled brown head poke round the canvas.

"Now then old girl, let's take a look at you, shall we?"

Goldie stood as still as she could while James examined her leg, but no matter how gentle he tried to be it was impossible not to cause her pain.

"It's a clean fracture of the cannon bone, it's not come through the skin. I believe it can be plated."

James stood up to his full height and faced Tom Drummond. "If we can get her to Newmarket in the next few hours I believe we can save her life." James had never sounded more determined.

"Yes!" Trevor clenched his fist. I could feel my cheeks creasing into a grin.

"We've got to strap it immediately. There's no time to lose."

"I disagree." Tom Drummond stood with his

arms folded and his feet apart in defiance. "Number one. Even if the operation is a success, which is a long shot, she'll never be able to show-jump again. Number two. She's an old mare; she's no good for breeding or anything else for that matter. And number three, the owner informs me she's not insured for medical bills, so I pose the question: just who is going to pay for it?"

The cowboy hat nearly fell to the ground when James admitted what it would cost.

"If you think I'm laying out two thousand pounds to save her life when she'll never be able to jump again, you've got to be joking."

Goldie's owner was obviously not one of life's great benefactors.

"We'll pay for it!" said Sarah.

Ross's eyebrows flew up into his fringe and I knew what he was thinking. The Hollywell funds were at an all-time low since we'd bought more land and ten ponies from a bankrupt trekking centre. I doubted we'd have enough to cover it.

"And we'll buy Goldie for the price you paid for her. On the condition that she retires to Hollywell Stables."

For the first time Tom Drummond actually looked nervous.

"Victor!" Suddenly a woman pushed through a gap between the ambulance and the screens and I instantly recognized her as the woman in the

14

multicoloured hat who'd been at the Hollywell stall.

"I'm Mrs Rawlings, Victor's wife," she said in a commanding voice. "And yes, we'll take your offer. It sounds very fair."

I think I was the only one to notice Mr Rawlings' chin quivering and Drummond's teeth gritted so hard his jaw looked like a clamp.

"Mel, we'll need four rolls of gamgee and elastoplast," James ordered. "Blake, you'll have to hold her still. Sarah, we'll need a vehicle to get us down, a four-wheel drive. Ring the Animal Health Trust and tell them we're coming! We'll be there in three hours."

Drummond stormed off in a filthy temper. Within half an hour we had Goldie bandaged and loaded into the trailer, ready for the most important journey of her life.

"I'll follow in the car," Mrs Rawlings insisted. "James says I'll need to sign forms, fill in questionnaires, that sort of thing."

"What about me?" Mr Rawlings gaped, pink and puffy in the face and completely out of his depth.

"Take care of Jessica. And you'd better tell her about Goldie."

We clambered into the blue Range Rover and pulled out of the arena with the horse ambulance hitched up behind. Most of the crowds had dispersed and two of the stewards were roping off the "bridge" with some red tape. You could still see Goldie's skid marks and the ground all cut up where she'd fallen.

"The idiots," Blake hissed. "Anybody with half a brain could see this would happen."

We drove through the collecting ring at ten miles an hour. Many of the horses were still milling around waiting for the class to recommence. Daniel Lamond was slouched by one of the jumps, chatting up two girls, and he just shrugged as he saw us go past. Was that the right attitude for a professional sportsman, to win at all costs?

Trevor was staying behind to dismantle the stall and search for Katie and Danny who still hadn't appeared. Sarah was in the front with James, and Ross and Blake were in the back with me. It was going to be a long haul.

Spectators turned and watched as James made his way on to the main thoroughfare past all the new tractors and expensive car displays. Way up above us two hot air balloons hovered in the calm blue sky and the Household Cavalry was on parade in one of the other rings. That's all we'd see of the county show for this year.

"OK," James said, as we turned on to the main road out of town. "Newmarket here we come!"

It was hours before we even saw any signs for one of the most famous racing towns in the world.

James said that when he was young he dreamed of being one of the top vets in Newmarket. I was amazed at how many racehorses we saw filing down the narrow roads, often as many as thirty in one string. James had us in hysterics when he said that most people in Newmarket were short because over the years everybody who had moved there dreamed of becoming a jockey.

We drove down more leafy lanes overhung with rich red copper beech trees and squirrels running from one side of the road to the other. More racehorses passed us round the next corner and Ross swore he'd just spotted Henry Cecil riding along on a pretty grey arab.

"Look, there it is." Sarah pointed ahead and we all fell quiet as the famous Animal Health Trust came into sight. Blake, Ross and I crossed our fingers for good luck as the Range Rover swished up the sand-covered drive and we followed the arrows straight round the back for the special Clinical Unit.

It was just how I expected, with wide open spaces and immaculate brick-built stables painted in Labrador yellow and Buckingham green. Horses were popping their heads over high doors and Goldie neighed from inside the trailer, rocking it slightly on its axle.

Blake insisted that a bright bay stallion in the nearest box was a runner in this year's Derby, and when I popped my head over the door I saw a huge creamy white pot on its leg plastered well up over the knee.

Two veterinary nurses scrunched across the drive from a nearby office, followed by a man in a white coat consulting a clipboard.

"It's a clean break. But it's difficult to predict her chances – I'd say fifty-fifty."

Goldie had been led into an empty stable and one of the nurses was making her comfortable. The surgeon who was going to perform the operation was jotting down notes. "She's a very brave horse, I'll say that for her."

Mrs Rawlings was in the main office giving details of Goldie's past history.

"We'll operate tomorrow morning so expect to hear from us sometime after lunch – one way or the other."

I'd only known Goldie for a few hours but already it felt as if we were leaving one of the family.

"She's in the best of hands." Ross tried to make me feel better as we both stood stroking her neck. James was busy talking to the surgeon about X-rays and Sarah had gone off to find Mrs Rawlings.

"We're going to have to go soon." Blake leaned over the door, passing on James's message.

18

"But we might never see her again." The words slipped out before I realized it. We all knew that the operation was going to be incredibly difficult; if it had been her pastern or one of the small bones in . . .

"There's nothing more we can do." Ross put his arm round my shoulder, reading my thoughts. "She's been given a chance, that's the main thing."

I patted the little white star on her forehead and kissed her muzzle. "Good luck sweetheart, be brave."

We left the smell of clean woodshavings and disinfectant behind and stepped out into the drive where a thin mist of drizzle had started to fall.

Mrs Rawlings was already in her Mercedes saying goodbye to Sarah. "You've got my address and phone number. I'll expect to hear from you."

The engine purred into life and the electric window was closing as Blake shot across to her side and whipped open the car door.

"You still haven't told us how she made such a miraculous recovery." His fingers were clutching the paintwork, the knuckles showing white.

Mrs Rawlings opened and shut her mouth, completely taken aback. "I don't know what you're talking about."

"Last week at the Windsor show, I saw Goldie. She couldn't walk."

"I've already told you," she spat out, clearly

annoyed. "You obviously saw another horse. Goldie was fine. Now would you please let go of my car door?"

"She's lying." Blake was adamant. His dark eyes blazed with contempt as the Mercedes became a dot and then completely disappeared. "She's hiding something. And I for one intend to find out what."

The journey back seemed even longer and twice as tiring. We stopped at a transport café and had hamburgers which tasted like cardboard and weak coffee. We were starving and as stiff as boards by the time we'd offloaded the Range Rover and trailer and crawled up the Hollywell drive in our own car.

"Home at last." James slammed the door and Big Boris stuck his head out over his stable door, trailing a forest of hay and looking totally content.

The yard was deserted, but a tantalizing waft of fish and chips drifted from the kitchen and we dived for the back door as if we'd spent three months at the North Pole.

"So you finally made it," said Trevor, drowning a double helping of chips in tomato ketchup. Katie was feeding a battered sausage to Jigsaw, our golden Labrador. Up on the kitchen units, Oscar and Matilda, our two cats, were picking at some morsels of fish on a saucer with all the daintiness of a duke and duchess.

"Yours is in the oven." Trevor slapped Ross's wrist as he tried to grab a handful of chips. "And I've left the plates warming."

"We'll make a housewife of you yet." Sarah reached for the oven cloths and yelped when her fingers went right through the material.

"Jigsaw had hold of them earlier," Trevor said by way of explanation. "And where's the vinegar?"

We told them all about Goldie and Newmarket and the Animal Health Trust, until Katie was steaming with jealousy and complaining that we should have tried to find her and Danny.

"Serves you right for skiving off the stall," I said, sticking my tongue out.

James immediately started drawing diagrams of Goldie's leg on a sheet of kitchen roll, and Danny screwed up his face when James said they used metal staples instead of stitches and Goldie would need about a hundred. I wiped the slobber from Jigsaw's mouth (he was drooling over the remains of Oscar's fish), and Blake asked to see the address for Mrs Rawlings.

"So what did you two get up to?" Sarah looked pointedly at Katie and Danny while fishing in her handbag and pulling out a compact and a clothes peg.

21

Danny started stuttering and Katie pretended to get hiccups to change the subject and asked Trevor to put some keys down her back.

"I'm not getting involved!" Trevor put his empty plate in the sink, and as luck would have it the phone rang and he bolted for the hallway determined to make an escape.

"Katie?" Sarah cocked an eyebrow at my nine-year-old sister and within seconds her elfin face went bright pink.

"It wasn't our fault," she squeaked, suddenly really anxious. "You'd have done exactly the same."

"What on earth . . . ?"

I don't know whether it was the sudden silence or just pure coincidence but the most deafening screeching-bleating noise had struck up from behind the washroom door.

"It sounds like a baby crying," Ross ventured. Oscar shot through the cat flap and Jigsaw flew under the table.

"*Katie Foster!*"

Sarah flung open the door to reveal two beady, wickedly mischievous eyes glaring at her from the top of the laundry basket.

"I knew it," she shrieked. "I just knew it"

A black and white baby goat with funny, sticking-up ears and a pale pink nose barged through her legs and skidded across the kitchen tiles, ram-

22

ming his tiny head into Ross's left knee. Sarah reappeared from the washroom as pale as paper, holding up her best silk skirt ripped into long thin shreds. James and Blake made a grab for the wriggly little neck just as it disappeared into Jigsaw's bowl of tinned dog food.

"His name's Spikey." Danny rubbed at the nobbly black and white head now held firmly in James's iron grip. "Nobody wanted him. Apparently he's a bit of a handful."

I was just about to declare this the understatement of the century when Trevor marched back in looking shocked, completely ignoring the eighteen-inch dynamo who was now busy chewing at James's hair.

"That was the Animal Health Trust on the phone," he said. "There was something Mrs Rawlings didn't tell us . . ."

"Let me guess." Blake took the words right out of his mouth. "They've just taken a urine sample and Goldie's been pumped full of Phenylbutazone. In other words," and he paused for dramatic effect, "she's been drugged up to the eyeballs!"

Chapter Three

"How did you know?" We all sat in a dazed state taking in the new turn in events.

Sarah scooted back from the conservatory where she'd put Spikey, and James went to ring the surgeon.

"Calculated guesswork." Blake passed round mugs of tea. "I knew right down to the pits of my boots that it was Goldie I saw last week. She couldn't have recovered that fast – it had to be drugs."

Phenylbutazone is a fine white powder commonly known as Bute, which acts as a pain-killer. It is often given to old retired horses with joint problems or horses in a lot of pain from illness. It is also illegally given to competition horses to keep them in the show-ring.

"But that's terrible!" Katie's bottom jaw had dropped open. "How do they get away with it?"

Blake explained that unlike racing, where winners are automatically tested for drugs, in show-jumping, especially at county level, it is quite easy to dope a horse and get away with it. He even knew one yard where they fed a horse sixty aspirins a day to keep it sound.

"It's unbelievable," said Ross, sweeping a hand through his black hair.

"These horses cost a fortune to keep on the circuit," Blake continued. "If Bute can keep them going, then to the owners it's worth it."

"Well, I think it stinks," I said, dropping four sugar lumps into my tea and stirring frantically.

"Yes, but Mel, what's better? A horse well looked after and able to continue enjoying his work, or being put down?"

"Nature tells us when it's time to retire," I snapped. "If a horse needs Bute then fair enough, but it should be rested, not slave-driven round endless courses of jumps."

"Hear, hear." Ross raised his mug. "Whatever happened to my shrinking violet of a sister?"

"The operation's going ahead." James came back into the kitchen. "The Bute won't have any effect. At the moment she's resting and everything seems OK. It was Mrs Rawlings who tipped them off."

"So she knew all the time." Blake's face hardened.

"What I want to know," said Katie as she fetched a chocolate cake from the fridge, "is how they get hold of the bute in the first place."

*

"Mel, don't let her wind you up, she's not worth it." Trevor poked his head over Queenie's stable door. I was grooming her so ferociously hairs were flying out in all directions.

"Ouch," I howled as the metal scraper grated against my bare leg. That was all I needed, another red mark to add to the jungle of thistle scratches. Soon I'd be able to do a dot-to-dot on my thighs.

"Mel, will you stop being so hard on yourself? You're playing straight into her hands."

I knew Trevor was right but somehow it didn't make me feel any better. The cause of my aggravation was a fifteen-year-old girl called Nicki Harris with raven-black hair and dazzling good looks, who at this precise moment I'd have liked to pack off on a one-way ticket to planet Mars.

"Maybe she's not that bad." Trevor grinned and I promptly lobbed the dandy brush at him.

From the moment Nicki had come to work at Hollywell Stables she'd made it quite clear that she was only interested in Blake and his show-jumpers. We'd advertised for ages for voluntary help over the summer holidays but as soon as people found out there was no riding they lost interest. Most of our horses and ponies were old, lame or not suitable for riding. What they needed most was love and attention and proper care, and as the sanctuary grew bigger and bigger we were becoming less equipped to provide this.

26

Nicki had seemed the obvious answer. She was bright and enthusiastic and had worked at the local riding school. Ross was immediately bowled over. Trevor hated her from the very beginning.

What had driven me mad this morning was that she'd made some heartless remark about Goldie being yet another useless old nag and suggested the best place for Spikey was the freezer. At this moment Goldie was fighting for her life on an operating table and all she cared about was dragging Blake down to the local shop for choc-ices.

"It's not fair, Trevor. What on earth does Blake see in her?"

It was a typically hot sticky August day and I didn't know how we were going to get through the next two hours until we heard about Goldie.

Sarah had gone off to the bank and James was working. All the horses were out in the fields, and Trevor was planning to draw straws as to who was going to start the creosoting. We'd painted all the stables but the new post and rail fencing looked as parched as paper. It was important we kept the sanctuary looking as smart as possible to impress the constant stream of visitors.

I was just about to rush into the house and answer the phone when Katie shot round the corner in a state of hysteria clutching a lead rope. "It's Spikey," she screeched. "He's gone!"

The original plan was to put Spikey in the

orchard with Snowy, our old donkey, but Snowy had gone berserk and Spikey had ended up being moved into the garden. That was a disaster too; within ten minutes he'd dug up all the bedding plants and leapt in the fish-pond.

James said he was a British Alpine and would probably have been put down because nobody wanted billy-goats, especially ones with misshapen ears and a personality problem like Spikey.

"He's on the muck heap," Danny yelled as a flurry of dirty straw spewed out like a muck spreader.

"Right, that does it," I yelled. "Spikey, I've had enough." Trevor went to answer the phone which was still ringing away and I ran across to the muck heap and leapt on top, still in my shorts and flip-flops.

What I didn't expect was the little monster to butt me on the back of my legs, sending me sprawling head first into a pile of fresh manure. "Spikey, I hate you, do you hear? You need roasting for this. I'll never forgive you."

Chaffy bits of straw stuck to my bottom lip and I was vaguely aware of a haze of midges zooming in round my head ready to go in for the kill. Spikey's beady eyes almost looked apologetic as he stared down and then he quickly decided it was some kind of game and leapt on top of me.

"Way to go, Mel."

I'd have recognized that silly tinkling laugh in Timbuctoo and would rather have died than look up into Nicki's laughing, taunting face with her perfectly glossed lips and mascara-coated eye-lashes. Even worse, my own brother and Blake were cracking up too.

"Go on, have a good laugh, why don't you?" I screeched, dust-blackened and stinking like a pig farm. "I think it's absolutely hilarious." I stormed off to the house in a serious huff and swearing I'd never see the funny side of anything again.

Trevor gave me a double-take in the hallway and then charged up the stairs, grabbing hold of my arm. "That was Tom Drummond on the phone," he hissed. "He wanted to speak to Sarah."

"Did he leave a number? Did he say what it was about?"

"Give me a break, Mel, he just sees me as the dork with the purple hair."

"Maybe he's genuinely concerned about Goldie," Katie said later, as we sat in the yard, trying to catch the sun.

"And pigs might fly," Ross tutted. "He'd already got Goldie packed off to the abattoir before she'd even been X-rayed."

"Bribery," said Danny. "It's the only thing left. He wants to bribe Sarah."

"Well I don't like it." Blake threw down a copy of *Horse And Hound* which was plastered with news about Daniel Lamond. "I wouldn't trust that toad as far as I could throw him."

"Don't you think you're over-reacting?" Nicki stretched out her long legs and batted her eyelashes in Blake's direction. "I mean, it could be about anything, not just Goldie."

I inhaled sharply and tried to resist scratching at the mountain of midge bites on my neck.

"What other reason could there be?" I said. "He's hardly one of our avid supporters."

Spikey strained on his lunge rein, which was attached to the outside tap. We'd given him a wash but he still smelt awful. I'd doused myself in Sarah's expensive French perfume and now felt on the verge of fainting as it cloyed my nostrils.

It was a quarter to twelve. An hour and a quarter to go.

"What if she doesn't survive the anaesthetic?" I whimpered.

"The trouble with you, Mel, is you worry too much." Nicki pulled down the straps on her vest top to expose perfectly formed sloping shoulders. "Now if it was me . . ."

"Anyone for lemonade?" Ross opened a couple of cans, desperate to diffuse the situation.

Blake said he'd still got a Coke, and Katie gave me that knowing sister-to-sister look.

"Anyone for sun lotion?" I volunteered, practically throwing the bottle at Nicki.

"Blake, could you possibly ... I can't quite reach ..."

The little cow, I thought. She's doing it on purpose.

Nicki lazily flicked a ladybird off her arm and inched closer to Blake.

"What if her heart won't take it?" I suddenly sat bolt upright in the deck-chair. "What if she's too old?"

"Mel, stop it. We'll never get through the next hour like this." Ross stood up, visibly on edge. "Let's talk about something else."

"Like what?" I shot back, unable to picture anything but Newmarket and those ultra-clean, disinfectant-filled stables.

"Sarah's fortieth birthday."

It was Saturday, August 14th. Next weekend. Sarah was a Leo, which explained that wonderful mass of red hair and dynamic presence.

"It's a secret." Katie excitedly made notes in her horsey diary. "We're planning a party."

Nicki's finely arched eyebrows rose in immediate interest.

For weeks Sarah had been obsessed with her age; examining her imaginary wrinkles, having James in hysterics when he caught her looking at herself in the sheen of a metal saucepan. "You're forty, for heaven's sake, not eighty," he grinned. "Anyway, beauty is in the eye of the beholder."

"So my neck really does look like a turkey?"

She insisted she was going to spend the whole of her birthday hiding under her duvet and if we wanted to buy her anything then it had to be a fitness video or an exercise bike.

"So a party it is then," Trevor had tormented her.

But unknown to Sarah, the idea had taken root. We'd already written out the invitations and made a start on a fantastic red and white banner.

"We'll need loads of balloons and streamers," Katie said. "And crisps and peanuts by the lorry-load."

"What about a theme?" Ross said. "Fancy dress or something?"

"Oh God," Nicki snapped irritably. "When you said a party I thought you meant a real rave, not a tea party!"

"Why do you have to be such a bitch?" I suddenly flew off the handle. "What's it got to do with you anyway – who said you were even invited?"

I could feel the blood thudding in my head and my cheeks flooding with colour. Nicki just gaped, looking really embarrassed. I couldn't help it. I was furious. And realizing that everybody was staring at me I charged off to the tack room.

Minutes later, Blake stormed in. "You didn't have to be so rude. She doesn't have to be here you know; she's working her guts out for nothing."

"Oh, don't give me that rubbish," I shouted. "You don't see her when she's painting her toenails and cursing the older ponies. She only shows you her goody-two-shoes side. She's a flirt and a cow and you're lapping up the attention."

I was gasping from the sheer passion of my temper and I realized I'd backed myself into a corner with nowhere to go.

"Mel, I never thought you could be like this." Blake made it worse by keeping his cool and looking at me like a disapproving schoolteacher.

"Well, I'm not perfect, OK? I'm not the sensitive, shy retiring little soul you think I am. I've got feelings and I'm not sitting back and watching you pander to her whims."

"There's no talking to you when you're like this." Blake was aghast. "I don't know what you're talking about. You're obviously seeing something that's not there."

"Oh, shut up and go away," I yelled, tears prickling hot and painful behind my eyes. "Just go, Blake. I've had enough of you."

At precisely that moment Sarah's red MG sports car stormed up the drive and the telephone burst into life. It couldn't be the Animal Health

Trust – there were still forty-five minutes to go. Unless . . .

Sarah flew into the house and Blake and I just stood looking at each other with blank expressions.

"I think," Blake finally broke the silence, "we'd better go inside."

"She's made it!" Trevor burst out of the back door, unable to contain himself. "The little cracker," he bawled, "she's pulled through!"

"You're kidding!" Blake and I could hardly believe it.

"Sarah's talking to the surgeon now," Trevor grinned, suddenly turning away as his eyes started to fill up. It was really odd, a fifteen-stone tough hunk of a nineteen-year-old getting all emotional over a strange horse. "She's made it, Mel, she's gone and shown them all."

"She's not out of the woods yet." Sarah kicked off her shoes which bounced into the dog basket, and started rummaging through a pile of papers. "The bad news is she can't come home for two weeks. But the bone's been plated, it's been a success!"

"She'll need a nice blanket." Katie started planning. "And some mints, apples, carrot cake – we can post it to her."

"Why not just get the fairies to take it?" Nicki,

who'd been quiet up to now, angled a dig but only Trevor and I heard her.

"Trevor, we need your car. Quick, I'll explain on the way." Sarah ran a hand through her hair and tried to look calm.

Trevor had recently rebuilt an entire car from the junk yard, which bumbled along at forty miles an hour. But at least we could all get in it.

"Nicki, I need you to stay behind. Keep an eye on Katie and Danny. James should be back soon." Sarah reclaimed her shoes which Jigsaw had just discovered and was about to sink his teeth into.

"Where are we going?" Ross looked as surprised as the rest of us.

"To Honeycomb Grange," Sarah read from a tatty piece of paper. "To visit Mr and Mrs Victor Rawlings!"

Chapter Four

"So it's quite simple." Sarah was explaining how owners obtained supplies of Bute.

Usually in every yard there were horses who required pain-killers at some time. It was even known for a competitor to buy in a couple of dud horses.

"The vet prescribes the necessary Bute," Sarah went on. "That's all on the level and above board. But the administration is totally in the owner's hands. All they have to do is siphon off some sachets for one of the other horses. The great thing about Bute is there's no side effects."

"It's immoral," Ross said. "Somebody should try and do something."

"But most show-jumpers are on the level." Blake turned round in the front seat. "It would be like finding a needle in a haystack, and there just isn't enough money."

"You haven't told us what we're going to see the Rawlings about," I said. "He doesn't strike me as the type to make a confession."

Sarah dug around in her handbag and passed

over a signed cheque. "I'm also hoping Mrs Rawlings will spill the beans. That woman knows everything. She's definitely the key."

"Here, turn left here." Sarah waved frantically. We'd been on the road for about half an hour, cutting across town and heading through the suburbs into the country. This was definitely a money part of the county; every other house looked as if it was worth a fortune.

"Trevor, can't you make this old bus go any faster?" Sarah urged. "We would like to arrive before next Christmas."

"Right you are, Mrs F." And Trevor shot the car forward at an extra ten miles an hour.

We were seriously backfiring as we turned up a long drive to pull up in front of a pink mansion with roses round the porch and an immaculate garden.

"Maybe we ought to take our shoes off," Ross joked, and I quipped back that the lawn looked as if it was regularly dry-cleaned.

"Just one thing." Ross turned to Sarah as we piled out. "How did you talk the bank manager into giving us a loan?"

"Oh that was easy." Sarah brushed off the question. "I just told him I was going to win the Romantic Novelist of the Year Award."

"You did what?"

But Sarah was already marching across to the

stable yard looking every inch a force to be reckoned with.

"My wife is in bed with a migraine." Mr Rawlings was furious that we'd just turned up unexpectedly and only softened when he saw the cheque. "I'm glad the horse is all right," he muttered. "Jessica will be pleased."

"But it doesn't solve the mystery of the Bute, does it?"

We were standing in the stable yard where there were about ten loose boxes. A couple of grooms were sweeping up, trying to listen in.

"I've already told you." Mr Rawlings' words were clipped and measured. "I know nothing about it and if you've got nothing more to say I'd like you to leave."

Mr Rawlings was getting edgy. He was dressed in tennis whites and we'd just dragged him off his own personal court where he'd been playing doubles with some friends. Without his cowboy hat he looked older and fatter in the face and he was twiddling with his tennis racket as if he wanted to hit us over the head with it.

"Don't try and lay the finger of blame on me."

"So how did it get into her system?" Sarah carried on regardless. "Don't tell me a guardian

38

angel flew down and poured it into her evening feed."

"I've nothing more to say."

"I'm informing the BSJA," Sarah said. "And we've got the surgeon's report. There was definitely a strain in the near tendon. It could have been that which caused her to fall."

"I've got nothing to hide. If somebody put some dope in the horse's feed, then I know nothing about it."

"A little bird tells me you want to get into local politics." Sarah went in for the kill. "This kind of publicity wouldn't do you any good."

"Get off my property." For the first time Mr Rawlings looked rattled. "If you don't leave this minute I'll call the police. And get that heap of junk off my driveway."

His face was set in a hard line now. We'd pushed him to the limit. Thankfully Sarah knew when to call it a day and started backing off towards the car.

"Don't ever take the liberty of calling here again." Mr Rawlings turned on his heel and marched back to his group of friends, who were sitting on the front lawn looking decidedly edgy, not to mention curious.

"Come on gang, it's time to depart," said Sarah, glancing round. "Now where's Trevor got to?"

Suddenly we heard a toilet flush from across the other side of the yard and Trevor appeared looking apologetic. "Sorry Mrs F, I was taken short."

The two grooms had disappeared and even the horses had put their heads in, keeping well out of the way. We were no longer welcome.

"Well, at least we've paid for Goldie." Blake tried to lighten the atmosphere. "And we've probably warned him off ever trying a stunt like that again."

We climbed into the car, arguing about who was going to sit in the front, and Sarah tried to wind down the back window but the handle came off in her hand!

For a fraction of a second I thought I saw Mrs Rawlings at an upstairs window gazing down at us, but then there was nothing, just a curtain half drawn across.

"This place is amazing." Ross took one last look at Honeycomb Grange as we backfired out of the drive. "Do you realize there isn't a speck of dust in sight?"

"It's not so clean any more." Trevor turned round, grinning like a Cheshire cat. "I didn't like to mention it, but we've left about three pints of engine oil on the drive."

*

"Trevor, you're a marvel." Sarah stared down at her lap, completely lost for words.

"I found them pushed down the back of some feed bins. I could hardly believe it myself."

We were chugging through yet another immaculate village with huge yew hedges, which are so poisonous to horses, when Trevor decided to drop his bombshell. He passed Sarah three empty silver foil sachets and there was no mistaking their original content – Phenylbutazone.

"But it's not enough," Blake said a few minutes later, his face etched with frustration. "Every show-jumping yard in the country has probably got these packets stashed away somewhere. It doesn't mean anything. It doesn't mean they're doping their horses."

He was absolutely right. And we all knew it.

"But at least it's a start," I said, still bristling from our earlier run-in and determined to think positive. "Goldie was drugged, that much we do know. All we've got to do now is prove who did it."

"Oh yeah Mel, and that's going to be the easiest thing in the world to do, isn't it?"

Back at Hollywell Stables all the horses who usually came in for a feed were milling round the gate looking panic-stricken, thinking they'd been forgotten. A radio was blaring out from the tack room and Spikey was creating bedlam in the coal house. The only parts of him that weren't jet black were his beady little eyes.

It soon became obvious where the problem lay. The whole of the kitchen floor was under a good inch of water and Katie and Danny were busy mopping up with every towel they could get their hands on. Nicki grabbed a cloth as soon as we walked through the door.

"My kitchen!" Sarah howled as a stray slipper floated past.

"It was an accident." Nicky put on her sweetest face. "I didn't realize . . ."

It turned out that the glass on the washing machine door had cracked because Nicki had thrown in all the dirty horse rugs without bothering to fasten the buckles down with elastic bands. Of course she swore blind I'd never told her to do this and promptly burst into tears.

"Look," said Sarah, casting an arm about aimlessly in bewilderment. "It's been a hard day for all of us. It's nobody's fault. Just one of those things."

Katie scowled and I rescued Jigsaw's food bowl which was full of water.

"I really should be getting home." Nicki pulled

back her hair in a velvet band which perfectly complemented her dark colouring. "I've missed my bus."

"I'll drive you home." Blake leapt up, and I was even more gobsmacked when Sarah gave him the keys to her sports car.

"James hasn't rung to leave a message," Nicki deliberately stirred. "I've not heard anything. He must be working too hard, getting forgetful. Next thing he'll be forgetting birthdays."

She smiled demurely and picked up her cardigan. Sarah's brow furrowed and just for a second her eyes flickered across to the calendar on the opposite wall. The 14th of August was marked in red.

"She's awful," Katie whispered later, when we were soaking up the last of the water with bed sheets. "All the time you were out she just sat around telling us what to do. She had Danny doing all her jobs."

"She's got to go," I said, grinding my teeth.

"Yes, but what can we do?" asked Katie. "When Blake and Ross think she's fantastic, we desperately need the extra help, and she's doing Sarah's typing . . ."

Trevor came up behind us with two big steaming

mugs of tea, and put a comforting hand on my shoulder.

"You know what they say," he said, putting on his wiser than wise voice. "Give her enough rope and she's sure to hang herself."

"Yeah, yeah, Trevor, but something tells me our little miss Nicki is just far too clever."

Ross and Blake went off to the fish and chip shop and would no doubt be gone for ages because the girl who worked there thought they were the equivalent of Tom Cruise and Keanu Reeves and always pretended the fish wasn't quite ready.

Mrs Mac, our secretary and indispensable organiser, was away on a two-week cruise with her family and we were having a serious job coping without her. The Hollywell fan mail was growing out of all proportion and we hadn't had a decent meal for days. Mrs Mac had left a freezer full of home-prepared meals coded in different coloured tubs, but Sarah had lost the sheet of paper saying what was what and at the moment the only thing thawing on the draining board was a watery Rhubarb Surprise.

James walked in later looking completely exhausted. The floor was drying quickly but there was still the odd puddle here and there and it was as slippery as ice.

"You wouldn't believe the day I've had," James groaned, burying his head in his hands. "Surgery was absolute murder."

Sarah tried not to look upset, but it was a losing battle. Her bottom lip was quivering like a jelly and I could see she desperately needed a hug and reassurance. "You could have let us know you were going to be late," she said.

James rubbed his eyes and gave her a steady stare.

Ross and Blake came in with bags of Indian take-away.

"The chip shop has closed indefinitely," Blake said. "We've probably eaten them out of every spud in the county."

"If you must know," said James, "I've been discovering some pretty thought-provoking facts."

"I knew I'd heard the name before," James explained. "I just couldn't remember where."

We were all reeling from what James had told us, the implications slowly sinking in. I dug my teeth into an onion bhaji, wondering how people could get away with it.

"Tom Drummond." Sarah said the name out loud as if weighing it up.

"I was suspicious from the beginning when he was so keen to have Goldie put down. He was almost nervous, running scared."

"I never did like him," said Trevor, borrowing Sarah's spectacles to read the report from the Royal Veterinary College.

It was dated two years ago and contained information on a formal hearing of one Tom Drummond – an MRVCS, very lucky not to have been struck off.

Apparently, James told us, the disciplinary body always published details of any such trials and posted the full report to every vet in the country.

"At the time it was a wonder Drummond got off, but in the end there just wasn't enough proof."

Tom Drummond had been accused of fraud, falsifying insurance documents and also of being at the centre of a drugs ring in Newmarket. People paid him a fortune to get what they wanted and he willingly accepted. He'd take backhanders from anybody.

James said he personally was once offered two thousand pounds to officially state a horse unfit for use and then later when it went up for sale to say the same horse was sound.

"It's outrageous," Ross said. "I never thought vets could be so dishonest."

"Very, very few," James said. "It hardly ever happens. Anyway, as soon as I remembered all this, I rang Drummond's office and spoke to his receptionist, pretended my name was Rawlings, asked if she could check my account and bingo, Drummond has been out to see Goldie three times in the last six months."

"Sounds like we've got our man." Sarah's eyes were glittering.

"But are you sure we're not just putting two and two together and getting five?" Ross said. "What if he's gone straight?"

"I've looked into that as well." James leaned forward conspiratorially. "He's just taken a massive loan out to set up a new practice. He's in debt up to his eyeballs. And there's something else . . ."

We all waited as James caught his breath and carried on almost in a whisper. "There are rumours starting to buzz around, nobody knows for sure, but I think he's started up the same racket. What I do know is that he's trying to undercut everybody's prices and he's skimping on equipment. There have even been some complaints about his emergency service. One of my neighbour's friends swears he unplugged the phone . . ."

"The man needs locking up." Sarah was ready to go to war.

"He's a crook, I'll admit that." Thinking about it made James frown.

"So," Katie said, twiddling with the tablecloth and looking pensive. "If all this is true ... why does he want to talk to Sarah?"

Chapter Five

"He threatened me." Sarah collapsed in the armchair with no springs. "Said if I started spreading stories I wouldn't know what had hit me. He's vicious, James. In fact he scared me to death."

I'd never seen Sarah so rattled. She was positively trembling.

"I'll kill him." Trevor snorted like a bulldog. "Nobody speaks to Mrs F like that."

"It's OK, Trevor, calm down." James pushed him back into his chair. "We need to stay rational, it's no good having slanging matches."

Katie put the stethoscope on his chest and said that his blood pressure was soaring.

"That's for his heart, you fool." Ross took the plugs out of her ears.

"Really, I'm fine," said Sarah. "If he thinks he can talk to me like that and get away with it then he's wrong."

"There's nothing more we can do tonight," said James trying to take charge. "Let's look at it in a fresh light tomorrow morning. Then decide what to do."

"Yes boss," Sarah joked.

The next day dawned bright and cheerful but soon descended towards disaster.

The first thing that went wrong was Sarah's surprise exercise video arriving by parcel post and coming within seconds of Sarah opening it. I whisked it out of her hands and buried it under some papers, cackling away that it was just one of Blake's show-jumping videos, nothing to get excited about.

What I didn't realize then was that the video I thought was Sarah's birthday present was actually something else, something far more sinister. Something that was going to mean the difference between getting off scot-free and prosecution for a certain Mr Tom Drummond.

Then Nicki arrived, decked out in the tightest pair of fawn jodhpurs I'd ever seen, and new black riding boots to match.

It was part of the agreement that in return for Nicki's help, Blake would give her a free lesson. As much as I hated to admit it, she was actually quite a good rider. Last week she'd cleared nearly four foot on one of Blake's other horses, Royal Storm. But Colorado was a different kettle of fish; he was quick, sharp and temperamental. Nicki had pestered Blake until she was blue in the face and he'd reluctantly agreed to let her ride him. I was the only other person who'd ever ridden Colorado.

"Keep your heels down and your hands as light as a feather." Blake checked the girth and accidentally brushed against Nicki's leg. She gathered the reins together, grinning at me from under the velvet riding hat.

"We should have cut the stirrup leathers or put itching powder down her back," Trevor grinned as Colorado clattered out of the yard.

We were supposed to be helping Katie with Angel and Holly, our mare and foal, but we couldn't drag ourselves away.

"Just five minutes won't hurt," I giggled and we sloped off like two sleuths. I was still carrying this week's copy of *In The Saddle* which had a centre spread of Blake holding Colorado and looking dark and sultry. He'd been named Show-jumping Hunk of the Year and Sarah had pinned another copy on to the fridge door with some Blu-Tack. Blake had been mortified.

"It says here that horses only sleep for seven out of twenty-four hours," I said, flicking to the quiz page and shifting my bottom on the hard ground. "So why is old Boris permanently snoring?"

Colorado went surprisingly well at first. He had his head tucked in and was tracking up behind, moving smoothly into canter.

"You've got to give it to her," Trevor said. "She does look good on a horse."

Blake had her doing twenty-metre circles and

lots of transitions and then popping over small fences. It was only early morning but it was already getting hot.

We were sauntering back to the stables when we heard all the commotion. Suddenly Colorado charged into the yard, stirrups flying, riderless and his reins dangerously close to his legs. Chickens went scrabbling in all directions and Spikey started screaming his head off.

"Steady boy, whoa, whoa!" Colorado eyed me warily as I reached for the rubber reins and slowly stroked his brown and white shoulder. His long mane was thrown over both sides of his neck, and sweat was starting to trickle down from underneath. "It's all right sweetheart, nobody's going to hurt you. There, there, sssh now."

Blake came sprinting up from the field, stony-white with fear, and immediately started examining Colorado.

"It's OK," I said. "He's all right, he's not hurt."

Blake wasn't satisfied until he'd felt every inch of his body and trotted him up to see if he was lame. Colorado had always meant everything to Blake and the idea of him being hurt was incomprehensible. To say that he wrapped him in cotton wool was an understatement.

Apparently Nicki had been turning into a small spread when a bot fly had zoomed round Colorado's legs and sent him wild. Instead of reassuring him, Nicki had slapped him with the whip and Colorado had bolted towards the hedge.

"You poor baby." I stroked Colorado's throbbing nose. Bot flies are wasp-like insects which come out in August and try to lay their yellow eggs on horses' legs and under their tummies. Most horses go crazy trying to run away, and many an accident has been caused by them.

"So where's Nicki now?" I asked, undoing Colorado's grakle noseband which was all soggy with green slime.

What?" Blake looked vague.

"You know, Nicki? The junior answer to Joan Collins?"

"Oh yeah, um, she's still laid out in the hedge."

"Of all the miserable, conniving, deceitful horses I've ever ridden . . ."

We literally had to lift Nicki out of a five-foot thorn hedge and neither Trevor nor I could keep our faces straight. Somehow she'd managed to get sprawled in the middle, a bit like getting stuck in a sofa with no springs.

"I hate him. How dare he chuck me off like that." She was spitting out bits of leaves and twigs and didn't look nearly so glamorous.

"Oh, stop moaning and pull yourself together." Trevor was losing his patience.

Usually, when you fall off a horse, it's the done thing to get up as soon as possible and keep a stiff upper lip. Not Nicki, she was going to milk it for all it was worth.

"You'll not get into Blake's good books talking like that," Trevor warned. "Now dust yourself down and go and get cleaned up."

"Don't you tell me what to do." Nicki flashed her amber eyes and retrieved her whip from the long grass. "You're only the groom. Everybody knows you're as thick as two short planks."

The back of my hand shot out before I even had time to think. I swiped Nicki a stinging blow right across the left cheek and stood back and watched as her eyes nearly popped out with shock. "I've been meaning to do that for a long time."

"You, you . . . I don't believe you just did that." She was spluttering and gasping like a little kid. "W-wait till I tell Blake."

"I honestly don't think he'd be interested."

"You're crazy," she snarled, holding a hand up to her reddened cheek, her springy black hair flattened down from her riding hat, mascara clogging her eyes. "You need to see a shrink."

"Sticks and stones . . ." I warned.

"If you start acting like a decent person, you might get treated like one," Trevor told her and then marched off.

"I'll get you for this," Nicki threatened. "If you think I was trying to take Blake away from you before, then wait and see what I'm capable of. You're not going to know what's hit you."

She stood, feet apart, lips drawn back in temper, eyes dancing with venom. I was thinking I'd just set off a time-bomb. Surprisingly I felt as cool as a cucumber. I even allowed myself a faint smile.

Blake opened a gate in one of the distant fields and turned out Colorado.

"Do your worst," I muttered, swivelled on my heel and stomped back to the stables.

"I think you'd better sit down for this." The local RSPCA Inspector and Police Constable stood in our kitchen looking deeply anxious. "It's got to be kept top secret. The slightest inkling could scare them off for good."

"Wow!" Ross collapsed back in a chair as the Inspector started to tell his story.

"They don't usually start until three o'clock in the morning. They block off the traffic with old gypsy wagons and vans. They always choose dual carriageways or bypasses. There's more room you see, for more runners."

I was stunned into silence. And to think that this was going on throughout the country and we didn't know anything about it.

"It's all undercover," the Constable added. "And obviously completely illegal."

"Around ten to fifteen ponies run, and the betting is massive, huge sums of money change hands. We suspect a chap nicknamed Mad Morris from Newcastle is the ringleader. We know from a tip-off that he moved here about a year ago. Inside information told us he had a superb pony called Teddy who used to win everything. Nobody knows what's happened to him."

The idea of organized trotting races in the dead of night on motorways was so preposterous I couldn't even begin to imagine it. According to the Inspector the ponies either trotted at great speed or "paced", which was an artificial gait whereby instead of moving diagonally the hindleg and foreleg on the same side move forward together. It was completely unnatural and the only way to get a horse moving like that was to put him in hobbles, special straps.

"It's unbelievable that they manage to get away with it." We'd all heard of loads of cases of cruelty over the last year but this was something else.

"It's so dangerous," Sarah mumbled.

"We'd like you to keep your ear to the ground. If you hear of anything suspicious, anything at all . . ." The Constable shuffled his feet, clearly upset.

"Most of these ponies end up crippled," the

Inspector was more hardened to facts. "We've got a description of Teddy," he flicked through his notebook, "a bay pony about thirteen hands with a white blaze? A bit of a character by all accounts. Chances are he'll wind up in a place like this, that's if he's still alive. The last pony we rescued in a raid had fallen and broken his back—"

"Well, we won't go into that now," the Constable quickly interrupted when he saw our faces. "If you can just keep a look-out. The man we're after is called Tommy Morris."

"Will do." Sarah showed the two men to the door.

"I don't think I'll ever be able to look at a dual carriageway in the same light again," I said instinctively picking up Oscar who was staring at us wide-eyed, and giving him a cuddle.

"The sordid details of the underworld." Ross shook his head.

"Just how can people do it?"

We were all subdued for the rest of the day and Trevor kept well out of the way, with his head under Sarah's sports car fixing the exhaust. I was wracked with guilt about slapping Nicki even though Ross said she deserved it. It still didn't make it right for me to hit her. I'd never done anything like that in my entire life.

Blake spent the afternoon schooling all four of his best show-jumpers and only broke off to guzzle three cans of Coke and talk to Ross. In ten days' time he'd be back on the circuit and it was vital he picked up a certain amount of points to get into the top twenty listing. It was also vital that somehow I patched up our tiff before it was too late. There was no sign whatsoever that he fancied Nicki and I'd completely flown off the handle.

"It's not going to be easy," Ross warned. And I knew exactly what he meant. When something bothered Blake he just retreated into his shell and nobody could get through to him. Sarah said he was an enigma and I insisted it was because he was a Scorpio. Either way I was going to have to eat humble pie.

Nicki was in the tack room when I unexpectedly barged in for a scoop of horse nuts. She had her back to me and was stretching upwards to reach the leather headcollars.

"We usually stand on one of the feed buckets," I said, trying to be friendly, a feeble attempt to break the ice.

"Oh yeah." She didn't turn round.

"Listen, I'm really sorry about earlier. I didn't mean to go that far." The words were out in the open before I realized it. "I just wanted to apologize . . ." My voice tailed off.

She didn't move for what seemed ages, and then slowly turned round with a hint of a smirk.

"That's OK, Mel, I got a bit rattled myself. Let's

just forget about it, shall we?" Her shirt still had grass stains down one side and there were scratch marks on her neck from the hedge.

"Yeah, fine," I said, and stumbled towards the door as if I'd got two left feet.

"Oh Mel, there's just one thing."

I turned round completely innocent.

"I'll be leaving an hour early today, I've cleared it with Sarah. So I won't be here for evening feeds."

"That's OK, we'll manage."

"Blake's invited me out to a restaurant."

"A little bird tells me you might need a friend." Sarah came up behind me as I leaned on the paddock fence. The rough wood of the railing grazed my cheek, but if I looked up she'd see I'd been crying.

It was a beautiful warm evening with a gentle haze of dying sun and all the ponies were crowded round the gate enjoying an early nap. Queenie and Sally were standing head to tail swishing off the flies, eyes half closed, each resting a hindleg.

"It's perfect, isn't it?"

"A little heaven," Sarah agreed, rubbing at Arnie's forehead and immediately getting covered in grease and grey hairs. "It's what we've worked so hard to create."

Every night I walked Jigsaw down into the fields and every night I marvelled at how happy and healthy all our rescue cases were, even the ones who'd been grossly mistreated like little blind Sally. They'd all found a pal and their own special place at the sanctuary. They never fought with each other or got jealous. It was as if through being a victim of cruelty they'd somehow grown wise and learned to appreciate every living moment. Trevor said it was like a permanent holiday in Majorca, which always made me laugh, but they deserved it.

"Pity we couldn't bring Teddy here," I said, breaking off a splinter of wood and digging it into the top of the rail.

"Yes, but Teddy's not what's really on your mind, is he?" Sarah got straight to the truth.

"No," I gulped, staring ahead at the reddened molten sky.

"You know once I thought someone was two-timing me." Sarah gently unpicked the knots in Arnie's mane while he stood and dozed. "I never did give him the chance to explain."

"What did you do?" I asked, suddenly curious.

"Oh, the usual thing, poured a spaghetti Bolognese over his head. Threw his car keys into a lake. Turned out he was innocent. We never could patch it up after that."

"I'm not surprised," I giggled.

"Yes, but it wasn't funny at the time. It broke my heart. What I'm trying to say, Mel, is don't leap to conclusions. Don't believe everything you see in front of you. It's often not the way it is."

"Give everybody a fair trial, is that what you mean?" I looked up despite my swollen eyes.

"It will come out in the wash, I promise you . . . Well, maybe not if Nicki's loading the machine." Sarah started to laugh, and hot tears welled up in my eyes.

"How is it," I said, giving her a massive hug, "that we all ended up with a fantastic step-mum like you?"

Chapter Six

"If you can't beat 'em, join 'em." I declared open warfare in the bathroom, clutching an eye-liner pencil and squinting into the mirror.

Katie sat on the toilet seat and pulled a face. "Mel, you look awful. You could pass for a witch."

"Katie, you wouldn't know. You're too young." I picked up the lipstick and drew a heavy line.

It was going to be another hot day but that didn't deter me from picking out a cream angora top and matching it with skin-tight black leggings. If Blake wanted glamour then that's exactly what he was going to get.

"Mel, I really don't think—"

"Katie, I've told you. I know best."

Downstairs Sarah was busy singing "Happy Birthday To Me Next Saturday" as if that wasn't the most obvious hint in the world, and James was ringing round colleagues trying to find out as much about Tom Drummond as possible. Spikey had somehow sneaked into the kitchen and was using his teeth to peel the tops off the milk bottles stashed on the floor.

"At least we're getting back to some kind of normality," Sarah said, beating up some vile pancake mixture which she insisted would be cordon bleu cuisine. "Blake's outside – he wants to talk to you."

A deep knot of nerves clenched my stomach. I couldn't go through with it, it was all a big mistake.

Sarah looked at me. "Mel, what on earth have you got on your face?"

I stepped outside into the bright sunlight and was immediately confronted by a scene I least expected. Blake was revving up his huge sponsored horsebox which took at least five horses, and Ross was carrying a pile of anti-sweat rugs and bandages from the tack room.

"I've only just heard," he leapt down from the cab, shouting over the roar of the engine. "There's an Irish-bred four-year-old going for a song on the south coast. I've got to pick it up tonight."

"But Blake?"

"I'll be back in a few days. Look after Colorado."

"Blake?"

"Don't panic. Here, catch this!"

He lobbed me a stars and stripes T-shirt which

he'd brought back from America emblazoned with "Have a nice day".

"Look after it for me," he yelled and clambered back into the cab.

I spent ten seconds gathering my thoughts before he stuck his head out of the window and gawked at my face.

"And for Christ's sake, get that muck off your face – you look awful."

Trevor insisted we went into town to track down a present for Sarah. Nicki had rolled up at lunch-time in the tightest T-shirt I'd ever seen and a new hair-do which must have cost a bomb.

As soon as she found out Blake wasn't there she stalked off to the barn in a seething fury with a snide comment that the meal had been wonderful.

"Ignore her," Trevor said. "There's got to be an explanation."

Sarah entrusted Trevor with the keys to her sports car and disappeared into the greenhouse to dwell on ideas for her latest saga. She was still insisting that she'd win the Romantic Novelist of the Year Award, and Goldie's medical bills were riding on it.

"Let's hit the road," Trevor urged just as the phone rang twice and then cut off in mid-flow.

"Must be a wrong number," I shrugged and reached for the seat-belt.

I didn't give it a second thought.

Town was heaving and the nearest we came to finding a birthday present was a horse portrait which was way over our budget. We got so desperate we even considered a lamp stand or a set of carving knives. Buying a card wasn't much better. Trevor couldn't decide between three jokey ones while I was intent on a purple badge which said "Forty Today".

I was still wearing my angora top and hovering under an overhead fan trying to cool off when I spotted Tom Drummond.

He was standing by the stationery counter flicking through a batch of half-price calendars. Nobody would have thought he'd been at the centre of a Newmarket drugs scandal, but then of course he'd never been proven guilty.

"Trevor," I hissed, backing into a promotional stand and quivering like a jelly. "Get over here quick."

Tom Drummond walked out of the store with three blank tapes. He hadn't noticed us. He marched straight through the shopping parade and disappeared from sight just as we paid for a two-foot size card with a picture of a dog on the front that looked just like Jigsaw.

"We'll write all the horses' names in it," Trevor said.

And even then they'd have to be small. We'd got more animals at Hollywell than in Noah's Ark.

We ended up buying a lovely leather briefcase with compartments for everything, and shiny gold locks. It was beautiful, and a vast improvement on anything Sarah had used before.

"We'll have to sneak it in when she's not looking," I thought aloud, batting an eyelid which had stuck together with cement-like mascara.

"Blake was right, you know," Trevor said, pressing a pedestrian light button. "You really do look a sight."

We saw him before he saw us. He was at the traffic lights in a green estate car biting his nails.

"That's him!" I shrieked, pointing through our windscreen and wondering why I was so excited.

Tom Drummond indicated left and pulled out into a stream of oncoming traffic.

"Hang on," Trevor yelled, and we wheeled out between two cars, narrowly missing a bumper.

"Trevor, what on earth do you think you're doing?"

We were four cars behind the green estate as we turned down the High Street.

"We've got an hour to kill." Trevor revved the little sports car forward. "It can't do any harm."

Considering Tom Drummond had threatened Sarah with legal action if she harassed him any further I thought it could do every harm.

"He'll spot us for sure," I squeaked. "What do you think we are, a detective agency?"

The leafy suburban streets gave way to open countryside as we rattled along at fifty miles an hour, trying to keep up. We were convinced he was heading for the Treebank Stud which bred racehorses, but instead of turning down the limestone track he cruised past and shot down a narrow lane.

"I told you I had a hunch." Trevor gripped the wheel. "He's up to something, I'm sure of it."

"Trevor, I'm not sure we should be doing this,"

The green estate slowed down and crept up a gravel track towards an old run-down barn and three mobile homes.

A man came out with two Alsatians and shook hands with Drummond, looking incredibly relieved. He was built like a rugby player, scruffy with a grisly beard and unkempt hair.

"Not exactly Buckingham Palace, is it?" Trevor whispered, winding down the window.

I insisted that we were far too close, but Trevor wouldn't listen.

"Look, what's he doing now?"

Drummond opened up the boot and lifted out a box of something or other and the three blank tapes. There was no sign of any horses on the property.

"Maybe he's come to treat one of the Alsatians?" I said, but then had doubts when they both charged off after a stick.

Drummond and the guy with the grisly beard disappeared into the nearest mobile home and slammed the door behind them.

"Now's our chance." Trevor pulled out the car keys and clicked open the tiny door. "Are you coming or what?"

We sneaked down the side of one of the buildings, which resembled an old-fashioned piggery. Sweat poured down my back like a waterfall, and my chest rose and fell in barely controlled panic. We could hear voices coming from the caravan and then a television being switched on.

We didn't find any horses. What we did find made us both catch our breath in alarm.

We slowly pushed open a half-closed door and peered into a large junk room with just a stream of light coming from a boarded-up window. It was dim and murky with a high ceiling and a cold concrete floor.

There in the corner was a green tarpaulin carelessly pulled over a lightweight structure which had flimsy bicycle-like wheels and a low-slung seat. Sprawled across one of the shafts was an equally flimsy harness, complete with reins and breastplate. The reason it was so light was that it was made out of black PVC plastic.

I'd never seen anything like it.

"It's a sulky," Trevor breathed, running his hand along the thin shaft. "And the racing harness to go with it."

In America sulkies are used for professional trotting races on proper tracks where thoroughbreds can reach incredible speeds, often nearly as fast as a racehorse.

"But there aren't any racetracks round here," I gasped, and then realized the implication of my own words.

Trevor stared at me.

"But I thought they used any old carts, not proper sulkies like this. It can't be, it's got to be a coincidence . . ."

Suddenly Trevor grabbed my arm and pulled me out of the door.

"Hurry," he hissed. "For God's sake, Mel. We could be in real danger!"

We skirted round the edge of the building in blind panic, my feet hardly touching the ground.

"Hey! Hey you! Come back!" The man with the beard plunged down the caravan steps, Drummond right behind him.

"Run, Mel, run!"

"I can't, I'm going to be sick." I'd never been more scared in my whole life. I could hardly move my legs. It brought back memories of when Ross and I had been in a scrap-yard running away from two thugs. "Trevor, I can't."

The sports car was exactly where we'd left it, pulled into the verge off the road, the doors still unlocked.

"Come on, quick!"

It was then that I heard Drummond's voice, loud and clear, bristling with authority. "Leave them be," he shouted, and then the most sickening part of all. "I know who they are."

"Trevor, he knows who we are. He recognized us!" We were sprinting along in the sports car not really knowing what we were doing or where we were going.

"Just imagine the scenario," Trevor said. "These horses get hammered on the roads, they need a vet, they need some kind of medical attention."

"But trotting races are illegal," I joined in. "Any vet getting involved would be struck off, unless he reported it."

"Tom Drummond's got no intention of reporting them." Trevor banged his fingers on the steering wheel in growing realization. "He's involved,

Mel, up to his eyeballs, and all he thinks about is lining his pockets."

The whole issue of the Bute was bad enough but trotting races as well ... "We've got to do something, we've got to stop him!"

The wind whistled through my hair until I thought it was going to be ripped off. "Trevor, slow down. We'll end up in a ditch."

We turned into Hollywell with our nerves shot to pieces and one thing on our mind: telling Sarah.

"And that's the long and the short of it," Trevor finished off. "Drummond's a bigger crook than we thought he was and I'll bet my best shirt the man with him was Tommy Morris."

Sarah struggled to take it all in. Katie and Danny were trying to read tea leaves and predicted more surprises to come, all because they'd spotted the shape of a fox in Danny's cup.

Ross was trying to ring a telephone number which Nicki had left on a sheet of kitchen roll, someone called Betty or Letty on a five figure number which had been written down wrong.

"Somehow, some way, we've got to get proof." Sarah paced up and down twiddling a strand of her red hair. "We're not going to let him get away with it, not in a million years."

I stomped upstairs to take off the hundredweight of make-up still glued to my face, and Katie raced up after me with more tales about Nicki and how terrible the whole situation was getting.

"We've got to set a trap for her," said Katie plonking herself on the edge of the bath. "Did you know she's been wearing Blake's stars and stripes T-shirt all the time you've been out?"

I grabbed hold of a piece of cotton wool and screwed it up into a tight ball.

"Mel, you're not listening to me." Katie waved her hand in front of my eyes in a desperate attempt to get my attention. "And you're using the tooth-paste instead of the cleansing cream!"

Sarah marched back in from the hallway after we'd decided on our latest plan of action. "I've just spoken to the housekeeper. It's not good news, I'm afraid."

She'd been trying to contact Mr and Mrs Rawlings about Goldie and Tom Drummond.

"They're not there," she said, and went on to drop the bombshell. "They've left the country."

Chapter Seven

The next morning we discovered that Katie and Danny were right about having another surprise. Only it wasn't pleasant, not by any standards. It was a horrible mess.

Sarah's sports car, her engagement present from James, was heaped to the very brim with rotting pig muck. It was all down the sides, over the wheel, it was impossible to see the interior. It was like something out of a horror movie, only we couldn't switch off by remote control, it was there happening right in front of us.

"It's ruined." Sarah's voice was no more than a whisper. "That's it – the end."

Ross put his arm round her shaking shoulders but could find no words.

"I think we'd better phone the police," said Trevor, taking the initiative.

"Have they any idea, the sentimental value . . . Just what they've done . . ." Sarah broke off.

"It's all our fault," I blurted out. "If we hadn't gone snooping, hadn't got caught."

"It's nobody's fault, and when push comes to

shove, it's just a car. It could have been one of you."

"But what kind of people could do this?" Ross shook his head in disbelief, slowly walking round the little car that Trevor had lovingly restored and Sarah cherished.

"Oh no, the brief—" I suddenly remembered that we hadn't taken out the present. It was stuffed under the front seat and we'd been waiting to smuggle it into the house when Sarah wasn't looking.

"Ruined." Trevor's eyes filled up, swimming with water. "The hours I put into that car," he whispered, and wandered back to the house, embarrassed by his own emotion.

"This should tell us more." Ross lifted a sticky, smutted envelope from underneath one of the windscreen wipers. Inside was a typed message which made us all gasp.

"TAKE THIS AS A WARNING. WE KNOW YOU'VE GOT THE VIDEO. IF YOU EVEN THINK OF INFORMING THE COPS IT WON'T BE JUST YOUR CAR WHICH GETS WRECKED."

Video? What video? What on earth were they talking about?

Sarah read and re-read the message with trembling hands. "I don't understand, what video?"

Trevor called us in for strong cups of tea and admitted he couldn't make head nor tail of it either.

We all agreed that we should tell the police. We had to, we couldn't be held to ransom by a thug and a crooked vet. And as Sarah said, this was way out of our league, it was downright dangerous.

"He's getting back in touch as soon as he reaches the police station," Sarah said collapsing into a chair. "And I've left a message for James."

It was half past seven in the morning and the day was just beginning. Ross flung some bread on the grill and raided the fridge for the margarine. "We've got to eat," he said. "We've got to come out fighting."

Sarah squeezed my hand as I forced back tears of anger and guilt. "I'm so sorry," I said. "James will be devastated." It seemed a lifetime ago since we'd returned from France and James had asked Sarah to marry him. We'd all been so happy and the car as a present had been so romantic.

"It will be all right," Sarah insisted. "It will, I promise."

Jigsaw put his head on my knee, eyes downcast, unable to work out what was wrong. Ross and Trevor mechanically went through the process of making breakfast and I twiddled with my hair. Sarah tried to joke that I was developing nervous habits. The atmosphere was terrible. Ross went through the motions of chewing a dry crust. Trevor drained and re-drained two huge mugs of tea. Danny, who hadn't said a word, lamely switched on the portable television in the kitchen and we listened to world news and watched a flamboyant chef making pancakes which Ross said were crêpes.

"I haven't seen her before," Katie squinted as a leotard-clad fitness expert took to the floor and started swirling her arms around to the music.

"The last thing on my mind is the battle of the bulge." Sarah bit her lip. She seemed to have lost half a stone in the last half hour.

"That's it!" Trevor leapt up, nearly knocking over the table with his bulk. "Mel, that video, the one you sent off for, it's the only answer. Where is it?"

Papers, newspapers, boxes of tissues, sun-tan lotion, everything went up in the air as we scoured the house for the parcel I had assumed was a fitness video.

"It's got to be that, it's the only answer." Trevor cleared a chair of papers in one fell swoop.

"Here!" Ross yelled. "It was under the cushion!"

It was a simple brown package, handwritten on the front to Hollywell Stables and marked Urgent. There was nothing to suggest who it was from. I'd obviously leapt to conclusions. There was nothing inside, not even a note, just a blank tape with a title scribbled out in blue biro.

We dived through into the sitting-room and Ross slotted it into the VCR.

"Fingers crossed." Sarah perched on the sofa, leaning forward.

The screen fuzzed into life with a snowy picture and then cleared to reveal a little bay pony being put into a sulky.

"I bet that's Teddy!" Sarah grabbed my arm, nearly cutting off the blood supply.

"That's the man that was with Drummond!" I almost screeched. "Tommy Morris!"

The video cut to another scene, this time on a road. It was night-time, there were horses and vans everywhere. People were shouting. There was a huddle of people round one particular horse which was laid on its side, and a tall man in a flat cap was pushing through holding a syringe.

"It's too cloudy," Ross howled. "I can't see their faces."

The picture crackled out to nothing.

"Was that incriminating evidence or not?" Ross leapt up and rewound the tape.

"I think we've just seen our first trotting race." Sarah looked deeply shocked.

"Who sent us the video?" I asked. "How did they know about it? What's going on?"

The postmark on the envelope was local. But what did that tell us? Nothing.

"Ross, play the tape back quick. I want to have another look at the guy in the flat cap."

The phone rang and Sarah was there after two rings. "Yes, constable, I understand completely."

"What did he say?" I was frantic as soon as she'd replaced the receiver.

"There's been a new lead." She grabbed hold of the Yellow Pages and started flicking through it. "They're convinced Tommy Morris has a sister who he's probably living with, someone called Betty."

"Betty!" Ross stood stock-still in shock. "The telephone number, the one Nicki wrote down wrong . . ."

"I could throttle her." Sarah stared at the five-figure number on the scruffy piece of kitchen roll. "The silly empty-headed birdbrain. Well, there's only one thing for it. We'll have to keep making up a sixth number until we get the right one."

"But that's like picking the lock to the Crown Jewels." Ross looked gobsmacked.

"Have you got any better ideas?"

Sarah peeled back a page in the Yellow Pages giving a rundown of video specialists.

"If we can just get the picture clearer, enlarge it maybe, I'm convinced that guy in the flat cap is Drummond. He's the same build, same posture.

If we can prove it, then bingo, we've nabbed him."

"No wonder he's resorted to dumping pig muck in our car," I said.

"Ouch, don't remind me." Sarah pulled a face.

"But who sent us the video, that's what I want to know."

"Isn't it obvious?" Ross looked up, the phone in his hand. "Betty, of course."

It was no good looking in the phone book. The police had already done that. Betty would be listed under her married name which could be anything from Anderson to Ziegler.

"I can't remember." Nicki stood in the kitchen pouting.

It was two o'clock in the afternoon and she'd just turned up for her shift. The police had come round earlier and taken away the video. They'd also jotted down directions to the place where we'd seen the sulky, but no joy apparently. Wherever Tommy Morris was, if that was indeed him, he wasn't at the mobile homes.

"I've told you, I can't remember." Nicki put on her most whiny voice. "She just sounded ordinary. She didn't say anything."

"And I suppose it was her who gave you the wrong number?" Ross was unusually scathing.

"Don't blame me," she snapped. "I've always got a million jobs to do. It's not my fault if you don't have enough staff."

It was so important when running a sanctuary to take every phone call ultra-seriously. It was usually mysterious phone calls or letters which led to saving the life of a horse or a pony.

"Anyway, Mel was rather slow about the video," she sniped back.

"OK, OK, let's not start fighting," said Sarah looking world-weary. "There's nothing more we can do."

Ross had rung heaven knows how many different combinations of telephone numbers, all to no avail. And the trouble was, while he was using the phone, Betty wouldn't be able to get through. That's if she tried ringing again, which was doubtful.

"I think Teddy's half thoroughbred." Katie smudged a sponge round Queenie's eyes, which were swollen up from the flies. "Did you see how thin his legs were?"

Nicki and I took out Colorado and Royal Storm for a gentle hack, following Blake's instructions to the letter. That was one of the fantastic perks of having Blake's show-jumpers staying at Hollywell: we could help with the exercising and fitness work. Royal Storm swung forward with the most wonderful long athletic stride. He wasn't nervous and uptight like he used to be when Louella Sullivan owned him. Blake had done wonders with his temperament and his abused legs. At least Nicki wasn't as bad as Louella; she wasn't cruel to horses.

It was boiling hot as we clattered up the Hollywell drive side by side. I was really envious of Nicki's new cool white riding shirt and pale blue cotton jods and seriously wondered if she'd won the lottery.

Trevor and Ross were still stripped to the waist shovelling pig muck on to the muck heap and looking glum with the hopelessness of it all. We'd moved the car as far away from the stables as possible because horses tend to go berserk at the slightest whiff of pig muck. I still hadn't worked out why. Spikey had been locked in a stable after he'd gleefully rolled in the worst of it and Ross had set the hose-pipe on him full blast.

Sarah wandered out in a trance, looking gloomy and dejected.

I carefully washed down Royal Storm's back where the saddle mark was, and scratched under his elbow, which he always loved.

"No news," Sarah said, taking the bridle. "Not a dicky bird."

She carried out a tray of fruit juice and a packet of Jammy Dodgers which the horses polished off because none of us had an appetite.

81

"It's the waiting I can't stand," she said.

"We did the right thing." Ross was strong for all of us. "We had to tell the police."

"Think of a number," Sarah said out of the blue, picking a dead fly out of her glass. "Any number from one to nine."

"Eight." I pipped Katie to the post. It was my lucky number.

"Right, I'll have one more go." She drained her glass and went back into the house.

"She's really upset about the car," said Ross, rubbing a hand over his chin. "I don't know what to say for the best."

I put the horses in the field, checked the water trough which was turning slimy green, and wandered back to the stables. I was in such a dream I didn't notice Katie until she was tugging at my T-shirt.

"It's Danny," she whispered. "He's really upset. I don't know what to do."

We went into the office, where Danny was sitting on the floor surrounded by the donation boxes which we'd had specially designed and had sent to schools, clubs, libraries, shops and so on. They were made out of cardboard with a slot in the top for inserting loose change. It said on the back to send the amount collected by cheque or postal order to our address. A lot of local people had filled up boxes and then dropped them off by hand so they could have a look at the horses at the same time. It was a mammoth job counting the coins out and putting them in order. Before Mrs Mac had gone on holiday she had shown Danny and Katie exactly what to do and they'd had no problems. Until now.

Danny was close to tears. Coins were piled up all over the place and empty boxes were stacked in the corner. It didn't take me too long to work out what had happened.

"It's OK, Danny, nobody's going to shout at you. Just tell me, how much is missing?"

He swallowed hard and fought back a sob. I hated to see him so upset.

"Two hundred pounds."

The words knocked me for six.

"Mel, are you in there?" Ross blasted through the door before I could even draw breath. "It's Sarah," he said. "She thinks she's on to something."

"I rang the number," Sarah explained, "putting in an eight. A woman answered and I asked for Betty; it was her." Sarah ran a hand through her hair in excitement. "As soon as I told her I was from Hollywell Stables she put the phone down."

"Not exactly the kind of response we wanted." Ross looked frustrated.

"So what now, do we tell the police or what?" I asked. I felt as if my brain was thrumming from overload, and I couldn't take everything in.

"I don't know," Sarah said. "I honestly don't know."

We were just walking back into the kitchen when the phone rang. It was almost eerie the way it broke the silence, almost ghostly, as if it had been reading our thoughts.

"I'll get it." Sarah twitched; she was a nervous wreck.

"Yes, speaking." She'd got her voice under control. "Yes, yes . . ."

Trevor leaned on my shoulder to get closer.

"I see, yes . . ."

We couldn't hear a thing. We didn't even know if it was Betty.

"No, no, of course not." Sarah waved frantically for a pen and paper. "Yes, I understand, we'll be alone."

She started scribbling down an address in spidery writing, leaning with the phone tucked under her chin. "Give us half an hour," she finally said and slammed down the phone.

"Yes!" She almost jumped into Trevor's arms. "We've got it!

"I presume that was the same woman ringing back," said Ross, trying to keep abreast.

Sarah kissed the piece of paper and quickly

pulled on her shoes. "Well come on, what are you waiting for?"

She hopped through to the kitchen, grabbed Trevor's car keys from the table and threw them straight at him. "We're on our way to find Teddy!"

Chapter Eight

"She sent the video," said Sarah, as Trevor crunched the gears forward and we shot down a narrow estate road which turned out to be a dead end.

"How on earth do you find this place?" We'd been travelling round in circles for the last half hour and all the roads looked exactly the same.

"Tommy Morris is her brother," Sarah said. "And he does own a pony called Teddy."

We turned into a road called Wimpole Street and hoped for the best.

"She's rung a few times and put the phone down, got cold feet at the last minute," Sarah explained.

"It's hardly surprising with a brother like Tommy Morris."

"So why is she deceiving him now?" I asked.

We came to a crossroads and took pot luck as to which way to turn. We were hopelessly lost in this huge estate and we were supposed to have met Betty ten minutes ago.

"Just keep going straight on." Sarah clung to the dashboard as we bounced over a ridge.

"Did she say anything about Teddy, anything at all?" I asked, dying to know about the little bay pony we'd seen in the video, and if he was all right.

"I don't know." Sarah's voice was low. "I think we've got to be prepared for the worst."

"There it is!" Ross pointed like mad at a sign saying Gordon Street and a house directly opposite with huge pottery shire horses filling the front windowsill. "Number six!"

As soon as we pulled up a woman came running out in faded pink slippers and a flowery slip-over pinny.

"I thought you weren't coming," she gasped. "I'd nearly given up hope."

She quickly led us along the garden path, saying that we hadn't got much time.

"But we've got the car," Sarah said. "Just tell us where he is."

Betty turned round with a look of surprise. "Oh no dear, we don't have to drive anywhere. Teddy's right here."

I nearly tripped over a paving stone in amazement. The garden was tidy but small, with neat little flower borders and a well-kept lawn – no place for a pony.

"He's over there." Betty pointed, her dress blowing up in the breeze. "In the garden shed."

None of us could speak. Nothing could take the shock away as Betty pulled back a small rusty bolt and pushed open the top half of a flimsy wooden stable door.

"Tom made this himself," Betty explained. "Just cut the door in two and screwed on some hinges."

The pony inside hunched back on its hindquarters and squinted, trying to focus in the sudden sunlight.

"He's not used to me opening the door at this time of day, are you baby. It's usually at least another hour."

Poor Teddy. I'd never seen anything quite like it. He was stuck in the shed, which had a loose scattering of straw and a bucket of water in the corner. The window was glass and made the shed a sun-trap, not to mention a death-trap if Teddy broke it with his nose. The wooden floor was soaked through with urine and the heat was unbearable. It was a tiny garden shed, not a stable.

"Why is he wearing rugs?" Sarah's voice cracked up before she could say any more.

It was a summer's day and Teddy was wrapped up in a blanket and quilt rug. His bright bay coat was soaked with sweat.

"Tom says he's got to lose some weight. He's in a big race this Saturday night."

I couldn't see much of Teddy's body, but for a thirteen-hand pony he looked incredibly lean and hard.

"He's fed oats, and the hay has to be the best, none of this off the verges or anything like that. He's well looked after."

"But Betty, he's in a shed." Sarah could stand it no longer. "He's got heat rash, he can hardly move."

For the first time Betty started to well up with emotion. "I know, I know. Why do you think I called you? Why do you think I sent the video?"

Her eyes were flooding with tears now. "And there's something else." She fished in the front pocket of her pinny and dragged out some silver foil sachets – Phenylbutazone. "I have to give him these twice a day. A big man drops them off in a month's supply. You see, what I haven't told you is that Teddy's crippled."

His hoofs were burning up. Ross and I gently felt down each foreleg with growing alarm. Even with the Bute the pain was still obvious.

"He's been racing most of his life." Betty pulled out a slice of white bread and started feeding it to him. "Nothing could ever beat him, none of the bigger horses. He was like lightning in that trap."

I ran my hand along Teddy's hard wiry neck and he looked at me with eyes that seemed to just accept his fate.

"He's a real little character you know, quite a star. But he's sixteen now, his legs can't take any more."

We led Teddy out on to the little patch of lawn and let him hobble around picking at the sweetest grass. I immediately started taking off his rugs and asking Betty for some water to wash him down.

"Tom will be back in an hour." Betty looked terrified. "He'll go berserk if he sees you here."

"There's no way we're going now." Ross spoke for all of us. "We're not putting him back in that shed."

Teddy was an exceptionally eye-catching pony, with a big white blaze down his face and two white socks behind. Even in pain he was really nosy and wanted to sniff at everything. His mane had been hogged, shaved off with clippers, which made him look younger. I vowed that when he was at Hollywell we'd let it grow back so it would keep the flies out of his eyes.

"I really think you ought to go," said Betty taking the lead rope from Ross. "I didn't want this, you don't know my brother's temper.

"How long has he known Drummond?" Sarah came right out with it. "Come on Betty, you know who I'm talking about, they're both in it together aren't they?"

"I . . . I . . ." Betty collapsed back on to a garden bench, her hands fluttering in her lap with nerves. "All I know is that a vet called Mr Drummond, the big man I was telling you about, treats Teddy.

He's got something planned for Saturday night, some kind of special injection."

Gradually in fits and starts the whole story came out. Teddy was entered for a big race on Saturday against two other experienced horses. Nobody expected Teddy to win. Everybody thought he was on the scrap heap. The betting would be in Morris's favour.

"They're convinced it will work," Betty said. "Apparently Drummond's done it before."

I could feel my eyebrows rising in shock and horror and I had to put my arm over Teddy's neck to try to convince myself that we weren't going to let it happen.

"But if they do that he'll be crippled for ever." My voice was a mere croak and I felt sick at the thought of it.

"Betty." Sarah knelt down. "If you want to help Teddy then you've got to tell us where the race will be held."

The next fifteen minutes were the most difficult of our lives.

"It's an impossible decision," I said choking back the tears. "We can't do it."

"Mel, we don't have a choice."

Teddy rubbed his forehead on my arm and then tried to drag me towards a clump of pansies, completely unaware that we were discussing his fate. His short little black tail swished at the flies, and a snail caught his attention under a stone.

"I really care about him." Betty was as upset as the rest of us. "He's just like a pet."

"It would only be for two days," Sarah said. "Just till the race. "We've got to catch them red-handed.""

"But you're asking me to deliberately get my brother into trouble."

"Betty, these races have got to stop. Somebody could get seriously hurt," Sarah pleaded.

Ross took the frayed lead rope out of my hand and started leading Teddy back to the shed.

The pony's boxy crippled feet dug in and a flash of panic shot across his face. A dog barked in the next-door garden and I looked away with my jaw set rigid.

"Mel, I need your help."

As soon as Teddy was back in the shed the light drained from his face. He swivelled round and tried to push at the door as Ross pulled back the bolt.

I stroked the top of his head, the bristly bit where the forelock should have been, the bit that Trevor said felt like a toilet brush. Up to now Trevor had barely said a word. He was too flabbergasted. It wasn't every day we found a crippled pony in a garden shed.

"Sarah's doing the right thing." He put a hand

on my shoulder. "For the sake of two days we can catch the ringleaders, put an end to it for good."

"And it's Teddy who's got to pay the price," I said gritting my teeth as a sob caught at the back of my throat.

"You've got to go." Betty bustled us down the path. "Tom will be back any minute, he mustn't suspect a thing."

Teddy's deep throaty neigh rang out up the garden with the obvious message not to leave him. Sarah walked faster and I closed my eyes, trying to shut out the noise.

"He always carries on like this when I leave him." Betty sounded almost embarrassed.

That was enough for me. I put my hands over my ears and ran back to the car, wondering for the millionth time how people could be so cruel to animals.

"Mel," said Ross, as he climbed into the back seat beside me.

"Sometimes . . ."

He put his arm round me. "I know," he said, kissing the top of my head. "It all gets too much."

"We made the right decision." Sarah marched up and down the kitchen floor. "Teddy will be all right, it's only another forty-eight hours."

James was in the kitchen with us, listening to

the story. We'd just finished talking to the police. "I'll ring them later," he said, "and arrange the final details."

I picked up Jigsaw's food, which had gone stale, and started shaking out more biscuits just for something to do.

"It's called nerve blocking," James started to explain. "From what you've told me it sounds as if Drummond is going to make two injections into the back of each fetlock. It's a bit like the injections dentists give, a local anaesthetic. It freezes up the feet within five minutes."

"And you mean after this, Teddy will be able to run completely normally?" Sarah was just checking out what we already suspected.

"It should last for about an hour. After that the poor lad will be in agony. And most likely crippled for life."

"But Morris and Drummond will have pocketed their winnings and won't care anyway."

"Exactly."

"And Drummond will have to be at the race to give this injection?"

"Yep. And if he gets caught he'll be struck off for life. He'll never be able to practise again."

"Not *if*, James." Sarah twiddled with the tea towel. "*When*."

The phone rang. Ross answered it. He came back in, his eyes shining with anticipation.

"We've got the place," he grinned. "Betty was true to her word. It's the main dual carriageway out of town. By the industrial estates." He paused to get his breath. "Three o'clock Sunday morning!"

Chapter Nine

Waiting was a nightmare. Thinking of Teddy in that hot stuffy shed. Betty probably a bag of nerves. The police arranging a raid. It was all so tense. So undercover.

We didn't know whether we were coming or going. Trevor had us scrubbing out Sarah's car for hours on end until every trace of pig muck had disappeared. Katie had the bright idea of sticking air fresheners down the back of the seats until the whole interior smelt like a florist's shop. Luckily the briefcase was OK. We'd pushed it underneath the passenger seat, still in its carrier bag, so it was unmarked.

Blake rang to say he was on a stud farm in Cornwall and one of the tyres had dropped off the horsebox. The Animal Health Trust kept us posted about Goldie, who apparently was eating them out of house and home – and all the staff had signed her pot. They didn't know when we would be able to pick her up, but at least the leg was healing. And of course none of us knew how on earth we were going to pay for it.

Thoughts of Teddy ran through my head at least every ten minutes and Ross said if I carried on at this rate I'd be a nervous wreck in no time. Katie and Danny insisted on writing out name cards for the two empty stables, one for Goldie and the other for Teddy. I couldn't help thinking we were counting our chickens before they'd hatched. There was still time for everything to go wrong.

"Mel, don't be such a worry wart. It's all going to go exactly to plan." Trevor finished polishing the steering wheel with a final flourish, and stood back to admire his handiwork.

"Well, now you've finished that," I said, "there's something I want you to do for me."

Trevor stared down at the home perm mixture with a look of horror.

"And before you say anything, I'm not going to change my mind."

We went into the kitchen. Sarah was out at a business meeting for the morning and Ross was there, trying to unravel a pile of stable bandages.

"Trevor, just put the whole lot on. If you dither any more we'll be here till Christmas."

"But I've never permed hair before. I don't think you realize . . ."

Ross started pacing up and down, still in shock about Nicki.

"But I always thought she was so nice, I can't believe she'd do that."

"You don't know half." Trevor re-read the instructions on the perm box. "She's had Mel and me jumping through hoops since day one ... There's no doubt about it, she's pinched the two hundred pounds."

"Fancy hair-do's, expensive jods, it all adds up," I said. "It's all to impress Blake."

"All right Mel, calm down. And at least try and keep your head still."

"And she's the only one who's been using the office." I dabbed at my neck with the towel.

"To do Sarah's typing." Ross was finally getting the picture.

"I think," said Trevor as he leaned back against the sink unit, "it's time we set a trap for Nicki."

"It's bizarre." Sarah barged into the kitchen in her sherbet lemon suit, clutching a bottle of champagne. Even Jigsaw woke up in surprise, wondering what was going on.

"Forget the Romantic Novelist Award," she shrieked, rummaging in the cupboard for some clean glasses and giving up and grabbing some mugs.

"Sarah, you're not making any sense!" Ross took the foil off the champagne bottle while Sarah flipped open her bag and pulled out a contract.

"Television rights," she croaked, eyes brimming

up with tears. "For my first novel. It's going to be on the telly!"

We were all astounded. It was straight out of the blue.

"I know, I know, it's all happened so quickly. I must tell James!" Sarah didn't know whether she was coming or going.

The champagne cork flew into the yucca plant before I'd had a chance to gather my thoughts. Sarah poured champagne into the mugs.

"You mean like Barbara Cartland or Catherine Cookson, a mini-series?"

"Yes, no, I mean, oh crikey, I think I'm going to cry!"

Trevor said he'd prefer a bottle of beer and the champagne bubbles were going up his nose.

"Stardom here we come!" Ross took a gulp. "I wonder if they'll use anyone from Hollywood?"

"Never mind about the actors," Trevor said. "Just think about the money."

"We can pay Goldie's vet bill," I blurted out, realization and relief sinking in.

"All we've got to do now is rescue Teddy," said Ross, looking at his watch. "In approximately twenty-four hours."

"Oh my God!" I suddenly leapt up in panic. "My hair!"

*

The last hour before we set off for the dual carriageway was a nightmare. We were all on the verge of hysteria and I honestly didn't think we'd have got through it without Trevor's silly jokes and Sarah's constant briefs on exactly what each of us should do.

It was one o'clock in the morning and I was wide awake and counting the seconds. Trevor was just about to make another joke about wacky hairstyles when I beat him to it and rammed a tea-towel in his mouth. I couldn't bring myself to look in the mirror it was so bad and when Sarah said I looked as if I'd been plugged into an electric socket I could have sat down and cried.

"Don't let Drummond see Mel," Trevor joked. "She'll scare him off for good."

The police had informed us that they'd identified both Drummond and Morris from the video. All they had to do now was pick them up in the act, along with all the other people involved.

"It's time to go." James looked at his watch. "Operation Teddy," he joked, but we were all deadly serious.

The police were already in position when we arrived. James went across to find out exactly what was going on, and we huddled in the car not knowing what to expect. It was a dark night with barely any moon, but of course the dual carriageway would be lit up with the overhead lights.

"There's no sign of anybody yet," said James as he came back to the car. "Come on, it's time to get into position."

We could hear the odd car zooming past down below but all in all it was pretty quiet. The embankment was much steeper than I expected and even Ross was puffing when we got near to the top.

"OK everybody, it's paramount we stay out of sight, and not even a murmur." James fiddled with a walkie-talkie which linked him up to the nearest police car. There were patrols on the roundabout and at each end of the stretch of road we most expected to be used for the race.

"This is nerve-racking," Sarah hissed as we crouched down on the damp grass in complete blackness.

"Just keep thinking of Teddy," I whispered, easing myself down on my stomach so that I had a good view of the road below.

"When you see things like this in films, they never tell you about cramp." Trevor rubbed at his calf muscle, his face all screwed up.

"Or cold ground, or bugs," Ross said. He was on the other side of me with a pair of binoculars.

"What time is it?" I asked, feeling as if we'd already been there for hours.

"A quarter to three."

"What if Betty's got it wrong? What if they don't turn up?"

The road below was deathly quiet. The last vehicle we'd seen was a lorry and that had been ages ago. A tiny spider scurried across my hand, making me jump back in alarm.

"Mel, will you keep your head down. You don't know who's watching."

The walkie-talkie crackled and hissed and a deep voice came over the line asking if everything was OK.

"Never better," James answered. "But still no sign."

It was getting breezy and I pulled my cardigan closer. Twenty past three and still nothing had happened.

"They've been tipped off." Trevor cracked the bones in his fingers and shuffled position. "They've probably gone somewhere entirely different."

"Don't say that," I gasped. "Don't even think it."

I knew we'd never forgive ourselves if we'd left Teddy in danger. I crossed my fingers and saw Sarah do the same.

"There!" James whispered. "The headlights!"

Slowly, almost at a snail's pace, a convoy of vehicles came up the inside lane. They were led by a blue truck with a two-wheeled trailer on the back, which pulled over into the edge. There were voices, shouting and unravelling of chains. Two vehicles further down there was a flat-backed trailer with the sulky on board and there, climbing out of the driver's seat, was Tommy Morris.

"Got him," Ross whispered, clenching his fist.

The walkie-talkie crackled into life. "Operation Teddy. Bide your time."

We had to wait until the race was just about to start. My nerves were jangling and they hadn't even unloaded the horses yet. The blue truck unhitched its trailer and drove off with a car to effectively block off the road.

There were more people milling around now. They seemed to be appearing from nowhere, spectators of an illegal sport, keen to make a bob or two on the side. Heaven knows how much money was changing hands in betting.

Then we saw the first of the runners, a grey horse about fifteen hands, stamping and whirling around, a lovely lightweight thoroughbred with a dark mane and tail.

"Where's Drummond?" Ross's voice grated as he held up the binoculars.

"Never mind about Drummond," I said. "What about Teddy?"

And then we saw him. He was led out of a tiny trailer, still wearing rugs, his forelegs bandaged and his tail tied up high like a polo pony. He looked so tiny against the grey thoroughbred.

"Eh up, I think we've got our third contender." Trevor pointed down to the furthest vehicle where a heavier black horse thundered down a ramp, already wearing its harness. It was altogether chunkier with high knee action, probably some Welsh blood crossed with a hackney.

"The stage is set." James gripped the walkie-talkie, waiting through anxious moments for the police go-ahead.

There was still no sign of Drummond.

Teddy stood very quietly by the side of the trailer taking it all in. His white blaze flashed in the shadows and he hardly seemed interested in anything.

"Poor little lad," Trevor said. "He looks well cheesed-off."

Morris slapped him on the rump and moved across to a huge man unloading the sulky.

"It's got to start soon," James hissed. "It's gone half past three."

The other two horses were already being hitched up to their sulkies. One looked very home-made with pram wheels and red paint. A single kick and I think it would have smashed to smithereens.

Morris was starting to look nervous. He quickly put on Teddy's blinkers and breastplate and arranged the crupper. A crowd of people by the main throng of cars seemed to be arguing over the distance and where the race would start.

"That big guy's taking the bets," Trevor said. "I'm sure of it."

The walkie-talkie burst into life: "We've got to move in soon, stand by."

"That's him!" Ross had the binoculars. "The guy in the white riding mac, it's Drummond!"

Before we had a chance to breathe, police sirens were wailing from all directions.

"Operation Teddy, go, go, go." James threw down the walkie-talkie and we pelted down the embankment.

It all happened so fast. Flashing lights, loud-speakers, men being bundled into police vans. It was chaotic. Our main brief was to get to Teddy as soon as possible, but now we were down on the road we'd lost sight of him.

Sarah cracked her leg hard on one of the road barriers and Ross had to help her up. "Go on Mel, follow James."

Two men charged past me with police officers behind them.

"This way, Mel." Trevor grabbed my hand and we crossed over the two lanes and I suddenly saw Teddy.

He was standing frozen, completely immobilized with pain and fear, his blinkered bridle half hanging off.

"Teddy!" I yelled, and raced across, flinging my arms round his neck.

He was sweating and trembling and immediately buried his nose in my chest for reassurance. "It's all right darling, nobody's going to hurt you. It's all over."

Morris was led off with his arms locked behind his back and his face set in stone.

"I'll get you for this," he said, suddenly wheeling round, half breaking free, his mouth peeled back in temper. "I don't care how long it takes, you'd better watch your backs. I'll be after you."

"Join the queue," said Ross looking at him with disgust. "We'll be waiting."

"I think this is what we're looking for." Trevor came out of the shadows carrying a small syringe. "I found it lying on the tarmac."

James immediately said it was loaded with anaesthetic.

"There's no doubt about it," the police constable informed us moments later. "Drummond's gone. He's vanished."

Our main concern was Teddy and getting him back to Hollywell. We'd think about Drummond later.

Ross and I took the plastic harness off and James unrolled the bandages. "Now then tiger, let's have a look at these legs."

The carriageway was quickly being cleared and in another half an hour nobody would be able to tell what had happened. There'd been seventeen arrests and the police were pleased. "It's a nasty business," one officer said to Sarah. "And it's been going on too long."

I unravelled Teddy's tail which was held up with black tape, presumably to keep it out of the way of the harness and the sulky. I never stopped patting him all the time James did his examination. He was safe now, he'd never have to go back in a garden shed ever again.

"I'll have to X-ray him of course," James said. "But I think he's got a chipped fracture."

"He'll be all right though?" I asked, getting tense.

"He'll never be completely sound, I think it's too bad to operate. But," James said, rubbing at Teddy's white forehead, "he'll be able to hobble round Hollywell happily enough. I think he'll have a good life."

"I bet he'll be banging at his stable door in no time," I said, relief surging through me.

"I bet he pals up with Goldie," Trevor grinned. "They've got something in common."

"I wonder if he likes Jammy Dodgers?" Sarah laughed, and then turned away because she was crying at the same time.

Trevor and I agreed to go and fetch the horsebox while James wrapped Teddy's worst leg in what he called a Robert Jones bandage.

It was already nearly six o'clock in the morning and I couldn't believe we'd been at the dual carriageway for so long. The early dawn was beautiful and the russet sky promised another fantastic day. I was so happy I didn't even think about being up all night. Trevor started singing along to the radio and looked hurt when I told him he sounded like a strangled canary.

"It's better than looking like a cat with its coat stuck on end," he laughed, looking at my hair and then immediately apologizing when my face dropped twenty feet.

"Stop at the nearest shop," I howled. "I need a paper bag!"

We were both surprised when we turned up the Hollywell drive. Blake's giant horsebox was parked in the yard and I saw a strange horse looking out over the nearest stable door.

"He must have travelled through the night," said Trevor, weighing it up. Blake often did this between shows and I knew he wanted to get back as soon as possible.

We got out, slamming the car doors, and that's

when we heard all the noise. It sounded like a real scuffle, and it was coming from Colorado's stable.

"Blimey." Trevor ran forward. "There's a fight going on."

It was the last thing we expected. Colorado was in a corner, cowering up against the wall. Blake had his back to us, his fist clenched ready to slam into someone.

"Blake, no. Leave it." Trevor yanked open the door and charged inside. It would take a tank to stop Blake. I'd never seen him so angry.

"Leave him be," said Trevor swinging Blake's shoulder round, and for the first time I saw the other man's face. He was pressed up against the manger, his face white, his nose running with blood.

Blake was like a madman. "Get off me!" He pulled away from Trevor's grip but couldn't break loose.

"Hitting him's not the answer," said Trevor as he finally got him under control.

The other man stood gasping, one hand holding his nose, fear sketched right across his face, his knees buckling in panic. It was Tom Drummond.

It was hard to believe at first. He must have come straight from the dual carriageway. There was no doubting the hatred on his face once he realized his life wasn't in danger. "You've ruined me," he growled.

"No, you've ruined yourself," said Trevor blocking the doorway. "You deserve everything that's coming to you."

Blake fished in the woodshavings and held up a syringe. He looked in cold horror, first at Colorado, panic-stricken in the corner, and then at Tom Drummond.

I suddenly understood what had been going on.

"He tried to kill him," Blake choked. "He tried to kill Colorado!"

Chapter Ten

"Barbiturates," James said later in the kitchen. "Totally lethal. Colorado would have dropped like a fly."

Tom Drummond had been taken off to the police station and Colorado was settling down, not knowing that he'd just come within inches of losing his life.

"He obviously made a bee-line for Colorado because he knew his value," James thought aloud. "He wanted to do the most damage."

Blake was slowly recovering and Oscar insisted on climbing up his shoulder and sat purring in his ear. Katie covered some toast in orange marmalade and wanted to hear the whole story again. She and Danny had been farmed out to a neighbour last night and were itching to know every detail. I swilled down some more black coffee and wondered how I was going to keep my eyes open.

Teddy was in the intensive care unit licking madly at the mineral mint block as if he'd just discovered a sweet shop. Katie insisted she was going to introduce him to Spikey, who in all honesty was more interested in watching the chickens.

"The relief is wonderful," said Sarah. She collapsed into a chair looking dreamy. "No more money worries, no more trotting races."

"Just pure bliss." Trevor rooted out some suntan lotion which had gone green round the lid. "I think we all deserve an easy day, don't you?"

Sarah was in full agreement, and Trevor insisted on carrying out the leather armchair from the sitting-room because the deckchair had been chewed up by Spikey. Sarah said she felt really self-conscious and what would people say if they saw her sitting in an armchair in the middle of the lawn?

"Just that you're eccentric," Trevor joked. "And they know that already."

"Mel, are you going to sit in the house all day or are you going to come outside and act normal?" Blake was trying to find a new bit in a box of old tack for his new horse which from the glimpse I'd had earlier was a real stunner.

I was fluttering round the house trying to tone down my hair and wondering what sarcastic remark Nicki would make when she finally arrived.

"You are a silly mare," Blake said, which always made me laugh. "You've got beautiful blonde hair, yet you insist on trying to look like a scarecrow.

And what's all this about me taking Nicki out to a restaurant? I've never heard so much rubbish in my life."

I couldn't stop grinning for the rest of the morning. Ross said I looked as if it was my birthday and told me to keep my feet on the ground or I might float away. All I knew was that Nicki wasn't just a thief but a liar as well, and I couldn't wait till Sarah sent her packing.

Unfortunately I had to wait longer than I expected. We all agreed that the best way to set a trap for somebody was to tempt them with an irresistible prize, a bit like a piece of cheese for a mouse.

We made sure Nicki had loads of typing to do, including drafts of our new newsletter, and also made sure she was left alone in the office with ready access to heaps of coins. Trevor had rigged up a camera which he'd borrowed off a mate who'd bought it second-hand. It was a real set-back when we realized it was as unreliable as Sarah's cooking and a complete waste of time.

Anyway for days Nicki showed no sign of helping herself to any money. Even Danny was beginning to think he'd got it wrong and we must have been burgled instead.

"Blake, when am I having my lesson?" Nicki strutted across the yard in buttercup-coloured jods about two sizes too small. "You did promise."

Blake said he'd been gritting his teeth and smiling at her so much his jaw ached and how much longer did he have to keep it up?

"She's not going for it at all," Ross hissed later that afternoon when Nicki still hadn't put a foot out of place.

Betty arrived around four o'clock to have a look at Teddy, and there were tears in her eyes when she saw him pottering round the orchard with Snowy, trying to reach the Granny Smith apples which were just a little too high up.

"He already looks different," she said, patting his neck which Katie had coated in fly spray. "He's getting back his old spirit."

"There's nothing like a touch of Hollywell magic." Sarah fiddled with her sunglasses which Snowy thought were edible.

"Tender loving care," I added, and swiped at a midge.

Suddenly Spikey started bleating his head off in the tack room.

"What on earth?"

"What's he doing?"

"I thought it was a baby," said Betty, spinning round in a state of panic.

"He's a baby all right." Sarah shot forward. "But not the controllable kind. Spikey!"

The scene that confronted us was utter bedlam.

Nicki was diving round the feed bins in a state of horror with Spikey charging after her, trying to butt her in the knees every time she made for the door.

"Do something," she shrieked, knocking over a tin of cod-liver oil. "He's gone crazy."

Katie and Danny were there within seconds and scooped him up just as he was about to ramrod Nicki's calves.

Trevor barged in and immediately started emptying Nicki's rucksack. A lunchbox flew across the floor followed by a lipstick and a hairbrush.

"Yes!" Trevor held up the bag of coins as if it were a trophy.

"I can explain," said Nicki, a little too quickly. "It's not how it looks."

"But it's every bit how it looks, isn't it?"

The atmosphere was terrible. You could have heard a pin drop.

"I suggest you collect your things and go." Sarah's voice was deadly calm.

Nicki was quivering all over. "You're not going to call the police, are you?" She didn't look a bit sorry.

"Just thank your lucky stars I'm not ringing them right now."

Nicki scrabbled on the floor for the lipstick and the rest of her belongings.

"Ah, if you don't mind, I'll take that." Blake reached forward for his stars and stripes T-shirt which was among the pile.

Nicki hastily did up the rucksack buckles and made for the door. "I've spent all the money. I can't give it back."

"Just go." Sarah didn't even look at her.

"You're wasting your time." Nicki reached the door and threw back one last dig. "Most of these horses should be put down. It's a waste of money."

We all stared in amazement. Sarah finally broke the silence when Nicki was half-way down the drive.

"If any of you ever keep something like this from me again there'll be big trouble, OK?"

"It's marvellous." Trevor poured out more shandy as we named Hollywell a Nicki-free zone. "We've finally got rid of her. I can't believe it."

"I wish I'd known," said Blake, looking wounded. "She's been all over me like a rash and I've only put up with it because I thought you guys liked her."

"Ah, poor Blake," I clucked, seeing the funny side now that Nicki was gone forever.

"What you call a serious breakdown in communication," Ross grinned, rearranging the fancy Union Jack flag which Spikey was wearing in honour of being such a hero. Katie was already convinced he was super-intelligent.

"I saw her take the money," Trevor said, putting a handkerchief on his head to keep the sun off. "It was purely accidental that Spikey decided to attack her."

"You've heard of Superman." Katie put on a deep voice. "Well this is Super Goat!" Spikey scowled at her and trotted off to check out the chickens. Jigsaw lay on the hot concrete watching him as if he'd just landed from outer space.

"What I want to know," I said, changing the subject, "is what are we going to do about Sarah's party?"

"It's going to take for ever," I howled as I tried in vain to handle a supermarket trolley which was fast getting out of control. Blake put in another two crates of Coke which sent the wheels skew-whiff, and the front nearly careered into a display of tinned beans.

"Balloons." Blake looked absent-minded. We must have balloons."

I set off in search of party sausages and ran into one of the local gossips who was sure to report back to Sarah exactly what was going on. I could see Blake down the next aisle signing autographs for two girls clad in jodphurs and trying to pull himself away, which was a losing battle. I still couldn't get used to him being so famous, although I had to admit to a great surge of pride.

"Next time bring a baseball cap," I grinned when he came back.

"Crisps, mini pork pies, picnic eggs, peanuts, nibbles," I read out. "You go that way and I'll go this."

Blake grabbed a pile of pony magazines and the daily papers. "OK, let's hit the check-out."

We collapsed in the car feeling emotionally battered and Blake was the first to pick up *In The Saddle*.

"There it is." He pointed with the car keys at a double-page spread attacking dangerous fences in show-jumping. After Goldie had broken her leg at the bridge, Blake had made a definite stand and was campaigning for safer courses. Everybody was behind him and there was nothing like public opinion to sway those who mattered.

"I don't think we'll be seeing any more ha-has," Blake grinned, opening up another magazine.

And thank heavens, because show-jumping against the clock is dangerous enough without creating more problems.

Back home it was even more chaotic than usual because Mrs Mac had just returned from her dream cruise.

"We can't tell you how much we've missed you," Sarah gushed.

"All I want to know," said Mrs Mac, casting a critical eye on our waistlines, "is have you been eating properly and what's been happening?"

"Oh," Sarah nearly burst out laughing. "Have you got three hours?"

"I'd better put the kettle on."

It was murder trying to keep preparations for the party a secret from Sarah. She kept appearing at the wrong place at the wrong time and we nearly got sprung twice. James was convinced she didn't know a thing because she kept wandering about, moaning that youth was over at forty and would James want her now that the wrinkles had set in?

The morning of the party I woke up with butterflies in my stomach and my mouth dry with nerves. We gave Sarah her cards and presents and then carried on as normal.

It was a big surprise to me though when at lunch-time Blake fished out the keys for the horse-box and announced that he and Ross would be back later.

"Talk about deserting the ship," I gasped.

"Mel, you'll be fine. Oh, and here, I meant to give you this later."

He handed me an envelope with "To Mel"

written in the corner. Inside was a card with three teddies and flowers on the front and a message: "Just To Say . . ."

I flipped it open and gasped again when I read the three special words. My eyes watered like a tap but I couldn't say anything because the pizza I was eating was stuck to the roof of my mouth. Blake winked and dived out of the door just as Sarah floated in and announced I was due at the hairdressers in half an hour.

"Mel, you look fantastic." Trevor was awestruck when I changed for the party at seven o'clock and came down the stairs dressed as a princess.

James had taken Sarah out on a pretend date and was going to blindfold her and bring her back here at half past seven. Trevor was standing at the foot of the stairs in a sumo wrestler costume and Danny was losing feathers all over the place from his Indian head-dress. Mrs Mac came in with another plate of sausage rolls and cursed for the hundredth time that nobody had told her it was fancy dress.

Guests were flooding in and the barn looked sensational. It was decked out with balloons and streamers and a big Happy Birthday banner over the door. Someone dressed as a Roman soldier was getting stuck into the sausages on sticks, but Mrs Mac had been cooking for ten thousand so I reckoned we could feed them for a week.

"Where are Ross and Blake?" I hissed to Trevor as we made our grand entrance.

"I don't know." Trevor reddened. "At the moment I'm just trying to stop this costume falling round my ankles."

I looked at my watch, which said twenty past seven, and started to get seriously worried. Surely they wouldn't miss Sarah's party? Where on earth were they?

We all hushed and held on to our drinks and James led Sarah up the yard ten minutes later. She looked radiant in a black velvet dress with her hair piled up, the star of the show. "James, if you're messing about . . ."

"Happy Birthday!" Party poppers went off and "Congratulations" struck up on the stereo. Sarah blinked in the bright light and then buried her head in James's jacket.

"I never suspected," she howled. "Not for one minute."

Trevor gave her another present, which turned out to be a new battery as a joke. Sarah clipped him over the head and Katie raced up to say that Justin Taylor had just given her a kiss but he couldn't have done it right because there were no bells ringing in her head. Danny clenched his fists and marched off to sort him out, only his head-dress fell off and was trampled on by a giant strawberry.

Suddenly an engine revved outside and someone said it sounded like a jumbo jet. I could recognize those air brakes hissing anywhere. We all dashed outside and Ross and Blake jumped out of the horsebox cab dressed as forties gangsters with false moustaches and black ties. "It's all they'd got left," Blake joked, looking particularly dashing and utterly kissable.

He wolf-whistled when he saw me and then he and Ross pulled down the ramp for the greatest surprise of the party. Goldie looked out over the partition, her soft eyes happy and content.

"The surgeon rang this morning," Ross explained. "She's made such fantastic progress she could come home early."

It was a special moment as Goldie clambered down the ramp, lifting up her plastered leg ever so carefully. She was home now, with one of the best vets to look after her and a whole team of doting assistants.

"It's the best show-stopper ever," said Danny, holding on to Katie's hand.

We all went back inside after everybody had given Goldie a pat and she'd settled into her new stable. James asked everybody to fill their glasses and said he and Sarah had a special announcement:

they'd set a date for the wedding, the 20th of October!

Mrs Mac started crying and we all applauded. "We'll have to start planning now," Mrs Mac snuffled. "We can't let anything go wrong."

"But it always does," Ross grinned.

"But it works out in the end," said Katie, looking dreamy.

The music started up and James led Sarah off on to the dancefloor.

"May I have this dance, Miss Foster?" Blake said, taking my hand.

"Well, if you insist," I grinned and I waltzed off with my arms round his neck and my feet hardly touching the ground.

"Feeling happy?" Blake gazed down at me.

"Delirious," I smiled back. "And I love you too."

"Funny," he said, frowning. "I was wondering when you were going to say that."

Books by Samantha Alexander

HOLLYWELL STABLES

RIDERS